THE PERFECT AFFAIR

ANGELA HENRY

Storm
PUBLISHING

Copyright © Angela Henry, 2024

The moral right of the author has been asserted.

Ebook ISBN: 978-1-80508-462-4
Paperback ISBN: 978-1-80508-460-0

Cover design: Lisa Horton
Cover images: Arcangel, Shutterstock

Published by Storm Publishing.
For further information, visit:
www.stormpublishing.co

ALSO BY ANGELA HENRY

Kendra Clayton Series

The Company You Keep

Tangled Roots

Diva's Last Curtain Call

Schooled in Lies

Sly, Slick & Wicked

Doing it to Death

Xavier Knight Series

Knight's Fall

Knight's Shade

Maya Sinclair Thriller

The Paris Secret

Middle-Grade as Angie Kelly

Labyrinth Society: The Versailles Vendetta

PROLOGUE

Whenever Terri Walsh opened an abandoned storage unit, it always made her palms sweat a little. Of course, it was a crap shoot. Often the units she bought were filled with nothing but old newspapers, bags of beanie babies, vintage Playboy magazines, and boxes of royal family memorabilia which, even when combined, didn't come close to covering what she'd paid at auction. But Terri had a good feeling about this unit. At least she did until the rusted lock finally popped open, and she switched on the lights of a nearly empty unit. Tears of disappointment welled up in her eyes. Unemployed and broke, she needed this unit to be profitable. Her last six hundred bucks had gone on a unit that should have been half the price, except that Ken, her asshole ex-husband, had shown up at the auction and purposefully kept bidding against her until the price had doubled. He was the reason she was living in her car while he'd moved into a house with her former best friend. She'd kept bidding because she thought Ken had known something she didn't about this unit. Turns out he'd known there was barely anything in it. She had to find something in here to turn a profit on. She had to get at least some of her money back – and she couldn't let him win again.

Terri angrily swatted cobwebs out of her way as she ventured further inside the musty unit, hoping the dust didn't trigger her asthma. Heavy metal racks lined the walls – at least she could sell them for scrap. Searching the boxes stored on the racks, she found outdated women's clothes, shoes, and purses, torn sheets, moldy blankets, and broken kitchen appliances. On the dirty floor beside were several boxes of old books. Sitting down with a sigh, she took the books out one by one and checked them out, just in case. It wasn't until she reached the bottom of the last box that she pulled out a book with a red and yellow cover. The title didn't register in her brain at first. When it finally did, she froze, quickly, jumping to her feet to hold it under the unit's dim light fixture. Opening the cover, she hoped against hope and... *yes!* The publication date was April 10, 1939. There was also a signature of Bill Wilson. She was holding a signed first edition of *Alcoholics Anonymous*, in pristine condition with the dust jacket still on.

The print run of the first edition was only 5,000 copies, and she'd heard of one going for $60,000. Letting out a whoop of excitement, she hugged the book tight against her chest and danced around the narrow space, bumping against a rack, sending a box almost crashing down onto her head. Carefully, she wrapped the book in a dust cloth, put it back in the box she'd found it in, and immediately went to lock it in the trunk of her car.

For the next hour, she meticulously examined every box. She came across nothing of value until she reached the very back of the unit, where a large six-foot horizontal freezer chest sat against the wall. It was coated with thick, greasy dust, but even so Terri was pleased. She could easily get a few hundred bucks for it. To her surprise, she found that the freezer was running. Whoever had owned this unit must have been paying a pretty penny for it. Storage units with electricity were rare and didn't come cheap. Without thinking, Terri lifted the lid, expecting to see ancient bags of frozen vegetables or packages of deer meat. Instead, a pair of sightless, clouded human eyes – the long lashes frozen stiff – stared up at her.

With a shriek, she let the freezer door fall shut. The thud echoed through the unit as she stumbled backward, tripping over a box and landing painfully on her ass. Like a startled crab she scuttled across the dirty floor before she could finally stand and run outside. After locking the unit with sweaty, trembling hands, she sat behind the wheel of her car shaking, unable to catch her breath. Pulling her asthma inhaler out of her purse, she put it in her mouth and pressed the plunger twice, sending the medicated mist into her mouth and lungs.

Once she was breathing normally again, she grabbed her cell phone from her purse to call 911. But she stopped. Her unit was now a crime scene. She'd watched enough crime shows on TV to know she wouldn't be able to take anything from the unit. There were cameras all over the place and they'd watch the footage and see she'd taken something from the unit and put it in her trunk. They'd make her give it back. It would be bagged up as evidence.

Terri groaned. She needed the money from the book, like yesterday. She couldn't afford to wait until the end of whatever investigation ensued when she barely had money for food, gas, and her meds. Would the book still be there when the investigation ended? Maybe it would be destroyed or claimed by some relative. Terri didn't know who'd owned the unit or how long the body had been there, but whoever was in the freezer wasn't going anywhere. Surely, they could wait a little longer to be found, until after she'd sold the book and left town. Once she was gone – long gone – she'd call the police and report it. Terri started her car and sped out of the lot, clipping a trash can near the exit, without turning back.

ONE

AARON NICHOLS

AFTER

December 5, 2023

Sitting in an interrogation room at the Oakmont, Ohio Police Department, waiting for almost an hour to be interviewed, I had plenty of time to think about the precise moment when mistakes are born. It's that moment you make a bad choice and end up someplace you have no business being – after that it inevitably all goes wrong.

I'm sure it's different for everyone. For some, it happens by degrees, a series of baby steps inching them closer to the edge until the next step sends them tumbling over the side. For others, it's quicker, like a drunk tripping outside a bar. In the end, it's not about right or wrong, it's about consequences. And the bigger question wasn't, why did this happen? It was, could I live with the consequences of what I've done?

"Thank you for coming in, Dr. Nichols. My apologies for the long wait," said Detective Melanie Alonso, entering the room with a notebook and file folder clutched in one hand.

I studied her as she pulled out the chair opposite me on the other side of the table and sat down. She looked to be in her late thirties, olive-skinned, tall and lean with a runner's build and long dark hair pulled into a ponytail. "Is there anything I can get you? Coffee? Bottled water?"

I'd have loved a coffee. I was exhausted from having gotten very little sleep for the past week. But I decided against it. I wasn't here for a social call. "No thanks, I'm good."

I didn't believe for a single second that making me wait for so long in this room wasn't intentional. As a black man, dealing with the police caused a knee-jerk sense of dread and panic and she knew it. I was regretting not bringing a lawyer. But I was already walking a fine line and didn't want to look even more suspicious than I already did.

"Then I'll get right to the point so as not to take up too much more of your time." She pulled a photo from the folder and slid it across the table to me. "Do you know this woman?"

I merely glanced at the photo, taking in the wide beautiful smile and the riot of honey highlighted brown hair and the laughing eyes. I didn't even need to look at it to know who it was, and my feelings of dread and panic collided violently with fear, loss, and anger. The windowless room was suddenly airless, and I was acutely aware of Detective Alonso's scrutiny. I let out a long breath before answering.

"Dr. Cara Morton. She one's of the English faculty at Roberson University where I work." I slid the picture back across the table. Then I braced myself for the question I'd been dreading ever since the email from the college president arrived in my inbox yesterday afternoon informing all college faculty and staff of Cara's disappearance, asking anyone with any information to contact the authorities, and warning us we might be interviewed by the police.

"When was the last time you saw Dr. Morton?"

"At the last faculty meeting before Thanksgiving."

"And I understand you're the chair of the English Department at Roberson. Is that correct?"

"Yes," I said, although technically it was no longer true. They had put me on paid leave.

"How well do you know Dr. Morton?"

I looked into the detective's eyes. Did she know? Of course, she knew. I came here knowing that. However, I was unprepared for how this question would affect me. How well did I know Dr. Cara Morton? Not as well as I once thought I did. Because had I known the woman I'd recently had an affair with – really known her – maybe I wouldn't be sitting in a police interrogation room being questioned about her disappearance.

TWO

AARON NICHOLS

BEFORE

August 17, 2023

I'm convinced whoever invented faculty meetings was a sadistic bastard. Not that those meetings don't have their place. But they always go off the rails about twenty minutes in. Nothing gets accomplished, and by the end, the only thing agreed is when to have the next meeting. But that's not why I hate them so much. I hate faculty meetings because it gives certain people an audience to bask in their own self-importance and act like fools. On this occasion, Dr. Helen Watford-Raines, professor of world literature, was reading a poem. A *poem*. She was supposed to give a report on the status of her online courses and if they might be open for enrollment anytime within the next decade. Instead, she read an ode to love, or maybe it was earthworms. All I know is she droned on for almost five minutes.

Helen's a hell of a professor. Really knows her shit. And she's a good friend. But she's a technophobe the likes of which I've never seen and forcing her to teach online is a cruel and unusual punishment for a woman who once thought a URL was some type of urinary tract infection. Of course, she could just say no. She's close enough to retirement and has already achieved tenure. But by saying no, she'd miss out on a prime opportunity to pretend she didn't know the open forum part of our faculty meetings was to give status reports on what we're working on. She'd call it a protest by a die-hard Luddite. But I know passive aggression when I see it. My wife Paige is the queen of passive aggression.

I'd been given a big helping of it that morning, in fact, along with my eggs and toast. The eggs were over easy. I like mine scrambled. And my toast was slathered in strawberry jam. I like good old grape jelly. And Paige, my beautiful wife of twelve years, knows this. Oh yes, I was being punished for not agreeing with her that our eight-year-old twins, Bailey and Bryce, should go to Highland Academy, an expensive private school where the yearly tuition for two kids cost more than a new car. And even if Highland offered buy-one-get-one-free tuition for twins, with Paige working part-time, and my associate professor's salary, there was no way we could swing it. But as far as my wife was concerned, I was dooming our kids to a lifetime of asking, "Would you like fries with that?" You'd think after more than a decade of marriage I'd be used to being on the receiving end of her... now what was it the therapist called it? *Sugarcoated hostility*. But apparently, I'm not.

When Helen finally finished her poem, followed by a smattering of applause and more than a few dirty looks and rolled eyes, my cell phone vibrated in my pocket. I pulled it out expecting a text from Paige reminding me to pick up the kids from their substandard public school – her words not mine – because she had work that evening. Instead, it was a text from Cara, or Dr. Cara Morton, who was sitting three rows behind me in the small auditorium.

Cara had just started at the college this summer and taught

Creative Writing and English 101. We'd met at a faculty retreat over the summer – a waste of a day where we took part in trust exercises involving falling backward and letting people catch you, leaving two colleagues almost concussed. Cara and I met over the boxed lunch. I'd put roast beef as my sandwich choice and had gotten a portobello mushroom sandwich instead. An unfortunate mix-up given that I'm deathly allergic to mushrooms. Cara got tuna salad instead of the turkey sandwich she asked for. She hates seafood. We traded and became fast friends.

The text she'd sent me was a gif of a pig twerking. No words, just an abundance of pink ham hock jiggling like the grape jelly I didn't get that morning. I let out a loud snort of laughter, earning me a scowl from several people around me, and jostled my coffee cup with my elbow, nearly tipping the whole thing over onto my notepad. And just like that, my day got much brighter. Well, at least for a minute, anyway. I quickly texted her back:

> THNX a lot! Lunch?

But I didn't get a reply because suddenly everyone was clapping and looking at me.

"Congratulations, Dr. Nichols," said Dr. Alan Peters, who taught Literary Theory. He shook my hand, pumping it up and down like he was jacking up a tire, and the others in my immediate vicinity followed suit. It took me a minute to realize I was just named acting chair of the English Department – and I'd missed the moment texting Cara Morton.

"Why are you so surprised? You told me they put you into the rotation last year," Cara asked me later around a mouthful of chicken taco. We were sitting on a bench on the college green eating a hurried lunch from the taco truck between our respective meetings.

Of course, I'd known they'd put my name into the rotation for department chair. Every full-time professor from the associate profs to the tenured full professors, employed by the university for at least ten years, had their name put into consideration to serve as acting chair, with each term lasting for two years. But beyond the ten years of employment, no one knew what other criteria were used to decide. Dr. Watford-Raines had never served, and she'd been teaching at Roberson University for twenty-five years.

"Yeah, but I never thought I'd actually get picked."

I wasn't putting myself down. I was a decent enough professor, served on many committees, advised a handful of students, and oversaw *Reflections*, the college's quarterly Student Literary Review. But I was hardly on the fast track. I hadn't published an academic paper in five years and rarely attended the faculty functions and mixers where ambitious faculty members who wanted to advance up the ranks rubbed elbows with the college president, deans, board members, trustees, and donors. I didn't care about schmoozing and kissing ass. Plus, I'm terrible at it. And now I was going to have to do that and more every day for the next two years. Suddenly, the taco in my mouth tasted like dirt.

"You okay?" Cara nudged my arm, and I quickly swallowed my mouthful of food and gave her a grin.

"Sorry. My future just flashed before my eyes."

"That bright, huh?" she deadpanned. We both laughed.

"Let's just say I see a lot of phony smiles and boring, ass numbing meetings in my future."

"Not to mention a pay increase, a big office, and being able to add department chair to your resume. And it won't be forever. Two years is going to fly by."

"Yeah," I conceded. "You're right. I guess I should be more grateful."

"Why did they announce this so late? Fall semester starts next week."

"They do it this way to keep the incoming chair from being unduly influenced by anyone with an agenda. There have been issues in the past with department chairs favoring one person or a group of people and accusations of favoritism, racism, nepotism, despotism, sexism, and any other ism you can think of. The theory is, if no one knows who the new department chair is until the semester starts, there's less time for someone to be in their ear with complaints and offers of quid pro quo."

"And has it worked?"

"Doesn't matter if it works or not if the board can prove they tried to address it. And I need to apologize to you in advance because, as the new kid on the block, you'll probably end up with a good chunk of my course load."

"Not if I can get the graduate assistant I requested."

"What GA?"

"The one I'm requesting now, Mr. Department Chair."

I laughed and finished up my taco. I was starting on another, my fourth, when a young woman of about twenty, her bronze skin glistening with sweat from running across the college green in the 97-degree August heat, ran up to us. She was one of my students, a junior named Jaida Reese. And I could tell by the concerned look on her face that she must have heard I was the new chair of the English Department. It had been less than two hours since it happened. How did she know already?

"Is it true?"

"Hey, Jaida." I stood up and gave the young woman a brief side hug. "Welcome back. How was your summer?"

"Forget about that, Dr. Nichols. Is it true you won't be teaching this fall? Did they really make you department chair?"

"I'm afraid so."

"You've got to be kidding me," she moaned. "And what about the lit review?"

The lit review was the furthest thing from my mind, and I had no clue what I was going to do about it when I knew I probably wouldn't have time to run it this school year. I'd named Jaida student editor for this academic year and had really been looking forward to seeing her shine, as she was easily one of my most talented students.

"I can't make any promises, but I'll try to keep *Reflections* running."

Jaida looked past me to Cara, sitting on the bench behind us, and gave her a curious look.

"Jaida Reese, this is Dr. Cara Morton. Dr. Morton joined the English faculty this summer."

"Nice to meet you, Jaida." Cara held out her hand, and Jaida instantly shook it as a smile lit up her face. Besides me, and Dr. Watford-Raines, Cara was only the third black full-time English faculty member teaching at Roberson. So, I understood Jaida's excitement at meeting her.

"Jaida's the lit reviews student editor this academic year, and I'm expecting big things from her."

Jaida rolled her eyes dramatically, but I knew by the sheepish smile she gave us, I'd flattered her. "Well, I gotta go. I left my parents at my dorm with all my stuff, and if I don't get back to tell them where everything goes, they'll have my room all jacked up. Nice meeting you, Dr. Morton."

Once she was out of sight, Cara gave me a big grin and a teasing nudge when I sat back down next to her. "You've got a fan."

"She's a good kid and a hell of a writer."

"Shit!" Cara said, jumping to her feet. "I've got a meeting in less than ten minutes. How about a drink later to celebrate?"

"Sorry. I'm on dad duty tonight. Paige has to work."

"Raincheck?"

"Definitely."

"And stop worrying. You're going to be a great department chair," she said, slinging the strap of her leather bag over her shoulder.

I watched her hurry across the college green, stylish as always in wide-legged gray trousers with suspenders and a black blouse, marveling at her ability to move so fast in the sky-high heels she always wore. She left a trail of expensive floral scented perfume in her wake and the smell made me smile. I watched her wait impatiently at the crosswalk, checking her watch and running a hand through her curly light brown bob. The sun shone on her hair, and I noticed she'd gotten blonde highlights.

As I continued to watch, a young man approached her. He was young, white, tall, thin to the point of being gaunt, and wore a baggy navy tracksuit with white stripes and a black base-ball cap. She looked stunned to see him and glanced around before putting a hand on his arm and guiding him away from the corner. I slid further over on the bench to get a better look. They were standing by a low row of decorative hedges bordering the college green. I couldn't hear what they were saying, but their body language said it all. The young man was angry and red-faced. He kept pointing at a sheet of paper in his hand, while Cara shook her head, her expression neutral.

I got up to go see what this kid's problem was when suddenly, the young man screamed, "Bitch!" at Cara and viciously kicked the shit out of a nearby trash can knocking it on its side and sending the trash inside sprawling all over the side-walk. Several passersby stopped to stare. By the time I reached where they'd been standing, the kid was hurrying back the way he'd come, and Cara was already across the street, half running to get to her meeting. I didn't take my eyes off her until she disappeared around the corner.

. . .

My new office was on the third floor of Tate Hall, the Arts and Sciences building. After getting the keys from HR, I'd arrived with a box of my stuff from my cubicle in the office I'd shared with four other faculty members on the fifth floor. The small room outside the department chair office was empty, and the door was ajar. I nudged it open and stepped inside. The office was easily twice as big as the one I'd been sharing for the last decade. There was a small seating area with a brown and green plaid love seat and a coffee table along the wall on the left side of the room with a large wooden desk and a leather wingback chair directly opposite it. The office's sole window behind my desk overlooked the college green with built-in bookshelves on either side. The burgundy wall-to-wall carpet and the worn furniture made the place look dated. But I didn't care. For the next two years, this office was mine. Maybe being department chair wouldn't be so bad, after all. I'd just sat my box of stuff on the desk when I heard my name.

"Dr. Nichols?"

A white woman wearing a long denim skirt, a pink T-shirt, and sandals, who looked to be in her late fifties, stood in the doorway. She wore her graying blonde hair pulled back from her face with a flowered headband. I'd never seen her before, but she was grinning at me like she knew me.

"Yes?"

"I'm Lynette Carson." The woman let out a nervous laugh. "Your admin assistant," she added when I continued to stare at her in confusion.

"Sorry," I said, crossing the room to shake her hand. "Nice to meet you, Lynette. HR must have forgotten to tell me that you'd be by today. But I'm glad you're here."

"My official start date isn't until next week. But I was here for new staff orientation and was hoping to meet you. Is there anything I can help you with?" Before I could answer, the phone on her empty desk rang, and she promptly picked it up. "Dr. Nichols' office. This is Lynette. How may I help you?" She listened for a minute before covering the receiver with her hand and asking, "Are you here? It's a Dr. Peters."

Although everything in me wanted to say no because I wasn't ready for my new role, I nodded for her to put the call through, realizing the currying of my favor had already begun.

I was heading to my second meeting of the day when my phone beeped with a text. It was Paige asking me to call her, probably to remind me for the umpteenth time to pick up the kids. Instead of being annoyed, I felt guilty because I'd completely forgotten to call her and tell her the news. My finger hovered over the box to reply before I shoved my phone back into my pocket. I wasn't in the mood to talk to her right now because of our argument that morning. I'd tell her about it later. But it turns out I wasn't the only one with news to share.

"What the hell do you mean, you quit your job?"

Paige had come home from work looking more relaxed than she had in months. That and the fact she was carrying a box of stuff that I recognized from her desk at work should have been my first clue that she'd finally done something she'd been threatening to do for years – quit her job as a nurse at the clinic she'd been working at since before we got married.

"What does it usually mean when someone says they've quit a job, Aaron?" She sat the box on the kitchen table and glared at me. I'm not sure what she thought my reaction to her quitting her job out of the blue would be, but clearly, I'd disappointed her.

"Okay. Let me rephrase that. Why the hell didn't you tell me you were going to quit your job when I called to tell you

about being named department chair?" After putting it off
longer than I should have, I'd finally called my wife earlier that
afternoon to tell her my news, and she'd given no indication
she'd quit the clinic.

"Because I didn't want to ruin your day," she snapped.

"Did something happen?"

"Nothing that I haven't been dealing with for years. I got
cussed up one side and down the other and called everything
but a child of God by a patient's family for a mistake a nursing
student made, and once again I got zero support from the nurse
supervisor. She wrote *my* ass up because the student is a
doctor's goddaughter. And the afternoon went downhill from
there. I just couldn't do it anymore. We're understaffed, and I'm
worn out. I tried to call you a few times today to talk to you
about it, and you never answered your phone. I wrote my resignation effective immediately on my break and then registered
for online classes."

"You're finally getting your nurse practitioner license?"

Paige gaped at me like I'd grown a second head. "Didn't you
hear a word I just said? I'm burned out, Aaron. I don't want to
be a nurse anymore. Dealing with sick, sad, and angry people
every day, not to mention asshole doctors, and getting no
support from people whose job it is to support me is turning me
into someone I don't like."

"Then what?"

"I'm getting a web design certificate."

"Web design? Since when do you want to design
websites?"

She didn't answer me. Instead, she leaned against the
kitchen counter, took a deep breath, crossed her arms, and
rolled her eyes.

"Seriously? That's it? That's all you've got to say. When you
called and told me about being named chair of the English
Department, I told you how proud and happy I was for you. I

didn't point out that you'd never once mentioned to me you wanted to be anything other than a professor."

"That's different. This wasn't something I applied for, Paige."

"But you could have turned it down, and you didn't. So, there was something about being department chair that appealed to you despite it not being anything you initially wanted, right?"

"Fine," I conceded with a sigh. "You're right. And I'm sorry, babe. You'd make an excellent web designer."

To say I was being disingenuous was an understatement. I just didn't want to argue. I took a step toward her and reached out to pull her into my arms. But she batted my hands away. The glare she gave me before going upstairs to get the twins ready for bed told me she wouldn't talk to me for the rest of the night.

An hour later, I poked my head into our bedroom and saw the twins were in our bed with Paige and all three of them were fast asleep, which meant a night either in our guest bedroom or on the couch. I opted for the couch. We were old friends, since I slept on it at least a couple of nights a month when Paige was mad at me, which she was a lot. It wasn't quite ten o'clock, and I was restless when I should have been celebrating. But maybe it wasn't too late. Knowing my wife slept like the dead, I grabbed my phone from the coffee table and sent off a quick text.

Is it 2 late for that drink?

I pressed send, before I could change my mind.

Cara took a sip of her apple martini and gave me a teasing grin. "And here I was thinking you couldn't come out after nine. Isn't this past your curfew?"

She wore tight jeans and a black halter top, exposing her toned arms and glowing dark, tawny skin. Her curly hair was pulled into a messy topknot. She was so stunning it made me nervous.

We'd met up in town at a bar called The Night Owl, a hole in the wall dive wedged between a laundromat and a pizza parlor. We were only two of about a dozen people in the place on a Monday night. Had the semester started, we wouldn't have been able to get in as it would've been wall to wall with students.

"And yet here I am." I knocked back a slug of my beer and tried hard not to show how irritated I was by her comments. I wasn't sure why it bothered me so much. Maybe this hadn't been a good idea, after all.

"Seriously," she said, putting a hand on mine. "I'm glad you wanted to meet up. I don't have many friends left here. Most of my friends from high school are long gone or married with their own lives and families. And it's hard to make new friends in your thirties."

"That's right," I replied. "You're from here. You never said what made you decide to move back after all these years."

"Had no choice. My dad has Alzheimer's and can't live alone. Eventually, he's going to have to go into a nursing home. But I want to keep him at home for as long as I can," she said with a faraway look in her eyes. "So, I gave up my dream job as head of the honors English program at a private school on the East Coast to come home and take care of a man who barely remembers who I am most of the time."

"I'm sorry, Cara. That's got to be rough. Who takes care of him when you're teaching?"

"Home health nurses, usually a different one every few months because he's a handful and drives them all crazy. Tonight, I got our neighbor to come sit with him. I really can't stay out too long."

"Sounds like you're the one with the curfew," I said, taking another sip of my beer. Unlike me, Cara let out a loud laugh that was contagious, and I laughed too. Or maybe it was the beer. I was on my second and ready for a third, either way I was suddenly feeling much more relaxed.

"And what about you? Where's home for you?"

As much as Cara and I talked, it was mostly about work. We knew little about each other's lives outside of the university. "Cleveland. Well, a suburb of Cleveland called Garfield Heights."

"Cleveland, huh? You miss it?"

"There are a lot of things I miss about Cleveland but not living there, especially in the winter. That lake effect snow is no joke."

"Such as?"

"Polish Boy sandwiches from Hot Sauce Williams, tailgating at the Browns games, clubs in the flats, and donuts from Jack Frost."

"But what about your family? Don't you still have family back in Garfield Heights?"

"Not anymore," I said, realizing I couldn't remember the last time I'd talked about my past. "Mom died of breast cancer when I was sixteen. Never had a relationship with my dad. He and Mom split up before I was born, and last I heard, he'd remarried and has another family, and is living his best life in Atlanta. My grandparents raised me, but they're both gone now too. So, there's nothing to go back to in the 'land'."

"I'm sorry about your mom, Aaron."

"Yeah, it was rough," I admitted, wondering if it was the beer or Cara that was making me open up. "But my grandparents made sure I had a damned good life and kept me out of the streets."

"And they'd all be so proud of you right now," she said, and I smiled. A strand of hair came loose from her topknot and without thinking, I reached out and tucked it behind her ear. I was suddenly self-conscious, like I'd exposed myself, and started talking to fill the awkward silence that ensued.

"What about your mom? I notice you didn't mention her."

"I would have if I knew where she was. She ran off with another man when I was five and I haven't seen her since. And you want to know the craziest part?"

"What's that?"

"To this day, my dad doesn't know that I know she left us for another man. He never told me that part, just that she'd left, and he wasn't sure when she'd be back. I heard some women gossiping about it at church. They'd seen her all over town with this man when my dad was at work. She wasn't exactly trying to hide it. Mom was a party girl, and my sweet, hard-working father must have been too boring for her. I don't think motherhood was her thing."

"That's pretty messed up."

"I know, right? My dad's a handsome man and a bunch of ladies from church tried to shoot their shot. I wish he would have moved on. But he kept waiting for Mom to come back," she said with a dry laugh.

"You ever try to track her down?"

"Nope." She took a quick sip of her drink and looked away. I took that as my cue to change the subject and then remembered what I'd witnessed after our lunch.

"What happened between you and that kid?"

"What kid?" She looked genuinely confused.

"Earlier on the college green when you left to go to class. I saw a young man come up to you and the conversation looked heated."

"Oh, him," she said, rolling her eyes. "He was in my English 101 class this summer and failed by a few points. He was trying to get me to change his grade. He even brought a grade change request form with him and was trying to get me to sign it. And I, of course, refused. He didn't take it very well."

"I saw that. And it wasn't cool. You know his name? Sounds like he may need to talk to a counselor to find out what's going on. We've got a lot of stressed-out kids on campus who don't know where to turn for help."

"I think it was Darryl or Damon. I really can't remember," she said, unfazed. I was confused. Why wasn't she taking the confrontation as seriously as I was?

"Well, if he approaches you again talking crazy, let me know. I feel for any student going through a hard time, but I won't hesitate to report him to campus police and have him tres-passed from campus if he does that again."

"Thanks, Aaron. I appreciate it. I'm betting he was just having a bad day. But thanks for caring." She reached over and squeezed my hand. The gesture made blood rush to my face.

"Promise me you'll let me know if he gives you any more trouble?" I still had her hand in mine. It was warm and dry, and I liked the way it fit so easily into my palm.

"I promise," she said, looking me in the eye. Suddenly self-conscious, I reluctantly let go of her hand.

We talked and laughed some more and before I knew it, it was midnight, and I didn't want to leave. I could have talked to Cara all night; I hadn't felt this relaxed for a very long time.

"Your wife doesn't care that you're out late drinking with another woman to celebrate being named department chair?"

"My wife cares about a lot of things. But my current where-abouts? Not so much." It wasn't true. Paige didn't know I'd left the house. But would she care if she did? And I was hardly going to tell Cara I'd snuck out like a teenager.

"She's not happy for you?" Her casual tone didn't match the intensity of her gaze.

"She is. But she's burned out with her own career." I briefly told her about what had happened earlier.

"Wow. That's too bad. Do you think she could be jealous that things are going well for you at work?"

"I don't know. Maybe." Until that moment, it never occurred to me that Paige might be jealous. She'd ended a career that she'd once loved on the same day I'd gotten a promotion. She'd acted happy for me. But was my wife truly happy for me?

"Be patient with her. She's going through a rough time. Make sure you give her plenty of time and space to figure things out on her own. But don't let anyone else's issues keep you from enjoying your new position. You earned it, and you should be proud of yourself." She picked up her recently refilled martini glass. The warmth in her eyes made me smile. "To Dr. Aaron Nichols, chair of Roberson University's English Department."

"I'll drink to that." I clinked my beer bottle to her glass, feeling a lot better than when I'd walked into the bar, and suddenly had an idea. "Why don't you take over *Reflections* for me?"

"Seriously?" Cara was genuinely shocked.

"You're more than qualified to run it. Your students love you, and there's no one else I trust to do it."

"You mean no one else wants to do it?"

"Honestly, there would be a lot of takers who'd only be in it for the stipend, and the kids would have to run on their own. I want someone who'd show up, be hands-on and work alongside them to make it great. And that person is you."

A bright smile spread across her face, lighting up the dim bar, and my stomach did a little flip-flop. "Oh, Aaron, I'd love that. Are you sure?"

"Absolutely. I can get the ball rolling first thing tomorrow." It had been a long time since Paige had been happy with anything I'd done for her. And Cara's gratitude felt so good I wanted to keep making her happy.

We finished our drinks, and I walked her to her car, which was parked just around the corner. "Thanks for meeting me tonight, and for the pep talk. You saved me from a night of feeling sorry for myself on the couch," I said, noticing for the first time how soft her lips looked.

"The couch? Poor guy. No wonder you needed to get out tonight. On the bright side, at least, you've got some good ol' make-up sex to look forward to." She winked at me and smiled.

My face flushed hotly in embarrassment because she'd just mentioned me having sex with my wife while I was busy staring at her lips. I'm not sure if she noticed me looking before she threw her arms around my neck and hugged me tight. When she pulled away, her cheek grazed mine and our eyes met, followed by our lips. Hers were soft, and she let out a little moan as the kiss deepened. It happened so fast. Overwhelmed by the feel of her breasts pressed against my chest, the heat of her skin, and the smell of her perfume, not to mention the wrongness of what we were doing made it feel so good. But then an image of my wife back at home with the twins popped into my head, and I gently pushed her away, breaking the spell, and Cara clamped both hands over her mouth in horror.

"Oh my God, Aaron. I am so sorry." She seemed genuinely appalled as she yanked her car door open and jumped into the driver's seat.

"Cara, wait!" I called out after her. But without so much as a backward glance, she started her car and pulled away from the curb, tires squealing, leaving me staring after her.

Half an hour later, I was back home on the couch staring at the ceiling wired and knowing I wouldn't sleep worth a damn, when my phone beeped with a text. It was from Cara.

I'm so sorry. It won't happen again. I promise

I thought hard for several long minutes before replying. Cara made me feel things I hadn't felt in a long time. Everything with her just felt easy. I typed out a message knowing it was wrong but not caring and hit send before I lost my nerve. It said:

Don't be sorry. I'm not. Goodnight, gorgeous.

THREE

AARON NICHOLS

AFTER

December 5, 2023

"I appreciate you being upfront about your involvement with Dr. Morton. As with all disappearances, time is of the essence when locating a missing person, and it saves us time when people are honest." Detective Alonso's expression was unreadable, and I instantly questioned whether I should have told her anything at all about me and Cara.

"I only told you because I figured you already knew. Why else would I be here?"

"I knew," she said without bothering to look up from her notes. "How long were you and Dr. Morton involved, Dr. Nichols?"

"Not long. Maybe three months."

"And how did the affair end? Was it amicable?"

"No."

"And why is that?"

I ran a hand over my face and sighed in frustration. This

was going to take forever to explain, and I wanted to leave. Despite the room being cool, a trickle of sweat rolled down the back of my neck.

"Look," I said, my hands clenched into fists in my lap. "I get why you have to ask me this stuff. And I'll answer all your questions. But you're asking the wrong questions."

"What questions should I be asking?" She put her pen down and gave me her full attention.

"You should be asking me who could have hurt her."

Detective Alonso raised her eyebrows. "You mean besides you?"

FOUR

CARA MORTON: AGED FOUR

1990

Cara peeked out from behind the couch she was hiding behind and suppressed a giggle. Hide and seek was her favorite game to play with her mommy, and Cara always won. Mommy could never find her.

"Now, where could my little girl be? Is she here?" Mommy dramatically opened the closet door. "How about here?" Cara watched her mother fling back the curtain from one side of the big picture window in the living room.

"I'm here! Mommy, I'm here!" Cara said, running out from her hiding place, laughing uncontrollably.

"There's my baby girl." Cara's mom snatched her up and swung her around, which was a mistake. Cara was instantly dizzy, and her stomach gurgled ominously. And then it happened before she could even tell Mommy she was going to be sick. She retched, and her mother instantly sat her down as she vomited onto the carpet.

"Oh, baby! I'm so sorry."

Cara continued to vomit all over the carpet and down the

front of her favorite pajamas, the ones with the teddy bears, as tears stung her eyes. She'd even thrown up on Mommy, which made her cry even harder. The sour stench of her own vomit made her vomit more. Her mother gently picked her up, carrying her into the bathroom. She stripped Cara out of the soiled pajamas, then changed her own clothes and gave her daughter a bath. Afterward, her mother put baby lotion on her, dressed her in fresh pajamas, her second favorite pair with the giraffes on them, and sat with Cara in the rocking chair next to her bed. Even though Cara was a big girl now and thought she was too big to be rocked like a baby, it felt good to be held.

"Sorry, Mommy." Cara's eyes drooped.

"Don't you ever be sorry, baby," Mommy whispered into her hair. "It's not your fault. Now close your eyes and go to sleep."

Cara fought sleep for a few minutes before burying her face against her mother's chest, inhaling her sweet floral scent, and drifting off to the sound of her gentle humming, wondering what was wrong with her and why she was always sick.

FIVE

PAIGE NICHOLS

AFTER

December 5, 2023

I waited until I'd dropped the kids off at school before I read the paper. We were one of only a few families on our block who still got it delivered. Aaron had gotten to it before I had and must have taken it with him when he'd left for the police station. I'm not sure why he thought taking it was going to keep me from hearing the details of Cara Morton's disappearance. I stopped and bought another one on my way home and spread it out on the kitchen island to read with my second cup of coffee.

Authorities Need Help to Find Missing College Professor

Police are searching for a Roberson University professor who has been missing for five days. Dr. Cara Morton, 36, was last seen Friday, December 2, after teaching an evening class on campus. A neighbor saw her arrive at the home she shares with her father around 7:30 p.m. However, when the home health nurse who cares for Dr. Morton's elderly father arrived the following morning for her shift, she found the front door unlocked and Morton's father alone in the house. He was unharmed. Morton's car was in the garage and her house keys and purse were all in the house. The only thing missing was her cell phone. Police say there was no forced entry or signs of a struggle. Gerald Morton, the missing woman's father, suffers from Alzheimer's and could not offer any answers of what had happened to his daughter and the recent storm over the weekend has hampered the search further.

I stopped reading, balled the paper up, and threw it in the trash. My stomach was in knots and a headache bloomed behind my eyes. I absently rubbed at the long, angry scratch on my left forearm and pulled the sleeve of my sweater over it, wondering how the hell things had gotten so out of hand and if our lives would ever be normal again.

SIX

PAIGE NICHOLS

BEFORE

October 4, 2023

I sat cross-legged on our bed, watching Aaron as he shaved in the bathroom. It was still early, and even the twins weren't up yet. This was the time of day I loved the most, when it was still and quiet. The calm before the storm and chaos that came with eight-year-old twins. Usually, Aaron would still be in bed with me, hoping for some morning sex. But he'd gotten up and showered before I'd woken up. He did that a lot lately. Seeing him now with a towel wrapped around his waist, I noticed something different about him.

"You're losing weight, babe."

"Is that a compliment or a criticism?" he asked without turning around.

"It's an observation. You look good." And he did. It wasn't just his weight. There was something else about him. He was a lot more confident these days.

"Thanks. I've been hitting the gym pretty hard."

I couldn't be sure, but I could have sworn the meaningful look he'd just given me was some kind of wordless dig about my own weight. For years now, I'd been struggling to lose the last twenty pounds after having the twins, and Aaron had never once made me feel bad about the extra weight. In fact, he'd told me he liked me thick. Figuring I was being paranoid, I decided to change the subject.

"When do I finally get to see your new office?" I'd been asking Aaron to see it since fall semester had started, and so far, there had always been an excuse why I couldn't. I realized that becoming department chair had come with increased responsibilities and workload, and I also knew my laid-back husband enough to know that he was probably feeling a bit out of his element, although he'd yet to admit it.

I could barely nail him down for the occasional lunch date and got the feeling he didn't want me stopping by his office, which confused me. Aaron had been teaching at Roberson for ten years and I often stopped by his office or met him for lunch or dinner on campus with the kids, since one of their favorite things to do was eat with their dad in the college cafeteria. I got up to make the bed, ignoring the fact he hadn't answered me.

"I'm going to be running a bunch of errands today. Why don't I swing by Marconi's and pick up some roast beef subs and we can have lunch in your office?" When he still didn't respond, I poked my head into the bathroom to see him sitting on the side of the tub, smiling down at his phone. Seeing me standing there, he instantly stood up.

"Did you hear a single thing I just said?" I asked, annoyed. But I wasn't just annoyed. Frustration and disappointment washed over me in waves.

One thing I'd been looking forward to when I'd quit my job was reconnecting with my husband. The stress of my work hadn't just taken a toll on me but our marriage as well. Aaron and I never seemed to be on the same page anymore, and I knew my anger and unhappiness were pushing him away and creating a wedge between us. But it had now been two months since I'd quit nursing. I was relaxed and happier and enjoying my online web design classes. I was really trying to make things right with Aaron. But nothing had improved. In fact, things were getting worse. My husband was never around, and when he was, he was distant and easily annoyed. There was always a meeting or crisis he needed to deal with, and when he wasn't spending late hours at work, he was at the gym. And worst of all, our sex life was suffering. My husband never turned down my advances, he just wasn't present during the act. When it was over, he'd roll over and go to sleep or get up and go work in his study. I blamed the stress of his new job and hoped it wouldn't be like this the entire time he was department chair.

I tried my best not to sound too accusatory. "And who are you texting at this time of the morning?"

"No one," he snapped. "Damn. I can't even get any peace in the bathroom." Aaron noticed how stunned and hurt I was because his face relaxed and he walked over and pulled me into an embrace. "I'm sorry, babe. Of course, I'd love to have lunch with you. Stop by around one. And make sure my beef is medium rare." He kissed the top of my head and walked into the bedroom to get dressed.

"Medium rare? Since when do you like your roast beef medium rare?" As long as I'd known my husband, he'd been a well-done beef kind of guy, not even a trace of pink. He looked back at his phone and didn't answer me.

An hour later, Aaron was heading out the door for work, after barely acknowledging me or the kids as we ate breakfast. Bailey called out after him.

"Daddy, my dance recital's tonight. Don't be late."

"You got no rhythm, Bailey. You dance like you got bees in

your pants," jeered Bryce, snatching the notebook his sister was writing in and holding it out of her reach. "And you can't write either. Your stories suck!"

"Give it back! You're just mad you didn't get picked for the writing program!" Bailey said and retaliated by punching her brother in the arm. They were seconds away from a full-blown fight.

But I was too busy staring at my husband. Aaron had frozen, his hand halfway to the doorknob. He let out a small groan and grimaced, and I knew he'd forgotten about the recital and was going to disappoint our daughter. Before I could say anything to him, the twins were shoving each other, and I quickly grabbed the air horn that sat on the kitchen counter and pressed the button, releasing an obnoxiously loud sound that got their attention immediately.

"Bailey Ann Nichols and Bryce Christopher Nichols, grab your backpacks and get into the car! If I have to repeat myself, there will be no dance recital for Bailey and no sleepover this weekend for Bryce. Move it! Now!"

The kids knew when the air horn came out, I meant business and scrambled to do as they were told. If only it worked on my husband. By the time I turned my attention back to Aaron, he was gone, without so much as a goodbye.

Later, when I showed up at his office at one with our lunch, his administrative assistant, who introduced herself as Lynette, told me he'd left for lunch around noon. Noticing Aaron's office door was open, I stepped inside and took a quick look around and was surprised it was so neat when he was such a slob at home. Then I tried calling and texting him and got no response. I left, embarrassed and trying not to show Lynette how upset I was, but she stopped me in the hallway.

"Mrs. Nichols. Would you like me to give Dr. Nichols a message for you?"

"No thanks, Lynette."

"Then I guess I'll see you tonight, then?" She gave me a questioning look.

"Tonight?" I repeated.

"The Fall Fling?"

The Fall Fling was a once a semester party for faculty, staff, and their significant others. It was a catered event hosted by Roberson's college president Colin Marshall and his wife in their home. Aaron and I rarely attended. But since he was chair of the English Department, he probably needed to make an appearance. And he couldn't be in two places at once, which meant he wouldn't be able to make it to Bailey's recital. Was that why he didn't bother telling me the Fling was tonight and why he stood me up for lunch? He knew I'd be mad he couldn't make the recital and took the path of least resistance? In the past, I'd have blown up at him for this. So, I guess I couldn't completely blame him for not telling me. But I didn't appreciate having to be the one to tell Bailey her father wasn't coming to see her dance.

I smiled at Lynette as if everything was fine. "Remind me of what time that is again."

"Cocktails start at 6:30 p.m. and the dinner buffet starts at 7 p.m. Here," she said, grabbing a cream-colored envelope from her desk and handing it to me. It was an invitation, complete with directions to the president's home at the far end of the campus.

"Thanks, Lynette. I'll see you tonight."

Bailey's recital was from six to seven. I'd have to miss the cocktails, but I'd be able to make it to the dinner to save my husband from having to make small talk on his own. I'd save the questions about what happened to my invitation for afterward.

. . .

When I arrived at President Marshall's sprawling mid-century split level at 7:15 wearing the only appropriately dressy outfit in my closet that still fit – a dark brown coat dress and a pair of black ankle strap pumps that were already beginning to rub my right heel raw – I didn't see Aaron anywhere. Finally, I grabbed a plate from the buffet and got in line behind one of the few people from his department that I knew.

"Hello, Dr. Watford-Raines."

"Paige," exclaimed the older woman as she balanced her plate with one hand and hugged me with the other. My husband might be nowhere to be seen, but at least she seemed genuinely happy that I was there. "It's so good to see you. You look wonderful. I love your haircut."

Helen Watford-Raines had a way of making people feel good about themselves despite their best efforts to the contrary. And I was feeling anything but good in a dress I'd last worn to a funeral. I don't know what I'd been thinking wearing a pair of shoes I hadn't worn since my sister's wedding five years ago either. I didn't know how much longer I could stand the pain.

"As do you, Professor, looking elegant as always." Helen was wearing a navy and cranberry paisley wrap dress that made her dark brown skin and bright white hair glow, and a pair of knee-length black boots.

"I missed you at the reading last month. I hope you can make the next one."

"What reading? I thought the next one wasn't until the end of the month." For the second time that day, I felt like a fool.

Roberson's English Department, with Dr. Watford-Raines serving as host, sponsored authors from all over the world to do readings and Q&As every semester, and Aaron and I always attended. It was something I looked forward to when my work schedule allowed. According to my schedule, Abidi Adesina, a Nigerian author whose debut novel I'd devoured, was supposed to do a reading at the college later that month. I was looking forward to meeting her and having her sign my copy of her book.

"Abidi had a family emergency and couldn't make her original date and couldn't reschedule for a later time. We hosted her virtually last week while she was on an airport layover on her way back to Toronto. I'm so sorry, Paige. I thought Aaron would have told you. When I didn't see you guys online, I figured you were busy."

"It must have slipped his mind." I forced a smile, wondering if it had really slipped my husband's mind or if he just didn't relay the information because it meant he'd not only have to talk to me but attend with me. Helen must have sensed my changed mood and put a hand on my shoulder with a sympathetic smile.

"And where is Aaron? I barely see him anymore since he became department chair."

I frowned. "Really? Not even at faculty meetings?"

"Only the very first one at the start of fall semester. I've stopped by for a chat several times, but he's always in a meeting with the president, or a dean, or trustee, or budget meeting. I just hope he's not getting in over his head. Chairing an academic department isn't for the faint of heart. How's he coping with it all?"

I felt my face flush slightly in embarrassment. How could I admit she probably saw as much of my husband as I did? Even when I saw him, he was so checked out, he may as well have not been there. Thankfully, I spotted Aaron out on the deck. His back was to me, but I could see he had a drink in his hand, and he was laughing at something someone had said. I quickly sat my empty plate down on the table.

"Speak of the devil," I told her, gesturing toward the deck. "It was great seeing you, Dr. Watford-Raines."

"Tell that husband of yours to stop by my office once in a while," she called out as I walked away, and I turned and waved to let her know I'd heard her.

I headed up the steps and out onto the deck, expecting to see my husband with a group of English faculty. Instead, I found him standing a little too close to a very attractive woman I'd never seen before. She had a similar skin tone as me but looked younger and twenty-five pounds lighter, with a curly highlighted bob that fell just below her chin. She wore a sophisticated dark gray jersey silk jumpsuit with ankle-length tapered pant legs. A wide black leather belt cinched in her already tiny waist, and her four-inch fire engine red Mary Janes made her almost as tall as Aaron. Diamond heart earrings dangled from her ears. A slight breeze carried the scent of her expensive floral perfume to my nose.

Aaron leaned in close, listening to whatever it was she was telling him. I couldn't see my husband's face, but I already knew from back in the day when we dated, he was making her feel like she was the only one who existed. I knew that feeling but couldn't remember the last time I'd felt it. She finally noticed me standing there and gave me a brief quizzical look. She didn't know who I was, which made me suddenly think of something I'd noticed when I stopped by Aaron's office for lunch earlier. There had been no pictures of me and the kids in his office. A cold, hard knot formed in the pit of my stomach. But I forced myself to take a step forward toward my husband.

"There you are. I've been looking for you everywhere." I slipped an arm around Aaron's waist, and he was so surprised he stiffened immediately and almost dropped his drink.

"Paige?" He extricated himself and took a step back, looking from me to whoever this woman was.

"Hi, I'm Paige Nichols." I held out my hand for her to shake. She immediately clasped my hand in both of hers. The gesture caught me off guard and the warmth in her expression made me briefly doubt what I'd just witnessed. But it was Aaron's obvious discomfort that made me realize something was up.

"It's so good to meet you, Paige. Aaron has told me so much about you. I'm Cara Morton."

"Dr. Morton is one of the English faculty," Aaron added, and I couldn't tell if he was trying to distance himself from her by calling her doctor or if he wanted me to know this woman had a PhD.

"Oh, I remember now. You started over the summer, right?" Aaron had mentioned Cara to me more than once when she'd first started at the college but had said nothing about her since fall semester started, and he'd left out the part about her being quite so pretty. I couldn't remember the last time he'd mentioned her.

"Yes, that's right? And Aaron tells me you're an aspiring web designer? How exciting."

She looked friendly enough, and she was still smiling warmly at me. But she made the word *aspiring* sound like a putdown. "I should have my certificate by next spring," I replied, as if her question was perfectly innocent. "If you know anyone looking for a website, make sure you send them my way."

"I certainly will. But in the meantime, how about a drink? I'm heading down to the bar. Can I get you anything, Paige? I hear President Marshall made a big pitcher of martinis."

"Yeah, I was telling her the president's martini recipe is famous." Aaron nodded slightly in my direction.

Her? When the hell had I gone from being Paige – or his wife – to a pronoun? I didn't know what kind of expression I had on my face, but they were both looking at me strangely.

"A white wine would be great, thanks," I finally said, and noticed she and Aaron didn't make eye contact as she passed us.

"What are you doing here?" he said as soon as we were alone. "Where are the kids?"

"With Ros. And wow." I really looked at him for the first time since I'd gotten there. He was wearing one of the expensive suits he'd bought since becoming department chair. He was even wearing cologne I'd never smelled on him before. And while he was slimmer and much more stylish and handsome, this Aaron was a stranger to me. What happened to the man who lived in sweats and jeans, was soft around the middle and smelled like soap. Suddenly, I wanted that guy back.

"What? Why are you staring at me like that?"

"Because you really aren't happy to see me, are you? And why wouldn't I be here? I'm your wife. You should have told me tonight was the Fall Fling. I shouldn't have had to find out from your admin assistant when I showed up with food for our lunch date that you blew off."

"Oh God, Paige. I am so sorry. A last-minute meeting came up and..."

"Stop it, Aaron!" I hadn't meant for it to come out so loud and angry, and I glanced around to make sure no one had overheard. If anyone had, they were polite enough not to stare. "Lynette already told me you were at lunch. If you're going to lie to me, make sure you're telling Lynette the same lie."

"Look," he said, putting down the glass in his hand on a nearby table and turning to give me his full attention. "I knew how mad you'd be when you found out I couldn't make Bailey's recital and I didn't know how to handle it. I'm sorry. I'm really am."

"Here's the thing," I said, taking a step toward him and lowering my voice. "I went to the recital and made it here in time for dinner. It's all about priorities. And I can't believe anyone here tonight would have begrudged you going to your daughter's recital and arriving a little late, except maybe Dr. Morton." Aaron didn't like that last part and glanced away. His face was tight and angry. Seconds after I'd uttered Cara's name, she was back on the deck with a white wine spritzer for me and a bottle of craft beer for Aaron. When the hell had he started drinking craft beer?

"This was the last one. I remembered how much you liked it when they served it at the faculty mixer last month, so I grabbed it for you." She handed the bottle to Aaron.

He took it wordlessly and practically drained it in one gulp. Why he was drinking craft beer wasn't the point of that little exchange. This bitch wanted me to know that she'd been spending so much time with my husband that she knew his likes and dislikes. She wanted me to know that they were close, as if that wasn't already apparent.

"Well, I don't know about you guys, but I'm starving, and they just put out more prime rib on the buffet, nice and medium rare." She gave Aaron a meaningful look.

We watched Cara go, and I drained my wine glass, sat it down on the table and glared at my husband.

"We should go eat," said Aaron. But he was glancing past me. I turned in the direction of his gaze to see Cara chatting with a handsome silver-haired man whose name I couldn't quite place. Peroni? Peters? I'd met him once and couldn't remember. Aaron could barely keep his eyes off Cara, even when he wasn't talking to her. Even when I was standing right there.

"I'll be back in a minute. I need to go to the bathroom first."

It was a lie. I really needed to pull myself together because otherwise I was going to burst into tears. Suddenly, the last few months made sense. Aaron's distraction, never being home, and the growing distance between us. It was her. Cara Morton.

There was a line for the bathroom in the foyer. I stood behind two other women I didn't know and couldn't help but overhear what they were saying even though they were talking low.

"Doesn't she drive a black Camry?" asked the woman with sleek blonde hair and glasses.

"Yeah, that's her car. And she's always parked right next to his silver Acura. Doesn't matter what parking spaces are open closer to the building. Wherever his car's parked, hers is right next to it. I usually see them walking out together after work every afternoon," said her companion, a woman with long dark hair pulled back from her face with a turquoise barrette.

"Isn't he married? I didn't think he was like that," said the woman in the glasses.

"They're all like that, honey," said the woman with the dark hair, before ducking into the bathroom the instant another woman emerged.

Aaron drove a silver Acura and I would bet every dime I owned that they'd been talking about my husband and Cara Morton. I no longer wanted to cry. Instead, white hot anger welled up inside me as thoughts of my husband – smiling, laughing, drinking fucking craft beer – with that woman made my fists clench. I walked straight out the front door, got into my Explorer, and called my husband.

"Where the hell are you?" he demanded. "Are you still in the bathroom?"

"I'm on my way home. And if you're not back in fifteen minutes, I'm changing the locks on all the doors." I hung up on him and started the engine.

SEVEN

PAIGE NICHOLS

BEFORE

October 5, 2023

"What did he say when he got home last night?" asked my sister Roselyn over coffee the next morning. She'd stopped by after I'd dropped the kids off at school because she could tell how upset I'd been when I'd picked them up the night before.

"That I was imagining things, and he and Cara are just friends." I made air quotes around the word friends. "Apparently, being department chair is stressing him the hell out and Cara knows what that's like because she ran an honors English program at some fancy private school on the East Coast. And she's helping him navigate it all."

Ros rolled her eyes and sighed. "He gaslighted the hell out of you."

"Pretty much."

"Do you think he's sleeping with her?"

"I don't know. But you should have seen them last night, Ros. Anyone who didn't know any better would have thought she was his wife, and I was the colleague. And I don't care what bullshit excuses he came up with. My gut is telling me something is different. I don't know what to do." My voice trembled. "I haven't been easy to live with. But I thought when I quit nursing, we'd find our way back to each other. I never thought he'd do something like this." A single tear rolled down my cheek and my sister reached out and squeezed my hand.

"I'm so sorry, P. I could just wring that idiot's neck. What the hell is he thinking?"

"He's not thinking. That's the problem." We were silent for a few minutes as we finished our coffee. "Have you and Jaz ever been through this?" My sister was a high school music teacher and her wife, Jazmine, was a former dancer and owner of the dance studio where Bailey took lessons. They'd met in grad school and quickly became inseparable. If they'd ever been through a bad patch, I'd yet to hear about it.

"No. Knock on wood. But there is someone you should probably talk to."

"Who?"

"Mom."

"Mom? Are you kidding? Mom thinks Aaron walks on water and any problems we're having are my fault. Have you forgotten the time she sided with him when we were arguing because he wanted another baby? We didn't speak for months."

"Yeah, I get she can overstep. But this is different, and I think you could really use her advice, P."

"Why? What do you know that I don't?"

My sister looked away and let out a breath before answering. "Remember when we were kids and Mom and Daddy sent us to spend the summer in South Carolina with Aunt Pat and Uncle James?"

"Of course, I remember. You were fifteen, and I was twelve. And you threw a fit because you missed band camp."

"God, I was such a nerd."

"Was?"

"Shut up," she said, irritated. "Anyway, I know the real reason they sent us down there for the summer, and it had nothing to do with wanting us to get to know our cousins better."

"Then what?" I asked, not catching on.

"Daddy had an affair."

"What? No way! Daddy would never..." I began before my sister held up her hand.

"This is the reason I never told you. I loved Daddy too. But he wasn't perfect. He cheated on Mom at least once that I know of."

"How do you know he cheated on Mom?"

"Because I'm not like you. I can't sleep through a tornado. When they were arguing late at night, it always woke me up. Remember Daddy would go out to meet the fellas at the bar after dinner?"

"Yeah, I remember. It was every Friday night. And he was always home in time to kiss us goodnight."

"Until he wasn't," she said. Her mouth set in a hard line for a moment before she went on. "He started going out on Saturday nights and weeknights, too, coming home drunk after midnight. One night, Mom followed him. She went out ten minutes after he did and told me not to open the door for anybody." She paused to take a sip of her soda. "Turns out the 'fellas' was a chick from accounting. She caught them in the backseat of Dad's car. It had been going on for months when she found out. Don't you remember the one morning Mom ever served us breakfast on paper plates? She always used to say paper plates were only for picnics and barbeques, and anybody using them every day was just too lazy to wash dishes. You asked her what was up with the paper plates, and she burst into tears? Come on. I can't be the only one who remembers that."

"I remember, but not why," I conceded, not liking where

this was going.

"That's because when they got home, they had the mother of all arguments and Mom broke every plate in the house. Daddy got banished to the basement and two weeks later, they dropped us off in South Carolina for the summer. They obviously worked it out because when we came home, Mom was pregnant with Tyler."

It had never occurred to me to wonder why my parents had had another child in their forties. I'd just assumed it was a happy accident. Had giving my father the son he'd always wanted been the reason they'd stayed together? Tyler was our mother's favorite. But was it because he was the baby of the family or because his birth had saved her marriage? My parents had remained married until my father's death from a heart attack the year after I'd given birth to the twins.

"I really wish you hadn't told me this." It was bad enough that my husband was cheating on me. But to find out the father I'd adored had cheated on my mom was more than I could stand.

"I never planned on telling you. But I don't want you burying your head in the sand either."

"What are you talking about?" I asked angrily.

"Look, I believe you. I think Aaron is being shady as fuck. But you need to find out for sure. Because he won't confess. And he won't stop as long as he thinks he's getting away with it. He's going to keep gaslighting you and doing whatever he's doing with this Cara woman. You need to know for sure so you can figure out what you're going to do."

I knew my sister was right. But what would I do when I found out for sure? Leave? How would I support myself and the twins? I had no job and no money saved. The truth was, I didn't want to find out whether Aaron was having an affair because what would I do then? What would happen to us, our kids, to me?

. . .

I was still thinking about all of this when Aaron showed up unexpected at noon with a bag of tacos from the campus taco truck.

"Hey, I thought we could have lunch and talk," he said, looking subdued and uncertain.

I simply stared at him as he spread out a variety of tacos on the kitchen island. Wordlessly, I got plates and glasses from the cabinet, and a pitcher of iced tea from the fridge.

"It's not craft beer, but it'll have to do," I told him as I sat across from him and poured iced tea into two glasses. He grimaced.

"I am really sorry about last night, Paige. I feel horrible."

"What exactly are you feeling horrible about, Aaron? Lying to me, neglecting me and the kids, or your so-called friendship with Cara Morton? And since when do you wear cologne?" I angrily took a bite from a soft chicken taco, barely tasting it.

"All the above," he replied, shocking me. I stopped chewing and stared at him.

"You're involved with her? You admit that you're cheating on me? Are you sleeping with her?" Tears filled my eyes and blood pounded in my ears. I'd known in my heart it was true, of course, but hearing him confirm it was still hard to bear.

"No! I swear to you I've never slept with Cara. But—"

"But what?" I shot back.

"We have gotten close. Maybe a little too close. I never meant for this to happen."

I felt strangely numb. "Do you have feelings for her?" I hated how weak my voice sounded. Hell, I hated he'd put me in a position to ask if he had feelings for another woman.

"Maybe a crush, but nothing else. Like I said, chairing the English Department has been even more of a challenge than I thought it would be. I'm getting a lot of pushback from some of the older faculty members about changes I'm wanting to make. And a lot of these people I'd considered my friends, and they're actively trying to sabotage me at every turn. Cara has been a lifesaver."

His words were a punch in the gut. A *lifesaver*? I was his wife. Wasn't I supposed to be the lifesaver? "Cara helping you out at work is one thing, Aaron. But you've changed. You're never around. You never confide in me anymore." I softened, ever so slightly. "I didn't even know you were struggling at work. And you've got all these new tastes and interests you never had before Cara came along."

Aaron hung his head and looked away. But he didn't deny what I'd just said, and suddenly my stomach was in knots.

"What about you? You've changed too. Why do you want to design websites? Where did that even come from?"

"Did you forget that I helped design the clinic's website?" Aaron looked embarrassed and didn't reply, so I had my answer. "There's good money in web design. I thought I'd try it." It came out more defensive than I'd meant it to. I was aware my career change had taken him by surprise, but he was not about to turn this around on me. "If it doesn't work out, I can always go back to nursing."

"And you didn't feel the need to explain that to me? I'm not the only one at fault here, Paige."

"All I did was push you away," I replied, furious. "And, yeah, that was wrong. But I didn't go out and find another man to make me feel important and validated."

Aaron gave me an incredulous look that caught me off guard. "That's what you think I did?"

"What I think is that you're having an emotional affair." I looked up and the anger on my husband's face made me flinch. But it was quickly gone, replaced by resignation because he couldn't deny the truth of what I'd just said. The silence that ensued made the blood pounding in my ears almost painful.

"You've been so distant and angry, Paige. I never felt like I could do anything right in your eyes. It was just... easier with Cara, and it was nice to have something just for me."

Aaron's words had pierced me to my core. But as bad as I felt for neglecting my marriage, I wasn't about to take all the blame.

"Did you ever wonder why I was so angry? Did you ever think to ask me what was going on or how my day was before you started unloading your day on me? No, you didn't. Did you ever offer to cook or go buy something for dinner after I'd worked a double shift at the clinic so I could have a hot bath and an hour to myself to decompress?"

"Babe, I'm—" Aaron began, but I talked over him, unable to stop now that the flood gates were open.

"Did it ever occur to you to offer to clean up the kitchen after dinner instead of disappearing into your study? All you do is work and come home, Aaron. Once you hit that door, your workday ends while I worked full-time and then came home to cook, clean, and take care of you and the kids after taking care of other people all day long."

Aaron sighed waiting for my tirade to be over, looking everywhere but at me. Was he even listening to me?

"And you don't listen!" I shouted to get his attention. "How many times have you forgotten to pick the kids up from school? Then you get an attitude when I remind you a million times. So, you'll have to excuse me if I'm not joining your little pity party because, frankly, I'd love to have something just for me. And no matter how distant and angry I may have been, I don't deserve this. Marriage is messy and not always easy. Either you suck it up and deal with it, or you leave. You don't betray your vows."

Aaron hung his head. "Babe, I... I'm sorry. I'm not perfect."

I rolled my eyes. "Wanting you to be honest and here for me and the kids has nothing to do with being perfect, and if you don't know that, there's no point in having this conversation."

"I just want—"

"What are we going to do about this?" I said, cutting him off again. I was in no mood to hear any more of his bullshit. "Because I'm trying. If you won't meet me halfway, then why am I bothering? I'm fighting for us while you're sneaking around drinking craft beer and eating half raw meat with Cara Morton." Now that I knew the truth, her name felt like poison in my mouth.

"What would you like me to do? Just tell me what to do." He ran a hand over his face and stared at me, his expression unreadable.

"That should be obvious. No more Cara. You need to cut her off before you find yourself someplace you don't want to be."

"And where is that?"

"Without your wife and kids." And there it was. Roselyn had asked me what I was going to do, and in that moment, I knew. I refused to play second fiddle to any other woman. And I wouldn't beg. Either Aaron wanted to be with me and the kids or he didn't.

Surprised by what I'd just said, Aaron got up and came around to my side of the island, pulled me to my feet and wrapped his arms around me. I resisted for a moment, then reluctantly hugged him back. The hug felt nice, despite my hurt and anger. It had been a long time since I'd gotten such a tight hug from Aaron.

"We can fix this," he said softly stroking my hair.

But he hadn't said what I needed to hear.

"And Cara?"

He didn't answer right away. Then he pulled back, looking me straight in the eyes, and said, "I promise to end things with her."

And I desperately wanted to believe him.

EIGHT

PAIGE NICHOLS

BEFORE

October 7, 2023

From my car I watched the entrance to Nova, a new restaurant that had opened downtown over the summer, feeling like a stalker. Aaron had brought me here for my birthday in September. But he'd been too preoccupied and distant for me to enjoy it, checking his phone every few minutes and barely paying me any attention. I didn't even get the earrings I'd wanted. Instead, he'd given me a wallet I hadn't asked for and didn't need. When our server brought me a complimentary birthday brownie à la mode for dessert, Aaron had looked up from his phone long enough to join in the singing of a wildly out of tune rendition of 'Happy Birthday'. After I blew out the sparkler stuck in the middle of the brownie, the servers again wished me happy birthday with practiced smiles as they quickly dispersed, and my husband's attention was back on his phone. In the past, we would have shared the brownie. Instead, I ate it alone, too annoyed to offer him any. Once it was gone and I was licking the spoon, he'd given me a look of surprise.

"Babe, you ate that whole thing? It must have been at least a thousand calories."

The look I gave him could have curdled milk. "Probably more," I said. "And, you know what, *babe*?" I got up and threw my napkin on the table. "It was easily the best thing about tonight because your company was shitty. I'd have had more fun with a coma patient." I left him there and took an Uber home. Worst birthday, ever.

Now, a month later, I found myself back there, sitting in my car and trying to get up enough nerve to go inside. I'd followed Cara Morton here and watched her walk in, followed by several other stylishly dressed black women. There was an event being held tonight. Most likely on the third floor, which the restaurant rented out. I grabbed my cell phone from my purse and called Nova's number. It rang forever, and I'd almost hung up when a breathless woman answered.

"Nova, this is Allison. How may I help you?"

"I'm attending an event at the restaurant, but I can't remember if it's tonight or tomorrow."

She paused as she checked the system. "The only event we have scheduled this week is the Gamma Rho Nu mocktail mixer in the loft tonight from six to eight."

"That's it. Thanks." I hung up and got out of the car.

Gamma Rho Nu was an African American sorority I'd intended to pledge when I was in college, but it never happened. My aspirations fell victim to a terrible decision that put my life on hold for nearly a year. Something I've never told anyone about, not even Aaron.

"What am I doing here?" I muttered as I headed across the street. Although, I knew exactly what I was doing here. Spying on Cara Morton. I should have just stalked her on social media like a normal scorned wife, but here I was in the flesh. I don't do anything by half.

"Mrs. Nichols?"

The sound of my name made me whirl around guiltily. A pretty, young black woman with long knotless braids that fell down her back approached me, smiling brightly. She wore skinny jeans and yellow Doc Martins that matched the yellow and gray Gamma Rho Nu T-shirt she wore underneath a dark gray cropped leather jacket. It took me just a second to realize who she was.

"Jaida? Reese?"

"Yep. I wondered if you'd remember me. How are you?"

"I'm fine and, of course, I remember you. I didn't know you were a Gamma."

She fell in step beside me, and I had no choice but to walk inside with her. I'd met Jaida a few times at the author readings I'd attended with Aaron at the college. She was such a lovely young woman and one of Aaron's favorite students.

"Third generation legacy. My mom and my grandma are Gammas. Are you here for the mixer?"

"I am." My cheeks hurt from my tight smile. Why had I come here? I just wanted to leave.

"Then you must be thinking about pledging, right? We have a very active graduate chapter."

"I am thinking about it. I almost pledged in college, but life got in the way."

Jaida gave me a curious look, waiting for me to continue, but I didn't. It wasn't the kind of story you shared with a stranger.

"Well, I'd better get up there, Mrs. Nichols. I'm supposed to help serve the mocktails and I'm late. It was nice seeing you."

"I will and it was nice seeing you too, Jaida." She smiled and headed up the steps to the loft above.

Nova was in a converted warehouse with a large open floor plan, exposed brick walls and ductwork, and metal pipes installed in an intricate crosshatch design on the ceiling. A bar occupied the back of the first floor, with small round tables for customers who didn't mind not being seated in the main dining room.

To my left was a hostess station and directly in front of me were the stairs. Muted sounds of voices and music drifted down the metal staircase. A few more women had come in behind me and made their way upstairs, glancing at me as I stood frozen in place, unable to put my foot on the first step.

I willed my trembling legs to move and climbed the stairs until I was standing in front of a yellow sandwich-board sign. It had dark gray lettering, the Gamma Rho Nu colors along with the sorority emblem and the picture of the speaker for the mixer, a smiling light-skinned black woman in her late fifties. She had a salt and pepper pixie cut that was longer on the top and sides which flattered her long narrow face. She was heavier, with noticeable lines around her eyes and mouth, but had the same small gap between her front teeth. Until that morning when I'd spotted her during my tour of Highland Academy, I hadn't seen her in twenty-one years. But I'd know her anywhere, Dr. Natalie Drew. And had I known she'd be here tonight, I wouldn't have come. Panic gripped me as beads of sweat popped up on my forehead. I needed to go. *Now*. I spun on my heel and ran smack into Dr. Watford-Raines, nearly knocking her backward.

"Helen!" I reached out and grabbed the older woman's upper arm to steady her and pull her back from the top step before she fell. "Oh my God. I didn't see you. I am so sorry." I bent to pick up her cane, which had clattered loudly to the floor. "Are you okay?"

"I'm fine." But she didn't look fine. Helen pressed her hand to her chest like she was trying to slow down the frantic beating of her heart.

"Are you sure?"

"Positive," she said, catching her breath and letting out a shaky laugh. "No harm done, but I could ask the same of you."

"What?"

"Girl, you look like you swallowed a bug. I kept calling you as I was walking up here. Didn't you hear me?"

"No. Sorry. And if you're sure you're okay, I should probably go." Panic coursed through my veins, making me antsy to put this place and Natalie Drew behind me. Although, I thought I had already done that twenty years ago.

"Oh no, you don't." Helen grabbed my hand and pulled me into the room behind her. The strength of her grip surprised me. "You owe me a very large drink. It's the least you can do for almost, as my students would say, yeeting me down the stairs."

"But..." I began. Only Helen wasn't having it and wouldn't let go of my hand.

"No buts. Let's find a seat. Besides," she said in a low whisper, "I hate these things and would love someone to talk to."

"Then why did you come?"

"I'm the graduate chapter president." Helen's eyes rolled heavenward as she pasted a bright smile on her face. To my horror, she chose seats in the front row, near the podium where Natalie Drew would be speaking. Would she recognize me after all these years?

Helen excused herself and left me sitting at the table while she worked the room.

I took the chance to check my phone. Aaron had already called twice and left a message saying he'd picked up the kids, asking where I was and if I was okay. I tossed my phone back into my purse, feeling like a fool. He'd told me that morning he had a meeting after work. It had only been a few days since the Fall Fling and finding out about him and Cara Morton. He said he'd cut her off, but had he? All day long, I'd imagined that the meeting had been an excuse to spend time with her. I'd dropped Bryce at basketball practice and Bailey at her ballet class, and on the way home drove past Tate Hall to see if I could spot my husband's car parked behind the building. It was, and I was even happier not to see a black Camry parked next to it. But that didn't mean he couldn't still be seeing her.

I'm not sure what I thought spying on my husband was going to accomplish. I couldn't make him do the right thing. But I needed to know if *I* was doing the right by giving him a second chance. I was pondering whether to wait in the adjacent parking lot and see who Aaron left the building with when a familiar figure exited Tate Hall from a side door, rushing to the lot with a phone pressed against her ear. It was Cara Morton. Her car sat two rows ahead of mine. She opened the driver's side door, tossing her black leather tote into the passenger seat, and got behind the wheel.

Five minutes passed before she finally started the car and pulled out of her spot. She was already at the light, about to turn right, which would take her downtown, when I started my car and followed her. I tracked her to the street in front of Nova, where she parked and then walked across the street to greet an older black woman. I pulled into the pay lot across the street and parked just as Cara and the other woman walked inside.

And now here I was, glancing around the dimly lit room, having followed the woman my husband had an affair with. Was this a good idea? Of course not.

Soft jazz music was coming from the loft's speakers, making the atmosphere seem a lot more relaxed and mellow than I was feeling. Jaida and several similarly dressed Gammas were mixing and serving mocktails from a small bar cater-corner to the podium, and those not interested in virgin drinks had brought their own up from the bar on the first floor. I noticed I was one of only four women in attendance not wearing Gamma yellow and gray. Even Helen wore a dress similar to the one she'd worn to the Fling with a yellow and gray paisley print. Despite scanning the crowds, I didn't see Cara anywhere, not sure exactly what I'd do if I had. After seeing Natalie Drew's picture, I'd almost forgotten about Cara. After what seemed like forever but was probably only ten minutes, Helen returned and settled into the seat next to me.

"What would you like to drink?" I gestured toward the bar.

"Honey, I need something a hell of a lot stronger than a virgin margarita. Let's get a real drink downstairs when this is over. But just one or all hell will break loose."

"What do you mean?"

"I'm alcohol intolerant. I shouldn't be having it at all, but one gin and tonic never hurt anybody."

What was I doing here? I needed to get home to the kids and started to tell Helen this when she got up and headed to the podium as the music stopped, the lights in the already dim room darkened and conversation slowed to a halt.

"Soros and future Soros, I am so thankful to welcome you all this evening to our first Gamma Rho Nu mixer in two years." Enthusiastic applause met Helen's words of welcome.

I clapped, too, and glanced at my watch as a floral scent suddenly caught my attention, followed by a soft tap on my shoulder. Cara Morton was sitting behind me. Her eyes narrowed slightly, and a smirk lifted one corner of her mouth. The look was gone in an instant, replaced by a smile. She mouthed hi and gave me a little wave. Had Aaron told her I knew about them? I'm guessing he hadn't because why would she be so friendly? Anxiety made me light-headed. I wanted to bolt from the room. Instead, I gave her a nod and tossed a hand up. I noticed when I saw her outside that Cara wasn't wearing Gamma colors either. Her black suit should have made her blend into the background. Instead, the dark color made her highlighted hair, bright red lipstick, and flawless skin stand out even more than all the women in the room wearing bright yellow. There were at least two dozen other chairs she could have sat at. Why sit behind me?

As if that wasn't bad enough, by the time I'd turned my attention back to the podium, Helen was gone and in her place was Dr. Natalie Drew in a dark gray dress with a yellow and gray Hermes scarf draped around her neck, held in place by a pearl brooch. With Cara Morton behind me and Natalie Drew in front of me, I was literally between a rock and a hard place, confronted by my past sins and reminded of my tumultuous present. I took deep breaths to calm my nerves. Trying to look anywhere except at the woman in front of me, while being keenly aware of the scrutiny of the woman behind me. Cara's eyes on me felt like ants crawling up my back.

Natalie Drew smiled and scanned the crowd while waiting for the applause to die down. Her gaze swept past me and for an instant I was relieved, thinking she hadn't recognized me. Then she did a double take, pinning me with her intense gaze, eyes squinting slightly in the darkened room as if she were trying to figure out if she was seeing who she thought she was seeing. It lasted maybe five seconds, and I was praying no one else noticed. But someone had.

"Do you know Dr. Drew?" Cara had leaned over my shoulder and whispered in my ear. Her warm breath on my skin startled me.

I shook my head and reached down for the bottled water sitting next to everyone's seat to relieve my dry mouth. But my hands were shaking so badly I dropped it. Cara reached past me, picked up the bottle and handed it to me as Dr. Drew began her presentation on women's heart health.

"Are you okay?" Cara whispered with a concerned tone.

"Fine. Thanks." I lifted the bottle in acknowledgment, hoping she'd shut up and leave me alone. But then again, I was the one who'd followed her here. I was the one who didn't belong.

The presentation lasted twenty excruciating minutes, during which the doctor read from her PowerPoint slides while glancing at her notes. I sensed seeing me had thrown her off her game. She seemed a little less enthusiastic than she was before she'd spotted me, and avoided looking my way again. When the presentation was finally over, women approached Dr. Drew to meet her and ask questions, including Cara, and I used the opportunity to bolt. Before I headed down the stairs, I looked back to see Cara and Natalie Drew staring after me. Cara was glancing from me to Dr. Drew with an amused expression on her face.

"Paige? Are you leaving already?" Helen was coming up the stairs, and I realized she'd never come back to our table after introducing Dr. Drew.

"I'm so sorry, Helen. I need to get home. But I promise you a raincheck on that drink soon."

Without waiting for a reply, I brushed past her, eager to get away from both Cara and Natalie Drew, the woman who'd been my mentor and friend in college.

Until I'd slept with her husband. And almost ruined my life.

NINE

AARON NICHOLS

AFTER

December 5, 2023

"Me? I'd never hurt Cara, Detective. I wasn't talking about me."

She looked up at me, blinking. "Then who?"

"She had a run-in with a home health nurse who'd left her father home alone. She ended up firing the woman, and she was also being harassed by a young man."

"You mean the one who accosted her on the college green?" Alonso asked, perusing her notes.

"Yeah him. And that wasn't the only time."

She frowned. "But she told you that was about grades, right?"

"Right. But there was a lot more going on there."

Alonso quirked an eyebrow at the frantic tone of my voice. I sat back in the chair and looked down at my lap, unable to meet her gaze. When I finally looked at her the expression on her face had gone from relaxed and neutral to hard and wary like she didn't believe a word coming out of my mouth. I was blowing it. I needed to calm down. But there were things I couldn't tell her if I wanted to walk out of this police station.

"All right." She sat her notebook down, put her elbows on the table, leaned forward, and said, "I'm listening."

TEN

AARON NICHOLS

BEFORE

October 13, 2023

I loosened my tie, pulled it from around my neck, balled it up, and threw it across my office the minute I'd closed the door behind me. Another meeting that ended with me on the hot seat having to explain once again why I was implementing the changes I proposed. The same six full-time faculty members I was answering to were refusing to attend the training I'd set up. If it were just pushback over learning unfamiliar software by a handful of faculty, that would be one thing. But these six faculty members regularly complained to the president of the faculty senate about how I was doing my job. And the only person I'd been able to talk to about any of it had been Cara.

I hadn't exactly lied to Paige when I told her I wanted to fix our marriage. In all honesty, she'd caught me off guard when she'd shown up at the Fall Fling and noticed the vibe between me and Cara. It was pretty hard to hide. But fixing it meant cutting Cara off completely. And that was proving to be impossible, as we were on many of the same committees and attended all the same meetings. We hadn't really talked since the night of the Fling. It was clear she knew something was wrong and was keeping her distance. But it didn't help when all I wanted to do was talk to her. I missed our lunches and texts, her laughter and the smell of her perfume. I missed her coming to see me after contentious meetings to give me long full body hugs. I missed the softness of her skin and the feel of her lips parting underneath mine when we kissed. When I told Paige I'd never slept with Cara, I was telling the truth. But I wanted to, badly. Instead, we'd been making out like teenagers every chance we got.

None of this was Paige's fault. And the crazy thing was, I still loved her very much. I just wasn't sure I was *in love* with her anymore. I was trying to be more present, spending more time with her and the kids, but it was an effort. Though she wanted us to be close again, I couldn't help but hold back about my work problems. Paige, meanwhile, was becoming more like the woman she'd been when I first met her: laid-back, fun-loving, and spontaneous. That should have made things easier, but somehow it felt like I was being disloyal to Cara. It had been a whole week since we'd spoken when my desk phone rang. Hoping it might be Cara, I picked it up immediately.

"Yes?"

"Dr. Nichols. Dr. Peters is here to see you."

I tried not to sound too disappointed. It was only Lynette.

"Send him in." Peters was the last man I wanted to see. He was the ringleader of the rogue faculty members sidestepping every bit of my authority. I'd just come from a meeting that ended with Peters and me in a shouting match. I couldn't believe he had the nerve to show his face in my office now. At least he had the decency to look embarrassed when he walked in.

"What can I do for you, Dr. Peters?" *Besides fucking right off*, I thought but didn't say. I didn't bother offering him a seat because I wanted him out of my office as soon as possible.

"Dr. Nichols. I just came to apologize and say how truly sorry I am for my appalling behavior. That was completely uncalled for, and I'm ashamed of myself."

"Thank you. I'm sorry for how out of hand things got, as well. And I hope you'll reconsider taking the training for the new communication system."

Peters simply stared at me and shook his head before answering. "I know you think I'm just an old man who doesn't want to learn anything new. But the cost of that software is going to put a huge dent in the department's budget and use up funds for programs that we've always counted on to help boost our enrollment."

"You're referring to the study abroad program?"

"You know I am."

"The pandemic put a hold on that program for at least another year. It may not be back for a while, if at all."

"What do you mean?" exclaimed the older man, visibly puffing up, his face reddening.

"I won't sugarcoat this. Enrollment is down at colleges across the country. The university is looking for programs to cut to save money. Unless our enrollment is up next year, the study abroad program is on the chopping block."

"You don't know that."

"It's my job to know that." I wasn't a fool. Peters was the faculty coordinator for the study abroad program, which paid him a nice, fat stipend and allowed him to take all expenses paid trips to the host countries to accompany the students enrolled in the program twice a year.

"Our study abroad program is one of the most prestigious in the country. I'm sure there are plenty of other programs we could cut that would benefit the college's bottom line."

"Such as?"

"The programs that aren't bringing in the quality students that this university needs."

"You mean the programs targeting minority students?" Roberson's study abroad program wasn't popular amongst the minority student population. It attracted mostly white students. The kinds of students that Dr. Peters obviously felt belonged at Roberson.

"That's not what I said. Stop trying to make this about race," Peters blustered. It wasn't what he'd said, but we both knew it was exactly what he'd meant.

"I'm done arguing about this. But I will tell you something I'm surprised you weren't already aware of. Money for the software program I'm proposing and money for the study abroad program come from separate accounts. Nothing we spend on new software impacts the college's budget for academic programs.

Peters' eyes darted to the ceiling, and he rocked back slightly on his heels. He was considering what I'd just said as confusion flitted across his face. I let out a frustrated sigh and broke it down further for him.

"Cutting the study abroad program has nothing to do with buying something that falls under a technology expense. But thank you for your money saving suggestion, Dr. Peters. I will certainly pass it along to President Marshall at the next budget meeting."

Peters glared at me and then turned to go. He reached for the doorknob, then stopped and turned to me. "You know, this wasn't the way things were supposed to be."

"Excuse me?"

"Your being named department chair."

"What are you talking about?"

"When you were selected, everyone thought that, because you were so laid-back and unambitious, you'd be easy to work with and you'd support the interests of the faculty above all others, and be an ally to us. Instead, you're an arrogant control freak playing fast and loose with the college's money."

"In other words, you thought I'd be a puppet you could control." I turned to face him completely. "Let me be very clear, Dr. Peters. My job is to make sure this department runs smoothly, and to support everyone who works here, from the tenured faculty to the administrative assistants. We all serve the students and no one, least of all me, has the time to deal with personal agendas."

"Personal agendas, huh?" said Peters, taking a step toward me. "Well, let me give you a piece of advice, my boy."

"And what would that be?" It took everything in me not to bitch-slap this racist old fool.

"Everyone knows about you and the lovely Dr. Morton. So, I wouldn't be getting up on my high horse if I were you. Even dogs know not to shit where they sleep. And I hope for your sake it doesn't get back to the president. You know how he feels about anything that could bring even a hint of scandal to this university."

He was gone before I even had time to register what he'd just said. I stared after him in shock. Had I heard him right? Everyone knew about me and Cara. How? We'd been so careful. At least I thought we had. Hoping Peters was just a bitter old bastard blowing smoke out his ass, I grabbed my jacket and headed to the cafeteria for lunch. I was passing by what I thought was an empty classroom when I heard raised voices and stopped to listen.

"But you promised!" said a male voice.

"We talked about this. You know I can't right now. Why can't you understand that?" replied a female voice, a very familiar female voice.

I stepped inside the classroom to see Cara and the same kid who'd accosted her on the street at the start of fall semester. He had her pinned against her desk, and her face was pale and pinched with fear. Anger and panic jolted me into action, and in two strides, I was across the room and shoving the kid away from Cara. He lost his footing and fell backward onto his ass before scrambling to his feet and running out of the room.

"Are you all right?"

Cara merely nodded, letting out a breath. "I'm fine. And you shouldn't have done that. I had it under control." She slung her purse over her shoulder and pushed past me.

"That's not what it looked like to me," I called after her. "And wasn't that the same kid who harassed you before?"

"I'm going to be late for a lunch meeting, Aaron, and I don't have time to talk because you've suddenly remembered I exist."

"Cara, please. I'm sorry." I truly meant it. In keeping my promise to Paige, I was hurting a woman I cared a lot about. And I hated it.

She stopped and turned to me. Tears shone in her eyes. "Did I do something wrong? Because you've been treating me like the past two months never happened."

"Of course not," I spluttered. The sight of her tears made me feel like the bastard that I was. "But we need to talk."

Cara blew off her lunch meeting, and we headed to a diner a few blocks from the campus. Things were awkward and tense at first, but we quickly fell into our familiar rhythm. I told her what happened with Paige after the Fling.

"I guess that explains why she was acting so weird when I ran into her last week."

"You ran into Paige? Where?" This was the first I'd heard about my wife running into Cara. But it didn't surprise me that she wouldn't have mentioned it to me.

"At the Gamma Rho Nu mixer last week," she said, looking down at her glass. "And I'm sorry I was such a bitch to her at the

Fling. But she caught me off guard when she showed up out of the blue and put her arm around you."

"I know." I wanted to reach out and squeeze her hand but was unsure of how she'd respond. "Believe me. I had no idea she was coming."

Cara sighed and shook her head. "She never comes to campus, and it felt like she was trespassing on our territory. I got angry and lost my cool."

Just then a server came to the table and took our orders. I waited for him to leave before turning my attention back to Cara.

"If that feels anything like what I felt seeing you flirting with Peters, then I completely understand."

"Flirting with Peters?" Cara looked genuinely confused to the point I almost questioned what I saw at the Fall Fling. "Seriously? What are you talking about?"

"Never mind," I said abruptly, beginning to feel like an overly sensitive idiot. Why had I brought that up when we were finally talking again?

"Please don't tell me that ignoring me for the past week was you pouting because you saw me talking to Dr. Peters at a party. I talked to lots of people that night. You don't own me, Aaron." Her face was hard and angry, and she gave me such a look of contempt that I almost flinched.

"No, I told you what happened with Paige." I lowered my voice and looked around. "Why are you being like this?"

"Because you're a married man who goes home every night to your wife and kids. I'm a single woman who can do whatever the fuck I want." She paused before lowering her voice. "And even if I was flirting with Peters, that's my business."

Jealousy flared inside me. The server returned with our food, and we ate in angry silence for a few minutes. Not that I tasted much of the cheeseburger I'd ordered. I just wanted Cara and me to go back to the way things had been before.

"This has gotten complicated, hasn't it?" she finally said, pushing aside her barely touched salad.

I nodded. "You have no idea."

She reached across the table and laced her fingers through mine. "Look, I'm just happy to spend time with you, Aaron. I'm not trying to complicate your life."

I hadn't realized just how starved for Cara's touch I was until I felt the warmth of her fingers. If ever there was a time I felt like a complete and total asshole, it was now. I'd made love to my wife that morning before breakfast, and here I was holding hands with Cara at lunchtime.

"And *I'm* not trying to own you," I replied.

"Sorry, I didn't mean to be such a bitch." Her voice was softer, more like how it usually was. "I've had a shitty morning."

"Me too." I told her about what Dr. Peters said, and she threw her head back and let out a harsh, humorless laugh.

"I hope you aren't worried over anything that hypocrite has to say. He's a joke and they want him gone. The dean keeps scaling his course load back because they want him to retire."

"I guess that explains why he's so hot to hold on to that stipend he gets from the study abroad program."

"That's not the reason." She gave me a knowing smile. It was the first time I'd seen that smile in a week. I'd almost forgotten just how beautiful she was. "I heard he has a girl-friend in Paris, which is why he's so hot to accompany the students to the Sorbonne, when they could get there quicker and easier on their own. Apparently, she teaches Renaissance Art, and it's been going on for years. Mrs. Peters is the one with all the money and an ironclad prenup. So, he has to cheat overseas."

I gently pulled my hands away from hers. For a long time, I said nothing, and Cara realized she'd touched a nerve.

"Hey, I didn't mean—"

"Do you think I'm like Peters?"

She didn't answer right away. "Only in circumstance but not in character. You're a good man, Aaron Nichols. If you weren't, you wouldn't be struggling with this."

If that was the case, I must be a hell of a guy because I was struggling hard trying to be a good husband and father while carving out time for another woman. Yeah, I was a prince all right.

I quickly changed the subject. "You never told me who that kid was."

"His name is Devon Lloyd," she replied, looking down at her drink. "He's at Roberson on a full track scholarship, which he's about to lose because he can't keep up with his coursework."

"How'd he even get in if he can't do the work?" I was still furious at this kid for what I'd seen him do to Cara.

"Did you get a good look at him? I'm pretty sure he's on drugs. And being able to do the work isn't the issue. He's a bright kid. He excelled in my English 101 class this summer," she said, not looking at me as she speared a cherry tomato with her fork. "But something changed, and he stopped showing up. I had to give him an incomplete. The next time I saw him was when he approached me on the college green, and I couldn't believe how bad he looked."

"And what was his issue this time? I heard him say you promised him something."

Cara's head jerked up in surprise, her eyes briefly widening before she shrugged and gave me a half smile. "His track coach came by to see me and gave me this sob story about how Devon was the first one in his family to go to college and he really needed to keep his scholarship, or he'd have to leave school. I agreed to let him turn in his final paper from summer so the incomplete wouldn't drag his GPA down. And guess what?"

I shook my head. "He never turned it in."

"No, he didn't, and I've given him two more chances to turn

it in. Today, I told him he was out of chances, and I would no longer accept the paper." She sighed deeply. "He'll have to retake the class, which is what I should have told his coach to begin with."

"I know you feel sorry for the kid because he's going through a hard time. But his behavior is unacceptable, Cara. What would have happened if I hadn't walked by? This needs to be reported to campus police."

"I know." Cara looked me straight in the eyes. "I'm going to file a report after we leave."

"Promise?"

"Didn't I just say I would?" she snapped, catching me off guard with her irritation. "I'm sorry, Aaron." She quickly grabbed my hand and squeezed it tight. "I didn't get much sleep last night and I get cranky when I don't get my eight hours in."

This was the first time Cara had ever lost her cool and snapped at me, and I wondered if she was still mad about me ignoring her for a week.

"Everything okay? Are you feeling all right?"

"Yeah, I'm fine," she said, but she didn't look fine. She still seemed irritated. "Something happened the other day, and I'm not sure how to handle it."

I squeezed her hand, glad she was letting me in again. "What's going on?"

"It's Jaida Reese."

"Jaida?" I said in surprise. "What about her?"

"I gave her the grant check we got from the Marsden Foundation's Creative Writing Fellowship to take to the cashier's to deposit in the lit reviews bank account and, according to them, they never received it."

"Wait a minute," I said, sitting up straight in the booth, letting go of her hand. "I wrote that grant last year. It was for $10,000."

"Yeah, and now it's gone."

Gone? Was she fucking kidding me? "And you think Jaida stole it? Why did she even have the check in the first place? I usually handled all the checks and cash that went into the lit reviews account."

"I got slammed with back-to-back meetings that day, and she volunteered to deposit the check for me. I know I should have found the time to do it myself. But she insisted on helping me out and I let her."

"That doesn't sound like Jaida. I've known her since she was a freshman. She's a good, responsible kid. That's why I named her senior editor for the academic year. Have you talked to her about it?"

"She denies it. She says she had the check and the only place she stopped on her way to the cashier's office was the library, and when she got to the cashier's, it was missing from her bag."

Frowning, I tried to make sense of what I was hearing. I'd put Cara in charge of *Reflections* – and I'd named Jaida editor, two women I trusted, who should have made a winning combination. How had a large sum of money gone missing on their watch? "Someone must have known she had that check, then followed her to the library and stole it. Maybe I should talk to her."

Cara's jaw tightened in annoyance, which shocked me. Why was she so willing to believe Jaida Reese was a thief when she'd been singing the young woman's praises since she'd taken over at the Student Literary Review?

"That's probably a good idea," she said, quickly recovering her good mood of mere seconds ago. "I really need to report this to the campus police, but I'll hold off until you talk to her."

We left the diner thirty minutes later, and I walked her to her next class, stealing a long, deep kiss in the dark recesses of the second-floor stairwell before I headed to my office on the third floor. Despite everything I'd heard, I was feeling relieved and happy that we'd gotten back on track and that she didn't want more from me than I could currently give. I wasn't thinking about the future or having to choose between Paige and Cara. But that all changed when I arrived back in my office and found Paige waiting for me with a lunch basket wearing tight jeans and a black sweater that molded to her curves. She even had on a little makeup. She looked amazing.

"I hope you haven't eaten. My class got cancelled, and I thought it might be nice to surprise my hard-working hubby with some lunch. I brought us some chili and cornbread. I've even made your favorite chocolate chunk cookies."

"Smells great," I said, forcing my face into a phony expression of happy surprise as my wife laid the food out on the coffee table.

Realizing I probably had some of Cara's perfume on me, I quickly shrugged out of my blazer and draped it over my office chair before settling across from my wife to eat my second lunch of the day. I knew then I was a fool for thinking things could go on like this forever.

When I arrived at the Student Literary Review office later that afternoon, there were only two students working. Jaida and Beth, a freshman who had joined the lit review this fall. As soon as Jaida saw me, she burst into tears.

"I'm fired, right?" Her voice came out muffled because she was speaking through her hands, which she'd clamped over her face the minute she saw me.

"Come out into the hall so we can talk about it."

"It's okay," said Beth. "I'm on my way to class so you guys can have some privacy."

I gave her a grateful smile, and we both watched as Beth grabbed her bookbag and left the room.

"Tell me everything that happened, starting from the beginning, and don't leave out any details," I told her as I led her over to a nearby desk.

"I swear I didn't steal that money, Dr. Nichols. You know me. We had big plans for that grant money."

"If I believed you had anything to do with this, I would've reported you to campus police myself. But we need to figure out what happened to that money, which means you need to tell me everything right now."

She nodded, wiping her cheeks. "Dr. Morton gave me the check yesterday morning to deposit in the cashier's office."

"You mean you didn't volunteer to take the check?"

Jaida frowned. "Volunteer? No? Dr. Morton specifically asked me to take that check to the cashier's office. She said I'd be doing her a big favor because she was running late for a meeting, and she'd be busy all day. She didn't want it locked up here in the office."

Cara had been adamant Jaida had volunteered to take the check. Why would she lie to me? Anxiety knotted itself into a ball in my stomach. Someone was clearly lying. But which one of these two women, who I thought the world of, was lying to me?

"Did anyone else know you were taking the check to the cashier's that morning?"

"No." Jaida was adamant. "It was just me and Dr. Morton in the office that morning."

"Any reason you didn't go straight to the cashier's office before going to the library?"

"I was meeting a friend to study for a test. I didn't think it would be a big deal to take it afterward, since no one knew I had it, and it was in my bag."

"Was your bag ever out of sight while you were at the

library?" She chewed on her bottom lip and looked away. "Jaida?"

"Well, I went to the restroom once and had to step out to take a call. But my friend was still at the table with all our stuff."

"And how do you know your study buddy didn't leave the table while you were in the restroom or taking a call?"

"I don't, but she probably didn't, and there was hardly anybody in the corner where we were studying. No one ever goes back there."

I believed her. Roberson's library was old and had sections that were isolated and perfect for studying and extracurricular activities. Many couples took advantage of the darkened corners to hook up. Once, Cara had me meet her in the library and took me to a secluded corner on the fifth floor to make out. It had been sexy, risky, and exciting. But thinking about it now made me slightly sick to my stomach. And then another thought hit me.

"What about before you left the office?"

"Before?"

"Yeah, after Dr. Morton gave you the check, was your bag left unattended in the office?"

She thought for a few seconds before answering. "I got a phone call from someone asking about submission guidelines. He had a ton of questions, and it took me forever to get him off the phone. My bag was in my desk drawer."

"And where was Dr. Morton during this call?"

"She left maybe two minutes after I answered the phone. No one came in after her. I got off the phone, locked up, and left for the library."

"Anyone hanging around outside the office?"

"Not that I noticed. But I was in a hurry because I was running late. Am I going to have to pay the money back? I swear I didn't steal that check." Tears made her voice tremble, and I held up a hand.

"We'll figure it out, I promise." I didn't have the right to make her any promises, but I knew she hadn't taken that check.

Her head fell. "Dr. Morton must be so disappointed in me."

"I seriously doubt that." It was a lie. I thought of Cara's disgusted expression as she was telling me about this mess. Meanwhile, Jaida was still desperate for her approval. I left the lit review office so deep in thought, I almost barreled right into Beth.

"Sorry, Dr. Nichols."

"Hey, Beth." I couldn't help but notice the serious look on her face. Beth was an enigma. Quiet, and much younger-looking than the average college freshman, she'd attached herself to Jaida, who didn't seem to mind that the younger white girl followed her around like a puppy.

"Can I talk to you for a minute?" she practically whispered.

"As long as you don't mind walking back to my office with me so I can grab some folders for a meeting. What's up?"

"That's okay." She paused. "I can stop by your office later when you have more time."

"Are you sure? Is everything all right?"

"It's just..." Her voice trailed off as she looked at something beyond me. I followed her gaze. Cara was talking to one of the adjunct English faculty.

"Never mind." She turned on her heel and darted down the hallway.

"Beth! Hey, wait up." I hurried down the hall after her, finally catching up to her as she waited at the elevator around the corner.

"I'm sorry to have bothered you, Dr. Nichols. It's nothing." She seemed flustered, like she might burst into tears. "I was just overreacting. Midterms are coming up, and I'm just stressed out."

"Are you sure? It sounded like you had something impor-tant to tell me." I knew there was something she wanted to share, though I wasn't sure how many more revelations I could take that day.

The young woman seemed torn and chewed her bottom lip. She wouldn't look at me.

All at once she said, "It's about a faculty member."

"Which faculty member?" The question seemed to make her even more hesitant. When the elevator door slid open, she rushed inside, and pressed the button.

"I'm late for class. Are your office hours still one to three?"

"Absolutely. But you can stop by my office anytime if you need to talk. And if you don't feel comfortable talking to me, I'll find you someone else." She merely nodded as the elevator door slid closed. I had a feeling Beth wouldn't show up during my office hours that afternoon. And I was right.

ELEVEN

AARON NICHOLS

BEFORE

October 17, 2023

A few days later, as I lay in bed wide awake and staring at the ceiling, my phone vibrated with a text. I glanced over at Paige, who was fast asleep, before looking at my phone. It was from Cara. She'd been texting me pictures at the same time every night, mostly smiling bathroom selfies. Tonight, though, it wasn't a picture. It was a video.

I slipped out of bed and went downstairs, grabbed a couple of beers from the fridge, and laid on the couch before pressing play on the video. In it, Cara was wearing only a lacy red push-up bra and a matching thong. If I thought she looked amazing with clothes on, she looked even more incredible with next to nothing on. There was soft music playing in the background, and it looked like she was in her bedroom. She swayed seductively to the music for a few seconds before unclasping the bra, pushing each strap down slowly and letting it fall to the floor. Swigging the beer, I couldn't look away and didn't want to. I slid my hand down the front of my boxers to take care of the instant erection I'd gotten once I'd pushed play.

I didn't realize my mistake until early the next morning when something heavy hit my chest, waking me abruptly, and I almost fell off the couch. It was a duffel bag. My black duffel bag that I take to the gym. Paige stood in the middle of the room. It wasn't until I got up from the couch where I must have fallen asleep last night that I noticed she had my phone in her hand. The empty beer cans sat by her feet.

"Paige?" I began slowly while staring at my phone in her hand.

Her face was hard and angry. She must have woken up, found me gone and come down looking for me, only to find me asleep on the couch with my hand down my pants. I always slept deeply after a few drinks. She'd used my thumb while I was out cold to unlock my phone, and seen all the texts, pictures, and that damned video. All of it proof that I was a fraud.

"The kids will be up in half an hour. I want you gone before they come down for breakfast." Her voice was flat and emotionless.

"Babe, listen to me. Whatever you saw on my—"

"Did you hear me? I'm not interested in your sorry, lame ass excuses! It's bad enough you lied to me and have been lying to me for weeks! But you're down here jerking off to that nasty bitch's videos just feet away from me and the kids?" She was looking at me like she didn't know me anymore. "What if one of them had come down here and seen you?"

"I never meant," I began, but stopped when I saw the look in her eyes. My wife was beyond caring about anything I had to say. And there wasn't much I could say. I had no defense. The pain in her beautiful eyes cut me to the core.

"I know you don't give a damn about me. But if you care at all about your kids, you need to go because I don't know how much longer I can stand to look at you without causing you bodily harm. Get the fuck out!" She was practically vibrating with anger, and it scared me. I'd finally pushed her too far.

I tugged on my jeans. "What will you tell the kids?"

"Don't worry. I won't tell them their father is a lying, cheating, conniving asshole." Paige walked over to the door to the garage and held it open.

I grabbed the duffel bag and stuffed my feet into my tennis shoes by the door. Once I was in the garage, Paige slammed the door shut behind me without another word. It was only then that she broke down. The sound of her sobbing on the other side of the door was like a knife in my heart. How could I have caused so much pain to the woman I'd vowed to love and cherish? A minute later, I backed out of the driveway and sped away from the heartbreak and misery I'd caused.

I drove around for over an hour, not sure where to go or what to do. I finally found a Holiday Inn Express near the airport. I could have easily gotten a room on campus in guest housing for visiting professors and lecturers. But I didn't want anyone knowing Paige had put me out. News like that would spread through the faculty and staff like wildfire. I didn't leave the hotel room except to get something to eat and to buy a couple of pairs of pants and a few shirts. The only things in the duffel bag were workout clothes, body wash, and deodorant.

I spent the rest of the morning trying to call Paige. But she wouldn't pick up. Finally, in the early afternoon, someone picked up the phone. But it wasn't Paige. It was my sister-in-law, Roselyn. I braced myself for the worst. Roselyn didn't suffer fools and was very protective of her younger sister.

"She doesn't want to talk to you."

"I just need to explain, Ros. Please put her on the phone," I begged.

"Explain, what? How you were supposed to cut that Cara chick off, and you're still involved with her, while pretending you want to save your marriage to my sister. I thought you were a better man than this, Aaron."

So did I, I thought bitterly. "I swear to you, I have never slept with Cara. Things just got out of hand because I was going through so much stress at work. I know that's no excuse, but I love Paige and the kids so much. They're my entire world."

"Well, you just blew up your entire world. I have never seen my sister so hurt and upset. And it doesn't matter whether you were fucking her! You were still cheating."

"How are the kids?" My voice was thick with shame. "Do they know?"

"No. Paige told them you're away at a conference."

I felt a deep surge of gratitude. I couldn't bear it if the twins found out the truth. "What do I do?"

"Leave her alone," Ros replied firmly. "She's in no state for your bullshit right now. Try calling her back in a few days when things have calmed down." She hung up before I could say another word.

Ten minutes later, I got a text from Cara.

Did you like my video?

Instead of replying, I turned my phone off. I was exhausted and trying to figure out how I'd gone so quickly from being a loving husband and father living with my beautiful family, to a lying, cheating bastard banished to a hotel room at the airport. And what made it all ten times worse is that I still wanted to be with Cara despite all the damage it was causing. I needed to talk to someone and, as much as I hated to admit it, that someone was Cara. I needed to feel like something other than a fuck-up right now, and she was the only one that had the power to do that. I needed her smile and the kindness in her eyes like I needed medicine. I hated hurting Paige. But maybe our marriage was already over. Maybe now was the time to explore what things could be like with Cara.

I'm not sure why I didn't call Cara before arriving at her house that afternoon. I'd only been to her house once before when I dropped her off when her car was in the shop. I sat parked on the curb for probably fifteen minutes before I got up the nerve to head up to her door. Her black Camry sat in the driveway. I rang the doorbell and waited, but no one came to the door. I heard voices coming from the back of the house and took the cobblestone path that led to the backyard. An elderly man who I knew must be Cara's father was sitting with his back to me at a round glass table on the covered patio. Cara was standing over him, red-faced and angry. Before I could call out a greeting, she swung her hand out and cracked her father hard across his left cheek. The elderly man cried out in pain and his hands instantly flew to his face. Shock stopped me dead in my tracks. I must have let out a gasp, because Cara instantly looked up and saw me standing there with my mouth hanging open.

"Aaron?" she called out after me as I turned and headed back to my car, feeling sick to my stomach. "Aaron! Please stop! It's not what it looks like."

"Really? Because it looked self-explanatory to me, Cara!" I didn't stop to look at her until I got to the driver's side door. I suddenly realized this was how I must sound to Paige, trying to explain the unthinkable.

"Please let me explain. Please."

"While you're at it, explain why I shouldn't call social services on you for elder abuse." Cara looked like I'd punched her. She leaned against the side of my car and ran her hands through her hair.

"We had a terrible night. I came home from work and found

out that his nurse had left him home alone. He got out of the house. It took me almost an hour to find him in the woods behind our property. And then he was up all night wandering the house and I didn't get any sleep because I was afraid he'd find a way out of the house again." Her voice broke and I thought she might cry, but she wasn't finished talking.

"Then the nurse had the nerve to show up here this morning for work like nothing had happened. I fired her on the spot. Dad's already shit himself twice today. I had to clean him and the house up and I'm exhausted, Aaron. Then I tried to feed him his dinner. He said the food was too hot, then threw the plate at me and spit in my face. And I just lost it." Cara leaned forward and gently touched my arm. "I never meant to hurt my father. I know it's not his fault, but I don't know how much more of this I can take."

For the first time since I'd gotten there, I really looked at her. Pieces of spinach were on her shirt, kernels of rice were in her hair, and spittle was on her forehead and cheeks. My anger gradually disappeared. I'd overreacted and here I was causing another woman I cared about pain. I reached into my glove box, got a tissue, and gently wiped her face and picked the food out of her hair. Then I gave her another tissue to blow her nose with and pulled her into a tight embrace, letting her sob against my chest.

Afterward, I helped Cara get her father cleaned up and fed before settling him in front of the TV to watch a football game. With her father's attention on the TV screen, Cara took my hand and quietly led me down the hall to her bedroom. We'd barely gotten the door closed behind us before our mouths met and we were tugging each other's clothes off. Cara pushed me down onto her bed and straddled me, grinding her crotch against my erection as she reached behind her back and unsnapped her bra. To my horror, I came before I could even get my underwear off. Cara felt the dampness and looked down to see the stain on my light blue boxers, and sighed in disappointment. Instantly, I grabbed her by the hips, coaxing her up on her knees and pulling her toward my face. She grabbed the headboard of the bed, and I pushed the damp crotch of her panties aside as she lowered herself onto my mouth. She arched her back and moaned as I filled her with my tongue.

As we laid cuddling in the dark, I told Cara what had happened with Paige, and she invited me to stay the night. But as good as being with her felt, I couldn't get the last image of Paige's face out of my head. I turned Cara down and headed back to my hotel room. It didn't occur to me to wonder until much later that if Cara had all that going on the night before, when did she have time to make that video?

A week went by, and I was still at the hotel. Paige hadn't accepted any of my phone calls. It was probably a good thing because I really didn't know what I was going to tell her. But I missed my kids like crazy. I'm not sure how long Paige told them I would be gone for, but clearly, we were going to have to come to an arrangement so I could see them soon.

Meanwhile, Cara and I were getting even closer. Although we still hadn't slept together, after I'd made a mess of things last time, we had lunch together every day and dinner at her house most evenings. On my first day back at work after being put out, I was paranoid, thinking that everyone on campus would know. In reality, we were on fall break, and there were no classes for the week, which freed me up to spend even more time with Cara.

I knew I was doing all the wrong things. I should've spent time away from both Cara and Paige to decide what the hell I was going to do. But Paige was making it one hundred percent clear that she didn't want to see or talk to me. And Cara couldn't get enough of me. The next week I decided I'd given

Paige enough time to calm down, and I needed to get some more of my stuff. I went back to the house and was relieved Paige hadn't changed the locks. She was in the kitchen sitting at the island drinking a cup of coffee and looked thinner than the last time I'd seen her, with dark smudges under her eyes, which made me feel terrible. She was wearing leggings and an over-sized Ohio State T-shirt. When I walked in, I half expected her to throw the cup of coffee at me, but she didn't. She just stared at me like I was a stranger. I would have preferred to dodge the coffee cup.

"We need to talk," I told her.

She didn't even look up. "About what, exactly?"

"I want to see the kids."

"I'm not keeping you from your kids. You know where they are five days a week from 8:30 to 3:30. You can pick them up or drop them off at school whenever you want." She spoke coolly, without any emotion. Then she went in for the kill. "But be prepared to tell them the truth about where you've been and why, because I'm not covering for you anymore."

We were silent for several agonizing moments while she continued to sip her coffee and stare into space. I didn't know what else to say. I couldn't beg her not to tell the kids when she was right; she shouldn't have to cover for me. She didn't seem inclined to say anything else to me, so I headed upstairs and packed some more of my clothes in an overnight bag. Paige finally spoke again as I headed out the door into the garage.

"You want to know what the most fucked-up thing about finding that shit on your phone was?"

"Paige, I am so—" I began. But she didn't let me finish.

"Goodnight, gorgeous." She put the coffee cup down, got up, and walked over to the garage door. "Goodnight, gorgeous. That's how you were ending your texts to that bitch. You obviously forgot that was how you used to end your texts to me when we were dating. Or maybe you remembered and didn't care to come up with anything original like bye, bye, beautiful or sleep tight, slut. You had to give her something that belonged to me."

Her voice broke, and it felt like a knife through my heart. Paige was never meant to see those messages.

"I'm sorry." It was all I could say, but I knew it wasn't enough.

"Do you love her?" She stared hard at my face, trying to read my emotions.

"I don't know." I hung my head, unable to meet her gaze. And when I finally looked up, my wife slammed the door in my face.

I was on my way to meet Cara for lunch when she called me.

"Hey, something's come up and I'm going to have to cancel lunch," she said, sounding breathless and on edge.

"Everything okay?" I asked carefully. "You sound off."

"Yeah, I just need to take care of something."

"You sure?" Cara rarely sounded anything other than calm and in charge. Now she sounded anything but, just like in the diner days before.

"Jesus! You're not my dad. I said I'm fine," she snapped.

I was taken aback. "Okay. I guess I'll see you later then?"

"Yeah." She hung up, and I stared at my phone.

What was that about? Was it her father? Had another nurse quit, or did he wander away from the house again? All she had to do was ask me for help. Was she too proud? Or was there something else going on? I couldn't just leave it. I had to make sure she was okay.

I was sitting at a traffic light, headed to Cara's house when I saw her black Camry fly by, going in the opposite direction. By the time the light changed, I'd almost lost her. But I caught sight of her driving down a side street and took the first chance to turn my car around, following at a distance. Where was she going in such a hurry? She was blocks away from her house and nowhere near campus. Finally, she pulled into the parking lot of an old, abandoned factory. At that point, I regretted turning my car around. Something was telling me she wouldn't appreciate being followed like that. So, I parked on the street in a spot where I had a clear view of her car, where she was unlikely to see me. Cara stayed in her car. She just sat there. What was she doing? A few minutes later, a tall, thin figure in jeans and a black hoody walked around the corner of the building and got into the passenger side of her car. *What the hell?* Without going closer, I couldn't see what was happening inside the vehicle. Five minutes passed before the figure emerged from the car. As he did so, the hoody fell back, revealing his face. It was Devon Lloyd. Fear gripped me. I jumped out of my car. As I crossed the street, I tried to see if Cara was okay. But she must have been hunched over because she was still hidden from view. Was she hurt? What had just happened?

"Hey! What the hell did you do to her?" I called out after Devon as I sprinted toward the car.

The young man turned and smiled, flipping me the bird with both hands before running and disappearing back around the side of the building. Rushing to Cara's car, I pulled the passenger side door open, blood rushing through my veins, not sure I wanted to see what I was about to discover. Had the kid attacked her again? Had I watched it happen without intervening? But as I looked inside the car, I didn't see Cara injured – or worse. Instead, she was bent over the center console with a rolled-up dollar bill.

"Oh my God," I whispered as her head jerked up and she stared at me with glassy, dilated eyes, cocaine crusting both her nostrils.

"Aaron? What are you doing here?" She fumbled with her door handle, trying to get out.

I took a step back stunned by what I was seeing. I felt like I'd been punched. "What the fuck, Cara?"

She managed to get the door open and clumsily ran around the car toward me. "I can quit anytime. I just need a little every once in a while. Stop looking at me like that!"

"All those times I saw you with that kid had nothing to do with grades, did it? You were buying drugs from him? You lied to me, Cara!"

"Oh, so the liar doesn't like it when someone else lies to him. Is that it?" She threw her head back and laughed. It was like a mask had fallen off, and I was seeing her for the first time.

I looked at her. Really looked at her. Was this the real Cara? Where was the beautiful woman I'd thought I was falling in love with? Her nose was bright red and running. She wiped it with the back of her coat sleeve and licked her chapped lips. The wind had blown her hair into disarray. She wasn't wearing makeup and acne dotted the mottled skin of her cheeks.

"Who the hell are you?"

Her eyes flashed with fury. "I'm the same woman who's been by your side all these months listening to you bitch and moan about how your wife doesn't get you and how the faculty hates you. Me! And now you find out I'm not perfect, and suddenly I'm a problem?"

Then reality set in. "You were the one who took that check, weren't you? The reason the check was missing from Jaida's bag when she got to the cashier's office is because you stole it from her bag while she took a phone call. She didn't even realize it was already gone when she left the office. How could you do that to her? That kid worships you. You could have gotten her expelled and arrested!"

"But she wasn't, was she?" she said dismissively, as if it all meant nothing. "You made sure of that when you turned into her knight in shining armor and ran to her defense. I bet you're fucking her, aren't you?"

"So, you did steal it." Somewhere deep in my subconscious, I always knew she had taken the check. I just didn't want to believe it. I came up with all kinds of justifications and excuses in my mind, so I wouldn't have to admit to myself that there was something wrong with Cara. It had been subtle at first, just flashes of unease here and there. But now – finally – my eyes were wide open.

"Prove it." The defiant and unrepentant look in her eyes made my heart hurt. How could I have gotten it so wrong? Where was the kind, beautiful, intelligent woman who had been my rock these last few months, who I'd been willing to risk it all for?

"I... I've got to get out of here." I headed back to my car to the sound of Cara's screams.

"You have no right to judge me! Come back here! Aaron, please!"

I went straight back to the motel. When I got to my room, I was so numb I couldn't even remember driving there. I sank down on the edge of the bed, head in my hands, feeling like a sucker. How could I have been so stupid? The Cara I thought I knew had never existed. She only showed me what I wanted to see. I didn't know her at all, not really, and I was about to lose my family over a fantasy that didn't exist. Was anything she'd told me true?

I took out my laptop and logged on to Roberson's student directory and looked up the name Devon Lloyd. The search came up with zero results. My heart dropped even lower. Next, I pulled up a photo of the university's men's track team, to discover there was no Devon Lloyd on the team. She'd lied about that kid being a student. Of course, she had. What else had she lied about? What hadn't she lied about? I immediately packed my shit and checked out of the motel. Meanwhile, Cara was blowing up my cell with texts that I ignored. Then I went home.

I found Paige sitting on the couch watching TV. I walked across the room and knelt in front of her. My wife looked at me like I was a leper. How the hell was I going to fix this?

"I know I screwed up, and I'm not sure if you can ever forgive me. But I'll do anything to fix it. Anything. Just tell me what I need to do." I laid my head in her lap and sobbed. She didn't push me away, which gave me hope.

"Anything?" she asked, lifting my chin to look me in the eye.

"Anything. I swear."

Her eyes widened in surprise. "Then give me your phone."

I handed it over without hesitation and watched as Paige pulled up Cara's last text message, which had come in mere seconds ago, and typed out a reply. Then she showed it to me.

It read:

> I need to repair my marriage and regain my wife's trust. I will not be contacting you again, and I ask that you not contact me. Please respect my decision. I will not be responding to any further attempts to communicate with me. Aaron.

"If you're truly serious, hit that send button," said Paige, as a single tear slid down her cheek.

And without hesitation, I did.

TWELVE

CARA MORTON: AGED FIVE

1991

A sound woke Cara up. It was nighttime, and she'd been in bed since morning, having missed another day of kindergarten. Missing school made Cara sad, and she hoped her friends would still remember her when she came back. Her tummy hurt, but not as badly as before. She sat up a little to see if she was dizzy, but she wasn't. So, she sat all the way up in bed. Her hair was stuck to her forehead from where she'd been sweating. When she pushed the covers off her to get out of bed, a strong scent filled her nose. She'd wet the bed again. Her face burned with embarrassment. She was too big to still be wetting the bed. At least most of it had dried, only leaving a damp spot behind, and even her pajamas weren't that wet anymore. Where was her mommy? Usually, she would have checked on her by now. She heard the sound that had woken her up again and walked over to the bedroom door, pressing her ear to the wood. It sounded like crying.

Cara opened the door just a crack and listened. It *was* crying. Someone was crying in the living room. She finally crept out of her bedroom and tiptoed down the hall and peeked around the corner into the living room. But Mommy wasn't there. She wasn't the one who was crying. It was her daddy, who was sitting in his chair in front of the TV with his face buried in his hands. He was crying hard. Cara walked over to him and did what Mommy always did to her whenever she cried. She patted her father on the back.

"Don't cry, Daddy. It'll be all right."

Daddy's head instantly lifted, and his face contorted as he grabbed Cara and held her tight. "You're going to be all right, baby girl. I won't let her hurt you anymore."

Cara had never seen her daddy cry, and it scared her. "Where's Mommy?"

"Mommy had to go away. It's just you and me now. And I won't let anybody hurt you again. Do you hear me?"

Cara just nodded because she didn't know what else to do. She had no idea what Daddy was talking about. All she knew was that she wanted her mommy and had just been told she was gone.

"But when is she coming back?"

"I'm sorry, baby." Daddy pushed the damp tendrils of hair off her forehead. "She's not coming back."

Then Cara started crying too.

THIRTEEN

PAIGE NICHOLS

AFTER

December 5, 2023

I should have gone to the police station with Aaron for moral support. But that's not the only reason.

I just don't trust my husband anymore. He's lied to me so many times in the last four months I hardly know what's real anymore. When he begged me to let him come home, I thought all this was behind us. I thought he'd missed me and the kids after our time apart, and had chosen us over Cara. That was a lie. I found out the real reason he'd come home when I went through his briefcase and found a copy of his written police statement. It detailed exactly what had happened between him and Cara for his sexual harassment case. Turns out, she's a coke-head. A drug addict. It shouldn't have been a surprise given the way she came after us, like someone incapable of rational thought. The funny thing is, Cara could have been a gambling, sex, shopping, alcohol, food, or even a porn addict and my husband would have tied a cape around his neck and gone into superhero mode to save her from herself. But drugs were where Aaron drew the line because of what happened to his mother.

Of course, he doesn't know I'd discovered the real reason he came home. I know he's not in love with me anymore, and I'm not sure I'm in love with him either. But we were very much in love once, and I see glimmers of hope that we could be again. I see them every time he's with the kids, and when he flirts with me like he used to, and when we go out for our therapist-mandated date night. But we'll never find our way back to each other if he's sitting in a prison cell.

The problem is, I know he's not telling me everything that happened at the police station, just like he never told me everything that had happened with Cara. If I'd gone with him to the interview and insisted I be there when they questioned him, I'd know everything they'd asked and his answers. In truth, I'm not just afraid of what Aaron might have told the police. I'm also worried about what evidence the police have about Cara. Do they know who she really is and what she's capable of? If not, should I tell them everything she's done to us? If they find out themselves, would I also have to tell them what I did?

FOURTEEN

PAIGE NICHOLS

BEFORE

November 5, 2023

"I absolutely did not cancel the reservation for Nichols at 2:30. Are you trying to tell me I called and canceled this reservation?"

I was standing at the counter of the Bounz Houz loaded down with balloons, paper plates, cups and two dozen chocolate fudge cupcakes. It was the twins' ninth birthday and I had reserved a spot at the Bounz Houz for the party. It was a new trampoline park, and the kids had been begging me to take them for months. But now they were telling me that not only was my reservation canceled, but they were fully booked for the day.

"Actually," said the young woman behind the counter, who looked barely out of her teens. "We got an email." She clicked around on her keyboard and then turned the screen to face me. I saw an email canceling our reservation for today signed with the name Paige Nichols. But the email address was funichols@webnet.com. *Cute.*

"That's not my email address. And I've got guests who will be here in less than an hour. Please tell me you have someplace I can host my kids' party. Please. We don't even need a private room. We can set up at a table in the corner."

She sighed and rolled her eyes in annoyance. "Let me see if there are any cancellations, ma'am."

She turned her computer screen back around and started clicking on the keyboard again. I knew she didn't believe I hadn't canceled the reservation. Panic was setting in, and I took a few deep breaths. I knew who had done this.

Cara Morton.

Ever since Aaron ended things with her, she'd been making our lives a complete misery. First, making trouble for Aaron at work. Next came hang-up phone calls on our landline, to the point where we finally just got rid of it. And now this bullshit. Panic gave way to rage. If she wanted to fuck with Aaron, fine. He deserved it. If she wanted to take shots at me, I didn't care. But now she was messing with my children. And I wasn't having it.

"Ma'am, we have a cancellation, but it's not until 3:00. Is that okay?"

"Absolutely. And thank you so much."

Later, as I mingled with the other parents and started setting up the table for all the pizza I had ordered, I watched Aaron sitting at a table, looking grim. I told him what happened as soon as he arrived with the twins. I knew he was blaming himself. It had been almost a month since he'd ended things with Cara. We were in marital counseling, and he was sleeping either on the couch or in the guest bedroom. Once the kids were in bed, we'd retreat to our separate areas because he didn't want them knowing anything was wrong. Things were still touch and go with us. There were days when I looked at him with so much love and gratitude for getting a second chance. But then something would trigger me, and the resentment would come flooding back.

One day, we were on our way home from dinner at our favorite Mexican restaurant and the song that had been playing in Cara's video came on the radio. One minute we were laughing, and the next minute I was sobbing and raging at him, asking how I could ever trust him again. Our counselor told us that this was normal. She even warned Aaron it would happen and to be prepared for it. She also told him to be patient. To his credit, he was doing all of those things. Our counselor told us that this was a process. And it could take two to three years to get past the affair. But when shit like this happened, I wasn't sure if I would ever get over his affair. It had only been a month since I'd let him come back home, and I was staring down the barrel of at least two more years of feeling this way. I didn't know if I could do it.

"I am so sorry, babe," said Aaron, coming up behind me and putting his hands on my shoulders pulling me out of my thoughts.

I told him to stop beating himself up because it wasn't his fault. But we both knew that it was. If he hadn't gotten involved with Cara, this would never have happened. I also knew that throwing it up in his face constantly would not help us heal. And I desperately wanted us to heal. I knew the marriage that we had before was gone, but I wanted something new and better. Something bulletproof.

"Isn't there anything we can do about her? She almost ruined the twins' birthday."

"There might be if there was proof. But there isn't any. I think we're just going to have to wait her out."

"What if she doesn't stop? How long are we supposed to put up with this?" Aaron gave me a look, and I knew what was coming next.

"I could try talking to her again."

"Yeah, because it worked out so well last time. That's exactly what she wants, Aaron. She keeps doing this shit to provoke you into contacting her."

"You could come with me."

I scoffed. "You honestly think she would talk to you if I were there?"

"We could try."

"I'm willing to try anything at this point," I told him. "But if she comes after the kids again, I swear to God, I won't be responsible for my actions."

"Daddy, come jump with me," said Bailey, tugging on Aaron's hand. I watched my daughter lead her father over to the nearest trampoline pad.

"Everything okay?" asked Roselyn. She was still treating Aaron like the enemy and knew all about the hell Cara was putting us through.

"Same shit different day."

"What did the crazy bitch do this time?"

I pulled her off to the side and explained the near disaster that almost happened with our reservation.

"How did she even know about the party or where it's at?"

I hesitated, swallowing hard before answering. "I posted about it on Facebook."

"What? Are you insane?"

"I wasn't thinking!" I snapped, feeling like an idiot as tears pricked my eyes. "I just wanted to give the kids a nice birthday party and put all this shit behind us for one day." My sister pulled a tissue from her purse and handed it to me.

"This has got to stop, Paige," she said softly. "She's escalating."

"You think I don't know that? She's being slick because none of this stuff can be traced back to her. For all we know, she could've hired someone to harass us."

"Have you even talked to the police about a restraining order?"

"They told us that unless there was a direct threat from her, there was nothing they could do."

"You mean until one of you ends up dead? Man, Aaron sure knows how to pick 'em," she commented without thinking and then instantly grabbed my hand by way of an apology. But I pulled away.

I knew my sister was just concerned, and I wasn't mad. She was absolutely right. I was just tired of having to deal with all of this crap while trying to save my marriage at the same time. Because every time Cara harassed us, it made it that much harder to forgive Aaron. I wondered if she knew that, and whether it was the whole point of what she was doing. I was certain she didn't want him back. She just wanted to burn his life to the ground for breaking up with her.

"You still haven't called Mom, have you?"

"Not yet. I'm not looking forward to that conversation."

My mom and I weren't exactly close. She was a lot closer to my siblings Ros and Tyler. I was always a Daddy's girl. Although she'd deny it, my mom resented me for my closeness to my father. By the time he passed away, I already had a family of my own, which prevented me from drawing closer to her in my grief. I had Aaron and the kids. Before, when she showed up after the twins were born to help me with them, all I could feel was her judgment and disapproval of my parenting choices, while my dad was just happy to be a grandpa. Then, when the twins were four, Aaron thought we should have another child and got my mother on his side, which was a huge mistake. Any little nigglings of baby fever I may have had at that point vanished the moment my mother opened her mouth about me giving my husband another child.

I was nursing full-time plus taking care of four-year-old twins and the house. Aaron was barely helping me at all because he had a full class load and committees. And he was opposed to hiring a cleaner because of the bad experience he'd had with the one he'd hired to clean his grandmother's house while she was dying of cancer. The woman had robbed her. So as far as I was concerned, him wanting another child was a slap in the face. Of course, no one knew I was struggling. I kept that to myself, making everyone think I was okay until I wasn't. Smiling when I felt like screaming. Laughing and then crying in the bathtub later. Aaron should have known. And now this. I wished I could confide in my mother about what was going on in my marriage. But I just figured that all I would get was blamed.

"I know she can be difficult. But you really should give Mom a chance and get over this resentment. She's only human too. And she did the best she could. Mom wanted to do things with her life, but Dad never wanted her to work. She was raised to be submissive and let the man be the head of the household."

"You mean until he cheated on her, right? Because it didn't sound like she was being submissive then." Ros and I both laughed.

"You got that right! Head of the household or not, she put Daddy in his place and got rid of that other woman."

"What do you mean, got rid of that other woman?" I asked. "I just assumed she faded into the woodwork when Daddy broke things off with her."

"Nope, she was doing the same stuff Cara is doing. Making trouble for him at work. Calling the house nonstop. Remember when Sammy got hit by a car?"

"I loved Sammy. Please don't tell me..."

"She poisoned him," Roselyn said, cutting me off. "I overheard Daddy telling Mom he'd found him dead behind the garage, along with a can of dog food that had rat poison in it. They both lied to us and said Sammy got hit by a car."

"That bunny boiling bitch!" I shook my head. "Sounds like Mom and Dad lied to us about a bunch of shit."

"Don't be like that, P. They were just protecting us. You know damned well you wouldn't be telling your kids about this kind of stuff. They don't know you and Aaron aren't sharing a bedroom anymore, right?"

I shrugged. "I have no problem with them knowing. There's a way you can tell kids stuff without telling them every gory detail. Nothing wrong with telling them their parents need to work on some things without telling them exactly what those things are. Aaron is the one who doesn't want them to know. And it has nothing to do with protecting them. He doesn't want them to think less of him and I get that. But it still bothers me."

"You really need to talk to Mom. I'm not exactly sure how she did it. But she got Daddy's former side chick to leave us alone."

"Can we talk about this later? I don't have the energy for it right now. This is supposed to be a party, remember?"

"Yeah, let's go bounce our frustrations away," she said, taking off a shoe before abruptly stopping and turning to me. "Hey, you never told me how the tour at Highland went. When do the twins start?"

Never, I thought but didn't say because it was just another thing I didn't want to talk about. Before I could respond with something vague and noncommittal, there was a frantic tug on my hand.

"Mom! Come quick! There's something wrong with Dad!"

Bryce practically pulled my arm out of the socket as he pulled me toward the table where everyone had been eating pizza and cupcakes. Aaron was sitting on the bench with a crowd beginning to form around him. His complexion was ashen. His eyes were wide and bulging. He clasped both hands around his throat as he struggled to breathe. Panic gripped me as I ran to my husband, pushed past the onlookers, and crouched down in front of him. I knew immediately what was wrong.

"He's having an allergic reaction! Where's my purse?" I frantically looked around for my purse, remembering I had an EpiPen with me. It had been a long time since Aaron had had an allergic reaction, and I knew he wasn't always good about carrying his EpiPen with him. So I always had one with me.

"Here it is!" My son thrust my bag into my hands. It took seconds to locate the EpiPen. I pulled off the cap and jabbed it into Aaron's outer thigh. Within seconds, it took effect and Aaron's labored breathing slowed down as he took big gulps of air. Minutes later, his breathing was back to normal.

"Ma'am, do we need to call an ambulance?" asked a concerned young man whose name tag identified him as Danny, the manager.

"No," gasped Aaron as his breathing started to return to normal. "I'm good. No ambulance," he insisted.

"He should be okay now." I turned to face the young man. "But he's deathly allergic to mushrooms, and I specifically asked that none of our pizzas have mushrooms."

"I am so sorry, ma'am. I took care of your order personally, and there were no mushrooms on any of the pizzas that you ordered."

I opened my mouth to call him a liar. Because mushrooms were the only thing that Aaron was allergic to. But my husband grabbed my hand and shook his head. He didn't want me to make a scene and ruin the kids' birthday. The twins were standing next to their dad, looking close to tears. He was right. There was no need to ruin my children's birthday by making a scene when I could just as easily handle it quietly while they enjoy their party.

"I'm fine, everyone. And you two go play. You've still got almost an hour left before the party ends." Aaron stood up and smiled. Five minutes later, the crowd that had formed disbursed, and the kids were back, happily playing with their friends.

"What happened?" I kept my voice lowered even though I wanted to shout. I wasn't mad at my husband, but I wanted to know how the hell he consumed mushrooms. I tried to push the thought of what would've happened if I hadn't had that EpiPen in my purse out of my mind.

"No clue. One minute I was chowing down on a slice of pepperoni pizza and the next thing I know my lips were tingling and my throat was closing."

I picked up the plate that had been in front of him with a slice of half-eaten pepperoni pizza. The only thing that was on it was cheese pepperoni and some herbs. No mushrooms. In fact, I checked all the pizzas, and the manager had been correct. There were no mushrooms on any of the pizzas. How the hell did he have an allergic reaction when he hadn't eaten any mushrooms? Had he developed a new allergy?

"Are you sure you're all right? I can have Ros take over while I take you to the ER." Aaron shook his head no. But he still looked a bit wobbly to me.

"I'm going to get you some water. Don't move." I grabbed a plastic cup from a stack next to the drinks dispenser and filled it with water.

"Excuse me, ma'am. Is your husband going to be okay?" It was a woman whose daughter was having a party on the other side of the room.

I gave her a weak smile. "He's fine, thanks."

"Good. I reported the strange woman who was hovering around your table a little while ago."

My head jerked up. "What woman?"

"There was a woman at your table when they first brought the pizzas out and she had a little shaker. It looked like pepper. She shook it on all the pizzas. I thought nothing of it because a lot of people bring stuff here. I mean, this place is great, but the pizzas are kind of bland. I always bring packets of Parmesan cheese and pepper flakes with me when we come here. Then your husband got sick, and she wasn't anywhere around, and I just wondered."

"What did she look like?" Apprehension tap danced its way up my spine and my stomach knotted up.

"I couldn't really tell. She was wearing a baseball cap with her hair tucked up underneath and sunglasses."

"Sunglasses?"

"I know, right? Who wears sunglasses indoors? And they weren't the glasses that transition to regular glasses. They were definitely sunglasses."

I looked around wildly but didn't see any woman wearing a baseball cap and sunglasses anywhere. It had to be Cara. Who else could it have been? She had to know that Aaron was allergic to mushrooms. What the hell had she put on the pizzas?

"Thank you so much for letting me know." I told the woman, who smiled and nodded. Then I headed back over to my husband and gave him the water. I noticed the pizza he'd eaten before he got sick was gone, as were all the other empty plates and boxes.

"What happened to the piece of pizza you were eating?"

"Some kid came over and cleaned it all up a couple of minutes ago. Why?" I filled him in on what the other woman had told me.

"Someone put something on the pizzas?"

"Not someone, a woman. Cara! She could have killed you, Aaron. And we're still no closer to being able to prove she's harassing us. Maybe you're right and we should go talk to her."

We looked at each other, and I knew my husband and I were both thinking the same thing. Ros was right. Cara Morton was escalating.

FIFTEEN

PAIGE NICHOLS

BEFORE

November 7, 2023

I waited until Monday after Aaron had gone to work and I'd dropped the kids off at school to FaceTime with my mother.

Mom still lived in Florida in the same condo she and Dad retired to three years before he died. I had assumed that she would move back to town. But she loved Florida and didn't miss the change in seasons, and had no intention of ever moving back to Ohio. She had a full life in Florida, complete with friends, hobbies, and volunteer work. Needless to say, she was a busy woman. So, it surprised me to find she was home that morning. She was sitting on the balcony of her condo dressed in a floral print T-shirt and jean shorts. It had been a while since I'd seen her and noticed she'd stopped dyeing her hair. It was now more gray than dark brown, but she was wearing it in the same sleek updo she'd been sporting for the last twenty years. Never a hair out of place. I'd rarely ever seen her hair loose and often thought my mother's hair represented the only thing in her life she could entirely control.

"I wondered when I was finally going to hear from you," she said instead of a greeting. That's when I realized: my sister had already spilled the beans.

"I guess you already know what's going on."

"I'm only surprised you didn't call me sooner. I guess I can't blame you for that."

That was as close as my mother would ever come to acknowledging the emotional distance between us.

"If you're calling me, can I assume you and Aaron are trying to work things out?"

"I'm calling because Ros keeps insisting I talk to you because you know what I'm going through." I didn't want to commit to anything involving Aaron to my mother, especially since I wasn't all in on this reconciliation. I was going through the motions for now. Every morning when I opened my eyes, I felt different. Sometimes, old feelings come flooding back. On other days, all I felt was anger. But after what happened at the twins' party, I was in fight mode.

"I do. Your daddy was the love of my life. But we went through a bad patch, and we both dealt with it differently. I threw myself into the church. And he threw himself into the arms of another woman who paid him attention and boosted his ego," she said dryly, then took a sip from her mug before continuing. "He'd lost out on a big promotion that should have been his to the son-in-law of the company president. He took it hard, and I admit I probably didn't do a good job of comforting him. But he found someone else for that."

"How did you get past it, Mom? Because I'm not sure if I can."

"You can. But I won't lie and tell you that it's going to be easy or that it's going to be quick. Even after I forgave your daddy and stayed with him, and even after your brother was born, there was always a niggling feeling of doubt lurking in the back of my mind every time he was late coming home from work. Every time he volunteered to go pick something up for me from the store. Every time he had to work overtime. I wondered if he was seeing someone."

I'm not sure what I'd been expecting her to say. But I'd hoped it would be something more reassuring, like a guarantee I'd be able to get past what Aaron had done. "And how did you get that feeling to go away? Marital counseling?"

"Marital counseling wasn't really a thing back then, Paige. If your man was stepping out, you either shut up and let him cheat in peace or you went and talked to your pastor. Neither of those things appealed to me. I suffered in silence and those feelings never really went away. I don't want that for you."

We were both silent for several seconds while I took all that in. I realized my sister had been right. Mom was just human. And we had a lot more in common than I'd realized.

"How did you find out he was cheating? What made you follow him that night?" I asked softly. Mom looked taken aback for a moment, and it dawned on me that this was a conversation she never thought she'd have with me.

"Well," she said, glancing away. "Aside from the fact that he was going out most nights and coming home late drunk, he was in another world most of the time, a world where you, Ros, and I didn't exist. He was distant and angry. I couldn't do anything right. He started criticizing everything about me. Even then, I still didn't suspect it was another woman until one day I was in the basement doing laundry. Your daddy left his CD player on. When he wasn't going out at night, he'd be in the basement listening to CDs."

"I remember that CD player. Ros and I weren't allowed to touch it."

"Well, I touched it," she replied grimly. "I ejected the disc and saw that it wasn't something he bought. Someone had made the CD for him, and the label had little hearts drawn all over it and was signed Love, J. That's when I knew. It was like someone had punched me in the stomach. I couldn't breathe. I don't know how long I sat crying in that basement. I waited for him to leave that night and then I went to the bar he used to go to."

"Skipper's?"

"That's the one. He was already inside when I got there, but I waited outside in the car and sure enough, twenty minutes later he came out with a woman I recognized. Her name was Jan. She worked in accounting at his workplace, and I remembered meeting her at the company picnic. She wasn't much to look at in the face, but she had a big old butt, and she dressed to show off her... assets," she said in disgust. "She was a good fifteen years younger than him too. He had his arm around her waist as they went out to his car and got in the backseat. Didn't take long for the windows to fog up. That's when I grabbed the baseball bat I'd brought with me and busted out all the windows on the car."

"No, you didn't!" I struggled to picture my strait-laced mom with a baseball bat going ham on Dad's car. But I understood that kind of pain and rage, and in that instant, I hated my father for putting her through that.

"Yes. I mostly certainly did! You should have seen those fools scrambling to get out of that car. Her top was off, and your daddy's pants were falling down. He was trying to calm me and get the bat away from me, but I kept right on swinging. People were coming out of the bar to see what was going on. I remember someone grabbing me from behind and your father finally getting the bat away. I kicked him in the balls and told him not to come home."

I tried hard to get the image of my father in the backseat messing around with another woman out of my head and failed. "But he did come home."

"He did. I was sitting on the couch when he finally returned an hour later, yelling at me about how much *I* had embarrassed *him*."

"Is that when you broke all the plates?"

"Every last one, including his mama's china."

"But you guys worked it out. Things got better, right?"

"They did. But like I said, it came at the cost of my peace. When the dust settled, your daddy was as sorry as any man could be. He spent the rest of his life trying to make up for what he did. But I never completely trusted him again." She paused. "I hope you're seeing a therapist separately from your marriage counselor."

"I am," I replied, leaving it at that. Technically, it was true. I'd gone to one session with a therapist but felt so raw afterward I never went back. I knew if I told her that, she'd nag the hell out of me until I did. But I would go back, eventually. "Ros said there was some trouble with that Jan woman?"

"She couldn't let him go." Mom shook her head and gave me a hard look. "She was in an unhappy marriage and thought your daddy was the answer to all her problems. When he broke up with her, she lost her mind. Hang-up phone calls. Keyed your daddy's car. Made complaints about him at work trying to get him fired. And other stuff," she said, her voice trailing off.

"Sammy?"

Mom's eyes widened in surprise. "How did you know about—"

"Ros overheard Daddy telling you he found Sammy behind the garage."

"It killed your daddy to lie to you two about your dog. And as far as I was concerned, that was the final straw. That woman came to our house. She was in our yard, and she poisoned our dog. She could just as easily have hurt you or your sister. And I wasn't having it. Your father had done everything he could to let her down gently. He was a married man, and his place was with his family."

"What did you do?"

"Something I probably shouldn't have. But I was desperate. I wasn't thinking about the consequences." My mom looked uncomfortable, and that wasn't something I was used to seeing. She wouldn't meet my gaze.

"Mom?"

She let out a sigh before replying. "I told her husband."

"Seriously?" I'm not sure why it surprised me she would go to those lengths, especially when I know how she must've been feeling.

"I didn't know she was in an abusive marriage. Your daddy never wanted to talk about her. He felt guilty for what he'd done to the both of us. But I felt like I had no choice because she wouldn't stop, and things were getting worse. So, I wrote him an anonymous letter letting him know she was stepping out on him but never said with who."

"What happened?"

"Well," she said, shoulders slumping as she looked away from me. "It was bad, Paige. I don't want to talk about it."

"Mom, whatever it was, it wasn't your fault. How were you supposed to know what would happen to her? She gave you no choice." Mom looked down at her lap and was silent for so long. I leaned forward in my seat. "Mom? Are you okay?" She finally looked up, tears shining in her eyes.

"For a long time, I didn't care about what happened to her just as long as she was gone. But I'm older now and I'm more empathetic toward her being caught between a rock and a hard place. A husband who beat her and a lover who no longer wanted her. She must've been desperate."

"I'm not so sure she deserves your compassion after what she did to poor Sammy."

My mother's eyes hardened. "What about your situation? Isn't there anything the police can do?"

"Not unless she makes a direct threat to us. She's smart. All the crap she's been doing is hard to trace back to her. Aaron wants us to go talk to her together. But that's just going to piss her off more. She doesn't have a husband I can talk to about making her stop either."

"What do you know about this woman?"

"She has a PhD in English and teaches at Roberson. Before that, Aaron said she ran an honors English program at some private school on the East Coast. But I don't know the name of the school or what city it's in. I'm not sure if she's ever been married. As far as I know, she doesn't have kids."

"You need to fight fire with fire. Find out something you can use as leverage against her to make her stop."

Where was she going with this? "Like what?"

"Like anything that would cause her to lose something important to her. Do you have any idea what that might be?"

"Her job, maybe? I don't know much about her. Aaron's just like Daddy was. He doesn't want to talk about her and gets annoyed if I bring her up."

"Then you have to do what everybody else does when you're trying to find out about somebody these days."

"Which is?"

"Come on now. Even an old lady like me knows that. Social media." I realized then that my mother was right. To find a way to make her leave us alone, I had to find out more about Cara Morton. As soon as we finished talking, I logged on to Facebook. I did a quick search for Cara Morton and wasn't surprised to find that she had a page. But it was private, and I couldn't see any of the pictures and posts on it. Next, I pulled up Aaron's Facebook page. To my surprise, his page was also private, even though we were Facebook friends. Suddenly, I understood why I couldn't see his page – he'd blocked me. Obviously, there was something on their pages that neither of them wanted me to see.

After I let him move back home, I had made Aaron give me all his passwords. I had no intention of checking his emails or his text messages ever again. I just wanted him to know that I could if I wanted to. But he rarely ever used Facebook and only had a handful of friends, so it had never even occurred to me to ask for the Facebook password. And he didn't offer it to me either. Luckily for me, he'd used the same password for Facebook that he did for his email.

When I finally got onto it, I was relieved to find there wasn't anything shady or incriminating on Aaron's page, just a handful of pics of the kids and me on vacation and holidays. There weren't any pics of him and Cara. But I did see that they were still listed as "friends" which stung. Shouldn't he have unfriended her? I clicked through to Cara's Facebook page from Aaron's page. Cara's page showed the life of a vibrant, beautiful woman in the prime of her life. She regularly posted smiling selfies and pics of her with students and colleagues at restaurants, bars, and other events. She obviously had an active social life.

She hardly looked like a recently dumped side chick. There were no cryptic memes or sayings about love and heartbreak and knowing your worth. If she was hurting over the end of her affair with my husband, she wasn't letting it show on her Facebook page. And then I saw why Aaron had blocked me. Until a month ago, he had liked or hearted most of her pics. There were DMs too. Lots of them. I was tempted to read them. But did I really want to scroll through their messages? It would be like picking at a scab and making the wound bleed again.

Instead, I went back to Cara's pictures. There were hundreds of them dating all the way back to her time as a member of the teaching staff at Parkdale Prep in LaDuc, New York. I kept scrolling until I came across a picture of her with an older white man. He was a handsome silver fox with cropped white hair and a beard and vivid green eyes. He looked to be in his fifties, but I could tell from the way his T-shirt molded to his chest that he had the body of a much younger man. The picture was at the gym, and they were both in workout clothes. I could also tell by the way his hand was on her lower back that they were more than friends. They were both smiling. Who was this man?

On a whim, I pulled up the website of Parkdale Prep and searched through the pictures on the site until I found him. His name was Paul Ramsey, and he was the head of Parkdale. The picture in his bio was him with his wife of twenty-two years, Joan, and their four teenage children, three sons and a daughter. I couldn't help but notice that in this picture, Paul Ramsey looked different. He looked like a middle-aged man in an ill-fitting suit, at least a size too small, with a chubby, round clean-shaven face. Not the muscular silver fox hottie he was in the picture with Cara. It was the same transformation my husband had undergone once he'd gotten involved with Cara. Wow. Mom had been right. How long had her affair with Ramsey lasted? Did she harass him and his wife like she was doing to us when he ended it? Did he end it, or did she? And did Joan Ramsey know? And more importantly, how could I find out?

SIXTEEN

AARON NICHOLS

AFTER

December 5, 2023

"Did your wife know about your affair with Dr. Morton?" Detective Alonso looked at me again with a neutral expression that she must have practiced to perfection.

"Yes, she knew."

"And how did she feel about it?"

"Paige didn't hurt Cara, Detective."

"I said nothing about your wife hurting Dr. Morton. I asked you how she felt about your affair. But I find it interesting that you felt the need to defend her so quickly."

"It hurt her," I told her, ignoring that last part. I'd put Paige through enough and didn't want her dragged into this mess.

"How hurt?"

"She asked me to leave our home, and we separated for a couple of weeks."

"But you reconciled?"

"Yes."

"And to your knowledge, did your wife ever confront Cara Morton about your affair?"

"Why are you asking me about my wife? I told you about two people Cara had issues with, and she had a cocaine addiction. She had things going on in her life that I didn't know about, which could have contributed to her disappearance."

"I've made note of that, Dr. Nichols. But you're not telling me everything, are you?"

Fear stiffened my spine. What else did Detective Alonso know? "What do you mean?"

"Here's the problem I'm having," she said as she waved at the two-way mirror. She got up from the table and went to the door where she was met by a short, stocky white guy with a buzzcut who handed her a laptop.

She set it up on the table, and we both watched doorbell camera footage of me arriving at Cara's house. Detective Alonso explained calmly that Cara's neighbor from across the street, who had been visiting her son in Hawaii for a month, had recently returned home and turned in the footage from her doorbell camera to the police. That footage showed me arriving at Cara's house the previous Friday, the evening she had disappeared. I sucked in my breath. I knew this video made me look guilty as hell.

"Would you like to explain this, Dr. Nichols? Because this camera footage is why you're sitting here. You won't do yourself any favors by continuing to lie to me," concluded Detective Alonso.

Anger welled up inside me as I realized how I'd been played. She'd asked me when I'd last seen Cara and I'd fallen right into her trap by lying. Shit. But the footage had only showed Cara and I arguing for a few minutes at her door. I never entered her house. But how was I going to prove that? The video cut off and didn't show me leaving.

"Where's the rest of it? You dragged me in here over a few minutes of incomplete doorbell cam footage?"

"No one dragged you in here. You came in of your own free will. What else am I supposed to think, when you lied to me about the last time you saw Dr. Morton?"

I didn't respond. Just stared stonily at her.

"What were you arguing with Dr. Morton about the night she disappeared?"

"She had called and begged me to come over. When I got there, she told me she wanted to go to an inpatient rehab facility in Cleveland and wanted me to drive her there because she didn't have anyone else she could ask. In exchange, she promised to drop the..." my voice trailed off. But Detective Alonso continued for me.

"The sexual harassment complaint? You're currently on paid leave from the university because Dr. Morton made a formal complaint of sexual harassment against you with the college, is that right?"

I nodded and ran a shaky hand over my face feeling even more like a fool for showing up without a lawyer.

Detective Alonso leaned forward. "Well, Dr Nichols, why don't you tell me about that?"

SEVENTEEN

AARON NICHOLS

BEFORE

October 27, 2023

Paige didn't know why I'd really come home, or that Cara wasn't the woman I'd thought she was. She was a drug addict, and she'd lied to me about Devon Lloyd. He'd never been a student, as far as I could tell. I even double-checked with someone in admissions, and they told me no one by that name had ever enrolled at Roberson. Of course, she had probably lied to me about his real name. Addicts lie. And the ease with which the lies regarding this young man had rolled off her tongue proved she was an accomplished liar.

If I had been paying attention, the signs of her addiction were all there. Her constantly running nose. Her moodiness. Her violence toward her father. I'm betting that wasn't even the first time she'd hit him. Taken separately, I could explain these signs. But now that I knew she used drugs, it all made sense. I just hadn't wanted to see it because being with her felt so good. I should have seen right through the illusion because

I'd been down this road before. Cara wasn't the only one who'd lied. I'd told her my mom had died of breast cancer. My grandmother was the one who'd died of breast cancer five years ago. My mom died of a drug overdose when I was sixteen. She'd been a heroin addict and had met my father in one of her many stints in rehab, but he got clean and turned his life around. My mom wasn't so lucky. My father's new life didn't include me, I'm guessing, because being a father to me meant being connected to a woman and a past he wanted nothing to do with.

By the time I was three, I was living with my grandparents. Mom got clean and got custody of me when I was twelve. But I was miserable and had to do things to cover for Mom when she fell off the wagon again mere months after I went to live with her. I lied for her. Scored drugs for her. Helped her shoot up in places that wouldn't show like between her toes. Stayed locked in my room with the TV volume on high when she brought home strangers to sleep with for drug money.

This went on for two years until I broke down at school one day and finally told the school counselor the truth. The school called social services who called my grandparents to come get me. When they went to the raggedy shithole I'd lived in with my mother, she was gone. I never saw her again until her funeral. They had found her dead from an overdose in a local park. I couldn't live that life again. And I knew as soon as I saw the fevered look in Cara's eyes, the cocaine caked in her runny nose, and the frantic tone in her voice when she lied about being able to quit any time, that it was over between us forever.

It's unfortunate that Cara didn't see it that way.

After I cut things off with her, Cara kept blowing up my phone with texts, to the point where Paige insisted that I block her. I felt like I owed her a conversation at least, but I knew my wife would go ballistic if I spoke to Cara again after my promise. Even so, I still had to work with her.

On my first day back at work after I'd broken it off, I'd barely gotten out of my car when Cara pulled into the spot right next to me. That had been our thing before everything blew up in my face. Parking next to each other in the parking lot so that it wouldn't look too suspicious when we walked out together in the evening and stood by our cars talking. After all, if we parked our cars next to each other, it would only be natural to have a conversation. That's how I justified it in my head. But people aren't stupid, and I'm sure everyone noticed how much time we'd been spending together. I just had my head too far up my ass to care.

Now, as Cara blocked my path, I regretted our little routine. "Please, Aaron. I really don't want to make a scene."

She was looking like her old self again, perfectly made up with her hair in an artful disarray of highlighted curls and her perfume mocking me with memories of the smell and taste of her skin. For an instant, and just for an instant, I questioned whether I'd truly witnessed what I'd seen in that empty parking lot. The woman standing before me hardly looked like a drug addict. She was just as beautiful as she'd ever been. And I almost forgot the lies that had come tumbling forth from her perfect soft pink lips. It was her eyes that snapped me back to reality. As put together as the rest of her looked, her eyes still told the story of what had happened. They still had that same frantic, fevered quality. And no amount of makeup, perfume, or expensive clothes could hide it.

I glanced around to check if many people were about to witness something that was probably going to get ugly. It wasn't a good look, fighting with your mistress in the parking lot where you work. It hadn't been a good look for a long time, the way I'd been carrying on with Cara, but how it looked to others hadn't bothered me when I'd foolishly gotten involved with her.

"I'm late for a meeting. But I've got some time later this morning. Can you stop by my office around 9:30?" I glanced at her, and she merely nodded.

"I'll come. But don't make me come looking for you, because I will. You can't lie to me and blow me off the way you did to Paige."

I wanted to tell her that the only reason I could get away with lying to and blowing off my wife was because she had loved and trusted me. But I didn't bother.

Later that day, after my meeting, Cara was already in my office.

"Dr. Morton is waiting for you," said Lynette when I walked into her small cubicle outside of my office. "I told her she was welcome to wait out here for you, but she said she would be just fine in your office." Lynette gave me a look that I couldn't quite decipher. But I'm sure she must've known about me and Cara. According to Dr. Peters, everyone did.

"That's fine. Thanks, Lynette." I walked into the office and pulled the door shut behind me to find Cara sitting on the small sofa with her long, slim legs propped up on the coffee table. Crossed at the ankles.

"I'm willing to forgive you. But you'll have to make it up to me." She uncrossed her ankles, pulled her skirt up high on her thighs, and spread her legs. She wasn't wearing any panties. I was stunned for several long seconds before turning away.

"Get out of my office now," I said as firmly as I could without yelling. "What the hell is wrong with you?"

She pulled her skirt down and jumped up from the couch. "I am so sorry. I don't know what I was thinking. I've just been so desperate these past few days. Why haven't you been answering my calls and texts? Is it Paige? Did she make you send that text because it didn't sound like you at all?"

"I can't do this anymore. It's wrong and I'm married. There's no future for us."

"Oh, so *now* it's wrong?" Her laugh was harsh and mocking. "Why wasn't it wrong three months ago? Why wasn't it wrong when you were kissing me and feeling me up in the stairwells and going down on me with my father in the next room? Why wasn't it wrong when I showed up here to comfort you after those meetings where you got ganged up on by Peters and those other old assholes? Why is it wrong now when it wasn't wrong then?"

"It was always wrong. The difference now is that I realize it was all just a fantasy. None of it was real. I didn't know who I was involved with, did I?"

Cara's jaw tightened and her eyes narrowed. "You are such a fucking hypocrite! I thought you were different. I thought you cared about me. But you're just like all the other lying ass men in my life!"

"Is your dealer included in that statement? Who is that kid? Because I know he's never been a student here."

Cara deflated like a balloon and sank down on the couch. She buried her face in her hands and sobbed. "I don't understand what happened. I thought we had something special. You told me I was the only one who understood you. You told me that most days talking to me was the highlight of your day. And now you're telling me that, because I do a little coke now and then, none of it was true?"

"Now and then? It's pretty clear you're an addict, Cara."

"Don't you fucking call me that." She jumped up from the couch and not a single tear shone in her eyes. She'd also conveniently not answered my question about Devon Lloyd.

"Is it because of your father? Is taking care of him too much for you? Or have you been using coke for a while now? I can help you find a rehab program."

"Don't you dare act like you give a damn about me or my

father. And the only rehab program I need is to break my addiction to spineless motherfuckers like you!"

"You need help, Cara. I want to help you. But things can't be the way they were. I'm sorry I let things get so out of hand. I wasn't fair to you or Paige."

Cara lowered her head, and, against my better judgment, I put my arms around her and tried to hug her. But she quickly pulled out of my embrace and gave me a contemptuous look before her hand shot out and cracked me hard across my left cheek. My hand flew to my face and my mouth fell open in shock. She had the same furious expression on her face as she did when she'd hit her father. Then she rubbed her nose so hard and fast it bled, a lot.

"Here, take these." I quickly grabbed a box of tissues from my desk, but by the time I'd turned back around, Cara was near my office door with blood running from her nose and over her lips, dripping onto her white silk blouse. She turned toward me, smiling, the dripping blood staining her teeth.

"You're about to find out that my bad side is not a place you want to be," she whispered before ripping the sleeve of her blouse at the shoulder and loudly shouting, "Don't you ever touch me again!"

Lynette came rushing into the room, almost colliding with Cara as she ran out. But Cara made sure Lynette had seen her bloody face and torn blouse before bursting into tears.

"Oh my God, Dr. Nichols! Is she okay? Should I go after her?"

But all I could do was stare at her and wonder what the hell had just happened?

True to her word, after that, things got bad at work. Cara had gone from being my ally to my enemy and was actively siding with Dr. Peters and his crew and questioning the job I was doing as department chair. If that had been all that she did, I could have handled it. But it only got worse when twelve days after the altercation in my office, I received a written notice in the campus mail. As soon as I saw the cream-colored envelope from the office of Linda Cole, the campus' Title IX coordinator, sitting on my desk, I knew I was screwed. I stared at it for a minute before snatching it off my desk and ripping it open. Cara had made a complaint of sexual harassment. I read the copy of Cara's letter of complaint that was enclosed multiple times, not believing what I was reading.

Dear Ms. Cole,

I am writing to make a formal complaint of sexual harassment against Dr. Aaron Nichols. The harassment started three months ago, right after Dr. Nichols was named chair of the English Department. On his recommendation, I took over as the new managing editor of *Reflections*, the Student Literary Review, which I accepted, not knowing that Dr. Nichols expected physical favors in return. Dr. Nichols would often corner me when I was alone in my office or in my classroom after my classes and touch me inappropriately without my consent. He made it clear that if I slept with him, he would help me advance even further at the college. He became angry when I refused his advances and threatened to remove me as head of the Literary Review.

On the 27th of October, Dr. Nichols called me to his office and again tried to pressure me into a sexual relationship. When I tried to defend myself against his advances, he persisted, which led to a physical altercation, resulting in my nose being bloodied and my blouse being ripped. I left his office bleeding and in tears, which was witnessed by Lynette Carson, his administrative assistant. I have feared for my safety ever since.

This kind of behavior is unacceptable, and I know Roberson

University does not condone this. I ask you to investigate this matter and put an end to this inappropriate behavior.

Sincerely,
Dr. Cara Morton, PhD

None of it was true. But I had to protect myself. I had to fight back, and I had to tell Paige.

"She's doing this because you broke things off with her. Didn't you tell them that?" Paige tossed the letter of complaint onto the coffee table in the living room. I'd waited until after the kids had gone to bed to tell her about the sexual harassment charge and that I'd been suspended pending an investigation.

"The university has no choice but to investigate. But I'll get to tell my side of the story."

"You sure seem calm for a man who could lose his job and reputation. This crazy bitch could ruin our lives with these lies."

"I know. I know, sweetie. But please don't worry." I pulled her into a tight embrace. And she let me hold her for a few minutes before pulling away.

"Don't worry? What I want to know is why you aren't worried? She's accused you not just of harassment but assault."

"Because if I assaulted her, why didn't she call the police? Plus, I have proof that everything that happened between Cara and me was consensual. I have all those texts, pictures, and that video she sent. Why the hell would a woman who is being sexually harassed engage in such behavior with her harasser? Those are questions she's going to have to answer."

"I hope for the sake of us all that you're right, Aaron." My wife walked away, disgusted with me, and I didn't blame her.

Despite my claims that I wasn't worried, I was worried as hell. I could lose my job and be labeled as some kind of pervert. Who would hire me if Cara won her case? I was the sole breadwinner in our household, and I had failed my family. I got straight on my phone to a lawyer I knew named Bill Watters.

Later that night, Bill let out a low whistle as I showed him all the texts and the video on my phone, as well as the letter accusing me of sexual harassment. When he was done, he looked at me and shook his head.

"I know," I told him, taking a sip of my beer. "I'm an idiot."

Bill suggested we meet for a drink to go over my case. Ironically, we were at The Night Owl, the same bar my affair with Cara had begun three months ago. If only I could go back to that night and make a different choice.

"And you've ended things with her, right?"

"Absolutely," I said, then added, "So, what do you think? Can I save my job?"

"Everything you've shown me is proof of a consensual relationship with your accuser and suggests her anger when you ended it. It's what happened in your office that's going to be tricky to prove. Did anyone else witness what happened?"

"Just my admin assistant and she only caught the tail end of it when Cara ran out of my office bleeding and in tears."

"But she never reported it to the police?"

"No."

"That's a point in your favor, although she could just claim she was too afraid to report it."

"Bullshit. You read that letter. She was asking the Title IX committee to put an end to my so-called harassment. Calling the cops and having me arrested for assault would have done that, yet she didn't call them because I didn't assault her."

"She may not have filed charges because she'd already achieved her goal."

"Which is?"

"Fucking up your life. This is the MeToo era, man. The

accusation alone is enough to ruin lives. You need to ask yourself if saving this job is worth it when there are going to be people who believe this woman, even if you're exonerated. Her intention is to cause damage, and it has."

"So, I'm supposed to just quit and let her win? Are you crazy? I'm guilty of a lot of shit, but I did nothing to Cara Morton that she didn't want, or encourage, me to do. I sure as hell didn't assault her."

Bill sat back in his chair and grinned at me. "Now that's what I wanted to hear. You're a fighter. Hold on to that righteous indignation. We're going to need it."

Bill Watters was old-school and reminded me of my grandfather. He even looked a little like him, with his cropped gray hair and wire-rimmed glasses. In his mid-sixties, he always dressed to a tee in tailored three-piece suits smelling of cigar smoke and expensive cologne. I could see my reflection in the shine on his gold cuff links. I had met him several years ago when he taught a legal workshop at the college. We were the only two black men in attendance. He told me if I ever needed legal advice, to call him. And here we were having drinks like old friends when I hadn't seen him in at least five years.

"How'd you end up in this situation, Aaron? You always struck me as being a straight arrow."

"Paige and I hit a rough patch, and I ended up someplace I had no business being."

"Oh, I feel you, man. I get it. But let me give you a piece of advice you didn't ask for and probably don't want."

"What's that?" I eyed him warily, in no mood for a lecture.

"I've been down this road many times. Loved having a wife and raising a family but always had a chick on the side. My wife Marion finally told me to either get help or get out. We were in marital counseling and things were better than they'd ever been. We were like newlyweds again. Then she died suddenly of a heart attack in her sleep and part of me died with her."

"Damn, Bill. I'm sorry, man. I had no idea your wife had died."

"Last year. A week before our fortieth anniversary. All those years chasing tail when I could have spent it with her." He shook his head. "Cherish you wife, Aaron. You don't know how much time you're going to have with her."

We drank in silence for a few minutes. Bill stared into his glass as his eyes watered with what I recognized as guilt and regret. I wondered if he'd have shared this story if he hadn't had so much to drink.

"Paige and I are working it out. We're in counseling and I think we've got a good shot."

"Glad to hear it," he said, perking up.

I'm guessing Bill didn't have many people to talk to. And suddenly I was getting antsy to leave. If I'd gone on seeing Cara, I could have been the one sharing my guilt and regret to strangers in bars while half-drunk. Bill must have sensed my discomfort. He tossed money on the bar for our drinks and stood up. I offered him a lift home and we walked out to my car together, which was parked across the street.

We'd gotten into the middle of the street, when the lights of a rapidly oncoming car blinded us. It sped straight at us, and I shoved Bill so hard out of its path, that he lost his balance and fell as we both hit the side of my car. His glasses slipped off and broke when they hit the street. The car had come within inches of hitting us.

"Are you okay?" I held out my hand to help Bill to his feet as I watched the black car make a hard right around the corner a block away. Maybe I'd had too much to drink myself, but I could have sworn I glimpsed curly light brown hair before the car had turned the corner. And the only person I knew with a black car and hair like that was Cara. Had she just tried to kill us?

"What the hell was that?"

"A crazy asshole." I didn't feel like sharing my suspicions with him. "Let's get you home."

After I saw Bill safely into his apartment, I left rattled and in no mood to talk. I was relieved Paige was already in bed when I got home. It wasn't until the next morning when I was taking the kids to school that Bailey pointed out something on my car I hadn't noticed the night before.

"Daddy, what's that on your car?"

Written on the trunk in what looked like red lipstick were the words: Goodnight, gorgeous.

"Dr. Nichols, are you sure you brought your phone to the gym with you?"

The head of campus security was giving me a doubtful look. I couldn't tell if it was because he truly didn't believe that someone had stolen my phone or if he was just too lazy to figure it out. I know I had my phone when I arrived at the gym because I always listened to music on it while I worked out. I had my Bluetooth headphones as usual, and I had just completed a five-mile run on the treadmill. I'd left my phone resting on it while I'd gone to the restroom. When I came back, it was gone.

"Yes, I'm certain. I was gone maybe five minutes."

I was the only one using the treadmill that afternoon and was one of maybe six people in the entire gym. I even went to the front desk and asked if anyone had turned in a phone. They had three cell phones in the lost and found, but none of them was mine. And that's when I called the campus police and reported it stolen.

"Excuse me, Dr. Nichols." To my surprise, it wasn't the young lady who had been manning the front desk when I arrived. But she was wearing the employee uniform of a gray sweatshirt.

"Beth? I didn't realize you worked here."

"Yeah, I just started last week. They said you lost your phone?"

"It's not lost. I think someone may have walked off with it." I tried to keep my voice calm, even though I wanted to scream; it wasn't Beth's fault.

"Do you have the Find My phone app on your phone?"

"I think so."

"I can show you how to find out where your phone is if you don't know how."

The campus security guy and I followed Beth back up to the front desk where she had pulled up Google and had me log in. Once I pulled up a map, I saw my phone was still at the gym. The three of us searched the place again, including the locker rooms. Beth suggested she ring my phone, which I was embarrassed not to have tried earlier, and I heard a faint ringing sound near the trash can next to the exit. Lo-and-behold, there it was.

"You don't want to file a report still, do you?" asked the campus security officer unnecessarily. I was certain that someone had stolen my phone, and for some reason had thrown it in the trash on their way out the door.

"No, that won't be necessary, officer, but thank you for coming by and being so willing to help me," I said sarcastically.

"Any time," he said and was gone.

"And thank you very much, Beth," I said genuinely. "You saved the day."

"No problem." She smiled sheepishly. "I have to do that at least once a month to find my phone."

I'd planned to stay longer and do some lifting. Instead, I took a shower, changed, and left. The whole time I was racking my brain trying to figure out why in the world someone would steal my phone only to throw it in the trash can. I didn't realize what had happened until two days later when I met with Bill a few hours before my hearing at HR for my sexual harassment case.

I was pulling up the pictures, text, and video that Cara had sent me to show Bill again. But I couldn't because they were gone. They had all been erased from my phone.

"Everything is gone," Paige asked incredulously. "All of it?" My wife looked horrified, and I couldn't blame her. I'd assured her I'd be able to prove my innocence and now that proof was gone. What the hell was I going to do? Bill had pushed the hearing to next week. But what happened when the next hearing came, and I still had no evidence?

"What about the cloud?" Paige asked. "Doesn't a backup copy of pictures and videos automatically get stored in the cloud?"

"Yes, pictures and videos are saved in the cloud. But I don't know of any way to retrieve deleted texts, and without the texts, the pictures have no context, and I can't prove a consensual relationship. Would Tyler know of any way to retrieve them?"

My brother-in-law worked as a programmer for a video gaming company in Seattle. Tyler was a teenager when Paige and I met. And in all the years I'd been with his sister, Tyler and I had never bonded. He was a highly intelligent guy but awkward, antisocial, and arrogant. He even refused to pronounce my name correctly. He called me A-a-ron from a Key & Peele comedy skit about a substitute teacher who mispronounced students' names. But if anyone would know how to retrieve the text messages from my phone, it would be Tyler.

"You're not exactly Tyler's favorite person at the best of times, Aaron. And after what happened, I doubt he'd spit on you if you were on fire, let alone help you get deleted texts off your phone."

"Does your entire family know?" I hadn't meant to sound so

defensive. Would I ever live this down? Was my lapse in judg-ment going to follow me around forever?

"No. And for the record, I didn't tell him. Mom or Ros must have. But I'll ask him about retrieving the texts."

"I'll check the cloud to see if I can at least get the pictures and video back."

There was a pause, then Paige asked, "When did you want to go talk to Cara?"

"Yeah, about that." I turned to face her. "I'm not sure that's a good idea."

"And why is that? It was your idea." Paige's eyes narrowed suspiciously, and I had to scramble to come up with a good excuse.

"Bill says stay away from her until after the hearing because she might say I'm trying to coerce or threaten her, and I agree with him."

"I guess that makes sense," Paige conceded. But she still looked suspicious.

I got on my phone and checked the cloud, only to discover every selfie Cara had sent me had been deleted from the cloud. Only the video she'd sent me the night before D-day remained. Why? Did whoever had stolen it forget to delete the video?

I heard Paige upstairs getting the kids ready for bed. I clicked play on the video, knowing that looking at the damned thing again was the last thing I should be doing. It was the first time I'd watched it since Paige had let me move back home. I'd watched it almost every night when I'd been staying in the hotel. But something was different about Cara in the video. It was her hair. I hadn't noticed it before, probably because I was too busy looking at the rest of her body. But it was darker, with no highlights. She'd had honey blonde highlights in her hair since the summer. Could she have been wearing a wig? I held my phone closer to the lamp on the end table. No. It was defi-nitely her curly hair. When did she make this video?

Swiping up on the video from the bottom, I saw the date that video had been created. It was two months before she'd started working at Roberson. She'd obviously made that video for someone else, not me. I shouldn't have been surprised. I never really knew Cara. But it still stung. Then another question occurred to me. Had she been the one to send me the video? She'd never mentioned it to me in person, so I'd assumed Cara was being shy about it. I had told her Paige had gone through my phone and seen everything but hadn't mentioned the video. If Cara had sent it, why hadn't it been deleted from my phone along with everything else? The only answer I could come up with was that she didn't know I had the video.

But if she hadn't sent it to me, who had and why?

EIGHTEEN

AARON NICHOLS

BEFORE

November 8, 2023

I didn't want to wait for Paige to talk to Tyler. I'd rather electric slide barefoot through broken glass than call him myself. But I had no choice.

"Well, if it isn't A-a-ron, the man who betrayed my big sister. What the hell could you possibly be calling me about? Are Paige and the kids okay?"

"Hey, Tyler. They're fine. And believe me, calling you was the last thing I wanted to do, but I really need your help, man."

"I'm not getting into the middle of your marital problems, bruh. If you're looking for character witnesses to talk to Paige on your behalf, then you're outta luck. 'Coz I never liked your ass, anyway."

"Paige and I are working things out. We're going to be fine. And I'm not calling about that."

"What do you want?"

I quickly explained about the video and if it were possible to figure out who really sent it.

"You're calling me to see if a video your side chick texted you was sent by your side chick? Man, you trippin'."

"Paige hasn't told you what's been going on?"

"I keep hearing the word 'bunny boiler' from her and Ros. I had to look it up. Man, you really know how to pick 'em."

"I'm not trying to make excuses. I know how bad I fucked up. And if I have to spend the rest of my life making it up to Paige and the kids, I will. But I wouldn't have called you if it wasn't important. Can you help me or not?" I heard him mumble something about me being a sorry mofo and thought he was going to hang up.

"Just as long as you know I'm doing this for my sister, not you."

"Understood."

"Was the text sent from her number?"

"Yes."

"Then she, or whoever had access to her phone, sent it."

"It couldn't have been sent by someone else, making it look like it was from her?"

"Someone could have either cloned or spoofed her phone or number and sent the video to you pretending to be her."

"What's cloning and spoofing?" He may as well have been speaking another language. I heard the condescending sigh that always came before Tyler, the tech geek, had to explain something he thought was common knowledge.

"Cloning is when someone copies the identity of a cell phone onto another cell phone and spoofing is changing a sender's details like their name to make a call or text look like it came from someone else."

"And how can I tell if the text I got was spoofed or from a cloned phone?"

"Only way to tell if it's cloned is to have access to the phone in question. Spoofing is easier to detect because you can't reply to it. You can't block the sender either. Did you reply to it?"

"Hold on," I told him and brought up the text with the video and typed out, *Who is this?* in the reply box and hit send. But it didn't go through. "I couldn't send it."

"Maybe she blocked you."

"Maybe. It said message not delivered. But," I began before Tyler cut me off.

"You sure you don't have another jealous side chick out there, playa? Maybe this wasn't your first trip around the block."

"There's been no one else." I let out a sigh, knowing I deserved all the shade he was throwing at me, but still feeling bruised by it. "But thanks for talking to me." I was about to hang up when he stopped me.

"Hey, seriously though, you probably won't be able to find out who sent it. But you might find out if they posted the video somewhere online."

"How?" I seriously doubted Cara would have posted that video online, but I didn't want to be rude and piss off my brother-in-law more than he already was.

"Take some screenshots of the video and do a reverse image search. If it's been posted online, it should pull up where it's posted. And if you don't know how to do either of those things, look it up 'coz I'm not tech support for cheaters."

He hung up before I could thank him.

It took me a little time, but I figured out how to do what Tyler suggested. I waited until after Paige and the kids had gone to bed, and I took several screenshots of the video. I did a reverse image search online. I didn't get lucky with any of them. The video was several minutes long, so I did another batch of screenshots. I was stunned when I got lucky on the third screenshot from my second batch. It was a screenshot of Cara cupping her breasts while only wearing the lacy red thong. She stared directly at the camera with her full pouting lips slightly parted. Unfortunately, when I clicked the link to the website where the picture had been posted, it had already been taken down for community violations. Someone had posted it in an online community for artists in a thread about real life inspirations for manga heroines. Lucky for me, although they'd deleted the picture, the thread was still up. Someone calling themselves Sanityis4Suckers had posted it back in May. Apparently, erotic pictures of real people weren't allowed, only nude art. I clicked on Sanityis4Suckers' name and was disappointed to see their profile was blank with no bio. But I could send this person a message. I quickly created an account under the name SadProf, then typed out a quick message:

Hello,
I'm interested in this pic you posted and am wondering where you got it, and if you know this woman?
SadProf

I attached the screenshot in question and hit send. Then went to take a shower. When I got out, I checked my account on the Manga Mania website and was stunned to see that I'd already had a reply.

Is D Love posting again? I'm her biggest fan!
Sanityis4Suckers

What the hell were they talking about? And who was D Love? Now I had a problem. I couldn't tell this person why I really wanted to know about this video. I'd never hear from them again. But what could I ask him to keep him communicating with me long enough to find out what he was talking about.

Hey,
You know her as D Love? I know her as Candy. Are you sure
we're talking about the same woman?
SadProf

Is this her?
Sanityis4Suckers

He'd included a link in the message which I clicked, taking me to a homepage of the website of a cam model named Devon Love, also known as D Love and, more recently, Dr. Cara Morton. Her website was listed on a bigger site called Make Me Cam and showed snippets of other videos, including the one sent to me. The last video had been uploaded in June but nothing since then. I would need to subscribe to access the video, which wasn't something I was willing to do. Paige and I have joint accounts, and she'd kill me if she found out. I was figuring out my next move when another message popped up from Sanityis4Suckers.

Well? Is it her?
Sanityis4Suckers

Yes! It's her! Any idea why she stopped posting?
SadProf

The reply was instant.

She had a stalker. Last session I had with her, she said it had
really freaked her out, and I sent her $500 and made her promise
to buy herself a gun. She just disappeared after that. I hope she's
okay.
Sanityis4Suckers

A stalker? Could that be why she'd disappeared? The thought made me sit up straighter on the couch. This might be the answer I'd been searching for. But then I'd thought back on how carefree Cara had always seemed. She led an active life if her social media posts were anything to go by. She wasn't a woman hiding and living in fear of a stalker. And I'm pretty sure that $500 went up her nose. Just as I was sure the name Devon Lloyd was a variation of her online persona of Devon Love. She must've panicked when I wanted to know what that kid's name was, and it was the only thing she could think of in a hurry. But I didn't have the heart to tell Sanityis4Suckers that. Whoever this person was seemed so infatuated with her I doubted they'd even believe me. I'd heard about guys who spent thousands of dollars on cam girls and got very little in return beyond vague promises of a relationship. Though who was I to judge?

I typed out a new message.

Did you ever get to meet her in person?
SadProf

No. She had a rule against meeting her fans in person. Only new girls desperate for money did that. And she was so popular she didn't need to meet fans offline.
Sanityis4Suckers

Will you let me know if she posts again?
SadProf

I didn't get a response.

I watched Aaron Nichols leave the police station. I had no choice but to cut him loose as we had nothing concrete to hold him on. He was right. The doorbell footage showed him arriving at Morton's house and arguing with her for a few minutes and nothing more because the battery had run out. Typical. I had officers canvassing the neighborhood and nearby businesses for more footage to create a timeline, but nothing had turned up yet. Meanwhile, I was still trying to get a read on Nichols. Who was this man? Well-respected college professor, sexual predator, or something even worse? I picked up on his anxiety and fear, but that was to be expected in his current situation.

"Well?" Came a voice from behind, startling me. It was my partner, Noah Richards.

Being the lead on this case, I had elected to conduct Dr. Nichols' interview on my own, feeling like he'd be more relaxed and open to talking if it was just the two of us in the room. Richards had been observing behind the two-way mirror. He hadn't been happy about the setup. But he'd get over it. My partner's toxic trait was thinking he was a more capable police detective having come from a family of cops. He'd gone straight into the police academy from a four-year stint in the army, while I'd gotten an Associates in Criminal Justice. My toxic trait was caring what Richards thought about *my* abilities as a police detective and letting it push me into taking unnecessary risks. I took the cup of coffee he held out to me.

"He copped to the affair quick enough. Though it wasn't like we wouldn't have found out, eventually. But he lied about the last time he saw Dr. Morton, and why lie unless you have something to hide?"

"And what about all the other stuff he told you about Dr. Morton?"

"Doesn't matter what I think. It at all needs to be followed up on." I handed him my notepad with the name that Nichols had given me.

He took the notebook and let his fingers graze mine in the process. My eyes quickly scanned the room, making sure no one had seen him. I knew I wasn't the first, last, or only detective sleeping with their partner. Neither of us were married, but I still didn't want the entire department knowing who was rolling out of my bed in the morning.

"On it." Richards winked at me. He'd taken a few steps before I stopped him.

"Hey. You never said what your take on Nichols was."

Richards shrugged. "He's a guy with a hell of a lot to lose because of a stupid mistake, and he's probably desperate for it all to go away. And we both know that desperate people are dangerous people."

Richards was right. Aaron Nichols was a desperate man, but the question was, how desperate. Desperate enough to make his mistress disappear? Possibly. He had told me much more about Cara Morton than I'd initially known. But was he telling the truth? And, more importantly, what hadn't he told me?

Fortunately, the answer to these questions came an hour later when Richards showed me a witness statement from a woman who owned a coffee shop downtown. She was certain she saw Aaron Nichols throw a black trash bag into her dumpster Sunday evening.

"And she's sure it was him?"

"Positive. Said he's a regular and she'd know him anywhere. She was surprised to see him on a Sunday evening. She lives in the apartment above the shop and heard someone in her dumpster, then saw Nichols from her window. Didn't think much of it until she read about Dr. Morton's disappearance and remembered seeing them together around town, and thought it might be connected. Want me to get him back in here?"

"Not yet. First, I want to know what was in that bag."

"Her trash got picked up this morning. And before you ask, she doesn't have a camera in the alley where her dumpster is."

"Shit," I said under my breath. "Send forensics over to process that dumpster." Gathering people to search the local landfill wasn't going to be easy, especially after the storm we'd just gotten. But I needed to know what Nichols had wanted to get rid of.

"You sure you don't want me to go pick Nichols up?"

"No. But let's put surveillance on him. I want to know everywhere he goes and everyone he talks to."

"What are you hiding Aaron Nichols?" I mumbled to myself. And if I found out, would I also find Cara Morton?

TWENTY

PAIGE NICHOLS

AFTER

December 5, 2023

I was taking a nap on the couch when Aaron got back home. I instantly sat up. He looked so serious as he sat down next to me on the couch.

"How'd it go? You've been gone for hours."

"I wish I knew."

"Do they know about—" My voice trailed off. I refused to say, you and Cara.

"Yeah, the detective already knew. I figured it wouldn't have been a good idea to lie to her."

"And your suspension and the sexual harassment complaint she filed against you?"

"I hadn't planned to tell her, but she already knew and asked me about it."

"Which is why you should have just told her upfront. This only makes you look like you're hiding stuff, Aaron." Annoyed, I got up from the couch. "You've told me everything, haven't you?"

"What do you mean?"

"Everything that happened with Cara. I won't get blind-sided, will I? Because I'm not sure how much more of this I can take."

"You won't. I promise you." Aaron pulled me into his arms, and I allowed myself to be pulled. I wrapped my arms around his waist, and as the fabric of my sweater rubbed against the healing scratch on my arm, I was instantly reminded that my husband and his former mistress weren't the only ones keeping secrets.

BEFORE

November 9, 2023

I'd given up on getting a reply from Joan Ramsey when she finally DM'd me two days later. I sent her a message through Facebook regarding Dr. Cara Morton and asked her to please contact me. Her reply was brief.

What is this about?

I quickly tapped out a reply and pressed send.

I'm sorry to bother you, but I'm hoping to speak with you about Dr. Cara Morton's time at Parkdale. Can I call you?

She responded an hour later with a phone number.

Call after 12 noon tomorrow.

I barely slept that night. Aaron had asked if I'd wanted to meet him for lunch, and I had to lie because I didn't want him to know I was digging into Cara's background. He'd probably tell me to stay out of it or I'd hurt his sexual harassment case. But what he didn't know wouldn't hurt him, and it could all be a colossal waste of time. I waited until 12:30, and my fingers shook when I punched in the phone number. It rang five times before a breathless woman answered.

"Hello."

"Mrs. Ramsey?"

"Yes."

"Hi. I'm Paige Nichols. I'm the one who contacted you about Cara Morton." There was no reply. Just heavy breathing on the line. "Mrs. Ramsey?"

"Sorry. Had to catch my breath. I didn't want to answer the phone in the kitchen so ran down into the basement."

"Is this a bad time? I can call back."

"Not at all, and I'd rather get this conversation over with. I'm sure you're probably a nice person, but any friend of that woman's is—"

"Mrs. Ramsey," I said, cutting her off. "Cara Morton is no friend of mine. And I wouldn't have bothered you if she wasn't trying to destroy my family. I'm desperate. I would appreciate any information you could give me about her."

"What happened?"

The floodgates opened, and I told her everything from the beginning, starting with Aaron getting the department chair position and ending with the sexual harassment complaint.

"Jesus," she whispered. "You could be me."

I continued, sensing she was ready to share. "I saw a picture taken at a gym of your husband with Cara on her Facebook page and kind of put two and two together."

"That would be his excuse to get out of the house. I think working out was foreplay for them. By the time I found out, it had been going on for months. When I confronted him, he packed his bags and left me for her."

"But you reconciled?"

"We did a few months later."

Our stories were eerily similar. "Was it because of her drug use?"

"No, her drug use just made him cling to her harder because he thought he could save her. She'd stop using long enough to convince him she was clean and sober, but it was all a lie. She never really quit. She just found better ways to hide it."

"Then what?"

"He found out she'd stolen from the school. She got ahold of his info for the school's bank account, then got an extra debit card. She slowly drained it of nearly $150,000, most of which went up her nose."

I had hit the jackpot. "Oh my God."

"And when he confronted her about it, she ended it and kicked him out of her house."

"Was she charged with theft?"

"No."

"Why the hell not?"

"Because she was smart. She wasn't the one who was taking the money out of the account. She had an accomplice."

"Do you know who it was?"

Joan Ramsey let out a bitter laugh. "You know, you're lucky, Mrs. Nichols. Cara is just coming for your husband. If she had just come after me and Paul, we could have handled it. But she went after our oldest son, Casey, and there was nothing we could do about it because at eighteen, he was legally an adult. If my husband was no match for that piranha, my son was even more susceptible. Cara knew my husband was losing interest and wanted to come back home, and she had a backup plan. Casey was already struggling with addiction when she got ahold of him. He was so in love with her he got money from that account whenever they wanted to score coke. He was the one on the camera from the bank's ATM. Not her."

"And there was nothing anyone could do to hold her accountable?"

"Paul set up a surprise mandatory drug test for all school employees. She knew she'd failed it and resigned in a hurry before she could be fired."

I made a careful mental note. A mandatory drug test. Why hadn't I thought of it before? "And what about your son?"

"Before she left, she made an anonymous call to the police about the money, and they arrested Casey, but he refused to admit that she gave him the card even after the police played the recording of the call she'd made turning him in. It was like she had a spell on him."

"Yeah, I understand that feeling," I said, more to myself than to her. "Then what happened?"

"We paid back that money from our personal account. Our biggest mistake was bonding Casey out and getting him into rehab. We should have left him in jail to get clean because he was barely in rehab a week when he ran away. I haven't seen my son in months. He's a fugitive and there's a warrant out for his arrest. And I blame my husband, Paul. He let that snake into our lives and now our son's life is ruined." Muffled sobs came from the other end of the line, and my heart broke for this woman, which made me even more determined to get Cara Morton out of our lives forever.

"I am so sorry, Mrs. Ramsey." I heard her sob on the other line and gave her time to regain her composure. It was almost a minute before she had calmed down enough to speak again.

"I'm not sure what information you're looking for or how I can help you. And I'm sorry for what you're going through, but please don't contact me again." She hung up before I could assure her I wouldn't.

She was wrong, though. She had helped me by giving me an idea.

"You did what?" Aaron stared at me incredulously as I told him about my phone call with Joan Ramsey.

But I couldn't figure out exactly what was causing his reaction. Was it because I'd found out the real reason he'd come home? Or was it because he hadn't been Cara's first rodeo? He had to know now that he had been nothing special to her. She was just looking for another victim, and he was merely low hanging fruit.

"Didn't you hear what I just said? Please don't make me explain this all over again."

"I heard you," he snapped.

"And?"

"And, what?"

I sighed. "Can you set up a surprise drug test at the university for the people in your department?"

"I probably could. But I'd have to have a damned good reason."

"I'd say getting that bitch out of our lives is a damn good reason, wouldn't you?"

"I still can't believe you called that poor woman out of the blue and asked her if her husband had an affair with Cara."

"Is that what's really bothering you? Or is it the fact that there was nothing special about your relationship with Cara? You were essentially just a means to an end. She never cared about you because she's not capable of caring about anybody. I'm guessing she used your affair to advance in the English Department. Am I right?"

I could tell I'd wounded him. "Why is it so hard for you to believe that another woman could've found me attractive?" he snapped.

"Oh, no, you don't!" I practically shouted at him. "Answer my question. Did she use you to advance at Roberson?"

"Maybe." He was trying not to look at me.

"Definitely. I read her statement against you. You named Cara the head of the Student Literary Review. That used to be your gig? I know you wouldn't have been able to continue that role after your appointment as chair. But I would've thought it would've gone to someone who'd been at the university a lot longer than a few months."

Aaron stared at me without speaking, and I knew I was right.

"Let me guess. You two were friends until you got named department chair, and that's when she really turned on the charm and things heated up because she knew being close to you could be good for her career. And for the record, this doesn't have a damned thing to do with me not thinking another woman would find you attractive. So don't try that shit on me again. I'm trying to figure out a way out of the mess you created, and I would like some cooperation, please."

Twisting the knife should've made me feel a lot better than it did. But the misery and regret coming off my husband in waves made me feel childish and small for throwing it up in his face that someone he'd cared about had been using him.

"I'm sorry." He looked away from me.

"And stop apologizing. Being sorry won't get us out of this mess. So, I'm asking you again. Can you order a surprise drug test for your department?"

"And, again, I'd have to have a damn good reason."

"Okay. Maybe not for the whole department. But is there a way you can order her to have a drug test?"

"Let's backtrack a minute. I would have to check the faculty handbook to see if failing a drug test would even be grounds for dismissal. They could just make rehab a stipulation for her to keep her job. And getting her fired may not even make her stop."

I sighed in frustration not wanting to admit he was right. Getting her fired might even make things worse. But we had to do something.

"Hey," Aaron said softly, sensing my frustration. "I'm not saying that it's not a good idea. But I feel like we need something more or something stronger."

"Joan Ramsey said that Cara got into the school's bank account and stole $150,000. Is she in charge of any programs with a budget that she could steal from? Because she obviously hasn't stopped snorting coke, and she has to pay for that somehow."

Aaron's jaw tightened and once again he wouldn't look at me. I knew I was right. She'd stolen money from the Literary Review's budget. I put my hand on his chin and gently turned his face toward mine.

"How much?"

"Ten thousand."

"Ten thousand?" I didn't mean to shout, and Aaron flinched.

"Not only that, but she tried to..." Aaron stopped talking abruptly and just stared off into space.

"Aaron?"

"What did you say Joan Ramsey's son's name was?"

"Casey. Casey Ramsey. Why?"

"You have a picture of him?"

I pulled up a picture of Parkdale Prep's website on my phone, found Paul Ramsey's bio with the picture of him with his family, and handed it to Aaron. He looked at it. At first, he grimaced, then a smile spread across his face.

"We got her, babe. I know this kid."

TWENTY-TWO

AARON NICHOLS

AFTER

December 11, 2023

It was the third time I'd had this nightmare in less than two weeks. I was in a darkened room, and I wasn't alone. There was a woman with me, but I couldn't see her face. I was in a panic because I couldn't make her stop crying. And I needed to because she was tearing me apart. Finally, in desperation, fear, and anger, I held my hands over her face until she'd stopped breathing. Then I woke up, covered in sweat and panting.

TWENTY-THREE

AARON NICHOLS

AFTER

December 12, 2023

After Cara's disappearance, I tried to avoid anybody I knew from the university. But it was getting harder. Oakmont was a dot on the map in a college town, and I couldn't swing a stick without hitting someone associated with Roberson, either an employee, student, or alum. Most days, I didn't even leave the house. I knew what they were all thinking. That I had done something to Cara because of the sexual harassment complaint. That I had gotten rid of her so she wouldn't testify against me and I could keep my job. But I may as well have lost my job. Even though I was still on paid leave and the final decision had yet to be made, I was done at Roberson University. The college president had lost faith in me, the faculty and staff no longer trusted me, students feared me, and everyone was gossiping about me.

Cara had told anyone who'd listen that she only got

involved with me because I was harassing her, and she was scared of me. She was very convincing. I'm sure she launched into one of her fake crying fits as she was doing the rounds. It didn't help that my own administrative assistant, Lynette, had backed her up, saying she'd overheard a slap and saw Cara run from my office bleeding. Despite the temptation not to, I was keeping my mouth shut. I couldn't wait to tell my side of the story at the hearing, bringing up her drug use and how she had abetted a known fugitive, Casey Ramsey, who I was certain was behind her disappearance. But there was a big problem with that plan, as Paige and I discovered from Detective Alonso who sat on our couch and delivered the news.

"He's in custody?" asked Paige excitedly. "Has he admitted to what he did to Cara?"

But I could tell by Alonso's impassive face that what she had told us was not good news.

"He was detained two weeks ago by immigration trying to cross the border into Canada with a fake passport. The name on his fake passport was not Devon Lloyd."

"What are you saying?" I asked.

"I'm saying the kid you saw with Cara Morton was not Casey Ramsey. Ramsey had been hiding out in the woods in upstate New York and living off the grid for months. As far as we can tell, he was never in this town."

"Meaning he was in custody when Cara disappeared on the second and couldn't have had anything to do with her disappearance." I felt my wife deflate next to me.

I had been so sure the picture of Casey Ramsey that Paige had shown me on Parkland's website was the kid I'd seen with Cara. They had the same height, build, coloring, and changes brought on by his drug use could explain any differences. I hadn't seen the kid in question since I saw him with Cara in that empty parking lot. He was wearing a hoody and didn't stick around long. If the kid I saw wasn't Casey Ramsey, then who the hell was he? I needed to find out soon. As he was no longer a viable suspect, that left me and me alone on the hook for Cara's disappearance.

A loud crash sounded from upstairs, and Paige quickly got up to check on the kids. I was alone with Detective Alonso. I started to speak but stopped. Something was holding me back from giving her information she needed to know. I would tell her about Cara being a Cam girl. But first I needed to consult with the only person at Roberson who was still speaking to me. After I walked the detective to her car and watched her leave, I hopped in my car.

"Aaron? Is something wrong? What are you doing here so late?" Dr. Helen Watford-Raines' disembodied voice spoke to me through her doorbell camera.

"I'm sorry to come by so late, Helen. But I really need to talk to you."

Seconds later, the door opened and Helen, wearing a purple velour floor-length robe zipped up to her chin, stood aside and let me enter her house. Helen lived in a two-story Tudor in the historic district of Oakmont. Her house was always clean but cluttered, filled with antiques, piles of books and cats. Hardly anyone knew Dr. Watford-Raines was a breath away from being a hoarder. The fact I couldn't see any one of the six cats I knew she had was testament to the sheer amount of clutter in her house.

"Come into the kitchen while I make some tea and tell me what you've dragged me away from my book about."

I had to move two large piles of books just to sit at the kitchen table while she put a kettle on to boil and rummaged around her cabinets for some mugs.

"Cara was a webcam girl. I think she was doing it to support a nasty cocaine habit."

She instantly stopped rummaging and turned to face me. "How do you know this?"

"Someone sent me one of her videos, and I was able to track it to a webcam site. She goes by the name D Love and has a large fanbase from what I can tell. But it doesn't look like she's posted on the site since May."

"Who did you say sent you this video?" Helen was looking at me skeptically.

"No clue. At first, I thought Cara had sent it to me." I looked away sheepishly. "It was when we were still involved."

"But now you don't think so? Who else could have sent it to you?"

"Helen, I wish I knew. I had no idea about this side of her life. But clearly if she didn't send it then someone who wanted me to know about her secret life did."

"Have you told the police about this?"

"Not yet."

"Good. Because if the media gets ahold of this, you know what will happen."

"People will stop looking for her."

"Cara's already at a disadvantage as a missing black woman. She's been missing for ten days, and it still hasn't made national news. When this gets out, people will blame her and say she had it coming."

"I know."

"I took part in the search of the woods around her house organized by the college. Quite a few people came out to help. But it was slow going with all the ice and snow on the ground. And I understand, considering what happened between the two of you and the damage she's done to your career and reputation, why you didn't show up to help, but it would have looked better if you had." She sat a steaming mug of tea in front of me.

"I wanted to. But Paige has been so freaked out over this, I was afraid she'd have a meltdown."

"You underestimate your wife, Aaron. I'm betting she would have been happy to help search for no other reason than to prove your innocence."

"Does everyone think I'm responsible?"

"No. You have some very loyal supporters amongst the faculty, staff, and students. But some people were wondering if you didn't show up because you knew where she was."

"Have you heard anything, Helen? Anything at all about Cara that could help me out?" I asked, quickly changing the subject. I was already well aware of how guilty I looked.

She considered my question for a few seconds before replying. "I did hear that the Monday after she was reported missing, Dr. Peters went charging into the Dean's office demanding Cara's office like he knew she wasn't coming back."

"What?" I said, completely taken aback, remembering the way Cara had been flirting with him at the Fall Fling. "Why? He has his own office."

"Yes, but hers is bigger and she was working in there alone because her office mates were teaching remotely this year."

"Do the police know about this?"

"I'm not sure, Aaron." She gave me a sympathetic look that managed to make me feel both comforted and embarrassed. "I heard this third-hand from someone else, and I have no idea how valid it is."

It was true that the Roberson gossip mill was like the telephone game. By the time a story made the rounds, what came out the other end bore little resemblance to the original story. But I was desperate. We were silent for a while as we drank our herbal tea. It tasted horrible, like wet leaves, but I would not offend Helen by not drinking it after I'd disturbed her evening.

"Well?" she asked me, not looking up from her cup.

"Well, what?"

"Do you know where she is?" She looked me in the eye,

pinning me with her gaze, like she was peering directly into my soul. I sighed and set my cup down harder than I meant to.

"No. I don't know where she is."

"I know," she said, smiling, and gently set down her own steaming cup. "I just needed to hear you say it."

"I also wanted to thank you, Helen."

"For what?" She seemed genuinely surprised.

"For believing I had nothing to do with Cara's disappearance. I know I'm an asshole for cheating on Paige and I brought this all on myself, but just because I cheated doesn't mean I'm capable of what people are thinking."

Helen gave me an unreadable look and shook her head before getting up from the table. She paced in front of the stove and kept glancing over at me like she was trying to decide something.

"What's wrong?"

"I've been feeling pretty guilty about something, Aaron. I'm wondering if it would have made a difference to what happened between you and Cara if you'd known about it."

"Depends on what it is." By the look on her face, it couldn't be anything good. I wasn't sure I wanted to hear more bad things about a woman I'd so recently cared about. She sat back down at the table before responding.

"I briefly dated Cara's father, Gerald."

This was the last thing I'd been expecting her to say. "Seriously? When?"

"It was maybe sixteen years ago, a few years after my husband John died and I decided it was time I rejoined the land of the living. A friend of mine from church introduced me to a very handsome and very charming man named Gerald Morton."

I remembered Cara telling me her father used to be a handsome man with no lack of female attention, but he'd never gotten over her mother. I'd assumed that's what Helen was going to tell me too. But I was wrong.

"And?" I prompted as she stared off into space.

"And we dated for a few months. He was the perfect gentleman and a hell of a lot of fun. Not a flashy man. Very humble and sweet. Hard-working and kind."

"So, what went wrong?"

"It wasn't just one thing. It was a culmination of things. First, it was his finances."

"You mean he was broke?"

Helen merely nodded. "I could never understand where all his money was going. He had his regular job at Century City but also worked nights and weekends cleaning office buildings. His house was paid for, and he was so proud of Cara for getting a full ride scholarship to Oberlin. He wasn't a flashy dresser, and he drove a ten-year-old car. He would never allow me to pay for our dates or go Dutch. But I knew he was in a lot of debt because I'd seen stacks of credit card bills at his house."

"Well, if he wasn't asking you for money, what was the problem?"

"Like I said, it wasn't just that," she snapped, and I could tell I'd irritated her.

"Then what?"

"Underneath all that charm, there was such sadness in him. I'd ask him what was wrong, and he'd blow me off. Then one night we'd had a little too much to drink, and he told me the reason his marriage ended."

"Cara told me her mother ran off with another man."

"That, and she was abusing Cara."

"What? Are you serious?" No wonder Cara hadn't wanted to talk about her mother.

"He caught her in the act when Cara was five. He never told me exactly what he caught her doing to Cara, but he kicked his wife out of the house, and that's the reason she left town with another man."

"Do you think being a victim of child abuse was why she was abusing drugs and everything else she was doing?"

"Yes, I absolutely do. Gerald blamed himself for not being able to protect his daughter from the one person he should have been able to trust. He had a hard time wrapping his head around the fact that his wife would hurt Cara."

"That had to be a hard pill to swallow." I wasn't sure what I'd do to anyone who hurt one of my kids. The thought of it made me crazy.

"I could be wrong, but if I had to guess, I think he was broke because he'd paid for Cara's counseling and rehab. I saw a statement from a treatment facility amongst the credit card bills. Had I realized how deep you had gotten with her, I'd have warned you. I heard the gossip going around campus about the two of you and didn't want to believe it. When I realized it was true, I buried my head in the sand and told myself it was none of my business. But you had a right to know who you were dealing with."

"How did things end between you and her father?"

"Badly. I'd fallen hard for Gerald. He made me feel alive for the first time since John died. I wanted to help him out. So, I offered to loan him some money to help him out of his financial mess."

I let out a low whistle.

"I know. I know. Not my brightest move. I truly wanted to help him. He was embarrassed and offended, and accused me of violating his privacy. But I'd done no such thing. Credit card bills were piled high on his kitchen counter for everyone who walked into that house to see. It didn't take a genius to figure out he had no money when he was working two jobs and none of our dates cost much more than twenty bucks. The accusation hurt me, and nothing was the same between us after that, and a few weeks later, it was over."

"Did you ever meet Cara while you dated her dad?"

"Not once. She was a junior at Oberlin, and I was supposed to meet her when she came home for Thanksgiving. But we'd broken up by then."

The sadness that filled Helen's eyes told me she was still carrying a torch for Gerald Morton. I reached across the table, grabbed her hand and gave it a squeeze. "If it makes you feel any better, my head was so far up my ass where Cara Morton was concerned, I doubt anything anyone told me about her would have made a difference."

"The heart wants what it wants," mused Helen.

"In my case, it was more like the ego wanted whatever would feed and validate it."

"Do you think I should tell the police what I've just told you?"

"They already know about her drug use, but I guess it couldn't hurt. They need all the help they can get."

I forced myself to finish the tea, and Helen walked me to the front door. A loud sound, like something falling, sounded from above us and I instantly peered up her staircase. Someone carrying a large box came rushing down the steps.

"Is everything okay? What was that noise?" Helen asked the person. It was Beth. She had a habit of turning up when I least expected.

"Sorry, Dr. Watford-Raines. I knocked over a stack of books in the hallway. Hey, Dr. Nichols," she added with a smile when she spotted me.

"Beth is staying with me for a while," Helen said when she saw the confusion on my face.

"I'm the new temporary housekeeper. My roommate at school is a psycho, and there's not another room available until spring semester. I had no place to go."

"And I'm in desperate need of help around here. Things just piled up when John was sick and by the time he died—" Helen threw up her hands in defeat.

Maintaining this big house all by herself must have been overwhelming, and I felt bad I hadn't thought to offer her help. I figured she liked the house the way it was and wouldn't have appreciated my offer.

"Nice seeing you, Dr. Nichols." The young woman flashed me a shy smile and disappeared into the kitchen.

I opened my mouth to speak, but Helen cut me off.

"Before you ask, I got this approved by student services. I'm also paying her on top of providing room and board."

"I wasn't going to ask you anything."

"Then what?"

"I was going to thank you for helping Beth. She's a good kid. In fact," I said, lowering my voice and glancing toward the kitchen door. "She's very intuitive. She tried to warn me about Cara back in the fall, and I didn't want to believe it."

"It's usually the quiet ones who see all the things everyone else misses," she mused with a faraway look in her eyes that made me wonder if we were still talking about Beth.

"Well, thanks for the tea and advice."

"Are you going to tell the police about Cara's secret life?"

"I think I need to. Someone from her other life might have done something to her."

"Agreed. I just hope they look just as hard for her after they find out who she really was. Oh, and before I forget," she said, opening a drawer in a table in the foyer and retrieving a pair of black leather gloves. "Paige and I met for lunch last month and she forgot her gloves at the restaurant. I keep forgetting to call and let her know." She handed me the gloves.

"Thanks." I took the gloves, wondering why my wife never mentioned she'd had lunch with Helen. I hadn't realized they were more than casual acquaintances.

We said our goodbyes, and I headed back home after getting some milk from the store. I didn't tell Paige where I'd really been because I valued Helen's opinion and wasn't sure my wife would appreciate me seeking another woman's advice when we were trying to rebuild our marriage. Paige gave me a blank look when I walked in with the milk. My wife's not stupid and knew I'd been somewhere else but didn't ask. We didn't speak for the rest of the evening and, for once, I was relieved.

TWENTY-FOUR

PAIGE NICHOLS

AFTER

December 13, 2023

Aaron is still lying to me.

He left the house right after Detective Alonso last night and came home forty-five minutes later with a gallon of milk. I'm not a fool. I usually have to ask him three times to pick up milk, and we usually run out long before he finally does it. On this occasion, we still had half a gallon of milk when he came home with more. Where had he gone? Did he follow Detective Alonso back to the station to tell her something he didn't want me knowing about? When was he going to realize it all got back to me in the end, anyway?

I won't lie. I'm afraid. Afraid of what he's hiding from me and what it means. I was also afraid for myself too because Aaron wasn't the only one keeping secrets. I had plenty of my own and with the scrutiny of the investigation, it was only a matter of time before they came out. I needed to talk to Detective Alonso myself, but before I did that, I needed to talk to my husband. With him still lying to me, however, I'm not sure I can trust him. Not nearly as sure as I was when I did something incredibly stupid. I just remember thinking that I didn't have a choice. But there's always a choice.

It had been bothering me. Why hadn't he wanted to join the search for Cara? I was more than happy to help search for her despite the looks and whispering I knew I'd have to deal with as the wife of a cheater whose side piece had disappeared. I could hear it now. *How can she stay with him? Isn't she afraid she'll disappear too? I bet they were in on it together.* I'd have even understood if Aaron had joined the search and asked me not to come. But I knew that, at least for a time, he had cared about Cara, possibly even loved her, or thought he did. Was he worried about her but didn't want to hurt me by admitting it?

When I asked him if he was going, he never answered. Instead, he spent the day cleaning out the garage and his car. He'd even done a load of laundry but forgot to take it out of the dryer. I found it still in there the next day. It was just a bunch of old dishtowels. But one caught my eye. It was rust colored. When had I bought dishtowels this color? Then I realized with a start the dishtowel wasn't rust-colored. It was heavily stained, mostly in the middle section, with the edges still showing traces of the original white. Was this blood? Because if it was, there had been a lot of it. I stared at the towel for a long time, bile rising in the back of my throat.

"Mom, can I have some ice cream? Daddy said to ask you." Bailey stood in the door to the garage, staring at me. "Mom?"

"Yeah, sweetie. I'll be right there." I'd tossed the stained dishtowel into the dumpster in the garage. After I took the kids to school the next morning, I dug it out and put it in a drawer in the kitchen.

TWENTY-FIVE

PAIGE NICHOLS

BEFORE

November 14, 2023

"And when can you start, Paige?"

"Right away. The sooner the better." I was sitting in the office of Ellen Mason, head of HR at Quality Nursing Solutions, a nursing temp agency.

I decided it was best to put my web design certificate on hold after the college suspended Aaron pending the investigation of Cara's sexual harassment claim. He was on paid leave, but who knew if he'd have a job to go back to after all this was over? We had some money saved and there was the twins' college fund, which I refused to touch. I needed to earn money now to offset the inevitable. Aaron hadn't said a word when I told him I was going back to nursing. He just looked sad and left the room. What could he say? This was all his fault.

And if I were honest, another reason I was going back to work was to have my own money in case my marriage didn't work out ultimately. Things with Aaron were still shaky and full of highs and lows. I wanted to forgive him and move on with our lives, but every time Cara pulled one of her stunts, it set us back even further.

"I'm sure we'll have something for you soon. In fact, what's the rest of your day looking like?"

"I'm free all day." And it was true. With Aaron not working, he could take care of the kids.

"Great. Then I'll probably be in touch with you with your first assignment at some point today."

"Thank you, Ms. Mason. I really appreciate this."

"I'm the one that should thank you. We are so short-staffed right now we need all the help we can get. If you know any other nurses who are looking for work, please send them our way."

True to her word, Ms. Mason called me with an assignment two hours later to work an evening shift at a nearby nursing home. Working at nursing homes was not my favorite thing, but the hourly rate with the nighttime differential was great, and the evening shift meant I wouldn't have to do much except administer meds and monitor the nurse's station.

When I arrived for my four to midnight shift, I discovered I was one of two nurses working that evening. The other nurse was also from Quality Nursing Solutions.

"Are there any nurses on staff here?" I asked Amy, the other nurse, an older white woman with short gray hair and glasses.

"All the nurses' aides are, but the nursing staff are temps. That way they don't have to pay benefits. It's how they keep costs down. Plus, they can't keep anybody for longer than a few months."

I didn't have to ask why. Nursing homes were notorious for high turnover. I took a dinner break around seven and walked around the grounds to wake myself up, as it has been a very uneventful shift so far. I was heading back inside, when I ran into someone I never expected to see. It was Aaron's administrative assistant, Lynette. We were both shocked to see each other and stared in silence for several long seconds, neither of us knowing what to do. It was me who finally broke the silence.

"Hello, Lynette. How have you been?" The older woman didn't quite know what to say to me. After all, Lynette's statement had helped to get Aaron suspended. She was a witness to Aaron's alleged assault on Cara in his office. She had only seen the aftermath, according to Aaron. And although I knew my husband was a liar and a cheat, I knew beyond any doubt that he had not physically assaulted Cara. But the board had based their decision on Lynette's testimony. It wasn't her fault; she had only relayed what she had witnessed. But I couldn't help but wonder what she had actually seen that day.

Lynette shifted uncomfortably. "I come here a couple of days a week to read to some residents."

"You don't owe me any explanations, Lynette."

"I know... I just..." She stared at me, her face flushing slightly. But whether it was with embarrassment or guilt, I couldn't tell.

"It's okay. No hard feelings. I know you did what you had to do. You had to report everything you saw that day. But can I ask you a question?"

"Sure," replied Lynette uncertainly.

"What exactly did you see that day?"

"It was all in my statement. I know Dr. Nichols should've gotten a copy of that. Did you read it?"

"I did. But I'd like to hear from you what you saw because what you're claiming you witnessed does not describe the man I've been married to for more than a decade." I didn't mean to put her on the spot, but my need to know the truth far outweighed any discomfort I might put her through.

She stared at me. "What do you want to know?"

"Just start at the beginning." I guided her over to a nearby stone bench just outside the nursing home's entrance. Lynette let out a sigh before turning to me.

"Dr. Morton showed up saying that she had an appointment with Dr. Nichols, and she was going to wait in his office. She just breezed right past me. I followed her and told her it would probably be best if she waited out in my office because I wasn't exactly sure when Dr. Nichols would be out of his budget meeting with President Marshall. But she said she was fine waiting in his office and shut the door in my face."

"How long was she alone in his office?"

"I'm not sure, maybe ten minutes, fifteen at the most. And then Dr. Nichols showed up, and I told him she was waiting for him in his office."

"And what was his reaction?"

"He didn't seem pleased, which was odd because I thought he and Dr. Morton were..." She flushed slightly as her voice trailed off.

"Close?" I finished for her. Lynette merely nodded. "And then what happened?"

"He entered and closed his office door. A few minutes later, I heard raised voices. They were arguing about something, but I could only make out a few words. Nothing that made any sense to me at first. Then their voices got louder. I heard Dr. Nichols tell Dr. Morton that she needed help."

"And what was her response to that?"

"She wasn't happy," said Lynette, looking away from me. "I won't repeat what she said, but it wasn't nice."

"Then what happened?"

"I heard a slap. And her screaming at Dr. Nichols to never touch her again."

"And that's when you ran into the office to see what was going on?"

"Yes. I didn't really know what to do until then, but after hearing the tail end of that argument, I decided I needed to go see what was going on. I went into the office and almost ran into Dr. Morton as she was running out."

"And she was upset?"

"She was bleeding, Mrs. Nichols."

"Your statement said that her nose was bleeding. And that she was very upset. So, I'm assuming you thought my husband struck her?"

"She was the only one bleeding. But now that I've had time to think about it, I realize that may not have been the case."

"Why is that?"

"Because a month prior to that, I ran into Dr. Morton in the restroom down the hall from the office and she had a tissue pressed to her nose. I could see that her nose was bleeding and asked if she needed any help. She just laughed and said her allergy medication made her nose dry and she got nosebleeds occasionally."

"I didn't see that in your statement. Why not?" Lynette's face reddened. I got the impression she hadn't meant to tell me that part. The question was, why not? And then she shocked me by bursting into tears.

"I am so sorry, Mrs. Nichols. I feel like this is all my fault." She buried her face in her hands and sobbed. I should have comforted her, but I was too stunned by what she'd just told me. As she continued crying, I put a comforting hand on her shoulder and asked her why she felt that way, when my phone rang. It was my brother.

"Excuse me, Lynette. I need to take this." I took a few steps from the bench we'd been sitting on and answered my phone, glancing back at Lynette to see her blowing her nose into a tissue. Before I could even say hello to my brother, he started talking. Telling me something that I certainly hadn't heard from my husband.

"He didn't tell you, did he?"

"No, he didn't. And you're sure he still has the video?"

"That's what he said. Look, I'm not trying to get in the middle of your mess, sis. And I'm not usually a snitch. But I just felt like you should know. I'm glad I called because I had a feeling he didn't tell you he'd called me."

I'm not sure why my husband didn't think my brother would tell me about their conversation. But I also knew that he was probably afraid, given their conversation. When Aaron told me that someone had stolen his phone and deleted all Cara's texts and photos, I'd naturally assumed he meant the video too. Why hadn't it been deleted? I hung up with my brother. But when I turned back to Lynette, she was gone.

After what happened at Nova, following Cara again had been a stupid thing to do.

Aaron told me that Bill, his lawyer, had told him to stay away from Cara, so she couldn't claim he was trying to intimidate her into dropping her allegations. But at the time I figured that didn't apply to me. I had rationalized I was doing it to protect my family, and it was mostly true. I also figured if I started following Cara around, maybe I'd have a chance at finding out something that would get her to leave us alone and withdraw her claim for sexual harassment. But truth be told, I was becoming obsessed with the woman my husband cheated with.

I'd just walked out of the grocery store when I spotted Cara heading into the hair salon across the road. Instead of going straight home after loading my groceries into the car, I sat in the car and waited. It took an hour and a half, but eventually she came out and got into her car. I followed her. I lost track of her two blocks later when I stopped at a traffic light and should have taken it as a sign to go home. It didn't take me long to realize that if I knew where she was at all times, eventually I'd catch her with her drug dealer. At least that's what I told myself. Our marriage counselor would've told me I was playing with fire, so I didn't dare admit my new obsession during our therapy sessions because Aaron would've gone ballistic. And rightfully so. I *was* playing with fire.

I managed to follow her for a week before she caught me. It was a few days before Thanksgiving. And I still don't know how she'd figured out what I was doing. I was being so careful. But one day it finally blew up in my face. I followed her to a coffee shop. I watched her go inside and then parked half a block away, waiting for her to emerge. She must've come out while I wasn't looking because she caught me completely off guard when she yanked my passenger side car door open and slid into the seat.

"You are so pathetic!" she spat at me. "Why are you following me?"

It was the first time I'd been in close proximity to her since following her to Nova. In the daylight, I could see she kind of looked like me, at least like the woman I used to be before I got married and had kids. Is that why Aaron was so drawn to Cara? Was he missing the old me? Old me used to drive a little red Miata and my hair, nails and wardrobe were always on point. Old me was always up for an adventure or a spontaneous trip away for the weekend and was down for sex whenever and wherever. Old me was free of commitments and could come and go as I pleased. My husband couldn't possibly have missed the old me more than I missed her. Didn't he realize that?

"What are you talking about?" I shouted back. "Get out of my car!"

"I'm filing a police report! You're just as crazy as your fucking husband! You're both stalkers."

"What the hell are you talking about?"

"You heard what I said. Aaron won't leave me alone! All the calls and texts and flowers and gifts he keeps sending me when he was the one who ended it! And now you're following me? I'm calling the police!"

"You're a liar! A liar and a coked-up whore! Get out of my car!" I screamed as rage caused blood to pound in my ears.

Instead of getting out of my car, Cara smiled at me. The bitch smiled at me. She was enjoying seeing me so out of control. She pulled out her phone, tapped the screen, and showed me a picture of a bouquet of pink roses in a glass vase. The message on the card attached to the yellow ribbon encircling the vase read:

I miss you A.

It felt like she'd struck me in the face. Were those roses from Aaron? Was he still lying to me? Whatever the truth was I couldn't let her think I believed a word she'd just said.

"You're a sad, lying bitch. I feel sorry for you."

"And you're a fucking hypocrite."

"What are you talking about?" But I knew exactly what she was talking about.

"I'm not the only one in this car who's fucked someone else's husband, am I, Paige? Dr. Drew and I had a drink after the mixer last month, and she told me all about you. About how you screwed her husband. You're no innocent victim, are you? You're no better than me."

"Get out of my car!"

"Why are you mad at me, Paige?" Her voice was soft, and her eyes were full of pity. "I don't owe you shit. I'm not the one married to you. I didn't make vows to you. It's not my fault you're a shitty wife who can't keep her husband satisfied. And don't blame me because karma caught up with you."

"Karma, huh? If that's the case, you've got plenty coming your way because you've done more than just screw other women's husbands. Where is Casey Ramsey? What have you done to that poor kid? Haven't you ruined his life enough?"

The smile on her face slipped just a little. And her eyes narrowed slightly. "You're the one who told the police that bullshit and had them coming to my house and the campus looking for some screwed-up kid I haven't seen since I moved here. And here I thought it was his sorry mama who'd told them I was hiding him. This is just more proof that you've been stalking me. I'll put that in the police report too."

"I don't care what you do. Just get the fuck out of my car and leave my family alone."

"I don't know what the hell you're talking about."

"Canceling my kids' birthday party. Putting mushroom flakes on all the pizzas. Aaron could have died! Don't you dare try to deny it. I know it was you."

I didn't wait for her to respond before I shoved her with all my might. I just wanted her out of my car. I didn't mean for her head to slam against the passenger side window so hard that she was stunned momentarily. She quickly came back to her senses, and her hand flew toward me. I raised my arm to shield myself. Her nails raked down my forearm, leaving a long, angry scratch.

"I don't know what you're talking about. I don't give a fuck about you, Aaron, or your damned kids. All I care about is making sure you go to jail for stalking me."

I was too busy staring at the blood oozing from the scratch on my arm to look at her. The next thing I heard was my car door opening and slamming shut seconds later. I watched Cara walk quickly down the street to her own car, jump in, and pull out of the curb so fast she almost hit another car. Then I sat there breathing heavily and shaking until, inevitably, the tears came. I rested my forehead and hands against my steering wheel until my breathing returned to normal, and I could drive home.

Later that evening, Bailey and I sat at the kitchen island

making beaded keychains for her teachers at school. As I listened to my daughter babble excitedly about the new story she was writing, I kept stealing looks at the front door.

"Mom, are you even listening to me?" complained my daughter.

"I'm sorry, Bailey. What did you say?"

"Should I put heart or flower stickers on the keychains?"

"Flower," I said absently. I was jumpy and on edge waiting for the police to show up and arrest me for assault or stalking or whatever the hell kind of story Cara was going to spin to them. And the saddest thing was that I wasn't as worried about going to jail as I was about what Cara had said about Aaron. Was she telling the truth? Did he want her back? Had he sent those flowers?

TWENTY-SIX

AARON NICHOLS

BEFORE

October 14, 2023

There was a soft knock at my door, and I looked up to see Beth standing in the doorway.

"Sorry to bother you, Dr. Nichols," she said, taking a tentative step into the room and looking around. "The lady that usually sits at the desk outside your office isn't there and I knocked, but you didn't hear me."

"Beth, come on in. My door is always open. Lynette must've stepped out for lunch or something."

"You're not busy?"

"I'm always busy, but never too busy to talk to a student. Please, have a seat." I gestured her toward the chair directly in front of my desk. She took her backpack off and sat down.

I knew very little about Beth aside from the fact that she was a freshman and good friends with Jaida, who had taken the younger woman under her wing. Being a freshman, I figured she had to be at least eighteen, but she looked younger. She wore no makeup, and her long light brown hair was pulled into a low ponytail with fringe framing her face.

"There was something you wanted to talk to me about yesterday. Is everything okay?" Beth started chewing on her thumbnail and looked down at her lap. "Is it your classes?" I prompted. "Are you having trouble with a professor?"

"No, I mean, yes. I mean, not me someone else."

"Someone else? You mean a classmate?"

"It's Jaida."

"If this is about the money that went missing—"

"She didn't steal that money," Beth blurted, leaning forward in her chair, her face reddening.

"I never thought she did." I was calm. Beth visibly relaxed and sat back a little in the chair. But she still seemed tense and on edge.

"Well, I'm worried about her. She's under a lot of pressure and that thing with the missing check has just about pushed her to the edge. And that other thing isn't helping either."

"What other thing?"

Beth seemed hesitant again, and I waited until she finally said, "It's Dr. Morton."

"Dr. Morton? What's going on with Dr. Morton?"

"Jaida worships her, Dr. Nichols. She wants to be just like her. But Dr. Morton..." Her voice trailed off, and she looked away from me.

"Dr. Morton what?" I wanted to pull the words out of Beth's mouth, but I needed to control myself and let her tell me whatever she needed to tell me, regardless of who it was about.

"She's not very nice to Jaida."

I frowned. "In what way? Can you give me an example?"

"I was there the morning Jaida was supposed to take that check to the bank. I came in early before my first class because I'd forgotten my English book and overheard them talking in the back room. I grabbed my book and left before they noticed I was there, but I heard most of their conversation."

"What did you hear?"

"Jaida didn't want to take the check. But Dr. Morton made it seem like she was the only one who was doing any work at the Literary Review and the least Jaida could do was help her out by taking it. It's not true! Jaida is practically running the lit review. We hardly see Dr. Morton. And when she comes by, she's moody, always in a hurry and criticizes everything we've done, then makes us do it all over again."

This didn't sound like the Cara I knew, but I wasn't about to say this to Beth and lose her trust.

"Does she treat everyone that way?"

"She doesn't really pay much attention to the rest of us. Just Jaida. She's always picking on her and making little digs at her. Jaida just smiles and acts like it didn't bother her, but I caught her crying in the bathroom. She was so excited about having Dr. Morton running the review. But she's a horrible person, a real narcissist."

"What do you mean?" Of course, I knew what a narcissist was. But I needed Beth to explain exactly why she was accusing Cara of being one.

"Another faculty member stopped by the lit review office when she was there one day and complimented her on all our hard work. Dr. Morton just stood there and smiled, she didn't acknowledge any of us and even talked about what a mess the review had been until she'd taken over. She's a user. And if there's one thing I know, it's users." Beth glanced at the clock on my desk and abruptly stood. "I'm gonna be late for class. I am sorry to bother you with this, Dr. Nichols, but I really needed to let you know what was going on."

"I appreciate you coming to me with your concerns, Beth. I will look into it and see if maybe we can get something resolved with the lit review." Had Cara really said the lit review was a mess until she'd taken over? Damn. That hurt more than it should have.

"Do you know the name of the faculty member who stopped by that day?"

"Some old guy with white hair," she replied with a shrug. "Had on a suit with a bow tie."

Peters. Why wasn't I surprised? But I couldn't deny the truth of what Cara had told me. I had no claim on her time and attention. Still, it stung.

"You won't tell Dr. Morton that I've talked to you, will you? And I don't want Jaida to know I talked to you either. It might make things worse for her. I don't think she realizes how not cool she's being treated."

"Not at all. Our conversation is confidential. Just between us."

"Thanks, Dr. Nichols. I'd better go." She headed out the door, and I watched her go, so lost in thought that I didn't even hear Lynette come in a few minutes later, not until she was standing in front of my desk.

"Dr. Nichols, I saw someone leave your office. Did you have an appointment that I forgot about?"

"It was an unscheduled meeting with a student. Believe it or not, some of them take advantage of my open-door policy."

"A student? Really? I thought it was..." she began, looking confused.

"Who?"

"Never mind. I must have been mistaken."

She went back to her desk leaving me wondering who she thought she'd seen.

I had Lynette cancel my meetings for that afternoon and went home. Was it true? Or did Beth misunderstand what she'd overheard and misinterpreted Cara's working style? Even if that was the case, I couldn't ignore Beth's concerns. The last time I'd spoken to Jaida, she was very stressed out and upset over the missing check. When I told her I could get the check canceled and reissued, she seemed relieved but still tense. It had been a few days since we'd talked so I headed over to the lit review the next morning to see how she was doing. When I got there, it was closed, which was odd. I gave Jaida a call. The phone rang several times before an unfamiliar voice answered.

"Hello?"

"Jaida?"

"No, I'm Jaida's mother. Who's calling, please?"

"Mrs. Reese, this is Dr. Nichols at Roberson. I'm trying to reach Jaida."

"I'm sorry to have to tell you this, Dr. Nichols. Jaida is in the hospital."

"Is she okay? What happened?"

"She tried to commit suicide."

TWENTY-SEVEN

AARON NICHOLS

AFTER

December 16, 2023

I waited until late afternoon on a Friday, when the campus would practically be a ghost town, to pack up my office. The day I was told of my suspension, I'd grabbed the most important things and dumped them in a box and left in a hurry, too embarrassed to linger. I think deep down inside I wanted to think I'd be coming back. But Lynette had called twice to ask me to get the rest of my things, which suggested my future with the college was decided and everyone knew it but me.

Something flashed in Lynette's eyes when she spotted me heading toward her. Was it fear? But then she smiled warmly, and I realized my paranoia had seen something that wasn't there. I was embarrassed and uncomfortable around Lynette. It was her testimony about that horrible day with Cara in my office that had gotten me suspended.

"Dr. Nichols. It's so good to see you. How have you been?"

"Hanging in there."

"I've left some empty boxes on your desk. I can stay if you need me to."

"No. That won't be necessary. I'll lock up when I'm done and leave the keys in your drawer."

"That'd be great." We looked at each other, not knowing what else to say. Damn, this was awkward. "Good night." She walked away, but before I could head into my old office, she stopped me.

"Dr. Nichols."

"Yes."

"I just wanted to say how sorry I am about all this. I went back to the Title IX committee and changed my statement. But I guess it was too late and I feel horrible about it."

"Why would you do that?" I was confused. I'd read Lynette's statement. She'd just recounted everything she'd witnessed that day.

"I thought about what I'd really seen that day. I never saw you strike Dr. Morton. I just assumed you had when I saw the blood on her face."

"It's okay, Lynette..."

"No, it's not. I saw Dr. Morton later that day and I know this is going to sound bad, but she seemed just fine. If what she claimed happened in your office had happened to me, I'd have gone to the police and filed assault charges. She was having lunch in the cafeteria with Dr. Peters, laughing like she didn't have a care in the world. And there wasn't a single mark on her face."

Hearing this a month ago would have filled me with jealousy. But now I just felt like a chump. "Don't worry, Lynette. I don't blame you for any of this. I was an idiot, and now I'm paying for it as I should."

"But at the expense of your career and reputation? Do they have any idea what could have happened to Dr. Morton? I've seen nothing on the news lately."

"All I know is that they're talking to everyone who knew her, and the search is ongoing."

"Well," she said, putting on her gloves. "I'm praying for you and your family."

"I appreciate that." I quickly ducked inside the office before she asked me anything else and made a mental note to tell Bill what Lynette had said about Cara's behavior later the day I'd supposedly hit her.

The office was the same as when I'd left it weeks ago. Looking around the office, I suddenly realized that despite my initial misgivings, I'd loved being department chair. It made me feel accomplished and important in a way I hadn't realized I'd needed. Now it was over because I'd let someone like Cara Morton into my life. But it hadn't been all Cara's fault. People like her could sniff out a person's weaknesses like a bloodhound. When I confided in her about being worried I wouldn't be able to manage being department chair, I handed her the blueprint for my downfall. And when I complained about my marriage, she instantly gave me everything I wasn't getting from Paige. I already felt like a fool, but when Paige told me about Cara and Paul Ramsey, I felt like the stupidest man on earth. How many others had she used? Could you even really say she'd used me when I freely gave her stuff because of how I felt about her?

I heard voices coming from somewhere down the hall and quickly shut the office door. I didn't want to endure any stares or more awkward conversations, so got busy packing up the office. Half an hour later, the only thing left to do was to go through the pile of campus mail in the tray on the corner of my desk. I quickly went through the stack of inter-campus envelopes, which were mostly invoices and forms to be signed that would have to wait for the new department chair, including one for the new communications software that I'd fought so hard for and wouldn't get to implement. I'd really been looking forward to making Dr. Peters take the training as a condition of his continued employment. The rest were catalogs from publishers and office supply stores, Christmas cards from those who hadn't heard of my suspension and other junk. I'd almost reached the bottom of the pile when a notice from campus police caught my eye. It informed me they had trespassed someone from campus and if I saw this person, I was to contact the campus police. I did a double take when I saw her light brown hair. Then I quickly grabbed the boxes I'd packed and left.

When I arrived at Helen's house, she was with a student. But this time it wasn't Beth. Because, as I'd just discovered, Beth had never been a student at Roberson.

"Did you know?" I asked, as I followed Helen into the kitchen, where Jaida was sitting at the table with a mug of hot chocolate. When she spotted me, tears welled up in her eyes, and she swiftly got up and threw her arms around me.

"I'm so sorry about the lit review, Dr. Nichols."

With Cara still missing, me on suspension, and Jaida no longer acting as senior editor, the lit review was on hiatus until spring semester.

"Forget about the lit review." I held her at arm's length to get a good look at her. "I'm more worried about you."

I hadn't seen Jaida since the check debacle, and after her suicide attempt, she'd been lying low and had finished the semester online. She was wearing an oversized black sweater with denim leggings and black Timberland boots. Aside from looking thinner with her long braids pulled into a topknot instead of loose around her shoulders, she didn't look like what she'd recently been through.

"I'm fine." She sat back down at the table and took a big gulp of her hot chocolate, avoiding my eyes. Helen and I exchanged looks. "Really. I'm good," she said when we continued to stare at her. "I shouldn't have let everything build up like that. I just got so overwhelmed."

"How's your therapy going?" Helen asked, as she handed me a mug of hot chocolate that wasn't so hot anymore. Jaida shrugged.

"It's okay. My therapist is cool. They put me on anxiety meds."

The three of us were silent until I remembered the reason I'd come by. "Is Beth still staying here?" I had addressed my question to Helen, but Jaida was the one who responded.

"She bounced a few weeks ago. I've been calling her since I got out of the hospital, and she won't answer. Her phone goes straight to voicemail. I'm really worried about her."

"So am I," added Helen. "She was only here a few days, and I came home from church the Sunday after she'd moved in, and all her things were gone. I haven't seen her since. But I had no idea she wasn't a student until the email from campus police went out."

"She always had a backpack full of books with her and was taking a full load this semester. At least that's what she told me," said Jaida.

"You didn't believe her?" As far as I could tell, Beth and Jaida had been inseparable. What had made her doubt her friend?

"She kinda lied a lot. And there was something just a little off about her. I mean, she was nice, and I liked her a lot, but she never talked about her family or anything."

"She alluded to being estranged from them. Until she moved in here with me, I'm pretty sure she was homeless," said Helen.

"Sometimes, she would sleep in my dorm room because my roommate was always with her man. But then they broke up and she and Beth didn't get along because she found out Beth was using her stuff, so she stopped coming to my dorm room."

"But that doesn't explain why she got trespassed from campus."

Now it was Helen and Jaida's turn to exchange looks. Jaida started to answer when Helen's doorbell rang.

"Must be the plumber. My bathroom sink is leaking." Helen left to answer her door, and I turned back to Jaida, urging her to continue.

"I'm the reason she got trespassed from campus," said Jaida, so softly I almost didn't catch what she said.

"But why?"

"Because she was the one who found me and called 911. We got into a big argument the day before, and I think she stopped by to clear the air. Instead, she found me unconscious. She saved my life, and when I couldn't get ahold of her to thank her, I called a friend of mine who's a student worker in the records office who looked her up for me. All I wanted was a contact number for her. Instead, campus police contacted me, asking me all kinds of questions about her. That's when I found out her name wasn't even Beth Jamison. They said she'd stolen some girl's identity, and the police were looking for her."

I let out a breath. "Do they know her real name?"

Jaida shook her head and took another sip of her hot chocolate before answering. "They wouldn't tell me. Just said to contact them if I see her again."

"Have you checked where she worked?"

"What job? Beth didn't work. She was always broke and borrowing money from me."

"But I saw her working at the campus gym. She helped me find my phone when it went missing last time I was there."

"She applied there, but she said they didn't hire her. Are you sure she wasn't just working out?"

"Only one way to find out." I pulled out my cell phone. I had the gym as one of my contacts since I'd been spending so much time there with Cara. The memory caused a lump in my throat that I quickly swallowed when the call connected. "Hi. I'm looking for a student employee by the name of Beth. Is she working today?"

"You must have the wrong number. No one named Beth works here."

"Are you sure? How long have you worked there?"

"A year. And we have a Brandi but no Beth."

"My mistake. Thank you." I hung up.

The sounds of Helen and the plumber heading upstairs floated down the hall into the kitchen. Jaida suddenly got up from the table.

"I gotta go. My parents are watching me like a hawk, and I told them I'd only be gone for an hour."

I walked her out to her jeep. She opened the driver's side door but stopped before getting in. "Could you do something for me, Dr. Nichols?"

"If I can."

"Please don't call the police if you see Beth. She needs help, not a jail cell."

I couldn't agree with her request. If Beth had stolen someone's identity, she needed more than either of us could give her. "Can I ask you something?"

"I never tried to unalive myself," she said, sounding beyond weary. "I was tired, stressed out, and I had a cold. I accidentally took a second dose of my prescription sleeping pills on top of some cold medicine. It was an accidental drug interaction. I hate that my mom told people I tried to kill myself before she even knew what happened. Now everyone thinks I'm depressed. And they're making me go to therapy."

"I don't think you're depressed. And that wasn't my question." She cocked her head to the side and waited. "Why did you and Beth argue? Did it have anything to do with what happened with Dr. Morton?"

"Huh?" Jaida looked taken aback.

"Beth told me she wasn't very nice to you. You don't have to answer if it's too personal."

"Oh, that," she said, rolling her eyes. "It's okay. And, no, it didn't have anything to do with Dr. Morton. I could never figure out what her problem was with me. But she was my boss at the lit review not my bestie. So, I just kept my head down and did the work."

"And Beth?" I prodded, not sure why I wanted to know.

"It's just I didn't have many people to talk to about this. Except Beth, or whatever her name is, and she basically told me I needed to grow the F up, be thankful, and quit chasing shadows."

"Uh... sorry. You lost me."

"I'm adopted," she blurted out loud. She looked around self-consciously. "I'm adopted, and when I was growing up, I didn't care about who my birth parents were or where I came from."

"But you do now?"

"Yeah, now I want to know. My parents have been supportive of me meeting my birth mother, but only if I reached out to her first to see if she wanted to connect with me and not find out who she is from one of those home DNA tests and then show up at her door."

"And?"

"And I wrote her a letter. Told her all about myself and how I'd love to meet her, then gave it to the adoption agency my parents used, and they forwarded it to her."

I could tell by the way her shoulders slumped how this story ended, and my heart broke for her. Tears filled her eyes, and she quickly wiped them away with the back of her hand and continued.

"I was so excited when I got a letter back a week later. But she didn't want to meet me. She said she was proud of me and happy I'd had a wonderful life and loving parents because that's all she'd ever wanted for me. But she'd made peace with her decision a long time ago and didn't want to meet me."

"And Beth didn't understand why you were so upset."

"Nope. She said I should be happy my birth mother didn't want to meet me because she'd recently met a family member herself. She'd been dying to meet this person her whole life, and it had been nothing but a disaster, and the woman was a horrible person. Said she was a real narcissist and used people. Then she called me selfish and said I was lucky to have parents who loved me because not everyone got to have that."

Jaida was still talking, but I'd stopped listening because the words Beth had used to describe this family member of hers sounded so familiar. She'd used the same words to describe someone else the last time I talked to her, and now I had to wonder if she'd been talking to Jaida about Cara Morton.

TWENTY-EIGHT

PAIGE NICHOLS

AFTER

December 17, 2023

I finally told Aaron about the confrontation between me and Cara. But I didn't tell him I had been following her or about the tussle that resulted in me shoving her and her scratching me. I just didn't see the point of making things worse. Or maybe I was in denial about how bad this could be for me, considering Cara's disappearance. His face went tight and angry, but in an instant, it was gone.

"Should we tell Bill?" I asked tentatively.

"Probably. Just to be on the safe side in case there was a witness who saw what happened and connects it to her disappearance. I just wish you'd told me sooner. Why didn't you?"

"I could ask the same of you."

"Meaning?"

"Tyler called me." That's all I needed to say to deflate Aaron like a balloon. "Why didn't you tell me you still had that video she sent you?"

"Because I'm not sure she sent it to me."

"Why?"

"Think about it. If she stole my phone or had somebody steal it and then wiped all evidence of our correspondence from it, why not delete the video too? And the only thing I can come up with is that she's not the one who sent it to me."

"Who in the world would send you a video like that of her?"

"Someone who wanted me to know about her double life."

"What double life?"

He walked over to his laptop and pulled up a website called Make Me Cam. He logged in and pulled up the profile of a woman named Devon Love. It was Cara. There were hundreds of videos of her as well as an option to have live sessions with her. I could barely wrap my head around what I was seeing.

"Does Detective Alonso know about this?"

"I haven't told her yet."

"Why the hell not, Aaron? She needs to know!"

"Because you know what will happen once the media gets ahold of this. People will stop looking for her. And I'll be under suspicion for the rest of my life. Until they figure out what happened to her, I'm the guy, Paige. They won't look for anyone else when I had the strongest motive to make her disappear."

"But someone from this double life of hers could be behind her disappearance. She may have even disappeared purposefully to get away from an obsessed fan. Alonso needs to know about this, Aaron. Like now. Today."

I understood why he felt the way he did. He was absolutely right. If word got out about her secret career, people would stop looking for her. But if I was under suspicion and in danger of losing my freedom, I wouldn't have held back on giving Alonso every detail about Cara Morton's life that I knew about. And, yes, the media would judge her, the public would judge her. But the police would find out eventually, anyway, probably from one of her regulars on that cam site.

"I know," he said with a weary sigh.

"Babe, the police already know about her drug use. They probably already know that she needed to feed the drug habit. And being on this site probably afforded her a way to pay for that habit." Aaron looked taken aback.

"What?" For a second, I thought he was about to argue with me. And then his expression softened.

"It's been a long time since you called me babe. I've missed that. I've missed us."

"Me too." And I meant it. I wanted things between my husband and me to be normal again. But they wouldn't be until we got out from underneath Cara Morton's shadow. Aaron pulled me into an embrace, and we stood like that for a long time before I took his hand and led him up the steps to our bedroom where we practically tore each other's clothes off and made love for the first time in what seemed like forever.

"I'll call Bill," he said afterward as we lay entwined in the bedsheets. "And then he can set up a time for us to go down to the station and talk to Detective Alonso."

I nodded in agreement not sure why I suddenly felt so uneasy.

The three of us met Detective Alonso at the station Monday morning, and I told them what happened with Cara in my car. When I was done, Alonso and her partner Detective Richards exchanged looks. Aaron must not have noticed the look.

"I also have some infor—" And that's all he got out before Alonso cut him off, her gaze laser focused on me.

"I'd like to thank you for coming in, Mrs. Nichols." Richards handed Alonso a folder, which she spread out in front of her. "It saved us the trip of coming to see you. We've uncovered some information that we'd like some clarity on."

"What kind of information do you need from my wife?

She's just admitted to having a confrontation with Cara." Aaron's brow furrowed in confusion.

"Mrs. Nichols, do you know a man named Jackson Drew?"

Cold sweat broke out along my hairline, and I'm not sure how many seconds passed before Alonso addressed me again.

"Mrs. Nichols?"

"Yes. I know him. What does he have to do with Cara Morton's disappearance?" I was more than happy to tell the detectives about my encounter with Cara. But I never intended to tell them about the Drews. How did they find out?

"He has nothing to do with her disappearance. But he has something to do with us getting a clearer picture of you, Mrs. Nichols."

"Who is Jackson Drew, Paige?"

Aaron put his hand on my back, and I had to resist the urge to shrug his hand away. I've told no one, including my husband, about Jackson Drew, or rather Dr. Jackson Drew. It was a part of my life that I desperately wanted to forget about. Because things could've ended up so much worse. Jackson Drew almost ruined my life and now here he was, two decades later, possibly about to ruin it once again. I could tell Alonso and her partner were betting this information would unravel me. But I wasn't going out like that. I sat up straight in my chair and looked directly at Alonso.

"He was one of my professors in college."

"And you engaged in an affair with Dr. Drew? Is that correct?"

"Yes, that's correct. But that was a very long time ago, and I don't understand why you're bringing this up now." Aaron's eyes bored into me, and I didn't dare look at him for fear of what I would see in his gaze.

"Your affair with Dr. Drew isn't the issue. It's what happened after the affair that we need to know about."

"What about it?" I was a fool for thinking they wouldn't

find out about me and Jackson. And I was angry. A woman was missing, and they were airing out my dirty laundry instead of looking for her.

"They arrested you for assault?"

"Assault?" exclaimed Aaron.

"Your wife assaulted Dr. Drew's wife, Dr. Natalie Drew, after he ended their affair. Isn't that correct, Mrs. Nichols?"

"It wasn't like that."

"And that's why I'm asking," said Alonso. "I'd like for you to explain what happened."

"Don't answer that, Paige," said Bill, speaking up for the first time since we'd arrived. "Detective, unless you are planning to arrest Mrs. Nichols, we've told you what we came to tell you and we'll be leaving now."

"Just make sure your client is available for further questioning, Mr. Watters."

The three of us left in silence and didn't speak again until we arrived at a nearby diner. Once seated, with cups of coffee in front of us, Bill took off his glasses and ran a hand over his face before speaking. Aaron just stared at me, his expression inscrutable.

"Is what she said true, Paige? Did you attack this guy's wife? Because if you did, you almost walked right into a trap, and they could use this info as well as what happened in your car with Cara Morton to establish a pattern of violent behavior, then use it to prove you're responsible for her disappearance."

I looked from Bill to my husband, licking my dry lips before sharing a story I put so far out of my mind, I'd nearly forgotten it.

"It happened when I was a junior in college. Jackson Drew was married to a woman I considered a friend and mentor. But I didn't know that at the time. Back then, my friend didn't go by Natalie Drew. She was still a nurse and going by her maiden name, Michaels. Jackson was new to the college and had just gotten his PhD. He was good-looking and charming, not quite forty," I said, not able to meet my husband's gaze. I wasn't sure why I felt so embarrassed. This happened so long ago, a good decade before I even knew Aaron Nichols existed.

"Go on," prodded Bill, making me realize I'd stopped talking and was staring off into space.

"He was my statistics professor, and I was having trouble in his class. He tutored me and we became close. I was twenty and had barely ever had a boyfriend. He paid me a lot of attention and seemed genuinely concerned about me. I was flattered. We became involved. But obviously we had to keep it a secret because professors dating students wasn't allowed. Then one day, about six months into my relationship with Jackson, I got a message from him asking me to meet him at a house I'd never been to before." I paused, my mouth suddenly dry, and I took a sip of my coffee. "I just figured we were meeting up for our usual secret hookup. But when I got there, he wasn't there. Instead, Natalie was there. I hadn't seen her in months because I was spending so much time with Jackson. That's when I found out Jackson was her husband, and the house was their house." I'll never forget the look of pain and rage in Natalie's eyes. She'd been kind and nurturing to me in a way I'd never gotten from my mother. I'd considered her to be a good friend."

"Damn," said Aaron so softly I almost didn't catch it.

"I swear to God I didn't know he was married. He never wore a wedding ring, and he sure as hell didn't act married. I never saw any pictures of them together, either in her office or his. I knew she was married. She wore a wedding set. But she never talked much about her husband. And like I said, he didn't wear a wedding ring. I never asked him if he was married. I just assumed he wasn't." I looked from Bill to my husband, searching their faces for traces of understanding, or sympathy. But Aaron just looked shocked. And Bill was impatient.

"Go on," our lawyer urged.

"When Natalie found out about us and confronted him, he threw me under the bus and said that I was an obsessed student who went after him until he finally succumbed to my charms. And when I told her I didn't have any idea that he was married, she slapped the shit out of me and called me a lying hoe. So, I slapped her back and left, but she called the police, and I got arrested for assault. And Jackson acted like I was a liar to save his own sorry ass."

"I am so sorry, babe. I had no idea you'd gone through something like that." Aaron grabbed both of my hands in his and squeezed them tight. I'm not sure what I was expecting from my husband, and it was a sign of how far we'd grown apart that I expected him to shame me. But I saw nothing but love in his eyes, which made my own eyes tear up.

"What happened after that?" asked Bill a bit impatiently, in no mood to witness our tender moment considering the circumstances.

"Nothing. The charges were dropped. I was released the next morning. I missed a week of classes. But by the time I felt strong enough to go back, Natalie had resigned, and Jackson got fired because it turned out I wasn't the only student he was messing with. There were at least two more. I drove past their house one night a few weeks later, and it was up for sale. And I never found out where they went or what had happened to them, and I didn't care."

"And that's all of it, right? I'm not going to be blindsided by anything else, am I?" Bill was looking at me so intensely I almost flinched.

"No. That's all of it," I told him.

"Then let's get this over with."

Aaron and I exchanged glances, and we followed Bill out of the diner.

· · ·

"You didn't know that Dr. Drew and his wife are now living here in Oakmont?" asked Detective Alonso.

We'd gone straight back to the station, and I'd just finished telling Alonso and her partner everything I'd told Bill and Aaron at the diner. But her question threw me for a loop. I knew they were in town. I found out back in October. Everyone's eyes were on me, waiting.

"Mrs. Nichols. Did you know Jackson Drew was living here in town?"

"Yes," I snapped without meaning to as frustration and irritation frayed my nerves. Ironically, I could now see why my husband was so determined to get out from under the Oakmont PD's scrutiny.

"In fact," said Detective Alonso, "he's the head of Highland Academy. I believe your children are on the waiting list for admission. Is that correct?"

"Yes, they are. And I didn't know Jackson was Highland's head. Or at least I didn't know until I went for a tour of the facilities that the academy gives to prospective students and parents. And you know what?" I asked no one in particular. "He didn't even recognize me."

"How do you know that?" asked Alonso.

"Because it was two decades and twenty pounds ago. My hair was a lot longer back then and dyed a different color. I wasn't married and still had my maiden name, Hamilton. My college friends didn't even call me Paige. Everyone called me PG and so did Jackson. I meant next to nothing to that man, and there were other women besides me. I looked him dead in the eye and even had a conversation with him, and he gave no indication that he recognized me. And I certainly never told him who I was."

"And then what?" asked Alonso, without looking up from her notepad.

"Once the tour was over, I left. I haven't seen or spoken to him since. The admissions coordinator called me a few days later to let me know the twins were on the waiting list for enrollment and if spots opened up for next fall, they'd call me."

"And you still wanted your children to attend this school, given your history with Jackson Drew?"

"Only until I found out Jackson Drew was the head. And had I gotten a call about open spots for enrollment, I wasn't planning on accepting."

"Detective, could you tell us how you found out about Mrs. Nichols and this Jackson Drew?" asked Bill.

"You can certainly ask. But I'm not at liberty to divulge that information."

"I have a right to know,' I cut in. "It's one thing for you to have found that old police report about what happened with his wife. But how did you know he was in town and that I'd run into him?"

Alonso gave me a long appraising look before glancing at her partner, Richards, who had so far remained silent. He shrugged before finally pushing himself away from the wall he'd been leaning against and sat down at the table directly across from me.

"Mrs. Nichols. Jackson Drew may not have recognized you. But his wife, Natalie, sure did. She was visiting her husband on the day of your school tour and spotted you and then saw you again later that evening at a sorority mixer. She made a complaint that you were stalking her that no one took seriously until Dr. Morton went missing and your husband's involvement with her came to light. And as you know, we look at every possibility."

I looked away from Richards, hardly able to stand the smug look on his face. At least I had my answer to why the twins weren't immediately accepted into Highland. Their grades were excellent, and all their teachers had given them favorable letters of recommendation. And with Aaron's promotion, we

could afford the tuition. Bailey even qualified for a dance scholarship, which would have lowered the tuition. Kids who didn't
have nearly as much going for them had received acceptance.
But why not my kids? And now I knew. Because I'd screwed the
married head of the school two decades ago. I honestly couldn't
blame Natalie for calling the police. After seeing me twice on
the same day, she must have freaked out and thought I was after
her husband again.

"If you've finished implying my wife had anything to do
with Dr. Morton's disappearance, I have some information that
might be useful," said Aaron. He quickly explained about
finding out Cara had been a cam girl. I thought the detectives
would appreciate the information, but they hardly blinked.

"We actually knew that," said Alonso. "We found out early
in the investigation when we searched her computer. But we
haven't released that info to the public for obvious reasons. I'm
more curious about how you found out."

"Dr. Nichols has no more information besides what he's
already told you. Now, if that's all," said Bill loudly, pushing
back his chair and standing. "We'll be going."

Aaron and I followed Bill out the door, but I glanced back to
see both Alonso and Richards staring after us with undisguised
looks of disbelief on their faces that sent a shiver down my
spine.

"You know you could have told me about this." We'd arrived
home and were still in the car. The drive had been uncomfortably silent.

"I know. I just wanted to forget about it."

And now I *really* wanted to forget about it, knowing that
something I did so long ago was going to affect my kids. Highland was the best school for fifty miles. They would have
thrived there. Bailey's interest in writing needed to be nurtured

beyond the once-a-year writing workshop she got at her current school. And Bryce was so bored with the curriculum he needed the challenge that Highland would have provided. But how would Jackson have acted toward my kids, knowing who their mother was? I thought back on my father's favorite saying whenever things didn't go my way. "Baby, what is for you will not ignore you," meaning if it was meant to be, it wouldn't have passed me by.

"And you didn't know this Jackson guy was the head at Highland?"

I sighed, suddenly so tired. "No, Aaron. I honestly didn't know. When I received the application packet in the mail, they listed a woman as head. They introduced Jackson Drew to us on the tour as the new head. He must have been so new to the position they hadn't officially updated their marketing brochures. I sure as hell wouldn't have applied if I'd known."

To be honest, if I hadn't been told his name, I might not have recognized him either. I wasn't the only one who'd changed in the twenty years since I'd last seen him. Jackson Drew was bald and much thinner than he had been back in the day. He was also clean-shaven, devoid of the sexy beard he'd sported that I used to love the feel of when he'd kiss my neck. His lack of facial hair revealed a weak chin and cheeks covered in deep acne scars. He was still attractive with a killer smile, which he unleashed on me and several other mothers during the tour. But my only reaction was to wonder what the hell I'd seen in that asshole.

"The man shouldn't be working anywhere. He's a predator." I slammed my hand angrily against the door, and when I did, the glove box popped open, and something rolled out onto the floorboard. A plastic container with a red top lay between my feet. "What the hell?" I picked it up. It was a cheap bottle of what looked like dried herbs. Aaron snatched it out of my hand

and stared at the label with such intensity, as his face hardened with anger, that he scared me.

"Are you fucking kidding me, Paige?"

"What?" But I didn't have time to say any more when Aaron thrust the bottle in my face. I read the label on the bottle. I was wrong. The bottle hadn't contained herbs. It was a bottle of dried mushrooms, and I realized with horror that this is what had been put on the pizza Aaron had eaten that had made him go into anaphylaxis at the twins' party. And now my husband thought I'd been the one who'd tried to kill him.

A quick check of the traffic cams on the street where Paige Nichols had her confrontation with Cara Morton corroborated her story. The footage shows Paige pulling into a spot half a block from the coffee shop she claimed she saw Cara Morton going into. Fifteen minutes later, Cara exits the coffee shop with her phone pressed to her ear and turns to her left, stopping in her tracks when she spots Paige Nichols' car. She makes a beeline for the car, pounding on the window before yanking the passenger side door open and getting inside. The camera couldn't pick up on what happened inside the vehicle, but less than five minutes later, Cara exits the vehicle, slamming the door behind her, and hurries away toward her own car. She pulls away from the curb so abruptly she almost hit another car in her haste to get away. Mrs. Nichols' car was still in the same spot several minutes later before she too started her car and left. Cara Morton was alive and well when she left Paige Nichols' vehicle, but the camera didn't pick up on what happened inside the car. But something else was bugging me.

"I know that look," said Richards.

"I'm just wondering how Cara Morton even knew that was

Paige Nichols' car. She's not the only one in this town who drives a silver Ford Explorer. I mean, she filed sexual harassment charges against Paige's husband and all the documentation that we've seen claims she was staying away from the Nichols. So, how the hell did she recognize Paige Nichols' car? It's a small town, they could've easily showed up at the same place coincidentally."

We watched the camera footage again, and that's when I finally realized Cara had gotten the phone call right as she was leaving the coffee shop. With the phone to her ear, she'd immediately turned to spot Paige's car half a block away.

"Someone called her and told her Paige was there."

"You think it was the mystery drug dealer?"

"Who knows," I replied. "But why have someone follow Paige Nichols?" I took a big sip of my coffee, knowing that even if I drank the entire cup and several more, it wouldn't combat my deep fatigue. I was exhausted.

"Maybe she was working with someone to frame both the Nichols for harassment. That way she could sue them and the college."

"You think this is all about money?"

"If not money, then what?"

I couldn't answer that. But I had a feeling this was about more than money or a discarded ex-mistress. It felt much more personal.

"Detective Alonso." A female deputy named Collins was standing in the doorway. "The team you sent to the landfill found something."

The words had barely left her mouth before I went charging down to the lab where a gloved crime scene tech was pulling items out of a grime-coated black trash bag that smelled like sewage. But I'd smelled much worse. It quickly became clear as the only four items in the bag were removed that the smell was coming from whatever filth had coated the outside of the bag.

Four items. Just four. As I donned gloves and examined them, excitement coursed through my veins. This had to be the trash bag Aaron Nichols had thrown in the dumpster.

"Think it's enough to get a warrant?" Richards had come in after me and stood next to me.

"Only one way to find out." I pulled my cell phone from my pocket to call the judge.

THIRTY

AARON NICHOLS

AFTER

December 19, 2023

It's one thing to find out about a married guy your wife screwed two decades ago. But it hardly compared to finding out your wife almost killed you. I got out of the car, wanting to put as much distance between me and Paige as possible. I still had the bottle of dried mushroom flakes in my hand and was gripping it so tightly it dented. Paige came running into the house behind me.

"Aaron!" she cried. "Stop. We need to talk."

"About what? How you almost killed me trying to frame Cara? Look, I know how frustrating things are, and I know you were desperate to make her stop. But damn near killing me wasn't the answer."

"What is wrong with you? How could you possibly think I'd ever purposefully try to hurt you? Not that the thought hadn't crossed my mind a hundred times in the last few months."

"Then how did this get in your car?" Paige didn't respond.

Instead, she stared at me like I was the stupidest bastard on the planet. Cara. Of course, it had been Cara. She must have either put the bottle of dried mushrooms in Paige's car the day of the party or when they'd had that confrontation in her car.

Before either of us could say another word, Ros and Jaz arrived with the kids and some Chinese takeout after a day of Christmas shopping and ice skating. Paige and I pulled it together enough to be present and polite, but tension still hung in the air between us like a thick fog. After settling the kids in front of the TV with their chicken fried rice, the adults retreated to the kitchen.

"And don't worry, Aaron, none of this stuff has mushrooms," declared Jaz, setting out boxes of sweet and sour ribs, egg rolls, shrimp lo mein, and crab Rangoon.

"Thanks, Jaz," I said, looking over at my wife, who was staring daggers at me. "And thanks for picking up dinner."

"No problem. Coming up with what to eat every night is a full-time job, and everyone needs a break," Jaz said, looking at her own wife meaningfully.

"Hey, I have no problem whipping up some cereal or peanut butter and jelly sandwiches a couple of nights a week. All you have to do is say the word and I am on it." Ros wrapped her arms around Jaz from behind and gave her a quick kiss on the cheek.

"I apologize on behalf of my entire family, Jaz," said Paige, looking a little less annoyed than she had when they'd arrived. "Mom gave the same cooking lessons to all three of us, but me and Tyler were the only ones paying attention. This one never made it past boiling water." Paige jerked her thumb toward Ros and sidestepped her sister's attempt to flick her in the ass with a dishtowel.

"Look, I was born to make music, not food." We all laughed, and I thought Paige and I had managed to hide the tension between us pretty well, but later Ros cornered me alone in the kitchen as I was cleaning up after dinner while Paige, Jaz, and the kids were in the living room.

"You guys okay? Did something else happen?" asked Ros.

"I'll let your sister tell you about it later."

"Is it about Cara? Have they found out anything about where she might be? And don't tell me to ask Paige because she doesn't want to talk about it."

"I can't get into it right now, Ros." I knew my sister-in-law meant well, but she was the last person I wanted to discuss this mess with, even though she'd always liked me much better than my brother-in-law ever did.

"Is this about what you called Tyler about?"

"Jesus," I said between gritted teeth. "Is there anything you guys don't tell each other?"

"Dude," she said, giving me an incredulous look. "You and Paige have been together for how long? Don't act like this comes as a big surprise. You already know how our family rolls."

"I know," I conceded with a sigh. "It's just hard talking about all this because I know it's my fault." Ros merely patted me on the back and went back into the living room. But she hadn't disagreed.

Once our guests were gone and the kids were in bed, Paige's hurt and anger at being accused of poisoning me came back full force. When she came back into the house from the garage, she threw a rust-colored dishtowel on the coffee table in front of me, then stared at me in disgust.

"What the hell is that?"

"You tell me. I found it in the dryer the day you cleaned your car. It used to be white."

It took me a few seconds to realize what she was getting at. I picked up the dishtowel and looked at the rusty red stains on it. "Is that blood?"

"I wouldn't know because I'm just a lowly poisoner. So, I'm

asking you what the hell you cleaned with that dishtowel to make it that color?"

"Babe, I'm sorry. I know you didn't put those mushroom flakes on my pizza. I was just freaked out when that bottle fell out of your glove box. I know you'd never hurt me."

"You didn't answer my question, Aaron. What is that? And why did I find it the day after you cleaned your car when you should have been taking part in the search for your ex-side chick?"

"What? Are you serious right now? You think I killed Cara and used this dishtowel to clean her blood from my car? Even if I did something to her, don't you think I'd be smart enough not to have held on to a bloodstained towel?" I could have told her how to get rid of bloodstained things. But I didn't dare.

"Lower your damned voice before you wake up the kids," she hissed at me. "And I thought you were smart enough not to have an affair. But I was wrong, wasn't I?" She turned on her heel and headed up the stairs.

"Paige. Come back here." I called out as loud as I dared. But she didn't come back. I put the dishtowel in the trash, burying it deep, and went to bed.

I'd forgotten about the account I'd made on the Manga Forever website when I got a notification in my email later that night. I had a message from Sanityis4suckers.

Sanityis4suckers: D Love's back on! She posted this earlier today!

Devon Love was back on Make Me Cam? How? Had Cara been hiding? Was she back? Could it all be over? There was a link included with the message. I hesitated for just a second before touching the link on my phone screen. A grainy video popped up immediately. The quality was terrible, but it showed a woman with Cara's height and build wearing a black lace bodysuit, sky high black pumps and a black lace mask covering her eyes. Her blonde highlighted bob framed her face in a riot of curls. She had a whip in her hand and was smacking the handle against her palm. At first glance, it certainly looked like Cara, but then the woman moved, and I could tell it wasn't her by the way she was barely able to navigate the heels she was wearing. The real Cara could run a marathon in high heels. When I looked closer, this woman was thinner than Cara. Whoever this woman was, she wasn't Cara Morton. The video only ran for about a minute and a half before a pay wall popped up, requiring me to put in my credit card info to unlock the rest of the video. I felt like the biggest idiot. I should have trashed the message. Instead, I grabbed my wallet from my pants on the floor and, against my better judgement, retrieved my credit card and entered the card number to unlock the video.

Once I'd entered my card info, the pay wall disappeared, and a message popped up asking if I wanted to restart the video from the beginning or continue where it had left off. I restarted it and could instantly see that the Devon Love imposter had also filmed this video in a bedroom. But it wasn't Cara's bedroom in the home she shared with her father. I glanced at the comments section under the video. Positive and salacious comments from fans glad to see her back in action numbered in the hundreds. But there was one anonymous comment that caught my eye. It read:

Who are you? Your ass is too flat, your tits are too small, and you can't dance for shit to be the real D Love! And what happened to the birthmark on your neck?

I wasn't crazy. This wasn't Cara. And how could I have forgotten about the birthmark? I'd kissed it enough times. Then another comment popped up in response to the comment questioning the woman in video's identity.

Bet this bitch hacked her account. Happens all the time. These sites don't do shit to protect these girls' accounts. They're always getting hacked and doxxed!

I quickly logged out and fired off an angry reply to Sanity-is4Suckers. Although I wasn't sure why. It wasn't his fault.

Sadprof: Anyone with eyes can see that's not her!

It surprised me to get an immediate response that made chills run down my spine.

Sanityis4Suckers: Sorry. Goodnight, gorgeous.

What the hell? My spine stiffened in alarm and my palms were suddenly sweaty as the shock of those three words nearly made me drop the phone. I couldn't breathe for a few seconds and had to wait for my hands to stop trembling before replying.

Sadprof: Who is this?

Sanityis4Suckers: Goodnight gorgeous. Goodnight gorgeous. Goodnight gorgeous. Goodnight gorgeous

Sadprof: Who are you? Do you know Cara Morton?

I waited for a response for hours until I finally fell asleep. I woke with a start from the same damned nightmare I'd been having on repeat to the thud of my phone hitting the floor. I couldn't move and lay there panting. It was still dark outside and gentle rain hitting the windows and roof cut through the predawn silence. My heartbeat finally slowed while I stared at the ceiling. This time I'd seen the face of the woman I'd smothered. It was Cara. She'd been laughing at me and wouldn't stop. I'd just wanted her to stop when I put my hands over her face and stopped her laughing for good.

Eventually, the sounds of Paige getting the kids ready for school floated down from upstairs, and I retrieved my phone from the floor and checked my Manga Forever account for a response from Sanityis4Suckers. But there were no messages. The entire chat thread between me and whoever the hell I'd been chatting with last night was gone. Not only were the messages between me and Sanityis4Suckers gone, but they had deleted their account.

Paige and I barely spoke while we ate a rushed breakfast of fruit, yogurt, and bagels. I made breakfast since she was running late to get to a last-minute assignment for the nursing service she was working for. I'm sure she was still thinking about what had happened last night because she barely looked at me.

"I can take the kids to school." It was a peace offering, and I was happy when she gave me a grateful smile.

"Thanks. That would help me out a lot. I'll also be working my regular shift at the nursing home tonight, so you'll have to pick them up and make dinner."

"On it." I told her as she kissed the kids and left. I remembered back to the days when I would get a kiss goodbye too. Man, how did I screw up my life so badly?

After dropping the kids at school, I headed to the gym and ran five miles on the treadmill, hardly registering the run as my interaction with Sanityis4suckers played out in my mind repeatedly. The first messages I'd sent this person had been in my inbox of my Manga Forever account. And now they were gone too. The only way I could think anyone would have access to my account was if my phone had been hacked or cloned. I didn't dare call Tyler again, and I realized last night's interaction was something Detective Alonso would want to know about. But why should I tell her? And what would I show her? Without the messages I had nothing to prove this person had contacted me. The video they'd sent me was poor quality, so I couldn't even be sure that the woman in it wasn't Cara. Maybe it had been her, after all? Her thinness and being unsteady on her feet could be explained if she'd been abducted, held against her will, drugged, starved and forced to make that video. And someone could have easily covered her birthmark with makeup. Had sending the video been an attempt to get money from me? And if this Sanityis4suckers person had Cara, then he had her phone, too, and probably saw the messages between us, which would explain the Goodnight, gorgeous. Shit! I slammed my hand onto the stop button on the treadmill, causing me to jerk to an abrupt stop. I had to figure out how to get those messages back.

After a shower and change of clothes I sat in my car and pulled up my Manga Forever account. At the bottom of the page, I noticed a link to chat with their help desk and immediately clicked it. A window popped up and someone identifying themselves as Tony greeted me and asked how he could help me. I quickly explained that all the messages had disappeared from my inbox.

Tony: We apologize for the inconvenience. We had a server outage last night and several thousand accounts were affected. We are working as fast as we can to get everyone restored.

A server outage? Typical. I guessed that was probably common with these kinds of sites.

Sadprof: How long will it take to get my messages back? It's very important.

Tony: I'll look at your account and see if I can expedite things. Can you give me your username and password, please?

I typed out my username and password and got a thank you from Tony before he disappeared for five minutes, though it seemed like he'd been gone forever. While I waited, I got three calls in a row from my lawyer, Bill. I let them all go to voicemail, not wanting to miss Tony when he came back. Finally, Tony was back.

Tony: I restored all of your messages. Is there anything else I can help you with?

Sadprof: No. And thanks so much for all your help.

I quickly signed off and pulled up my inbox to find all the messages between me and Sanityis4suckers had been restored, including the link to the video. I let out a breath of relief. This time, I took screenshots of all the messages. As I was pulling out of the parking lot, three police cars and an unmarked sedan flew past me, sirens wailing. They were driving in the direction of my house. The bottom dropped out of my stomach. I followed at a safe distance to see them head down my street and pull into my driveway. Alonso and her partner got out of the sedan and went to my door and pounded on it. My phone rang. It was Bill again, and this time I answered it.

"What the hell are police doing at my house, Bill?" I practically screamed into the phone.

"Where are you, Aaron?"

"I'm at the corner watching police kick in my door. What the hell is going on?"

"Why haven't you been answering your phone? I've been trying to get ahold of you. The police have a warrant to search your house."

"What the fuck are you talking about? I didn't do anything to Cara. Have they found her?"

"Are Paige and the kids at home?"

"No, the kids are at school and she's at work. I was at the gym. Look, I have evidence someone could have abducted Cara."

"Don't you go home either," he said, not even acknowledging what I'd just told him. "What's the nearest gas station to you?"

"The Shell station is about half a mile from my house."

"Great. Get there as quick as you can, and I'll come and pick you up and escort you to the station."

"Bill, this is insane! What evidence do they..."

"And for the love of God, don't let them see you or they'll detain you in front of your neighbors and the reporters that are bound to show up. Do you want your family seeing you being put in a police car on TV?"

"Hell no!"

"Then meet me at the Shell station in fifteen minutes." He hung up.

Five minutes later, I was at the Shell station parked behind the building when my phone beeped with a text message. I froze. It was the tinkling bell sound I'd assigned to Cara's texts to distinguish her texts from Paige's when we were involved. I couldn't move for a few seconds, and my hands shook as I looked at the screensaver on my phone and saw the text notification with the name Cara. I pulled up the text and read it.

> In trouble. Need your help. Please meet me at the Dalton motel room 12B ASAP. I'll explain everything. Cara.

I read Cara's message three times before finally pulling up her name in my contacts and calling her. But my call went straight to voicemail. Was this for real? Had I been right about the kidnapping? Was Cara alive? I started my car and pulled out of the Shell parking lot. The sound of someone frantically honking caught my attention. I looked in my rearview mirror to see Bill had parked by a pump and was frantically waving his arms, yelling my name. But I didn't stop.

In hindsight, I realized how stupid I was, leaving like that, but I wasn't thinking clearly. I thought the woman I'd had an affair with was being held for ransom. The Dalton Motel was a run-down shithole at the edge of town. According to Paige, it used to be a nice place in the early nineties before falling into disrepair. The only people who used it were people who didn't know any better and were desperate for a place to stay, or homeless people who scraped together a few dollars for a night's stay when the weather was bad. Students at Roberson would rent rooms to have parties in what they had nicknamed the Roach Motel. Even prostitutes didn't use it much anymore. I pulled in front of 12B and quickly got out and pounded on the door.

"Cara! It's me, Aaron! Open up!"

The door opened and the smell of cigarette smoke, urine, and greasy takeout food hit me in the face. I pushed past the smell and realized my mistake almost immediately as the door shut behind me. I whirled around to find the gaunt face of Cara's drug dealer staring at me from beneath the same black hoodie he'd worn when I'd seen him getting out of Cara's car.

"Cara texted me. Where the fuck is she?"

He held something lit up in his hand and turned it to face me. It was Cara's phone. What had this kid done to her? "I'm the one who texted you, asshole."

His smirk made me want to throat punch him. "Where is Cara?"

"You tell me, man."

"Why do you have her phone?" My phone had been bleeping in my pocket for the past several minutes. It had started right after I pulled out from the Shell station and Bill spotted me. I could imagine that he was going ballistic right now.

"I found it."

"Found it or stole it after you killed her?" I took a step toward him. But he stood his ground, glaring at me with feverish eyes. His skin was so pale I could see the bluish-green veins beneath the surface.

"Killed her? Fuck you, asshole. I found it in her office. We were supposed to meet, and I went to her office, but she wasn't there and never showed up. I figured she forgot it and took it to give to her. But I haven't seen her since."

"And you never thought to give it to the police? They've been looking for it. It could have evidence on it! Are you stupid or just crazy?" He looked down at the phone, like the logic of what I'd just said never occurred to him.

"Don't call me stupid!" He got right in my face and was so close I could see the blackheads on his nose. "But yeah, maybe I am crazy. Sanity is for suckers." His grin exposed yellowed teeth.

"You? You're Sanityis4Suckers? It was you all along?" I slammed him against the wall next to the door. "What did you do to her?" I finally noticed when his coat fell open that the image on his T-shirt was a character from Dragon Ball Z, one of Bryce's favorite manga's. Whoever this kid was he must also be a manga fan. No big surprise then that he'd be a member of the Manga Forever website.

"I didn't do shit to her! I didn't have a reason to hurt her! I needed her."

"You sold her drugs, but you'd never hurt her? You posted stills from that video of her online. But you'd never hurt her, huh? You're a liar."

"And so are you, married guy." He shoved me away from him. "Don't act like you're better than me when you're here in this hellhole looking for the chick you cheated on your wife with. Running to her rescue like I knew you would. Did you really think someone as classy as Cara would be in this dump?" He let out a laugh that turned into a coughing fit. I took a step back, and he rolled his eyes. "And I wasn't selling drugs to Cara. I was scoring drugs for her. It was her money, Einstein."

I sank down on the edge of the bed and ran a shaky hand over my face. I'm ashamed to admit there was still a part of me that wanted to believe the woman I came looking for was the real Cara. But this was Cara's MO. She was doing the same thing with whoever this young man was that she'd done to Casey Ramsey and his father, me, and God only knew how many others. Frustration took the place of my anger, and I just wanted to be out of this room and far away from this kid whose crime was the same as mine, getting too close to Cara Morton.

"What do you want? And if you haven't hurt Cara, then who the hell was that woman who posted on Cara's webcam account that you contacted me about last night?"

"I got no clue who that bitch is. I was just fuckin' with you," he grinned. And again, I wanted to punch him.

"Were you fucking with me when you sent me the first video of Cara?" The kid gave me a blank look.

"What are you talking about? All I did was post pics from that video on that manga site. I never sent the whole video to anybody, especially if they weren't paying me for it." He looked truly confused. He hadn't sent me the first video and Cara wasn't here. And I had more important matters to deal with than this stupid, strung-out kid. Then something else occurred to me.

"Were you blackmailing Cara? Is that why you posted her pictures on that manga site? Did she refuse to pay you and you got revenge on her?"

The kid sighed and let out a snort of laughter. "You don't know shit about me or Cara. And she was proud of being a cam girl. Said it made her feel free. I found that video on her laptop last time I was alone in her office on campus. She had all the videos she posted on her webcam account saved on her laptop," he said, giving me a bored look. "I only took that video because I knew an artist on that manga site who said he could draw her as a manga character. I was going to give the drawing to her as a gift, but everyone freaked out when I posted the pics, and I got a community violation and then I just forgot about it."

Did I believe him? I probably shouldn't have, but oddly enough, I did. Hadn't Alonso said they found out she was a cam girl by searching her computer?

"Why did you text me? What do you want?" I repeated. The acrid stench of piss emanating from the filthy carpet made my nose burn. I desperately wanted out of that room.

"What do you think?"

"Money?"

"Damned straight. I need to get out of this town. And I'm betting you'll pay to get this phone back, considering there's proof of your nasty little affair on it. All those sexy texts and pictures she sent you. It's all still on her phone proving you didn't harass her."

Instead of replying, I lunged at him, grabbing for the phone. He may have looked like skin and bones, but he was a lot stronger than I thought he would be, and he sucker punched me in the head. We grappled, and he momentarily broke free from me long enough to get the motel room door open, but I grabbed his coat which slipped off as he jerked away from me. He ran toward the street, and I followed behind. He was halfway across the parking lot when a speeding truck pulled out and clipped him, spinning him like a top until he fell flat on his back on the dirty pavement amongst pop cans, cigarette butts, and fast-food wrappers. I rushed over to him, panting hard. His groaning told me he was still alive. I could've left. I probably should've left. But I thought about his Dragon Ball Z T-shirt. He was just a kid, somebody's son. Cara's phone lay beside him, crushed to pieces under the wheels of the truck. The little side compartment that held the phone's SIM card had popped open and without hesitating, I pocketed it. Then I pulled out my phone and called 911.

"Kid, lay still. I'm calling an ambulance."

He didn't respond, and I noticed his shirt was ripped, revealing and round circular port in the top left area of his chest. My grandmother had something similar when she was battling breast cancer. It was a chemo port. And that's when I realized this kid wasn't a drug addict. He was a cancer patient and here he was lying unconscious in a filthy parking lot when he should be in a clean, safe environment focusing on getting better. I was so confused and no closer to knowing who this kid was and why he needed Cara. Instead of leaving, I waited with him until the ambulance arrived. As soon as it turned onto the street, I took off.

An hour later, I was sitting in the interrogation room with Bill. Although they hadn't charged me yet, I figured I was about to be.

"Do you recognize these items, Dr. Nichols?" Detective Alonso placed three items encased in plastic on the table in front of me.

One look and my stomach instantly knotted up. How the hell did they find it? The first bag held a light gray dress shirt with a blood smear on the right sleeve and three bloody fingerprints like tattoos on the front over where my heart would have been. I noticed a couple of small cuts in the stained part of the fabric where they'd taken samples for blood analysis. The second bag held a women's lacy purple thong, the third a box of unopened condoms, and the final bag a red gift bag.

"You were identified by a witness who saw you throwing a trash bag containing these items into the dumpster belonging to

Becca's Coffee Bar on the Sunday evening following the disappearance of Dr. Cara Morton."

"Don't try to deny any of this belongs to you," began the short, stocky white guy I recognized as the man who'd given Alonso the laptop the last time I was here. Alonso had introduced him as her partner, Detective Noah Richards. "Your fingerprints were all over the trash bag, the buttons on the shirt, the box of condoms, and the gift bag."

"And the blood belongs to Cara Morton," concluded Alonso.

"Aaron?" Bill's tone was a warning as I gaped at the items on the table.

"Fine," I snapped without meaning to. "The shirt is mine. And the panties and condoms were given to me in that gift bag by Dr. Morton."

"How did her blood get on your shirt?" asked Alonso.

"It was from when we had the confrontation in my office, when she accused me of assaulting her."

"You never mentioned getting her blood on your shirt during your previous interview," said Alonso. She was smirking, and I could tell she thought she had me cornered.

I'd told her most of what had happened. But had neglected to mention everything. It wasn't just Alonso I'd withheld all the details of my encounter with Cara from. I'd left it out of my statement to the Title IX coordinator and didn't mention it to Paige or Bill either. But I couldn't hold back any longer. Not with my freedom at stake.

"After Cara made her nose bleed, and after she whispered the threat about being on her bad side, she kissed me on the lips before I could stop her and pressed her hand against my chest leaving the blood behind. I wiped away the blood on my mouth with my shirt sleeve and quickly turned away so Lynette wouldn't see it when she came rushing into the room."

"And why did you leave this detail out of your statement?"

Alonso asked. She and her partner Richards were staring at me skeptically.

"Why do you think?" I asked, incredulous, my voice coming out much higher-pitched than usual. "Because if I'd told anyone about her blood on my clothes, it would have made me look guilty of assaulting her." The things she'd said and did that day were bad enough. But the blood took it over the top. I was also embarrassed because it made her look unhinged and, by extension, me for having gotten involved with her. What happened was already so crazy and messy and the stuff with the blood... I shook my head at the memory. "I just wanted to forget it ever happened."

"By tossing everything in a dumpster downtown after Dr. Morton went missing. Gotta admit your timing is pretty suspect," said Richards, looking over at Alonso who never took her eyes off me.

When the email from the college president about Cara's disappearance had arrived, my first thought was self-preservation. The trash bag with my bloody shirt and the unwanted gifts she'd given me were already in the trunk of my car. I'd stopped by the hardware store after the storm to get some salt for the driveway, then stopped by Becca's Coffee Bar on the way home because I knew she didn't have a camera in the alley that ran alongside her shop to dispose of the trash bag and my last link to Cara.

"And the condoms and the underwear?" asked Alonso.

"Gifts to lure me back after I broke things off with her. She'd left the gift bag with the panties and condoms in my office a few days after what happened in my office. And if you have my prints on the box of condoms and gift bag, then you had to have found her prints, too, right?"

There had been a card as well. It had read: *You know you still want me* signed with the initial C. I'd foolishly torn it up and thrown it in the trash. I'd have thrown the panties and condoms in the trash, too, but didn't want the custodian to see them because then it would be all over campus. And there was no way I was throwing it in my trash at home for Paige or the kids to possibly see.

It was before she'd accused me of sexual harassment and without the note, I couldn't prove Cara had given the gifts to me, which is why I never told Bill about it. Neither Alonso nor Richards confirmed or denied Cara's prints had been found. But I'm guessing I was right, or why not just arrest me already?

"Why are you still wasting your time on me? Cara could have been abducted."

I showed them the video on the Make Me Cam website.

"And who exactly is this supposed to be? The video quality is so bad I can't even tell who I'm looking at," said Alonso.

"Another cam girl taking advantage of Cara's large following could have hacked her account," said Richards, something already theorized in the comments on the video.

"Well, what about that kid at the motel who had her phone? He has to know where she is. He claims he found her phone in her office." I had seen no way around not telling them about what had happened earlier with the kid, minus the part where I stole the SIM card from Cara's phone. I'd hidden the SIM card in Bill's car on the way to the station to turn myself in.

"You mean the kid who's still unconscious with no ID found next to a phone so crushed we can't tell who it belonged to?" said Alonso.

"Why don't you just tell us what the hell you did to Cara Morton? Where is she?" asked Richards.

And if things weren't already fucked up enough, a knock on the door interrupted us. Richards answered it, and a uniformed officer handed a manila folder to him through the door. He opened the folder and scanned the contents before handing it to Alonso, who also looked inside before setting it on the table and putting her sole focus on me.

"Dr. Nichols. Do you know a woman named Shirley Doyle?"

What the hell? Panic knotted my stomach, and I clenched my hands under the table so tight my knuckles cracked. My recent bad dreams, the reason I couldn't sleep more than a few hours, all came down to this.

"What does she have to do with Cara?"

"Just answer the question," said Richards.

Bill cleared his throat and put a hand on my shoulder, but I was tired and just wanted this to be over with.

"She was a cleaner I hired for my grandmother while she was under hospice care."

"And you didn't feel the need to tell us about her accusation, that she saw you kill your grandmother?"

"Detectives, my client—" began Bill, rightfully indignant. But I held up a hand.

"It's all right," I told my attorney. "I got this." I took a deep breath before continuing. "If you know about Shirley Doyle, then you also know her accusations came after I caught her stealing from my grandmother and got her arrested?"

"Go on," said Alonso.

"Things started going missing about a week after I hired her. DVDs, small kitchen appliances, an MP3 player. The last straw was when my grandmother's wedding band went missing. She'd gotten so thin by that point she wore it on a chain around her neck. She never took it off. I suspected Ms. Doyle was stealing and set up a hidden camera in the living room, where my grandmother's hospital bed was, and filmed her stealing my grandmother's liquid morphine and replacing it with saline." The memory still made me so upset I had to take a few seconds before I could continue. "My grandmother died the day I captured that footage. I showed the footage to the police. But I told her if she just returned my grandmother's ring, I wouldn't press charges. She returned the ring in time for me to bury my grandmother with it, but she still got arrested despite my not pressing charges over the petty theft. It was stealing my grandmother's medication that got her a year in jail. She tried to get back at me by saying she witnessed me killing my grandmother."

Alonso and Richards exchanged glances, and anger took the place of my panic.

"What? You mean Shirley Doyle's record for stealing prescription drugs isn't in your little folder? So, you came at me about one of the most painful times in my life, watching my grandmother waste away to nothing in front of my eyes and not being able to do a damned thing about it?" I stood up abruptly, startling Bill and causing Alonso and Richards to stand as well, hands on their side arms. "If you're going to arrest me, then fucking arrest me!" My voice cracked as a sob tore at my throat.

"Please calm your client, Mr. Watters," commanded Alonso.

"Aaron." Bill's voice was stern, and I let him gently push me back down into the chair.

"We have to investigate these kinds of accusations when they arise during an investigation. And Ms. Doyle reached out to us after seeing you quoted in a news article about Dr. Morton's disappearance," said Richards, sitting back down at the table and leaning forward, his heavy jaw jutting out and his eyes boring into mine, watchful like he was bracing for another outburst.

I remembered that article. I'd been called at home to offer a statement about Cara's disappearance in which I gave the standard response of keeping Cara and her family in our thoughts and prayers, after which I got royally chewed out by the college's PR director and told if anyone else called wanting a statement about Dr. Morton, I was to refer them to her since I was still on paid leave.

Alonso and Richards were called out of the room by the same officer who'd brought them the folder.

"They can't detain you for much longer without officially charging you. And no more theatrics. Got it?" Bill hissed, staring at the door the detectives just walked out of.

Before I could respond, Alonso, minus her partner, returned. Her face was back to being an impassive mask, and her mouth was set in a hard line.

"Thank you for your cooperation, Dr. Nichols. You are free to go. But you will need to make yourself available for further questioning."

"Why? What happened? Have you found Cara? Is she alive?"

"Goodnight, Dr. Nichols." Alonso was clearly pissed at having to cut me loose. No apology for searching my home, impounding my car, and detaining me.

"And my client's car?" asked Bill.

"As long as no further evidence is found, your client can have it back after we've conducted our search," said Alonso.

"Let's go, Aaron." Bill quickly guided me out of the room and out the back door of the station to avoid the media, the curious, and true crime podcasters hanging out front who'd heard an arrest was imminent in the Cara Morton case and were circling like buzzards.

Paige was waiting for me when I got home. To my surprise, I saw genuine sympathy in her eyes, or maybe she was just tired of arguing and being angry with me. Either way, I felt relieved that I wasn't stepping out of the police station into a hell of my wife's anger and disappointment. I silently followed her into the house and stopped, staring in shock. The police had torn up our entire house. God only knew what they'd been looking for, but they didn't find it because there was nothing to find. The only thing they could have possibly found was Cara's SIM card, and that was in a tissue in my pocket after I'd retrieved it from the cup holder in Bill's car.

"In case you're wondering," my wife said, barely glancing at me as she got to work sweeping up the debris. "The kids are with Ros and Jaz. I think they should stay with them for a while. I'm wondering if I should even pull them out of school when the media finally finds out it was you they'd questioned."

"That might be a good idea," I told her. "I can make sure they don't fall too far behind."

I'm not sure when it hit me. Maybe it was when I saw the house torn up, or the thought of having to pull our kids out of school, or the sad, resigned look on Paige's face. But it was all those things and one more truth. Shirley Doyle may have stolen from my grandmother, but she hadn't lied about what she'd seen me do. The weight of the guilt I'd felt since that terrible day had been crushing me for years. Suddenly, my legs were wobbly, and I slid down the side of the kitchen island to the floor, staring at my hands and shaking and crying like I hadn't since my grandmother died, or rather since I'd killed her.

"Aaron?" Paige instantly dropped the broom and knelt by my side, pulling me into her embrace, soothing me and stroking my hair like I was one of the kids. I was the one who had screwed our lives up, yet here she was comforting me with all the love and care I didn't deserve.

Besides the home health nurse who came every day, I was my grandmother's sole caregiver in her last days. Paige offered to take care of her, but she had her hands full with the twins, who were toddlers, and her job. I wasn't teaching that summer and went to Cleveland to stay with my grandmother. She was in so much pain. Seeing her in such agony, the woman who had raised me like a mother, slowly ate away at me. Soon the pain meds weren't managing her pain, and she needed more and more. But the nurse was adamant that she was on a schedule and could only have so much. Neither of us had known Shirley Doyle was stealing her morphine.

That was when Grandma started pleading with me to help her die. She pleaded with me for weeks, to the point I could barely stand to be near her. Her sunken eyes, so full of pain, tore at my heart until one afternoon when I went to check on her, her pain was so great she was sobbing about wanting to be with my grandfather. I couldn't take it anymore. I pressed my right hand over her nose and mouth and held it there until she stopped breathing. It didn't take long. Minutes later, Shirley found me holding the body of the only mother I'd ever known and sobbing. I never knew if she had really witnessed what I'd done or was just looking to ruin my life when she ended up in jail.

I tried to tell my wife all of this, to confess what I'd done, but I could barely get any words out, until Paige finally put her finger to my lips and told me we could talk in the morning. My wife had called off from her shift at the nursing home that night to stay with me. She put me in the shower and even joined me, and afterward dressed me, then put me to bed. She curled up against my back as I drifted off to sleep, determined to fix what I had broken.

I was alone in our bed when I woke up the next morning around nine after the first good night's sleep I'd gotten since Cara disappeared. The sound of voices floated up to me from downstairs, and I quickly headed down to the kitchen to see Bill and Paige having coffee. A quick glance outside showed there were a few reporters and a news truck parked across the street, hoping to get a glimpse of the suspected murderer. They were both leaning over the newspaper as I walked into the kitchen, and Paige quickly folded it up and shoved it aside.

"Do you want some coffee?" I didn't answer and instead

reached past her to grab the newspaper. My own face stared back at me with the headline

ROBERSON PROFESSOR NAMED PERSON OF INTEREST IN CARA MORTON DISAPPEARANCE

I didn't bother reading the rest since I was the one living it.

"So now that I am in the frame for this bullshit, does it mean they're not going to look for Cara anymore?"

"I've been told that this is now a murder investigation, and they're looking for Dr. Morton's remains," said Bill. "And before you ask. I have no idea why they think Dr. Morton is dead."

Paige looked incredulous, and so did I. Either this was straight up karma for what I'd done to my grandmother, or I was the unluckiest asshole on the planet right now. Probably both.

There was another article toward the bottom of the page that caught my eye, and I instantly scanned it.

Police Need Help Identifying John Doe Hit-and-Run Victim

Emergency services were called to The Dalton Motel yesterday afternoon for a victim of a hit-and-run accident in the parking lot. The victim, a young white male estimated to be between the age of 18 and 25, was found unresponsive in the parking lot. Witnesses claim to have seen the young man struck by a truck that was speeding through the parking lot and didn't stop. Motel management could not assist police in identifying the young man as he paid cash for the room he'd been staying in and gave a fake name, and authorities found no identification on him. He is currently in serious but stable condition at Oakmont General Hospital. If you know this young man or can give authorities any information you are urged to call...

A picture accompanied the news article showing the young man lying unconscious in a hospital bed. But I'm not sure why they even ran the picture because he had an oxygen mask strapped to his face. You could barely tell what he looked like.

"This is the kid? Cara's drug dealer?" Paige was reading the article over my shoulder.

"Yes. But I'm confused."

"About what?"

I quickly told her about the chemo port in his chest. "Wouldn't the cancer center have a record of this kid? I don't understand why the police, or the hospital, haven't been able to figure out who he is. How many eighteen to twenty-five-year-old white male cancer patients could there be here in Oakmont?"

"Are they looking at this kid in connection to Cara's disappearance?"

"I wish I knew." I pulled Paige close, and she hugged me back even tighter. I found it ironic that me being in so much trouble was finally what was bringing us closer together.

"Now what?" Paige said, looking over at Bill.

"Now I need your husband to tell me *everything* he knows regarding Cara Morton, including the cam site stuff and anything to do with this kid. I need to know absolutely everything. No holding back this time. They want to charge you with murder, and the only reason they released you was because they didn't have a strong enough case and didn't want it falling apart in court, because they're only going to get one shot at this. If there is anything at all that you're holding back from me, I need to know right now."

I was silent for a few seconds.

"Aaron," snapped Paige.

"Fine." I went upstairs and got the tissue with the SIM card from my pants pocket and handed it to him. "It's the SIM card from Cara's phone."

Paige threw her hands up in exasperation. "Why would you take that, Aaron? Do you know how guilty that makes you look? Alonso is going to think you have something else to hide."

"Not to mention you took something from a crime scene," added Bill. They were both looking at me like I was insane. "Alonso and Richards are looking for any reason to charge you, and you've just handed them a big one."

"Look!" I slammed my hand down on the kitchen island. "You think I don't know it was a stupid thing to do? It was just lying there in the parking lot, and I wanted to make sure it didn't disappear. I wanted an advantage," I said in exasperation as Paige and Bill exchanged worried looks. "All I could think was that I now had proof that what happened between me and Cara wasn't sexual harassment! All I saw was a way to prove I'm not some pervert who made a woman disappear to keep from losing my job. Maybe if they see I didn't harass her, they'll know I'm not a murderer." I hated how my voice cracked as I spewed the faulty logic behind what I'd done. Maybe I had truly lost it. None of us said anything, and a tense, awkward silence filled the room, only to be shattered by the doorbell ringing.

"I'll get it." Paige quickly left the room.

"Aaron," said Bill, getting up and clapping me on the back. "I'm going to do the best I can to get you out of this mess. But, man, you can't pull anymore crap like this. I can't be caught off guard again like I was in that interrogation room yesterday. Understood?"

I nodded.

"I'm going to give this to my tech guy to see if he can get anything off of it before I hand it over the police."

I walked Bill to the back door as he'd parked in the alley behind our house to avoid the press. When I got back to the kitchen, Paige handed me a certified letter from Roberson's HR department. I tore it open and read it, not at all surprised by the content. Even so, it still felt like I'd been sucker punched in the nuts with brass knuckles. I'd been officially terminated.

Paige put her arms around me from behind. "We're going to get through this. I promise," she assured me.

"God, I hope so." I turned to kiss her on the cheek, then crumpled up the letter and tossed it across the room into the trash can.

"Hey," she began softly. "What was it you were trying to tell me last night? I've never seen you like that."

She stared at me so earnestly, and I realized I couldn't tell her. What I'd done was my burden to bear alone. "It was nothing. Everything just caught up with me all at once. I'm okay now." I gave her another quick kiss on the lips and headed upstairs to get dressed. After everything she'd already been through, my wife didn't need to know that her husband wasn't just a cheater. I was also a murderer.

THIRTY-ONE

DETECTIVE ALONSO

I took a gamble and lost. And I didn't know which was worse, having my ass handed to me by the prosecutor or having my ass handed to me by the chief?

I'd thought all I had to do was bring Nichols in and rattle his cage and he would tell us where Cara Morton was. I thought the evidence we found at the landfill would get a confession out of him. In reality, forensics don't work like they do on TV. The blood and the prints have yet to be confirmed and could take several days if not weeks to come through. I didn't have that kind of time.

Roberson's president was a good friend of the chief. He was putting pressure on him to get this solved and that meant the chief was putting pressure on me. None of the other information we'd dug up about Cara Morton's life was leading to her whereabouts. Yes, she was a cam girl on the side, most likely to feed her cocaine habit. But she never had a stalker that anyone knew of. She'd been using the stalker angle to scam money from her fans who'd sent her anywhere from $500 to two-grand to buy herself some protection, then seemingly abandoned the account when the well ran dry. There was no evidence she'd ever met up with any of the men in person.

My main suspect was Dr. Aaron Nichols, with whom she recently had an affair. An affair that ended contentiously and led to a claim of sexual harassment. Was the claim true? Who the hell knew? It was his word against hers. But when the bag with the bloody shirt was found at the landfill and we had a statement from someone claiming they'd seen him kill his grandmother, I figured we had our man. In my mind, it was enough to bring him in, and so I talked a judge into agreeing to a warrant. But then the video footage from a gas station near Nichols' house was finally turned over by the owner and showed he *had* stopped to get gas on his way home ten minutes after the footage of him at Morton's house. Clearly not long enough for him to have attacked her, killed her, and made her disappear. And nothing was found in Nichols' car or home. We had to cut him loose.

My other suspect was the kid, and he was still unconscious. And so far, no leads from the community had come in about his identity and his prints weren't in the system. The only thing the doctors could tell me about him was that he was dehydrated, malnourished, and had a staph infection. But despite having a chemo port in his chest, he didn't have cancer.

I was so distracted thinking about all of this that I collided with deputy Collins coming around the corner, sending the papers she was holding flying out of her hands.

"I'm so sorry, ma'am," she cried.

"No, worries. It was my fault," I mumbled, embarrassed as I bent to help her pick up the photos. They were multiple photographs of a body, each body part photographed in detail. "What is all this?"

"They found a Jane Doe in a freezer in a storage facility over in King County. They're trying to get an ID on her and sent these over."

"Homicide?" I asked, flipping through the stack of photos.

"Looks like it. They're trying to track down the woman who reported it because she owns the unit and skipped town before she called it in."

"Well, good luck with that." I told her, shoving the stack into her hands before hurrying off in search of a vat of coffee to drown my sorrows in, wondering when I was going to catch a damned break.

THIRTY-TWO

PAIGE NICHOLS

AFTER

December 20, 2023

As if what was happening with Aaron, his losing his job and officially becoming a murder suspect wasn't bad enough, I was in no mood to hear what I had just been told when I showed up for my shift at the nursing home the next night.

"Paige, I am so sorry. I just don't think it's a good idea for you to be here right now," said Sue Bryant, the director of Serenity Village Nursing Home, where I'd been working the night shift for the past week.

"Why?" I pressed.

"They brought Gerald Morton in this afternoon. Until his daughter's case gets resolved, they've been moving him around to different nursing homes and today they brought him here. And under the circumstances, I just don't think it would be appropriate to be in a nursing home where the wife of the prime suspect in his daughter's disappearance is working. If the media gets ahold of this, people could pull their relatives from the home."

To be honest, I didn't think it was appropriate either. But I was already here, and they were beyond short-staffed. The letter Roberson sent Aaron regarding his termination said he would receive a generous severance package. But we were going to need money, especially for lawyer fees. Bill was a nice guy, but he rarely did pro bono work. And my next nursing assignment didn't start for another week. That was if they'd even still want me since I was now the wife of a murder suspect. And there was no way in hell we were touching the kids' college fund.

"No problem, Sue, I get it. I do. But you guys need help. I'll have one of the other nurses tend to him this evening. But just let me work out my shift. And I won't be back."

I could tell she didn't know what to do. But three nurses had called off. It was after 4 o'clock and she had been there since before seven that morning. I knew she was ready to go home.

"I'll even sit at the nurses' station in the back, so no one sees me in case the media shows up to verify that Gerald Morton is here."

"Fine," she finally conceded. "Sam can sit up front, and I'll let him know if anyone calls or shows up inquiring about Mr. Morton that he can't discuss who's a resident at the facility."

"Got it. Now get out of here."

The rest of the evening went by quick enough. But an hour into my shift, Lynette showed up to do her rounds of volunteer reading for anyone who wanted it.

"Hello, Mrs. Nichols. How are you doing?" She could barely make eye contact with me and when I saw her, I wanted to turn and walk the other way, but that would've been rude, and why the hell would I do that when Aaron and I had nothing to hide? My husband was innocent, and I wouldn't act like he was guilty by avoiding people.

"Hanging in there, Lynette. Thanks for asking."

To my surprise, she asked nothing about what had been in the paper and didn't mention anything about Aaron being fired, and I was grateful for that. It was just business as usual, and that's exactly what I needed.

"I got a call this morning that Mrs. Jacobs passed away yesterday. She was the blind lady I would come and read to. Is there anyone else who might need someone to read to them?"

"I was so sorry to hear about Mrs. Jacobs. She was such a sweet lady. But I think Mr. Burns might like someone to read the Bible to him. He accidentally broke his glasses the other day, and his son won't be able to get a new pair for him until tomorrow. I'll just walk you up there and introduce you."

"Thanks. That would be great." She paused. "How's Dr. Nichols?" she finally asked as I walked her up to the second floor. "The college sent out an email announcing he was no longer working for the university. But everyone knows they fired him. It's so unfair. They didn't charge him with a crime and the college is throwing him under the bus."

"He's a fighter, Lynette. And I'm glad he's got you in his corner." I knew she meant well, but I really didn't want to talk about it anymore. I introduced her to Mr. Burns, a flirtatious eighty-year-old former pastor, and went quickly back to my station.

I had an hour left on my shift when the alarm sounded on the security panel at the nurses' station. The patient in room 24D had a tracker bracelet that had triggered the alarm because either they'd left the building or were trying to. I was the closest person to the nearest exit toward the back of the building and immediately headed there.

An elderly black man with snow-white hair wearing pajamas and a robe was frantically pushing against the door trying to get out, tears of frustration streaming down his cheeks. I hadn't seen this patient before, and a quick glance at the name tag encircling his wrist identified him as Morton, Gerald. Cara's father. Shit. I was really hoping I wouldn't have to have any kind of interaction with him while I worked my last shift here. I buzzed for Sam, the only other nurse on duty manning the front nurses' station, so he could take Mr. Morton back to his room and sedate him. But he didn't come, and I knew he was probably playing video games on his phone and ignoring the call button.

"Cara?" Mr. Morton was staring at me with wide, tear-filled eyes. "Cara?"

He thought I was his daughter and panic made my stomach do a flip flop. I gently took him by the hand and guided him away from the door, slowly walking him back to his room. My mouth had gone dry.

"Cara, where have you been? Where am I?"

"Mr. Morton. You're in a nursing home and I'm one of the nurses here. Now, let's get you back to your room." He allowed me to take him back to his room, and by the time I had him back in his bed, Sam finally showed up with valium and a small paper cup of water.

"Sorry," he told me. "Mrs. Tate needed her diaper changed. Mr. Ramsey wouldn't let me change the bandage on his infected leg unless I put a smiley face sticker on it, and it took me twenty minutes to find them, and there's a mouse in Ms. Riser's room that I'm positive she's been feeding. So, I'm late doing the meds run."

I felt bad for thinking he'd been on his phone. He looked exhausted.

"Here, Mr. Morton. It's time for your meds." He handed the elderly man his pill, which he promptly put in his mouth and washed down with the small cup of water, after which he stared right at me and then held out his hand.

"Sit with me until I fall asleep like you used to, Cara." I gave Sam a panicked look, and he whispered in my ear.

"Go ahead. I won't tell Sue. He'll be asleep in a few minutes and won't even remember you in the morning. Kinda like my last date." Sam left the room before I could protest, and I turned back to Mr. Morton, who still had his hand held out to me.

Reluctantly, I took his warm and slightly moist hand and sat down on the edge of the bed. He lay back against the pillows, still clutching my fingers.

His breathing slowed and his eyes fluttered shut. I waited a few more minutes until a snore escaped his lips before I extricated my hand from his and slowly got up to head to the door. When his voice stopped me.

"I am so sorry, Cara. I am so sorry."

I froze with my hand extended toward the doorknob. He was sorry. What was he sorry about? Did he hurt his daughter? He was the only person home with her the night she'd gone missing, and Alzheimer's patients could sometimes be violent. I slowly walked back over to the bed where he was staring at me with tear-filled eyes, sat down, and took his hand. And then I did something I knew I was going to feel like shit about later. But my family and I were fighting for our lives, and I needed to know.

"What are you sorry about, Daddy?"

"I didn't know. I swear I didn't know what she was doing." His voice was hoarse and barely louder than a whisper.

"Who Daddy?"

"Your mother. I didn't know what she was doing. I should've protected you. You're my daughter. My baby girl. I let you down. Shoulda never told you what she did because you were never the same afterward." He cried now. Fat sloppy tears it slid down his smooth brown cheeks. And I felt like the biggest asshole in the world. What did I hope to accomplish by pretending to be Cara?

Aaron had told me Dr. Watford-Raines once dated Cara's father and that Cara's mother had been abusing her. Aaron's association with Cara had been the equivalent of turning loose a wrecking ball in our lives. But she was a daughter and, from what I could tell, very beloved by her father at least. And here I was taking advantage of this poor man's terrible memories and regrets over not being able to protect his daughter. And the award for Horrible Nurse of the Year goes to Paige Nichols. Congratulations, Paige! And now I had to fix it, if I could.

"You did the best you could, Daddy. You didn't know."

"You don't hate me?" The surprise in his question brought tears to my eyes and I let them flow, crying for this man, for Cara, and for my own father, who I still missed desperately, despite his mistakes.

"I could never, ever hate you. I love you."

His eyes drooped again, but when I gently slipped my head out of his, he woke up again because he still had more to say.

"I made sure she stayed away from you. But then I got sick and she..."

"And she what? What do you mean, Daddy?"

But Gerald Morton was fast asleep.

"Where are my grandbabies?" asked my mother when Aaron and I Facetimed her after I'd gotten off from work. My mom was a night owl, and I knew she'd still be up. She was in her nightclothes, with a silk bonnet on her head, and a cup of chamomile tea sitting on her coffee table.

"With Ros and Jaz," I told her before taking a big sip from my glass of Moscato. The rest of my shift had been uneventful, but I couldn't stop thinking about what Mr. Morton had told me about Cara's mother. He'd been successful in keeping her away, but then he got sick and... And what? What had he meant, and could it have anything to do with Cara's disappearance?

"I'd have thought you two would be too busy getting Aaron out of this mess instead of calling me at almost midnight."

"Hi, Eleanor," said Aaron tentatively, not sure of the response he would get from my mother.

They hadn't spoken at all since this started, which was odd, seeing as how my mother was never one to bite her tongue over anything to do with her family. Sensing his apprehension, my mother's expression softened.

"Hello, son-in-law. I'd ask how you were doing, but I already know the answer."

Aaron smiled, and the tension broke. "Now, what is it you two want this late at night?"

"Did you know Gerald Morton?" I asked. Taken aback by the question, her right eyebrow lifted in surprise.

"Of course, I know Gerry Morton. Every woman in Oakmont knows Gerry Morton fine as he was back in the day. I hear he's still good-looking. He worked with your daddy. Why are you asking me about..." her voice trailed off as it hit her. "It's his daughter that's missing, isn't it?"

"Yes," Aaron and I said in unison.

"Did you know his wife?" I asked.

"No. He married a white girl almost twenty years younger than him when he was forty-six. Never thought he'd settle down. He fell hard for that girl, though. I think her name was Beverly, and she was a good friend of your daddy's friend, Janice." She said the word Janice with a bit of grimace before taking a sip of her tea as I looked down at my lap, still wincing from the knowledge that the father I'd thought was perfect had cheated on my mother.

"Who's Janice?" asked Aaron, looking from me to my mother on the computer screen. My mother didn't answer, and

I gave my husband a gentle nudge, a subtle hint to drop it. I'd yet to tell him about my father's affair. I was still processing it.

"We heard a rumor that Beverly was abusing their daughter. Did you ever hear anything about that?" I asked.

"It was all anyone could talk about for weeks. He caught her in the act from what I heard and kicked her out of their home, had all the locks changed, and filed for divorce. She was also seeing her ex-high-school boyfriend on the side, which was to be expected. Her family and friends cut her off when she married Gerry. I think she wanted her old life back. Being married to a middle-aged man, no matter how fine he was, couldn't have been fun for a woman her age."

"What did he catch Cara's mother doing?" asked Aaron.

"I couldn't tell you. He was extremely tight-lipped about it. All any of us heard was that he caught her doing something that caused him to kick her out and file for divorce. And it shocked me because the few times I saw Beverly out with Cara, she seemed to really adore that little girl. She and Tyler were even in the same preschool for a little while. But then she stopped coming."

"Why?" I asked.

"She was a sickly little girl. There was always something wrong with her, and from what I heard, they did test after test for everything from sickle cell to diabetes to leukemia and never figured out what was wrong with that child."

"They must've figured something out because she seemed healthy enough to me." I couldn't keep the sarcasm out of my voice. I didn't dare look at Aaron.

"Either that, or she just grew out of whatever was wrong with her. Tyler grew out of his asthma by the time he was in his teens. Anything is possible."

"I can't believe she didn't get custody of Cara. Did Gerald Morton have proof of what he saw her doing to their daughter?" I asked.

"Like I said, I think she missed her old life and with Gerald keeping full custody of Cara, she could start a clean slate with that ex-boyfriend of hers. It is a good thing she didn't try for full custody. I can't imagine why any woman in her right mind who called herself a mother would abuse a sick child unless..." Mom was thoughtful, like something had just occurred to her.

"What?" Aaron and I asked in unison.

"Unless Gerry knew she was running around on him. Everyone in town knew. Being cheated on causes a special rage in people, though women seem to be a bit more forgiving than men." She gave me a pointed look. "Gerald wouldn't be the first man to punish a cheating wife by denying her access to her child. She cheated on her husband. With the gossips in this town, it wouldn't be much of a stretch for people to believe she was a child abuser too."

"And he never remarried, right?" asked Aaron, quickly changing the subject being that he was now experiencing people thinking him capable of other horrible things since he was a cheater. And I have a feeling he already knew the answer to his question. I didn't know how deep his conversations with Cara got, but I'm sure she probably told him about her father.

"No. He changed after that. I don't think he trusted anyone else around Cara. As far as I know, he never dated much after that either. At least not like he used to back in the day."

"He must have been worried she might come back one day to try to take Cara," I said, more to myself than anybody else.

"I don't think he needed to worry about that. I'm betting Beverly slipped right back into her old white life and didn't give Gerald or Cara another thought."

"I made sure she stayed away from you. But then I got sick and she..." The last words Gerald Morton had said to me last night before he fell asleep suddenly came back to me. What had he meant?

"Paige?" My mother's sharp voice, accompanied by a nudge from Aaron, snapped me back to the present.

"Thanks, Mom. Sorry we kept you up."

"So, neither of you are going to tell me why you called so late asking me about ancient history? What does this have to do with Cara's disappearance?"

"We don't know, Mom. We're just trying to find out anything that might explain what happened to her."

"And with them focusing solely on me, they aren't searching for any other explanations," said Aaron wearily.

"They need to be looking in all directions, and not just this one," I added, suddenly angry, remembering how the police tore our house apart. I drained my wineglass in one gulp, earning me a raised eyebrow from my mother, which I ignored.

We said goodnight to Mom, and she promised if she could think of anything at all that might help us, she'd let us know. She also promised to pray for us. And I was grateful because we needed all the help we could get.

True to her word, when I woke up late the next morning to the smell of Aaron cooking sausage, I had a text message from my mother:

> You might want to ask Janice about Cara's mother. She moved back to town last year. And don't ask me how I know this. I just do.

Mom had told me she didn't know what happened to Janice after her affair with Daddy ended. But it wouldn't be the first time my mother had lied to me, and I didn't have the energy to wonder why. Besides, I was too busy staring at the name my mother had put at the end of her text. Janice Singleton. I knew this woman.

THIRTY-THREE

PAIGE NICHOLS

BEFORE

October 20, 2023

"Mrs. Nichols, Jan will see you now."

I followed the receptionist to a big bright office with large picture windows overlooking the Oakmont town square. Jan Singleton LPCC, a slim, attractive, brown-skinned woman with a salt and pepper buzzcut who could have been anywhere from late forties to early sixties, rose from her white leather chair to greet me. Her framed degrees, a BS in Psychology from Antioch and master's degree in counseling from Central State University, along with several other certifications, hung on the wall behind her. She wore a black turtleneck and a knee-length brown suede skirt with chunky heeled black leather ankle boots. Aside from the small gold hoops in her ears, she was unadorned, and wore no makeup. Oddly enough, I liked her instantly.

"Please have a seat, Mrs. Nichols," she said with a smile. I sat, and she set a gold timer on her desk for an hour.

Could I tell this woman everything I was going through in

an hour? My anxiety, my sleepless nights, my discovery that my husband was cheating on me with a younger, prettier, more accomplished woman, my feelings of failure. I knew I needed help. But now that I was here, I didn't know what to say.

"How can I help you?" Jan prompted gently when I continued to sit there staring at her. Her soft voice caused tears to fill my eyes, and I glanced away.

When I finally looked back at her, she'd come out from behind her desk and held a tissue box out to me. I snatched a few and gave her a brief wobbly smile before wiping my eyes and blowing my nose.

"My husband's having an affair."

"You think he's having an affair, or you know he's having an affair?" she asked, as she sat back down behind her desk.

"He's admitted to it and promised to stop, and then I found out he was still involved with her."

I'm not sure what made me wake up at five in the morning, only to realize Aaron was not next to me in bed. Figuring he probably gone to the bathroom, I drifted off to sleep again and woke abruptly less than an hour later to realize he still hadn't come back to bed. That was when I found him downstairs with his hand down his pants, his phone on his chest. Then I saw the video of *her*, dancing suggestively in her lacy underwear.

Aaron had lied to me – again. He'd made me think he was working on our marriage, that he wanted things to get better and only wanted me and the kids. To say I felt like the biggest idiot on the planet was an understatement. I was furious and just so done with his bullshit.

Once I'd told my new therapist what happened next, I looked down on my lap to see a pile of shredded tissues I didn't remember tearing up. I realized they were a representation of my marriage.

"Was this the first affair that your husband has had?"

"No clue," I told her truthfully. "He says it is, but his credibility with me is next to zero at the moment."

"And what are you hoping to accomplish by entering therapy?"

Her question surprised me. Why the hell does anyone come to therapy? To fix what's broken and find out why it broke. She noticed my expression and continued.

"The reason I ask is that I want you to have realistic expectations. Therapy is an exploration, a journey, if you will. It's not a magic pill, and it may take months, possibly even years, to address a lifetime's worth of emotional issues."

I understood what she was trying to say. She wasn't making me any guarantees that I'd get what I need from her as a therapist unless I made a commitment. "I don't need to unpack a lifetime of emotional baggage. I need a neutral party to talk to help me decide what my next steps should be. I'm lost and confused and so angry. I'm in a place I never thought I'd be in."

"In that case, the first thing I would advise would be not to decide anything regarding your marriage for at least three months unless you or your children are in immediate physical danger, or your husband is verbally or emotionally abusive. Is he abusive? Because if he is, I can help you and your children get to a secure location." Jan Singleton leaned slightly forward in her chair, invested in my answer. That's when I noticed the thin scar on her neck, just under her chin. She realized I'd seen it and self-consciously pulled her turtleneck up higher on her neck.

"No. Aaron's never been abusive. He's just a gaslighting, lying asshole."

"Gaslighting is a form of emotional abuse, Mrs. Nichols. It alters your sense of reality."

She was right. My husband had certainly altered my sense of reality. He'd made me think he wanted a future with me. Did he give Cara the same impression? Was he acting like he wanted a future with her too?

"Mrs. Nichols?" Jan Singleton was giving me a concerned look.

"Sorry, what did you say?"

"I asked if you felt safe with your husband."

"No. But not because he's ever been violent."

"In what way, then?"

"I guess because he's put another woman's wants and needs before mine. He didn't guard his heart or protect our marriage. It should have been the two of us against the world. But now it's the two of them against me, and as a result, I don't feel safe. Does that make sense?" I hoped she understood what I meant because I wasn't sure I even understood completely.

"Do you blame yourself for your husband's infidelity?"

"Maybe for helping to create the conditions that allowed it to happen. Until I quit my nursing job a few months ago, I wasn't easy to live with. I was angry and distant. But I absolutely did not deserve to be cheated on. I could have just as easily gone out and found a man to distract me from everything that was wrong with my marriage, but I didn't."

"Do you think your husband's affair was a distraction for him?"

"Aaron found an easier path and took it, not caring about the fallout to me, our marriage, or our family. He actually told me that things with Cara were easier."

"How did that make you feel?"

"How would it make you feel?" I hadn't meant to snap at her, but, seriously, who wouldn't have felt hurt by their husband making that kind of admission?

She leaned back in her chair, patiently waiting for me to answer. That's when I realized my answer wasn't as important as my need to acknowledge it and say it out loud. "It felt like a slap in the face, like everything I do for him, and our family, wasn't good enough because it wasn't always wrapped up in a pretty package. I'm only human. I get mad, and frustrated, and angry. I'm not always nice. I can be critical, and I complain a lot. But I'm also loving, and caring, thoughtful, and supportive, kind..." I looked down at my lap as more tears filled my eyes. I quickly wiped them with the shredded tissues.

"Cheating spouses often compare the affair partner's best qualities to their spouse's worst qualities and the spouse can never win. They do it to justify the affair to themselves. Often, the only way they can continue the affair is to demonize their spouse."

"He had no intention of breaking things off with her, did he?"

"Only your husband can answer that. But many cheating spouses are functioning under a tremendous amount of guilt for what they've done. But at the same time are still addicted to the emotional high they got from the affair. They re-establish contact and promises to the spouse to end it are broken. Ending an affair is a process."

"Then what do I do now?"

"Be kind to yourself. What your husband did was not your fault. Put you and your children first. I won't lie to you and tell you this is going to be easy. It isn't. Even if you decide to forgive your husband and work on your marriage, the marriage you had before is over. You also need to prepare yourself for the possibility of a new future and a new beginning."

"Have you ever been cheated on?" I'm not sure why I asked her that. Maybe I just wanted to feel like I wasn't alone. I didn't expect her to answer, but to my surprise, she did.

"I've been lied to, cheated on, beat up, stolen from, discarded, and almost killed," she said, absently touching the scar on her throat. "It's why I became a therapist. I found the strength to mend everything in me that was broken. And now, I want to help others do the same." Our eyes met, and she stared at me with such intensity that I had to look away.

The timer chimed. Our hour was up. Jan Singleton walked me to her door and told me she hoped to see me again soon. But I never went back.

THIRTY-FOUR

AARON NICHOLS

AFTER

December 20, 2023

I was surprised they'd taken so long to fire me. I thought that after Cara had filed her harassment claim, they'd kick me straight to the curb. But the college owed me a hearing, and I'd looked forward to defending myself. Being a person of interest in a kidnapping and suspected murder, however, was another matter entirely. I didn't blame them for firing me when they had a responsibility to protect the students, faculty, and staff from someone who might be dangerous.

If it weren't so fucked-up, I'd have laughed at how out of hand everything had gotten. Falling into a bottle to make the pain go away was so tempting. But I couldn't, wouldn't, do that to Paige and the kids. They needed my sorry ass. The dismissal letter I got from the university said I would receive payment for unused vacation, a severance package of two weeks of pay for every year I'd worked there. We weren't completely screwed with Paige working again. But when that money was gone, we'd need a plan B.

The media was camping out 24/7 in front of our house and the kids were still with Ros and Jaz. I hadn't left the house in days, and Paige was the one navigating the barrage of questions and cameras stuck in her face as she went to work. The only thing Bill's tech guy could pull from the SIM card from Cara's phone were text messages that would have confirmed I hadn't harassed her, and her phone's contacts list. They were going through the contacts list but so far had identified everyone except for a handful of numbers listed with only initials. I wondered if one of those was her drug dealer. There had been nothing else on the news about the kid, so I assumed he'd yet to be identified.

With nothing else to do, I got the Christmas tree out of the attic and set it up. I couldn't have cared less about Christmas. But I didn't want to disappoint the kids. We hid their presents in the attic, which we kept locked. And then it hit me. A while back I'd ordered Bailey a ballerina charm bracelet she'd been wanting for a long time and had it delivered to my office so she wouldn't see it. During my involvement with Cara, I'd forgotten to bring it home and left it in my desk drawer at work. Shit! I had to get that bracelet, or my daughter would be upset come Christmas morning, which meant I had to slip out of the house unseen and get to campus. But I couldn't do it during the day. I was pretty sure I was no longer welcome at the college. I could have called Helen to see if she could get it for me, but I know she left town during winter break to visit her sister. I could have called Lynette, but in all honesty, I was afraid of how people from the college would react. I didn't want to put them or me in an awkward position.

Paige was working an evening shift at a hospital the next town over and wouldn't be home until after eleven. I couldn't tell her about forgetting the one thing our daughter had really wanted for Christmas. I couldn't afford to be any more of a fuck-up than I already was in the eyes of my wife and kids. After I dragged the artificial tree down from the attic and put it together in its usual spot by the fireplace, I went into the garage and pulled my bike down from where it had been hanging on the wall since the last time I'd ridden it almost two years ago.

Darkness had fallen and a quick peek out the front door showed me the reporters camped out in front of our house had decreased by more than half. I guess they were tiring of waiting for something they wouldn't get, especially since the police had never charged me with anything. The journey to campus by bike was about fifteen minutes. It probably would've taken me a lot less time if I hadn't been so out of shape. I hadn't been going to the gym regularly since the affair ended and the strides I'd made when I was working out like a fiend were almost gone. I was back to being a middle-aged guy getting soft around the middle.

It was after seven and Tate Hall was mostly in darkness. The main entrance was unlocked, and I quickly slipped inside before anyone saw me. With a stab of panic, I saw that the elevator on my right was coming down to the lobby. So, I walked up three flights, instead. They hadn't asked me to return the key to my office, to my amazement. It wouldn't be *my* office for much longer, though. Helen had told me the college had named Dr. Peters chair of the English Department for the rest of my term, but he didn't start until January. I reached for my key but found the door already open, and the office light was on. Figuring there was no way around it, I gently knocked. But there was no response. I opened the door and looked inside. The room was empty. Peters had already made his presence known by taking everything I'd left and dumping it in a box that sat on the table in front of the couch. I remembered Cara sitting there trying to entice me back to her by flashing me with no underwear on. Before, I would've been excited, aroused. But thinking about it now just made me feel empty.

Eager to find the bracelet and get home, I searched the box and found the bracelet gift box amongst the clutter, but to my surprise it was empty. Shit! But was I really surprised? The bracelet was gold. Paige and I had an argument about buying Bailey such an expensive bracelet at her age. In the end, we decided Paige would hold on to the bracelet and Bailey could only wear it on special occasions until she got old enough to take care of it. And now it was gone. Probably given to one of Peters' granddaughters.

What the hell was I going to do? I checked around on the floor, just in case the bracelet had fallen accidentally, and searched every drawer in my desk. But I came up empty. The bracelet was gone. I had to get out of the office before Peters came back, putting me in a position where I'd have to whip his ass. I didn't need the trouble. Stepping outside the office, I heard voices coming from down the hall, so again I ducked into the nearest stairwell. The lights in the stairwell weren't on, so I didn't see the large mass lying on the floor until I tripped over it and went flying, falling flat on my face.

"What the—?" I pulled myself up to my feet using the handrail.

Feeling around on the wall for the light switch, I flipped it on, illuminating the stairwell to see someone lying on the third-floor landing. It was Dr. Peters. He was lying on his stomach and blood trickled from his forehead. His right loafer was lying in the middle of the stairway leading up to the fourth floor, meaning he must have fallen down the stairs. What the hell was going on now? I just stared at him, not sure what to do. When I regained my senses, I rushed to him and reached for the side of his neck to check for a pulse. Before I could touch him, he groaned, and I snatched my hand away. At the same time, I noticed something glittering from his pocket. It was the bracelet. Bastard! I *knew* he'd taken it. I pulled it free from his pocket and stuffed the bracelet into mine. A sound came from above me. Someone was coming down the stairwell and was seconds away from seeing me standing over a bleeding Peters. I didn't look back as I stood and ran out of the nearest exit.

Fifteen minutes later, I was back home, sitting on the couch. I pulled the bracelet out of my hoodie pocket and saw what I thought at first was a charm I didn't recognize. Upon closer inspection, I realized it wasn't a new charm. It was an earring, a dangling diamond heart earring. The hook was caught in one loop of the bracelet. I couldn't believe what I was looking at. This was Cara's earring. I held it to my nose and sure enough, there were faint traces of her floral scented perfume. The smell was like a punch in the gut. Even if the earring hadn't smelled like her, I'd have known it was hers because I was the one who'd given her the earrings. Why the hell did Peters have it in his pocket? And could it have anything to do with the story Helen had heard about Peters wanting Cara's office? Had he known she wasn't coming back? Had Peters killed Cara Morton? Or was he the victim? Had he fallen down the stairs – or had he been pushed?

The next morning, I checked the news and saw nothing about Dr. Peters being attacked or suffering from an accident. I called the hospital. He hadn't been admitted. I hadn't slept worth a damn all night wondering why he'd had Cara's earring in his pocket. I had to talk to him alone. Luckily, there were even fewer reporters loitering outside our house now, and I knew Paige wouldn't be up for a couple more hours. I rode my bike past Tate Hall and didn't see Peters' car in the faculty lot. But I knew where he lived. Did I dare go over there? He could call the police on me. He didn't need an excuse to make my life even harder than it was right now. Despite my apprehension, I pedaled toward his house. His black Range Rover was in the driveway of his sprawling brick ranch. And as luck would have it, he emerged from the front door sporting a bandage on his forehead. He was pale and had a livid purple bruise on his right cheek, but he was very much alive and sweet relief washed over me.

"Nichols?" He was completely shocked to see me. "What are you doing here?"

"We need to talk."

"If this is about my becoming department chair..." He tried to walk past me to his car, but I blocked his path.

"Does it look like I give a damn about you being department chair? I've got much more important things to worry about and so do you."

I held up the earring.

"You!" he spat out at me. "You're the one who pushed me down the stairs last night, aren't you? You could have killed me! I was in the emergency room for hours last night! It took five stitches to close the cut on my forehead and I've got bruised ribs and..."

"Man, shut the fuck up!" I interrupted. "Why would I push you down a flight of stairs? Not that you didn't deserve it for stealing my daughter's bracelet."

"Look," he said, sighing with resignation. "I've got some time before my doctor's appointment. Let's go inside," he said grudgingly.

I followed him into an immaculately decorated but dated house that smelled like cinnamon and pipe smoke. An over-weight beagle came waddling toward us as we entered the house, and Peters bent down to stroke its head affectionately before leading the way to the sunken living room with a Christmas tree in front of the window. Family pictures of Peters with his wife and two sons from their childhood to adulthood lined the mantel over the fireplace.

"I'd ask if you wanted a drink, but I know this isn't a social call."

"All I want to know is why I found you at the bottom of a stairwell in Tate last night with Cara's earring in your pocket?" I tossed the earring on the glass coffee table. Peters picked it up and sighed.

"For starters, I didn't think you wanted the bracelet, since you didn't take it with you. You took stuff of no value but left an expensive bracelet behind. What else was I supposed to think? And Cara forgot her earring at the hotel we were staying at a few days before she went missing. I never got the chance to return it to her." He saw my stunned expression and added. "I wasn't about to become a person of interest and have my life torn apart like you. I was on my way to put it in her office when someone pushed me down the stairs."

I was speechless. I was sure I'd heard him right. Peters looked amused.

"Please tell me you're not this stupid. Did you really think you were the only one?"

"What happened to not shitting where you sleep?" I asked, surprised at how calm my voice was despite the turmoil I felt inside.

"Cara could be very persuasive when she wanted something... or someone." He smirked.

"How long?" It shouldn't have surprised me that Cara was sleeping with other men and, like she said, I didn't own her. Hell, I was still sleeping with Paige when we'd been involved. Why had I thought we'd had something special? Why had I believed her when she said nothing was going on with Peters?

"It started the night of the Fling and had been going on until her disappearance. Which, as I said before, I had nothing to do with."

He was enjoying twisting the knife. I glanced beyond him at the papers on his coffee table with his name and address at the top. Then another thought hit me like a Mack truck. Peters first name was Alan. An A name, just like mine. His name was probably even next to mine in Cara's contacts list on her phone. If she'd been high or in a hurry or texting us both at the same time, it would have been easy to send the video to the wrong man.

"It was you," I said more to myself than to him.

"What the hell are you talking about?" Peters was looking confused and not quite as confident as he seemed only seconds ago.

"Cara sent me an explicit video I thought was for me. But it was for you, wasn't it?" It made perfect sense now. The reason she'd never brought up the video was because she thought she'd sent it to Peters.

"And so what if she did? She sent me lots of videos."

"Look," I said, beyond frustrated with this asshole. "Do you know where she is?"

"No," he replied with such a bored and unconcerned tone that it made me want to bury my fist in his face.

"Your concern for her is touching. Did you care about her at all?"

Peters rolled his eyes and let out a mirthless laugh. "Cara and I were a lot more alike than the two of you because I knew the rules."

"The rules?"

"Rule number one: Don't get attached. And rule number two: No man was ever going to lock her down and get all of her attention. She was a different woman for each of us. She saw you coming a mile away, my friend, a knight in shining armor in need of a damsel in distress. She was already tired of you long before you broke things off."

"If you knew all of that, then you knew she was addicted to cocaine, too, right?" I ignored what he'd said because he wanted to rattle my chain and I wouldn't give him the satisfaction.

"I'm very open-minded," he said, shrugging nonchalantly. "Everyone should fuck on cocaine at least once in their life." His shit-eating grin was more than I could stand.

"Fuck while high on cocaine, or fuck someone who has to be high on cocaine to fuck you?"

"Get out of my house," he growled.

"Was rule number three: Don't tell your wife? Because if I'm not mistaken, your wife is the one with all the money and a prenup. If she divorces you, you're screwed, right?" I said, remembering what Cara had told me. I took a step toward him, and he took a step back. "What happened? Did Cara threaten to tell her? Was she blackmailing you? Is that why you killed her? Did her earring come off in the process?"

"Get the fuck out!" he yelled, causing the beagle to sit up from where it had been lying by the fireplace and bark.

I bent down to pet the dog, and it instantly rolled over, exposing a big pink belly. "I heard she'd barely been gone before you went after her office like you already knew she wasn't coming back."

Peters face reddened as he clenched and unclenched his fists. "My office was being treated for toxic mold. I needed a place to work, and her office is empty. But now I have *your* old office. So that solved that problem, didn't it?"

"You know I'm going to tell the police about this, right?"

"Go ahead. I was at the Midwest College Association's annual conference in Chicago when Cara went missing and the police already know that." As he talked, he headed to the front door and held it open for me, and I left.

I was halfway home before I finally realized what was bothering me about what Peters had told me. Not the part about his affair with Cara. But what he'd said about being on his way to Cara's office to put her earring back. I'd found him at the bottom of the staircase that led away from her office. He was on his way back, not on his way there. And why had he suddenly decided to return the earring, anyway? Unless that's not the real reason he was in her office. Was there something in there that would incriminate him in her disappearance? As I slipped back into the house ten minutes before Paige got up, I realized I had to go back to the campus tonight and search Cara's office. At least that had been the plan until Bill called me.

"Now what?" Hearing from my lawyer was a double-edged sword these days. I was happy to have an excellent lawyer, but most of the news I'd gotten from him lately was anything but good.

"Camera footage from the Shell station near your house showed you getting gas less than fifteen minutes after you arrived at Cara Morton's house and since they searched your house and car and found not a single trace of Dr. Morton, looks like they're well on the way to clearing you of any involvement. That's why they cut you loose."

I sat down on the couch and buried my face in my hands. Could this nightmare really be almost over? Could a few minutes of footage from the gas station really put an end to all of this for me and my family? It seemed too good to be true. "But Cara is still missing. And until she's found or whoever made her disappear is caught, I'll still be guilty in many people's eyes. How are me and my family supposed to live like that?"

"One step at a time, buddy. This is a win, and you need to stay positive for Paige and the kids. I'll be calling you back later with more information."

Paige came down into the kitchen and was standing behind the couch while I was on the phone. "Bill?" she asked. I simply nodded as I put the phone down. Paige rushed to my side and put a hand on my shoulder.

"What's wrong? What's happened now?"

"Looks like I may have finally caught a break." I told her what Bill had said, and she burst into tears, burying her face against my shoulder. I put my arms around her and held her tight. But I just couldn't feel safe until they found Cara. I still had to search her office to figure out what Peters had been up to. And why he really had Cara's earring in his pocket.

THIRTY-FIVE

AARON NICHOLS

BEFORE

October 4, 2023

"What's this?" Cara looked down at the small purple velvet box with a look of confusion on her face.

"Open it and find out. Go on," I urged when she continued to stare at the box.

We were having lunch in her office. A risky move, but one of her office mates was working remotely and the other two were teaching all afternoon. So, Cara had the office all to herself. We had spread out a picnic lunch on her desk. Nothing fancy, just some sandwiches, chips, and a small cake I picked up at the bakery on my way to work. It was her birthday, and this was all the celebration I could give her. But I more than made up for it with the gift. She gave me a devilish grin before opening the box and gasping. Inside, nestled against the purple silk, was a pair of diamond heart earring set in white gold and dangled from a loop. The hearts were silhouettes with a sixth of a carat of diamonds lining the edge of the hearts and running halfway up the lever back.

"Aaron," she breathed. "They're beautiful. You really shouldn't have."

"Well, I did. Aren't you at least going to try them on?"

Cara gave me a serious look. "You know I can't accept these."

"Why? Don't you like them?"

"You know I love them. But..."

"You're special to me. And I want you to have something that shows you how I feel."

She finally gave me a big smile. "Thank you. You really shouldn't have. But thank you."

"Go ahead. I want to see them on you."

She took her own earrings off and put the earrings in the box on. Just as I'd suspected, they looked amazing on her.

"You look beautiful."

"Really?" she asked doubtfully.

"Come on. You know you're beautiful. Don't act all shy now."

Her laugh was like music to my ears. And she leaned across the desk and kissed me. "I think I'll wear these to the Fling tonight. I got a new outfit that these will be perfect with."

I thought about Bailey's dance recital that night and Cara must've noticed the look on my face.

"What's wrong? You're going to the Fling tonight, right?"

"Of course."

"You better. I still don't know that many people here and I'm allergic to small talk."

"Don't worry," I told her. "I'll be there to save you from any small talk."

. . .

When I arrived at President Marshall's house later that night, Cara was already there and looking amazing in a gray jumpsuit, red heels, and the earrings I'd given her. I didn't go home to change so I wouldn't have to deal with my wife and my daughter's anger and disappointment. I would make it up to Bailey and buy her the expensive charm bracelet she'd been wanting for Christmas. She'd be okay. I hadn't wanted to admit to myself that I really wanted to be here tonight for Cara to help her navigate her first Fling because I knew all too well how intimidating they could be, especially when you're the new kid on the block. But Cara was talking to Dr. Peters. He had his hand on her back and whispered something in her ear, which she laughed at. I watched them, feeling a stab of jealousy. When she spotted me from across the room, she made her excuses and came up to me.

"I was worried that you weren't coming."

"Sorry. I had a late meeting." I'd thought Cara and I would meet up and arrive together. I never heard from her and decided just to head to the party. I didn't know why I was so irritated to see Cara enjoying herself with other people. We'd been hanging out so much, I guess I didn't realize seeing her interacting with other people would bother me so much.

"Dr. Nichols," said Dr. Peters, who'd followed Cara over to where we were standing. He made a show of looking behind me. "Isn't your lovely *wife* going to be joining us tonight?"

I gave him a tight smile. "She had an event to attend with our kids tonight. She won't be able to make it."

"What a pity. Her name is Piper, right?" He knew damn well what her name was. He was just being an asshole. Cara flushed slightly and grabbed a glass of champagne from a server who was passing by.

"It's Paige," I corrected. I didn't ask where Mrs. Peters was. Everyone knew Simone Peters spent October through March in Florida in the couple's second home.

At the mention of Paige's name, Cara waved at someone across the room and, without a word, went to join them. So much for her not knowing many people. She seemed to know quite a few and had no problem mingling.

"That's right. My apologies." Peters gave me his typical shit-eating grin, glanced from me to Cara's retreating form, and walked away.

I made the rounds myself, stopping off to greet President Marshall and his wife Rita. I didn't catch up with Cara again until an hour later when I saw her standing alone on the second-floor deck. I tried not to make it look like I was making a beeline for her, but I made a beeline for her. She gave me a blank look when she saw me approaching, like I was a stranger, which was worse than if she'd looked angry. If she was angry, then I'd at least know she cared. The indifferent look made me feel like a nobody.

"Sorry about Peters. I think he's drunk." I gave her a smile, which she didn't return.

"He didn't say anything that I wasn't already wondering about. When you were late, I thought you were going to show up here with her."

"I was late because I thought we might come together. But I never heard from you."

Cara's expression softened. "I got my hair done after work, and it took longer than I thought."

"You look amazing. Love those earrings. Where'd you get them?"

"Oh, these?" she said, finally smiling. "From an admirer."

"An admirer, huh? And how do you feel about this admirer? Do you admire him too?"

"Well, I'm wearing the earrings. So, what does that tell you?" She took a few steps closer to me, reached out, and gave my tie a quick tug. We laughed.

"It tells me you like the earrings. But what about the dude that gave them to you?" I was smiling at her, waiting for her answer, when an arm unexpectedly encircled my waist.

It was Paige. And the night just went downhill from there.

THIRTY-SIX

DETECTIVE ALONSO

"I got bad news about that kid from the motel," Richards told me when I got back from my debriefing with the chief about the Cara Morton case.

The only difference from the last ass-chewing I'd gotten was a threat to pull me from the case if I didn't have another lead by the end of the week. Not only did the camera footage at the gas station near Nichols' house back up his story of only being at Dr. Morton's house for less than ten minutes, but his lawyer turned in the SIM card from Cara's phone that Nichols conveniently found in the parking lot of the motel. The text messages pulled from the SIM card corroborated his claim that his affair with Dr. Morton had been consensual and he'd received a call from her the day she went missing. The only thing we could get Nichols on was stealing from a crime scene and withholding evidence in an active investigation. The kid in the hospital, whoever the hell he was, was now our only lead. So, instead of asking what the bad news was, I glared at my partner until he flushed and told me.

"The hospital called. He's gone."

"Shit!" I slammed my notepad onto my desk. "When did he die?"

"Oh, sorry. I meant gone as in left the hospital."

I closed my eyes briefly and sighed. "When did he wake up?"

"The hospital didn't bother telling us he woke up late last night. Said they were letting him rest and were going to call us this morning, only by the time the nurse checked on him, he was gone." He quickly added when he saw the murderous look in my eyes, "But we got this from hospital security."

Richards opened the laptop on his desk and pressed a few buttons. A black and white CCTV video started playing. At first, it was just footage of an empty hospital hallway with the occasional nurse and people who looked like either patients or visitors walking down the hall and disappearing out of frame. Impatient to see something useful, I was just about to press fast forward when a thin young man wearing dark-colored warm-up pants and a hospital gown walked out of one of the hospital rooms, moving slowly but purposefully down the hall. The man had one hand on the wall for support as he disappeared out of frame. The next video showed him walking out a side door to the parking lot, after which the camera picked him up as he was getting into a dark gray Honda Accord that drove out of the hospital parking lot.

"Please tell me one of those cameras picked up the plate number."

Richards looked like he'd rather not reply. "No. Sorry. But the kid didn't have a cell phone on him, and there wasn't one found in that motel room he rented. The hospital switchboard showed he placed a call at about four this morning from his room."

"Have you found out who he was calling?" I asked impatiently.

"The number belongs to a Beverly Miller. We haven't been able to get ahold of her, but we got an address."

"Then let's go," I told him, grabbing my coat from the back of my chair and praying something good would come out of this visit to turn around my shitty day.

Only when we arrived at Beverly Miller's address, the apartment was empty. Whoever lived there had cleared out in a hurry and not paid their rent, according to the landlord.

"Hey, Alonso, back here."

Richards' voice was coming from the bedroom. I followed his voice and found myself in a room that looked like a makeshift hospital room with a hospital bed, IV poles, and a closet full of medication and medical supplies. Some of the medical supplies had a name on them. Serenity Village Nursing Home. Richards and I gave each other a look.

"Looks like Beverly Miller, or whoever was living here, was stealing medical supplies," I said.

"For who? That kid doesn't have cancer. Besides suffering from malnutrition and an infection, the doctors said there was nothing wrong with him. They have no clue what was being administered to him through that port in his chest."

"Maybe it's Beverly Miller who's sick."

"And maybe someone at Serenity Village Nursing Home knows who this woman is."

"Get forensics in here. And I need everything you can find on Beverly Miller."

THIRTY-SEVEN

PAIGE NICHOLS

AFTER

December 21, 2023

"Mrs. Nichols? I wasn't expecting you."

"I'm sorry. I stopped by hoping you might have time to see me. It's important."

"Please, come back to my office." Jan Singleton gave me a quizzical look and headed down the hall to her office.

"Thank you. I won't take up too much of your time."

"Is this about your husband?"

"No. It's about an old friend of yours from Century City."

She gave me an uneasy look. "Century City? How do you know I used to work there? That was thirty years ago."

"My father was Tim Hamilton. I know you knew him."

The older woman visible stiffened, and her face grew hard and wary. "If this is some kind of confrontation over something..."

"No!" I said quickly when she was about to get up and show me the door. "Whatever happened between you and my dad all those years ago is none of my business. I need to know about Beverly and Gerald Morton." She sat back down as confusion flitted across her face.

"Bev and Gerry? What about them?"

"Their daughter Cara is the Roberson professor who went missing and my husband is a person of interest in her disappearance."

Jan Singleton looked down at her lap. "I saw that in the paper. And I'm sorry you and your family are going through this. But I don't understand what her parents have to do with this? The papers said Gerry has Alzheimer's, and I haven't seen Bev since before they split up."

"What can you tell me about them? Anything at all that might help them find Cara will help. Please," I added when she continued to stare at me.

"Well," she said, and then sighed. "Bev Shepard was my friend for the few years I worked at Century City. We both worked in accounting. I was an accounts payable clerk, and she was the secretary to the department head. She had a huge crush on Gerry, and I had a huge crush on..."

"My dad," I finished for her. It surprised me I felt so detached about having a conversation with the woman whose involvement with my father had hurt my mother so much and could have torn apart my family.

"Yes," she whispered. "We also bonded over the fact that we were both in interracial relationships. My ex-husband was white."

"What was Bev like?"

"She was a nice enough girl," Jan said, shrugging. "Pretty. Funny. Friendly. Stylish. She had a lot of admirers at work, at least when she was at work."

"What do you mean?"

"Bev was always sick. She almost lost her job over absenteeism."

"What was wrong with her?"

"Honestly, nothing."

"Nothing? Was she skipping work on purpose?"

"I thought so at first. Thought she might have a man she was sneaking off to see. But she seemed loyal to Gerry."

"Then why was she missing so much work?"

"For the attention."

"What do you mean?"

"I mean, one day I saw her throwing up in the bathroom. She looked awful, and she ended up going home. I had to fill in for her taking notes for a meeting that afternoon and went to get a notepad from her desk drawer and found a bottle of syrup of ipecac."

Her meaning sank in. "She was making herself sick?"

Jan nodded. "I noticed a pattern. She'd only be out sick for three days because if you were sick over three days, you needed a doctor's excuse. Every illness she had miraculously went away after three days. When she came back, there were flowers, cards, and candy waiting for her from her boss and other guys at work who were in love with her. People would stop by throughout the day to ask how she was feeling. And she ate it up. Loved the attention. She was still living at home, and she told me once that the only time her parents ever paid her or her sister any attention was when they were sick. I first met her in the break room when she cut her hand real bad on a broken glass. Left a nasty scar behind on her palm and now that I think about it, she probably cut her hand on purpose."

"If she were your patient, what would your diagnosis be?"

"Ever hear of Factitious Disorder?"

"No. What's that?"

"You may know it as Munchausen Syndrome."

"When someone fakes illness or purposefully makes themselves sick?" I remembered learning about it in a college psych class.

"Right. Usually done for attention and sympathy."

"What happened to Bev?"

"She got pregnant, and Gerry married her, and she stopped working. We used to hang out occasionally, but she had a difficult pregnancy, and she was under a lot of stress from her family to leave Gerry and come back home. Her parents didn't mind her having a black friend, but a black husband and a half black baby wasn't something they'd ever accept. I tried to be there for her, but I had issues of my own I was dealing with, and we drifted apart. By the time she gave birth to Cara, I'd already left town."

Neither of us needed to mention what those issues were. But another thought came to me, one that made my stomach turn.

"I've heard that Cara was a sickly child, and they could never figure out what was wrong with her. You don't think..."

"Munchausen by Proxy, parents purposefully making their kids sick. Wouldn't surprise me."

"I was told Gerry caught her in the act, put her out and divorced her, and Cara got better after that."

We were both silent for a few seconds.

"I'm sorry, Mrs. Nichols. But I'm going to have to cut this short. My next appointment will be here soon." She got up, and I reluctantly did the same and followed her to the door.

"Thank you so much for your time. I really appreciate you speaking with me." I was out the door and halfway down the hall when she called out to me.

"Can you give your mother a message for me?"

I froze and slowly turned to face her. What in the world could she possibly want me to tell my mother besides an apology for almost tearing her marriage and family apart? But to my surprise it wasn't an apology.

"Please tell your mother that what happened to me wasn't her fault."

"Excuse me?" I gave her a quizzical look, and she continued.

"She sent a letter to my husband informing him of my affair with your father. But I intercepted that letter before he ever saw it and destroyed it. In fact, that letter made me realize how far I'd fallen to the bottom of the barrel. I contacted my sister in Dayton, who said I could come and live with her. My car was packed, and I was planning to be gone before my husband got off work." She was looking beyond me like she was watching the memory from afar.

"What happened?" I couldn't take my eyes off her face.

"He got home early and caught me, dragged me out of the car and beat the shit out of me. He'd slashed my throat when a neighbor pulled him off me. After my husband's conviction for attempted murder, I left town and hadn't been back to Oakmont in decades. My ex-husband served twenty years in prison and was still living here. He died last year. I decided it was time to come home. So, despite what your mother may have intended, that letter probably saved my life."

"Is that all?" I asked her softly.

"My life was a living hell, Paige. And I was looking for a savior and thought I'd found one in your father. I was just looking for a way out. Any way out. And honestly, he could've been anybody." She walked back into her office and, without saying goodbye, she closed the door.

"How does any of this help find Cara?" Ros asked. I'd called my sister on the way home from talking to Jan Singleton. I hadn't told Aaron any of this because I didn't want him to get his hopes up over something that might mean nothing. Plus, I knew he'd just tell me to stay out of it.

I told her what Cara's father had said to me at the nursing

home, conveniently leaving out the part about me pretending to be Cara.

"He could have been scared Bev would get custody of Cara and was paying her to stay away."

"Exactly," I said. "And Gerry now has Alzheimer's and can't take care of himself..."

"Cara may have cut off the money or not known about the arrangement her father had with her mother."

"But would Bev really have come back after all these years and killed her own daughter over money?" As a mother, that was unthinkable to me.

"If she was capable of making her infant daughter sick on purpose for attention, then she's capable of anything. Did she say anything about Sammy?"

"No, why?" I asked carefully.

"Why?" my sister repeated. "I don't care how many degrees that heifer has now. She killed our dog, P. I'd have at least given her a good slap for Sammy."

I didn't respond. "I'll call you later. I need to talk to Detective Alonso."

But talking to Alonso proved to be impossible. I tried all afternoon to get ahold of her, only to be told she was busy, and they'd give her my message to call me. So, I headed to my next appointment of the day for a conversation that was long overdue.

I'd been waiting for almost half an hour, sipping slowly on a glass of Moscato and periodically looking at my watch when Dr. Natalie Drew finally arrived at Nova's bar. Besides the bartender, a young black woman with a frohawk, we were the only patrons at the bar at 2:30 on a Tuesday afternoon.

"Perrier with lime," she told the bartender as she took off her long, black wool coat, revealing the burgundy cowl-necked sweater dress beneath it, and draped it across the barstool next to her. Once seated, she finally looked at me expectantly, without a trace of warmth in her eyes. But what had I been expecting? That she'd throw her arms around me, tell me all was forgiven?

"Thanks for coming." My nerves were shot, and I drained the rest of my wine in one gulp.

Her tone was suitably frosty. "I'm not sure why we couldn't have done this over the phone."

She picked at imaginary lint on her sleeve. And I took in how much she'd changed since the last time I'd seen her. Not the horrific confrontation in her home, but when she'd been a valued friend, mentor, and confidant.

I'd met Natalie Michaels my junior year when I was a physical therapy major and volunteered in the rehab unit at the university hospital where she was a nurse. We'd hit it off instantly, and I loved my time working in the rehab unit. Natalie called me a natural and urged me to change my major from physical therapy to nursing. I became a nurse because of her. I knew she was married to a man she called Jack. But I'd never met her husband and assumed Michaels was her married name. We'd had so much in common despite our twelve-year age difference. When I'd known her; she had a smile that lit up a room, a wicked sense of humor, and a contagious laugh. She was easily the smartest person I knew. And she was probably still all those things to people she loved and cared about. But that no longer included me.

She took a sip of her drink and gave me an impatient look. "Well?" Her voice was nasal and higher-pitched than I remembered. She hadn't sounded like this during her presentation at the mixer last month and I chalked it up to nerves. But her curt tone made my face flush hot with embarrassment.

"I didn't know your husband was the head at Highland when I went on that school tour, and I sure as hell didn't know you'd be at the Gamma mixer," I said, purposefully avoiding saying Jackson's name. "I'm a married mother of two and I have a hell of a lot more on my mind these days than you and your husband. I'd appreciate if you didn't report me to the police again because this is a small town and I'm sure this won't be the only time our paths will cross. But you have my word that when that happens, I will walk the other way." I pulled a twenty from my purse and was about to toss it on the bar when she stopped me.

"PG, wait."

I paused, noticing her confused expression, and surprised she'd called me by my college nickname.

"Police? What are you talking about?"

Was she really going to play dumb? "You reported me to the police for stalking after you saw me on the Highland tour and then at Nova on the same day."

"No, I didn't. Why would I do that?" She seemed genuinely confused.

"All I know is I was told a Dr. Natalie Drew made a report claiming I was stalking her and her husband."

Natalie relaxed and, in doing so, briefly became the Natalie I remembered. She let out a sigh and set her drink down on the bar. "You know, when you called me wanting to talk, I thought..." Her voice trailed off, and I instantly filled in the gap.

"What? You thought I was going to tell you me and Jackson were a thing again?" I let out a mirthless laugh. "Girl, I got off that train a very long time ago. I was stupid and naïve and whether you want to believe it, he played both of us." I'd been shoved off that train. Hard. But I didn't want to think about that part. Instead, I signaled to the bartender for another glass of Moscato.

"I know. And I'm sorry. You weren't the first or the last. But you were the only one I knew personally. The only one I considered a friend. I took all my anger out on you."

I had to ask. "Why do you stay with him?"

Natalie let out a short, bitter laugh. "Why are you staying in your marriage?" I shouldn't have been so surprised she knew about Aaron's affair with a woman who'd gone missing. Everyone in town knew.

"I love Aaron. He's a good man who made a big mistake and is trying to fix it." Natalie's eyebrows shot up and I quickly added, "And no, he didn't hurt Cara Morton."

She studied me for a few seconds while she sipped at her drink. "It must be nice to have that much faith in your spouse. I hope it's not misplaced."

"You didn't answer my question." I couldn't hide the defensiveness in my voice.

She took the lime wedge out of her glass and bit into it before finally replying. "I stopped loving Jackson a long time ago. I'm not sure he ever loved me. Our marriage is more of a business arrangement now. There are things we both wanted out of life that came easier by being married. He wouldn't have gotten his position as the head of Highland Academy if he'd been a single man. He comes from family money, allowing me to live a lifestyle I'd have never had on my own. And I'm not letting any of his little side chicks push me aside until I'm good and ready to go."

"Sounds lonely."

"I have a friend," she said, her eyes suddenly full of warmth that hadn't been there when she'd talked about Jackson. "Or at least we started off as friends, but it turned into something more. We met years ago at a medical convention in London. He owns a vineyard in the south of France. I spend as much time there with him as I can, and when I retire from my practice in a few years, Jackson and I will divorce, and I'll be moving to France permanently with a fat bank account. So don't feel sorry for me. I've got everything I need."

We were silent for a while before I remembered what she'd said. "Did you really not report me for stalking you?"

"You have my word that I didn't. But I think I might know who did."

I sat up on my barstool and leaned forward. "Really? Who?"

"Cara Morton."

"Cara? How do you..." And then I remembered leaving the Gamma mixer and Cara looking from Natalie to me and the amused expression on her face. She figured there was history between us and set out to find out what it was.

"Seeing you again after all these years really threw me for a loop. After the mixer, I ended up down here in the bar. I'd already had a few drinks in me by the time Dr. Morton sat next to me and bought us a round of drinks. And you know me, PG. I can't hold my liquor worth a damn. And she offered a friendly ear for me to bend."

"And you told her about me and Jackson."

Natalie nodded. "And about seeing you twice that day. She told me I should report you for stalking, and got annoyed when I told her I had no intention of doing that. There was something wrong with her, I could tell right away. I probably should have warned you about her. She must have been the one to report you pretending to be me."

"Wow," was all I could think to say. I should have known. That woman would stop at nothing to ruin our lives.

"I'm sorry. After seeing you again, I knew I'd finally have to face what I'd done to you."

And there it was, the elephant in the room even bigger than my having slept with her husband.

"You knew?" I asked quietly.

"I found out the next morning when I heard they had admitted you, and I accessed your medical records. You said you have children. So, I assume there were no complications from the... fall?"

I'd expected her to call it an accident, but to her credit, she didn't. I'd told the truth at the police station when I'd said Natalie and I had gotten into a physical altercation when she'd confronted me about Jackson. But what I'd never told anyone, including my sister, was that as I was leaving her home, Natalie followed me out the door screaming and shouting, and calling me names that still made me flinch when I thought back on the day. She shoved me, causing me to fall down the half dozen stone steps leading to their circular drive. I was scraped up and shaken, having sprained my wrist. But I drove myself to the ER, where I began to cramp and bleed in the waiting room. I'd been eight weeks pregnant and was having a miscarriage. I didn't even know I'd been pregnant. And worse still was that after they released me from the hospital, as I was walking from my car to my dorm and still bleeding from the D & C I'd received, I got arrested for assault and spent a night in jail. The charges were dropped, and they released me the next morning, but the damage to my emotional state was already done. I barely finished out the semester and never went back, opting to finish my nursing degree at the local community college after taking a year off.

"No complications. I have healthy nine-year-old twins."

"PG, I..."

"Don't," I said, holding up a hand. I didn't want to hear her apology. I'd forgiven Natalie a long time ago. Jackson was the one I blamed for putting us both in the position he did. And I blamed myself even more for being so stupid and trusting.

"And he wasn't worth any of it."

"No," I said, reaching out and squeezing her hand. "He certainly wasn't."

. . .

Aaron and I picked up the kids from my sister's later that day. We had our first dinner together in over a week. We still hadn't told them what was going on, but they knew, anyway, or at least some of it. The kids were oddly quiet when they got home and couldn't take their eyes off Aaron.

"Daddy, did you hurt that lady?" Bryce asked at dinner. Aaron's fork froze halfway to his mouth.

"Where did you hear that?" I asked my son. Aaron met my gaze and shook his head, then reached over and squeezed our son's shoulder.

"My friend Max from school said you hurt some lady, and you were going to prison." Bryce's bottom lip trembled, and tears filled his eyes. Aaron got up and knelt by our son's chair. Pulling him into a tight hug.

"Don't worry, little man. I didn't do anything wrong and I'm not going anywhere."

By this time, Bailey was also crying and jumped out of her seat to join the hug. Aaron put his other arm around our daughter and squeezed both of our kids tight.

"Come on now," I said. "This food is going to get cold, and no one's going to prison." But Bailey was still crying, looking from me to Aaron.

"Go ahead," said Bryce, nudging his sister. "Tell them."

"It's all my fault," said Bailey in a voice thick with tears.

"What's your fault?" I asked my daughter, which made her cry even harder.

"You are such a baby, Bailey," exclaimed Bryce, rolling his eyes.

"What's this about, baby girl?" asked Aaron, looking concerned.

"Bailey was in the garage looking for Christmas presents, and she knocked over an old can of red paint. I helped her clean it up with one of Mom's dishtowels and we kept rinsing it and rinsing and the paint wouldn't come out. So, I put it in the washer when Daddy did a load of laundry."

"And I overheard you arguing because you found the towel and thought Daddy killed that lady. And now you're going to get a divorce and Daddy is going to jail," said Bailey, before dissolving into tears again.

"And why would you be looking for Christmas presents? Santa..." I began before Bryce cut me off.

"Come on, Mom. We figured out you guys were Santa when we were seven."

We calmed Bailey down and finished dinner, neither of us able to look at each other after having accused each other of the unthinkable. But one thing was clear. We didn't trust each other at all.

"Are you going to work tonight?" Aaron asked, surprised to see me in work scrubs.

"I was already on the schedule," I replied, reaching for my coat, "and I can't call off tonight because we still need to pay Bill."

"It won't be like this forever. I'll get another job and you can go back to studying for your web design certificate. And..." His voice trailed off, and he looked away.

"And?" I prompted.

"And I hope when this is all over, we can work on us."

Did I forgive my husband for all he'd put me and the kids through? Mostly. Was I ready to just hand my heart back to him and trust him not to break it again? No. That would be a process. "Let's just take it one day at time and not make promises we can't keep."

Aaron nodded and kissed me on the cheek. He walked me to my car and watched me drive away. I'd reached the corner when my phone rang. It was Serenity Village. Why were they calling me?

"Hello?"

"Hey, Paige. It's Sam. Just a heads up. You might not want to come in tonight."

"Why?" I was still working under the radar at Serenity.

"The police are here. Something about stolen medical supplies from Serenity found at a crime scene. They're in Sue's office now. And..."

"And?"

"In all the confusion, Mr. Morton got out of the building."

"What? How?" I pulled my car onto a side street and parked. Alzheimer's patients all wore wrist alarms that alerted the staff if they tried to leave the building. There was a special key that had to be used to remove the bracelets.

"Damned if I know. That lady who comes to read to patients found his bracelet on the floor next to the back exit."

"Lynette?"

"Yeah, I think that's her name. I never really pay her much attention."

"What about the cameras? Did you look to see if one of them picked him up or which way he could have gone?"

"Those cameras are just for show for the families. They don't work."

I sighed with frustration. "Are you kidding me?"

"Look, we need to find him before the press finds out we lost him. We're already hanging on by a thread. They could shut us down and some of these people have nowhere else to go."

I saw what he was getting at. "You want me to drive around looking for him, right?"

"Pretty please. He shouldn't be too hard to spot. He's not wearing a coat, and he's got house slippers on."

What choice did I have? "Fine. I'll do it."

"Thanks, Paige. Here's his address. He could be trying to get back home."

"Why do you think that?"

"Because it was all he's been talking about all day. Going home. And not his heavenly home either."

After I hung up, Sam texted me Mr. Morton's address, and I drove slowly up and down every side street I could on the way to his house. If he wasn't at home, I'd have no choice but to call the police. I'd heard about too many cognitively impaired elderly people who'd gotten lost and never made it back home. And I also still felt like shit for pretending to be Cara. It's most likely why he was trying to get back home, thinking Cara was waiting for him.

Half an hour later, I finally arrived at the Morton house and parked in the driveway. There was no light on in the house, so I waited for a little while to see if he showed up. Serenity Village was a good three miles away on foot, although I supposed could have gotten on the bus or been picked up by a stranger. But it was only 30 degrees out and according to Sam he had no coat or regular shoes on. As every worst-case scenario flashed through my mind, a flicker of light in the house caught my attention. I looked again and saw nothing. Must have been my imagination. But only a few minutes later, I saw a flash of light again. This time there was no doubt. Someone was in the house. Mr. Morton must have gotten here and let himself in. I got out of the car and went up to the door and tried the doorknob. It was locked. I rang the bell. No response. I pounded on the door with the palm of my hand.

"Mr. Morton! Open the door! I know you're in there." No one came, and I went around to the back sliding door that led to the patio. I cupped my hands to look inside before knocking on the glass, and detected movement.

"Mr. Morton!"

It all happened so fast. One minute I was knocking furiously on the glass door, and the next thing I knew, the glass door slid open, and a hand reached out, grabbed me by the front of my scrubs and dragged me into the darkened house, shoving me onto the floor. It was pitch dark inside the house, and I could barely see the person looming over me.

A light switched on, and I locked eyes with the person looking down at me.

"What?" I managed to get out before my shock wore off. "What the hell are you doing here?"

THIRTY-EIGHT

DETECTIVE ALONSO

I was back at the station after spending most of my afternoon at Beverly Miller's recently vacated apartment, and then at Serenity Village Nursing Home. No one there had ever heard of Beverly Miller, but when we showed the staff her picture, they'd immediately identified her.

Serenity Village was so short-staffed, no one even noticed supplies had gone missing. I'd barely gotten to my desk when my phone beeped with an email notification. Forensics had sent me the report on the prints found in Beverly Miller's apartment. I quickly pulled up my email on my computer because my eyes were too tired to read the tiny print on my phone. Richards leaned over my shoulder, reading my screen.

"Shit!" he whispered.

Shit was an understatement. Beverly Miller was one name in a long list of aliases for a woman who was wanted in Indiana for fraud, theft, and tax evasion. There was a list of names she went by, including Beverly Miller and Beverly Rogers. The last name on the list caused Richards and me to look at each other.

Beverly Lynette Morton.

THIRTY-NINE

PAIGE NICHOLS

AFTER

December 21, 2023

"Lynette? What are you doing here? Where is Mr. Morton?"

"What am I doing here? I could ask the same of you, Mrs. Nichols. What are you doing here?"

"Mr. Morton has gone missing from the nursing home, and I came by to see if he was here. And you didn't answer my question."

"Gerry isn't missing. He wanted to come home, so I brought him home. Now why don't you have a seat here at the table and we can talk about this?" She held out her hands to help me up.

"Why would you do that? You're not his next of kin." What was she thinking, taking an Alzheimer's patient out of the nursing home? She had to know he wasn't in his right mind. "He needs to be at Serenity for his own safety. He's got Alzheimer's. He needs someone taking care of him."

"I'll be taking care of him. He's my husband, therefore, my responsibility."

"Husband?" I thought I couldn't have heard her right. It took me several seconds to connect the dots. "You're Beverly Morton? You're Cara's mother?" She looked nothing like the woman in the Century City company picture my mom had sent me. I wouldn't have recognized her just like Jackson Drew hadn't recognized me after all these years. I pushed her hands away, quickly scrambled to my feet, and pulled my phone out of my pocket. Quick as a flash, Lynette snatched the phone out of my hand.

"What is wrong with you? Give me my phone back!" I reached for it, and she held it out of my reach.

"Sorry, Mrs. Nichols. But I can't let you do that."

I stared at her in disbelief. "Where is Mr. Morton?"

"I was about to tell you. He's in here."

Lynette left the kitchen, and I followed her into the next room, which was a TV room. Sitting in a recliner in front of the TV was Mr. Morton, dressed in the same pajamas and robe he had left the nursing home in. The room was dark, and the only light came from the TV. That was the flicker I'd seen from outside. He glanced over at the two of us standing in the doorway and gave us a blank look.

"Mr. Morton? Are you okay?" But he merely stared through me and then went back to watching his football game.

"I need to get him back to the nursing home before they call the police. You had no right taking him."

"I have every right. I told you, I'm still his wife. We never divorced. And with Cara missing, I am his next of kin, and I am well within my rights to take him out of that nursing home."

"Then why did you remove his alarm bracelet and sneak him out the back exit if you're his next of kin?"

"That's none of your business," she snapped.

Before I could respond, a girl who looked to be about sixteen came rushing into the kitchen. She was thin and pale and had long, light brown hair pulled back from her face in a ponytail.

"Are you the doctor?" she asked me.

"Beth, I told you to go to your room."

"But Adam is getting worse. We need to get him back to the hospital."

"No!" Lynette's face was an angry red mask.

"I'm a nurse. What's the problem?" I tried to walk toward Beth when Lynette blocked me.

"Mom, please!" the girl cried. "Let her look at him."

I pushed past Lynette and followed Beth down the hall to the back bedroom. Lying on the bed was a young man, extremely thin, with sunken eyes and dark circles. He was sweating profusely. I rushed over to him, put my hand on his forehead. He was burning up with fever. His heartbeat was erratic. I recognized him immediately from my husband's description. This was the young man from the motel. The John Doe hit by the truck. The man that Aaron claimed had been selling Cara drugs.

"Your name is Beth, right? Who is this young man?" I asked the girl. "Has he been given any drugs? Is he an addict?"

"He's my brother, and he's got cancer!" said Beth, sitting on the side of the bed. "We got evicted from our apartment and they wouldn't let us back inside to get my brother's cancer meds. I think he's got an infection. He's always got some kind of infection because chemo compromised his immune system."

"You were the one taking medical supplies from Serenity, aren't you?" I whirled around to confront Lynette, who was watching from the doorway. And then an even more horrible thought came to me.

"What have you given him?"

Lynette feigned confusion. "What are you talking about? My daughter just told you what was going on." Her voice was flat. "Can you treat him or not?"

"He needs to be in the hospital, and you need to tell me what you've done to make him sick. Because I know all about you, Beverly, or Lynette, or whatever the hell you're calling yourself these days."

"What's she talking about, Mom?" Beth looked from me to her mother, confusion clouding her face.

"If you won't help us, then get out of my son's room." Lynette took a step toward me. There was fury in her eyes.

"Unless you want your son to die, you need to tell me what the hell you've been giving him to make him sick. Just like you did to Cara."

"Cara was sick!" Lynette screamed back. "They could never find out what was wrong with her, but she was a very sick little girl. Just like Adam." She looked over at her son lovingly.

"It's true," said Beth frantically. "He's sick! He's been battling cancer for years."

Not in the mood to argue with a crazy bitch and a deluded kid, I lunged for my phone, which was in her jeans pocket. But Lynette was quicker. She pulled the phone from her pocket and slammed it against the edge of the desk she was standing next to, cracking the screen.

"No!" I exclaimed. "Why did you do that? Do you want your son to die?"

"He won't die. Because you're going to treat him."

"Is Cara dead?" I watched her carefully. "Did you kill her? Where is she?"

Instead of answering, Lynette grabbed Beth by the arm, dragged her out of the room and slammed the door shut behind them, locking me inside with Adam.

I pounded and kicked on the door for almost five minutes, trying to get out. Adam moaned and doubled up on the bed. I knew what was coming next and rushed over to the bed, grabbing the trash can next to it in time for him to vomit violently into it, filling the room with a sour stench. I helped him lie back down and wiped his mouth with a napkin that was on the night-stand beside a bowl of what looked like broth.

"Who are you?" Adam's voice was raspy and low.

"Don't talk. I'm here to help. Have you taken any meds? Has your mother given you anything?"

"Just that." His eyes locked onto the bowl of broth on the nightstand.

I picked it up. There wasn't much left. I sniffed it and determined it was chicken broth. As the broth sloshed around the bowl, I saw a bright yellow smiley face design on the bottom about an inch wide. Not thinking anything of it, I set the bowl back on the nightstand when I remembered something Sam had told me about Mr. Ramsey. I put a finger in the bowl, running it around the edge of the smiley face. It wasn't a design. It was a sticker.

I tugged at the sticker and pulled it up from the bottom of the bowl and looked at the opposite side. Part of a bandage was stuck to the underside, a bandage dark with blood and pus. Lynette had taken part of Mr. Ramsey's discarded, infection-laden bandages and put them in her son's soup to make him sick. I instantly dropped the sticker and watched it float on top of the broth, the smiley face mocking me as I fought to keep the horror that seized me off my face. How could she have done this to her own son?

The door opened and Beth slipped inside. She had a bottle of water, a bowl of ice and a dishtowel. "Mom told me to bring you these. How is he? Can you treat him?" She looked at her now sleeping brother with obvious concern, then turned hope-filled eyes to me.

"Beth, listen to me. We need to get him out of here. He's very sick, and I don't have what I need here to treat him."

"What did you mean when you said my mom made him sick?"

"That's not important now. He needs help. Will you help me get him out of here?"

Beth looked torn and looked back at the door. "But how?" she whispered.

"Do you have a phone?"

Beth shook her head. "Mom won't let us have cell phones, and they have shut the phone service in the house off."

"Then you need to go get help."

"I don't know. Mom will know I'm gone and get mad." This girl was so scared of her mother she'd risk her brother's life to avoid her anger. What had Lynette done to these kids?

"Then I'll go." I got up and pulled the chest of drawers away from the only window in the room. Beth shoved the chest of drawers back under the window.

"What is your problem? Your brother is going to die!"

"Beth!" Lynette's voice echoed down the hall and the girl froze.

"You'll just leave and not come back."

"I swear to you, I won't. I need to get help..."

"Cara said she would help us too," said Beth, cutting me off. "But she lied." Beth's eyes filled with tears. "She used me and Adam. Made us do bad things for her. Acted like she cared about us and said we could come live with her. But she lied and now she's gone! She got what she deserved."

"Beth," I said slowly. "Where is Cara? Do you know what happened to her? Did your mom hurt her?"

"Mom!" At the sound of her daughter's voice, Lynette came rushing into the room. "I caught her trying to get out of the window."

Lynette walked over to the window and pulled the curtain back, revealing that the bedroom window had bars over it. There was no way I could have gotten out.

"Nice try. They had a break-in years ago, and Gerry had them installed on all the windows facing the back of the house.

Now treat my son." Before they left the room, Beth looked back and gave me an unreadable look.

I got Adam to sit up and made him drink some of the water, which he could barely keep down. I stripped him out of his sweat-soaked clothing down to his underwear and saw the chemo port in his chest. What had she been administering to him through that port? Or was it just a prop to make him and everyone else think he had cancer? He was so young. Seventeen if I had to guess. I used the rest of the water to wet the dishtowel and filled it with ice cubes to wipe his body down with to reduce his fever.

"Did Cara send you? Is she coming to get us?" Adam's voice was even weaker and raspier than it had been before, and his eyes were wide and feverish.

"Was she supposed to come get you guys?"

"She promised she would. But she wasn't good at keeping promises."

"Adam, how long have you known Cara?"

"My mom moved us here in the spring. Said she wanted us to meet our big sister. But that was a lie. I overheard her arguing with Cara."

"About what?"

"Money. Cara's father had been paying her a couple of grand a month. But then he got sick, and Cara took over his finances and cut Mom off."

"What happened after that?"

"Cara wanted to be a bone marrow donor for me. But Mom said no. Cara snuck me to the doctor behind her back and they said I don't have cancer," he said in a weak voice. He tried to sit up but fell back against the sweat-soaked pillow. "But that can't be right because I'm always so sick. But Cara changed after that doctor's visit. She said she'd become our legal guardian, but we had to do stuff for her."

"Like what?"

"Score coke for her. Steal your husband's phone and wipe all the text messages off it. Follow people and spy on them for her. Steal. She was mad when your kids' party didn't get cancelled. So, she had Beth put some stuff on the pizzas." He looked away from me at the wall next to the bed. But whether he was embarrassed or ashamed, I couldn't tell. Several seconds passed before he continued. "Each time we did stuff for her, we'd ask when we could come live with her, and she always had something else for us to do. I even downloaded the application for legal guardianship for her to fill out."

"Did she fill it out?" I asked, already knowing the answer.

"She kept telling me it wasn't the right time. It would never be the right time. She was a lying bitch. She's no better than Mom."

"Adam, do you know where Cara is?" He shook his head no. "Why come back to your Mom? Why not stay in the hospital where you were safe?"

"Beth was still with Mom. After I woke up in the hospital, I called home thinking Mom would be at work. But she answered the phone and told me if I didn't come back home, they were leaving town without me. I wanted to protect my sister. She still wants to believe Mom isn't a horrible person."

"I'm not a horrible person," said Lynette from the doorway. Adam visibly flinched. I hadn't even heard the door open and wondered how much she'd overheard. I stood and faced her.

"You've been feeding your son broth with an infected bandage in it. What else have you been doing to him? You made your daughter Cara so sick when she was a little girl that her father had been paying you for years to stay away from her."

"He was paying me alimony!"

"That wasn't alimony. That was stay-away-you-crazy-bitch money. Were you and Cara in on setting Aaron up for sexual harassment together?"

"Are you kidding me? Your husband's wandering dick got him in trouble. That had nothing to do with me."

"But the apple didn't fall far from the tree, did it? Cara's just like you. A manipulative, narcissistic liar worming her way into people's lives and destroying them. Only she picked strangers while you preyed on your own kids, making them sick so you could get attention."

"Mom? What's she talking about? Have you been making Adam sick?" Beth had come in behind her mother and took a step toward her.

"I told you it was her," said Adam, his voice sounding much weaker than it was moments before. "Why wouldn't you believe me?"

"Mom, why?" Beth's voice was full of tears.

"Shut up, Beth!" Lynette backhanded her daughter across the face and had drawn her hand back to hit the girl again when I grabbed the nearest thing to me, which was the bowl of soup and flung it at Lynette. She managed to deflect the bowl, sending it crashing against the wall next to the bed.

Lynette flew at me, her face contorted in rage. She caught me off guard and got a handful of my hair, tugging it so hard my eyes watered.

"Is this what you did to Cara? Attack her when she threw facts up in your face," I screamed, as I tried to pull her hands out of my hair without luck. "Did she remember what you'd done to her?"

Lynette was holding on for dear life until, in desperation, I kneed her in the gut. She let out a grunt, and I shoved her away from me so hard I lost my balance and fell back onto the bed, landing on Adam, who attempted to catch me. For a few seconds, the only sound was my heavy breathing and Lynette's groaning as she clutched her stomach. She straightened and was about to lunge for me again when the sound of sirens, faint at first, then quickly getting louder, stopped outside the house.

Lynette tried to run out the bedroom door, but someone blocked her path. It was Gerry Morton. He looked as angry and alert as I imagine he was the day he'd caught Lynette abusing their daughter. He raised an aerosol canister of bug spray and sprayed Lynette in the face.

"Get out of my house! I told you never to come back!" Tears streamed down the old man's face and Lynette shrieked in pain as the caustic spray hit her eyes and skin.

The sound of the front door being kicked in and police flooding into the house was music to my ears. And I gently took the now empty can of bug spray out of Mr. Morton's hand.

"Thank you," I told him. But his eyes were blank again and stared ahead at nothing.

I was back home two hours later. The kids were already in bed and Aaron held me on the couch as I shook and cried. I could have died tonight. They arrested Lynette, and she was being treated for chemical burns to her eyes and face. Adam was back in the hospital, in serious but stable condition, Beth was with social services, and Mr. Morton was safely back at Serenity. It could have been so much worse. But a sudden thought made me sit up.

"What's wrong?" Aaron stared at me in alarm.

Jan Singleton's voice echoed in my head. *"We met in the break room when she cut her hand real bad on a broken glass. Left a nasty scar behind on her palm..."*

When Lynette had offered me her hands to help me up from the kitchen floor. There was no scar on either of her palms. There was no way that woman was Beverly Morton.

FORTY

DETECTIVE ALONSO

"Anything?" asked Richards, as I emerged from the interrogation room after an hour of interviewing Beverly Morton. Her eyes and lips were swollen, and her face was an angry red from just above her eyebrows to her chin, chemical burns from the bug spray Gerald Morton had sprayed her with. They were shiny from whatever topical treatment ER had treated her with. But she'd live.

"Insists she's done nothing wrong. Apparently, she and Morton never divorced, and she's claiming the house is hers now. She has no clue what happened to Cara. Damn, I need coffee, preferably on a drip." A yawn split my face. I was exhausted, and this night was only going to get longer.

"She has no right to anything as far as Gerald Morton is concerned."

"What are you talking about? And where the hell have you been?" I couldn't keep the irritation out of my voice. Richards had a way of making me work for information, unveiling it slowly like he was Hercule Poirot, and I wasn't in the mood for it. Not when he was supposed to be in the interrogation room with me and never showed up.

"While you were in there with bug spray Bae, I got a call from Paige Nichols. She's convinced that's not Beverly Morton in there. Morton supposedly had a distinctive scar on her palm and this one," he said, gesturing toward the woman behind the two-way glass in the interrogation room, "doesn't."

At first, I was unconvinced by Richards' revelation. Perhaps her scar had healed, I thought, or maybe she was somehow covering it up. I was sure the woman I'd been speaking to was Beverly Morton. But then something clicked in my brain. I pushed past Richards and made a beeline straight for the young deputy I'd run into earlier who was sitting at her desk in the corner. She looked up in alarm to see me looming over her.

"Do you still have the photos King County PD sent around of that body in the freezer? With the close-ups of all the body parts?"

"Yes, ma'am." She quickly pulled the stack of photos from her desk drawer and handed them to me.

I flipped through them until I found the one I'd remembered. It was a close-up photo of a hand with a thick band of white scar tissue bisecting the right palm. "What else do we know about this victim?"

"The body was that of a woman in her late twenties who died from blunt force trauma to the head, and they estimate the body was most likely in that freezer for at least twenty years."

"Jesus," I whispered, as excitement hacked its way through the thick fog of my fatigue. "Paige Nichols is right. The woman we've got isn't Beverly Morton."

"Then who the hell is she?" asked Richards.

"I guess we're about to find out." Richards followed me back into the interrogation room, where I spread each picture out in front of the imposter. "Who are you? Because you're not Beverly Morton. This is Beverly Morton." Of course, there was no positive ID on the body in the freezer, but I wasn't about to tell her that.

She picked up the first photo, holding it up to her eyes that were nearly swollen shut. Once she realized who she was looking at, she gasped and dropped the photo. It fluttered to the floor and Richards bent to pick it up. Thick tears rolled down her red cheeks. "Bevy," she whispered. "My poor sister."

"Beverly Morton was your sister?" asked Richards before I could. She nodded.

"I'm Valerie. Beverly was my older sister. Gerry killed her."

"And for the record, who are you referring to as Gerry?" Richards asked.

"Gerald Morton, her husband."

"And why do you think Gerald Morton was the one who killed her?" I asked gently.

"Because she invited me over to their house for lunch that day, and I got there and found him leaning over her dead body, that's why," she said, suddenly belligerent. "He told me it was an accident. He shoved her. She fell backward, and her head hit the edge of the coffee table. But he was so angry, not upset like you'd think a man whose wife had just died would be. And when I ran to her side, she had bruises on her arms."

"And how did you go from grieving sister to stealing her identity? Why didn't you call the police?" Richards didn't bother to hide his disgust.

"I loved my sister! But she was dead and... and..."

"He offered you money to keep quiet and help him hide the body?" I asked.

"It was the least he could do for me! She was dead, and I needed to get away and get out of this shithole town. He paid me two grand a month to leave town and stay gone. There was nothing left for me here, anyway. Our parents never cared about us. And Bevy used to have to hurt herself, make herself sick to get their attention, but then that wasn't even enough. Then she started hurting me and pretending to be the loving older sister who took care of me. And then when she became a mother, I knew she was probably hurting Cara too. She owed me! She owed me!"

"Do you know where your niece is? Where is Cara Morton? Did you kill her when she cut you off from her father's money? Or did she figure out you weren't her mother and started asking questions? Where is she?"

"Where are my children?" She was looking around wildly like she'd just remembered she had children. She hadn't asked a single thing about either of them since we'd brought her in, and I wasn't about to buy her concerned mother act now.

"You mean the son you convinced everyone, including him, had cancer? After what Beverly did to you as a child, how could you treat your own children the same way?" There was no response. "And by the way, that was a very professional job you did inserting that chemo port into his chest."

"Yeah, where'd you learn to do that? YouTube?" asked Richards, twisting the knife.

Valerie didn't answer. Instead, she started ripping up the pictures on the table and screaming before grabbing her chair and swinging it around blindly. It took three officers to subdue her.

FORTY-ONE

AARON NICHOLS

AFTER

December 22, 2023

I've been told I'm no longer a person of interest in Cara's disappearance, but I knew people still thought I was the guy. I could tell by the way I was avoided, even by people I'd known for years. I needed professional references to apply for another job, and the only person who'd been willing to provide me with one was Helen. One last act of professional kindness before she retired at the end of the month.

It has been a few days since Lynette's arrest. I never had time to search Cara's office, and the buildings were now closed for the holidays. But I still had my master set of keys. Paige and the kids were with her sister doing some last-minute Christmas shopping, and I had several hours to myself. I couldn't ride my bike to campus because it had been snowing all afternoon, and the streets were too slick. I waited until the sun set and drove. I parked a block away from campus and walked the rest of the way.

Roberson's campus is one of the most beautiful campuses in the state of Ohio, but not so much in the dead of winter without all the students, staff, and faculty that gave it life. The bare trees, dark empty buildings, empty college green, and lightly falling snow made it look apocalyptic. I pulled my hoodie over my head and walked around to the one of the building's back entrances and was about to let myself in when I saw someone walking down the hall. It was Mr. Wright, the custodian. He saw me at the door, and I had no choice but to wave. Surprised to see me, he rushed over to let me in.

"Dr. Nichols? What are you doing here? It's good to see you."

"Hi. Mr. Wright. It's good to see you too. I forgot something when I packed up my office and was hoping someone would be here so I could get it."

"Come on in." He stepped aside so I could enter, and I immediately noticed how cold it was in the building. I'd forgotten they turned off the heat in the buildings when campus was closed.

"Thanks."

"No problem. Just make sure you're gone in the next half hour because I get off at six and I'll be locking the building up."

"I will," I told him as I got in the elevator.

The fourth floor was dark and creepy. I wanted to get this over with as quickly as I could. I used my master key to let myself inside Cara's office and shut the door behind me. I only had about twenty minutes to search, and I didn't even know what I was looking for. I knew the police would have already checked the place for anything connected to her disappearance, but there was every chance they'd missed something.

I grabbed papers from her desk tray that turned out to be ungraded term papers, notes from committees she was on, and what looked like personal mail to her father's address. I sorted through the mail, but aside from overdue utility bills in her father's name, nothing jumped out at me. I was starting to think coming here had been futile when I noticed Cara's black fur lined leather jacket hanging on the coat rack by the door. She'd started wearing that jacket when the weather got cold, and I hadn't seen her in a different coat the whole time I'd known her. Why was it here in her office and not at her house when that's where she'd supposedly disappeared from? There was no way she would leave it behind in the dead of winter. But I also hadn't seen Cara since my suspension. I supposed it was possible Cara switched to a different coat in that time. Even so, I searched through the pockets. Tucked inside an inner pocket, and folded up small so that it was easily missed, was an empty, business-sized window envelope. The return address was for Hope & Grace Adoption Agency in Springfield, Ohio. I frowned. Why would Cara have had this?

My phone rang, startling me. It was Paige.

"Are you at home?" she asked, a note of anxiety in her voice.

"No. I went to pick up a sandwich. Why?"

"You need to get home and stay there. They can't find Beth. She ran away from her foster home. She got really upset when they wouldn't let her see her mom. Alonso thinks she might come after us. I'm staying overnight with Ros and the kids here in Dayton. Promise me you'll be careful and if you see her, call the police."

"I promise," I said, pleased to hear my wife's concern for me. "But I hardly think I'm in danger from a sixteen-year-old."

"I'm serious, Aaron."

"I know. And I'm on my way home now. See you guys in the morning."

Once I hung up with Paige, I stored the envelope in my pocket, set the stacks of papers on Cara's desk, locked up her office and left the building just as Mr. Wright was leaving. On my drive home an accident forced me to take a detour down several side streets, right past where Helen lived. As I stopped at the corner, I glanced down her street to see a light on at her house. I knew she'd left town to visit her sister in Florida when the fall semester ended. So why were there lights on in her house? Realizing the empty house of Beth's favorite professor would be an excellent place for her to hide, I turned onto Helen's street and parked in front of her house. The light was on in the garage. I rang the doorbell and heard a sound from inside. When no one came to the door after several rings, I tried the doorknob and discovered the door was unlocked.

"Helen!" I called out as I entered, and heard a faint cry coming from the garage. I navigated the clutter and headed into the kitchen for the garage door, which was ajar. I heard groaning and pushed the door open to see Beth unconscious on the garage floor bleeding from the head. Helen was leaning against her car with her hand to her chest, panting like she'd just run a mile.

"Aaron," she said between breaths. "I just got home from my sister's, and she was in the house. I told her we needed to call the police, get her some help, and she attacked me. I hit her with this in self-defense." Helen waved her cane. "Is she alive?"

I knelt next to Beth and pressed two fingers to her neck and found a strong pulse. Relief flooded my body. Thank God! "She's alive, but we need to call for an ambulance, and I need to call the police. She ran away from her foster home tonight and they're looking for her."

I stood and pulled my cell phone out. As I did, I noticed Helen's luggage was sitting by the back of the car. Beth must have approached Helen just as she was unloading the trunk. Draped over her suitcase was her coat with her passport sitting on top of it. The trunk was still open. But if she'd just arrived home from her sister's, why wasn't she wearing her coat? And why did she have her passport? As far as I knew, her sister lived in the next state. She hadn't just arrived. She was leaving – and not just leaving town. She was leaving the country.

I took a step forward as something on the floor of the empty trunk caught my eye, sparkling in the dim lighting of the garage. A shiver ran down my spine as I realized it was an earring. A diamond heart-shaped dangle earring. As my eyes adjusted to the light, I noticed that there was also a large, faint brown stain on the carpet of the trunk. The kind of stain that would never come out. Helen slammed the trunk shut, and I took an involuntary step backward.

"I'm sorry, Aaron," she said, looking at the closed trunk. "None of this was supposed to happen. It just got so out of control."

"Helen. What did you do?" My voice was low and calm, but that's not how I felt inside. My heart was hammering.

She leaned heavily against the car and just stared at me.

Helen? No! This didn't make any sense. "Why, would you hurt Cara?"

For what seemed like an eternity, she didn't speak. "Gerry and I had gotten close again," she said finally. "Not romantically. We'd become good friends and were spending a lot of time together. I started noticing his memory loss and confusion and insisted he see a doctor. Rapid onset Alzheimer's. I was the one who called Cara and told her about her father and that he couldn't live alone, and suggested she apply for a position at Roberson. I even gave her a recommendation. She left New York and came home to take care of him and that's when she pretty much cut me off. She told me she had nurses taking care of him. It was a lie!"

"How do you know that?"

"Because I'd wait until she had class and go to Gerry's house, but there were never any nurses there. He'd be soiled, hungry, and confused and I found bruises on him. I threatened to report her for elder abuse more than once. But she couldn't have that. She'd lose his house and access to his money if he went into a nursing home. That's when she went searching for something to use against me and found out my secret."

"What secret? What could she have found out that you'd kill her for?" I took another step backward distancing myself more from the horror of what she'd done than from her.

"A couple of years after John's ALS diagnosis, I had a brief fling with his home health nurse. We had a great support system in the beginning, friends and family always checking up on us and offering help, bringing food by. But as time went on, people just stopped calling and coming by." She sighed. "I was lonely. It only happened a few times, and I don't even remember his name. But I got pregnant. I was in my forties. John and I could never have kids. But if it had been his child, I'd have kept it. I couldn't bring myself to get an abortion. So, I took a sabbatical from work. I hid my pregnancy and gave the child up for adoption. Then a few months ago, the thing that I'd been afraid of happened. The child I'd put up for adoption contacted me. She wanted to meet me, and that was the last thing I wanted."

Her words made the hairs on the back of my neck stand up. "Jaida? You're Jaida Reese's birth mother?" Helen simply nodded.

"But why reject her?"

"Because I didn't want to disappoint her."

"Disappoint her?"

"Look at me, Aaron. I'm not beautiful or stylish. I'm an old woman with a cane living in a house filled with cats and memories of a life I lived with a man who died a long time ago. I gave her – and all the joy she could have brought to my life – up for this." She held out her arms and looked around the garage.

"But how did Cara find out?"

"She had this one," Helen said, nudging Beth's still unconscious form with her foot, "snooping around. She came to me with a sob story about having no place else to go, and I welcomed her into my home. She was the one who offered to help me clean up the house. But she was taking anything she thought was important and giving it to Cara. One of those things was the letter the adoption agency forwarded me from Jaida. Cara confronted me in my office that night and demanded I rescind a complaint against her for elder abuse," she said, walking toward me. It took everything in me not to recoil. "When I told her I didn't know what she was talking about, she waved Jaida's letter in my face and said she was going to tell Jaida I was her mother. Then she told me not to worry because Jaida adored her, and she would be there for my daughter. She tried to leave my office. I wish I could tell you I don't remember what happened next. But I do. I've relived that moment every single minute of every single day since it happened." She finally looked up and her eyes were so empty it scared me more than what I'd just seen in the trunk.

"But it was self-defense, right?" I knew it wasn't, but something in me desperately wanted it to be true or for her to at least lie and tell me it was. Because if it wasn't, that meant the woman I'd looked up to, who'd been a friend and mentor to me, was not only a murderer, but had sat back and watched the police accuse me of a crime I didn't commit.

"It was self-defense, in a way. But I didn't do it for me. I did it to protect Jaida. I had hurt her enough. I didn't know how she'd take it if she found out that I was her birth mother. That her mother was someone she knew, and had rejected her not once but twice," she said, shaking her head as sadness and regret washed over her features momentarily, making her the Helen I'd always known and admired. "And I couldn't let that bitch get her hooks into my daughter. She had no right to play with people's lives because her mother hurt her. Before she even reached my office door, I hit her with my cane. It was just enough to stun her at first, but I hit her again, and again, and eventually she stopped moving."

"But I don't understand. One of Cara's neighbors saw her arrive home later that night."

"They saw her car drive by with a black woman behind the wheel and assumed it was her. It was me. I used an AV cart in the hallway outside my office to load her into my trunk. For once I was glad the college ran out of renovation budget before they installed cameras near my office."

She noticed my doubtful expression and let out a short bitter laugh. "You think because I use this cane that I'm physically weak? I'm not. I use the cane for balance. I was more than capable of getting her onto that cart and into my trunk."

"And then what?" I asked, wondering what type of lunatic thought being able to move a dead body alone was a flex.

"After I got rid of her, I went back to campus, got her car and drove it to her house, then cut through the woods behind her house to the nearest bus stop and caught a bus back to campus to get my car. And nobody paid me the slightest bit of attention because the weather was getting bad, and people just wanted to get home. Plus, I'm a black woman of a certain age with a cane and therefore invisible. You can probably figure out the rest."

"But how did Peters get one of her earrings? He told me they'd been having an affair, and she forgot it a hotel room."

"They were having an affair. With you out of the picture, she thought she could use Peters to advance at the college. And he was more than happy to screw her, but he didn't have the power or the inclination to help a black woman advance at the college. And he played you, Aaron. He didn't know whose earring that was. He said he found it on the AV cart when he used it to move his things into your old office and asked if I knew who it belonged to. When I said no, he said he'd take it to the lost and found. After I drove her car back to Gerry's that night, I was in such a rush to get back here to clean my office and get my car I hadn't even realized her other earring had come off, too, let alone that it had been lying on that cart since the night she died. I watched him put it in his pocket."

"And you panicked."

"I had to get it back, otherwise it was only a matter of time before he realized it belonged to Cara. You could see it in the picture that ran in all the papers. There was a risk he might have told the police where he'd found it. I called lost and found and he hadn't turned it in. So, I realized it must still be in his pocket. When I saw him walking down the steps, I didn't think about what I was doing. I just pushed him. But before I could search his pockets, you showed up."

"So now what? You just move on with your life and leave me holding the bag for everything you've done?" I stared at her in disbelief. This couldn't be happening. Helen had been my friend for years.

"I never meant for you to be accused of her disappearance. That was the last thing I wanted."

"Then come with me to the police station and tell them everything you just told me."

"I can't!" she insisted, slamming the tip of her cane against the garage's concrete floor, making me flinch. "But once I catch my flight to the Maldives, you can tell them everything I've just told you."

"So, they can't extradite you, and you get away with murder?"

"No one truly ever gets away with murder. It catches up to us all."

"Only if you have a conscience," I spat out at her. She flinched.

"If I didn't have a conscience, Cara Morton would still be alive to ruin the lives of everyone unfortunate enough to cross her path. Don't you stand there and tell me that, when she was putting you and Paige through hell, the thought didn't cross your mind. I did the world a favor. Hell, I did you a favor because you know she wouldn't have stopped until she'd completely ruined your life!"

"I wanted her gone, not dead. And what about Peters? You could have killed him when you shoved him down those stairs."

"And what about all the good I can still do to atone for what I've done? I'm volunteering in the underprivileged communities in the Maldives. I'm needed there."

I didn't reply to her bullshit logic about atoning for murder in paradise. Instead, I looked beyond her to where Beth had been lying. It was too late for Cara, but maybe there was a chance I could save Beth. But she was gone. I rushed past Helen to look around the garage, but Beth was definitely gone, hopefully to get help. The only sign she'd been there at all was a small bloodstain from her head wound.

"You're out of luck, Helen..." was all I got out because when I turned back to her, she struck me hard in the temple with that killer cane and everything went black.

When I finally woke up, I was lying on my back, cold, disoriented, and confused. My hand scrabbled feebly against the wet dirt and slush on my right side. My left hand encountered nothing but a void. My head hurt and my vision was blurry, but I could make out pinpricks of light high above and realized they were stars. I needed to get up. I needed to run. But I didn't have the strength. If I couldn't walk, I would just have to crawl. I tried to roll onto my stomach. But something was in my way. A pair of legs. A shadowy figure stood over me. Helen. I opened my mouth to yell for help, but the only sound that came out was a wheezing gasp, followed by a grunt. But the grunt hadn't come from me. It was Helen grunting with effort as she rolled me to the edge and shoved me over the side into the cold, black abyss.

I rolled downhill for what seemed like forever moving so

fast I couldn't catch myself or slow down. I scraped my palms in my attempt to grab hold of something, anything. Finally, something stopped me from rolling further down the hill. The hood of my winter coat had snagged on an exposed tree root, bringing my descent to an abrupt halt. I lay there panting and in pain, looking around to figure out exactly where I was. From what I could tell, I was at the bottom of a hill lying under a pine tree. I tried to sit up, but my right side was on fire, and dizziness nearly made me pass out. I was pretty sure I'd broken some ribs on my way down. But by far the worst pain was coming from my left leg, which was bent the wrong way with a shard of bone protruding from a rip in my pants. Seeing it, I briefly passed out. Melting snow from the tree's branches dripped in my face, waking me up. Sounds from the road above drifted down to me.

"Help! Help! I'm down here!" I screamed as loud as my ribs allowed.

The screaming cost me dearly as a sharp biting pain took my breath away. I had to get out of there. I recalled from the weather report on the radio that a blizzard was rolling in just after midnight. Once it started, no one except the city's salt trucks would be out, not to mention the dip in temperature. I'd be dead by morning. A faint ringing sounded somewhere behind me. With effort that brought tears of pain that blurred my vision, I pulled myself into a sitting position and looked toward the sound to see my cell phone lying in the snow a good fifty feet up the hill. I didn't care how much it hurt to move, I had to get to that phone. I scooted backward millimeter by millimeter, stopping every few minutes when the pain in my limp and twisted leg became unbearable. Covered in sweat and whimpering in pain, I laid back in the snow, glancing toward a flash of red in the corner of my eye to my left. I wasn't alone.

Thirty feet away, lying wedged beneath a snow-covered clump of bushes, I spotted a once familiar face. It was pale and lifeless. The blue lips were retracted back from the teeth. The honey highlighted hair I used to love running my fingers through was wet and plastered to her head. Her eyes were open and cloudy; her gaze fixed and staring at nothing. The vivid red scarf she'd won in a college raffle was around her neck. Instead of her signature floral perfume, I caught a sickly-sweet whiff of decomp mingled with the smell of wet dirt. Dr. Cara Morton was no longer missing.

I closed my eyes, and a sob tore at my throat. Why I was crying for a woman who'd been hellbent on destroying me and family was simple. I was crying for the little girl she'd once been. A little girl betrayed by her mother, the one person in the world who should have loved and cared for her, and instead let her down. I was crying for the moments we'd shared, the laughter, the friendship, the tenderness even though they'd been a lie. But mostly I was crying because despite the pain and destruction she'd caused, she didn't deserve to end up like this, discarded like a fast-food wrapper thrown from the window of a moving car. And neither did I.

"Dr. Nichols! Dr. Nichols, are you down there?" Came a voice from the road above.

"Here!" I screamed in a ragged voice full of pain and tears. "I'm here!"

FORTY-TWO

CARA MORTON: AGED 15

2002

"Why can't I go? All my friends are going!" Cara yelled at her father.

"You know why. You're too young to be hanging out with college boys," her father said, his voice weary.

Had Cara gotten ready at her best friend Jess's house, she could have avoided this scene. Instead, she'd thought she could slip out before he got home from work. But she was running late because she couldn't find her other shoe. She'd bought the wedge heels specifically to go with her new boot cut jeans and leather jacket. She was going to a concert in Cincinnati with her friends to see Ashanti, a concert her father had already told her she couldn't go to.

"Come on, Daddy. It's just one college boy. Jess's boyfriend, and he's cool. They're already on their way to pick me up."

"Then I'll tell them to go on without you. Now, go wash all that crap off your face."

"I'm fifteen! When are you going to stop treating me like a kid?"

"When you're no longer living under my roof, eating my food, and spending my money!" He yelled back at her. Her father rarely yelled at her, and they were both surprised at the bass in his voice.

"Then maybe I'll go live with Mom! I heard the ladies at church talking. You're the reason she was cheating on you! I bet you wouldn't let her do anything or go anywhere either! I'll find her and go live with her!"

Before she could even blink, his right hand swung out and cracked her hard across her cheek. Her hand flew to her face and her eyes instantly filled with tears.

"You want your mother, huh? Think your life would be better with her than with me? You have no idea who that woman really was." And then he told her the truth that he'd been hiding from her for years. As he spoke, Cara's eyes widened in shock and disbelief.

"You're lying!" she screamed at him.

"I'm not lying. I have no reason to lie about this. I caught her in the act putting bug spray in your soup. You could have died because of what she was doing to you. Remember how sick you always were? It was her. It was her all along."

"But why? What did I do to make her do that to me? I thought she loved me," Cara said, her voice barely a whisper.

"Oh, honey," he said, attempting to touch her, but she slapped his hands away. "You didn't do anything wrong. She wasn't in her right mind. Don't you think I'd love for you to have a relationship with your mother? I would never have done what I did if she wasn't dangerous. It's better this way. I just hope one day you'll understand." He left her standing in the living room in tears. No big surprise when her father didn't handle emotions well, especially tears. Ironically, her mother had been a pro at comforting her.

Cara ran into her room and slammed the door shut behind her. By the time she heard the car horn letting her know her friends had arrived to pick her up, she'd calmed down. But something had broken inside her. The one thing she could always count on were the memories of her mother, her warmth, her scent, her tenderness, her smile, her laughter when they played. All of it just for her. They were memories she took refuge in because memories were all she had left of her mother. Since the day she'd found him crying in the living room when she was five, Cara had always believed it was her father keeping them apart because he was jealous that Cara loved her mom more than him. But she realized now that if her mother had really wanted to see her, she could have called, written, or showed up at the house or her school when her father wasn't around. She'd done none of those things, which meant her father had to be telling the truth. She probably hadn't come back because what she'd done to Cara could have gotten her arrested. But now Cara was empty. She pinched herself hard on her forearm, trying to feel anything, anything at all. But there was nothing except anger and rage.

Cara listened, expecting her to hear her father telling her friends to go on without her. But the only sound she heard was the shower in the bathroom, so she grabbed her purse to go. Before she left, she pulled a bottle from her bottom dresser drawer. It was an almost empty bottle of perfume. Her mother's signature floral scent. She'd found the bottle in the bathroom closet a couple of years after her mother left. It was the only thing of her mother's her father hadn't gotten rid of. Whenever she was feeling down, she'd pull that bottle out and spray a little on her pillow and pretend she was burying her face in her mother's neck like she used to when she was little. But it had all been a lie. Not only had her mother been the one making her sick, she'd left with another man and had never looked back. Cara could no longer pretend her mother was going to swoop in and come get her one day. Because why would she do that when she'd never really loved her?

Cara sprayed herself with the perfume. But this time it wasn't to feel closer to her mother. It was to remind herself of what the woman she'd loved more than anyone had done to her, and to remind her never to love anyone like that again. She sprayed more perfume in the hallway and the living room as she left the house knowing her father would smell it, and hoping it made him feel as bad as she did because she hated him. Not because he hadn't protected her from her mother all those years ago, but because he'd shattered her illusions by finally telling her the truth.

FORTY-THREE

AARON NICHOLS

AFTER

December 26, 2026

After Valerie goes on trial for being an accessory in her sister Beverly's murder, they'll extradite her back to Indiana to face charges of theft for collecting money for her son's cancer fund, parental kidnapping, and identity theft. She'd raised over $50,000 for her son's cancer treatment and then disappeared. She'd been mainly living on the money Gerry Morton had been paying her once a month to keep quiet about Beverly's murder. Between paying Val every month and funding an expensive storage unit to hide Beverly's body, Gerry Morton was eternally broke. Adam and Beth, whose real names were Josh and Brittany Sumner, had reunited with their father, who they hadn't seen in years and had been told was dead. Turns out Valerie had disappeared with them when they were little after divorcing him, and he'd been searching for them ever since.

Beth, or rather Brittany, was the one who'd found me that night. She hadn't left Helen's house to get help, after all. She'd gone to get her phone. When Helen had hired her to help clean up the house, she'd hidden a cell phone at Helen's, keeping her mother from finding it. Thinking Helen was in Florida for the holidays, she'd run away from her foster home to retrieve it. She hadn't broken in. She'd walked into the garage as Helen was about to make her escape and had seen the earring and the stain in her trunk before I had, and Helen attacked her. I'll never know for sure, but I think I received the fate that had awaited Beth when I showed up unexpectedly and interrupted Helen. Beth had cloned my phone, which she'd stolen from the gym for Cara, before wiping all the texts and pics of her from it, leaving the video Cara had mistakenly sent me behind. In doing so, she could use the Find My phone feature to figure out where Helen had taken me and called the police.

"I saw you guys kissing in the stairwell at Tate one day." Beth told me when she stopped by to see me in the hospital after my surgery to repair the compound fracture in my leg. "You were always so nice to me, and I wanted you to win your harassment case. I left that video on your phone so you'd have proof. She acted differently around different people. She was always the nicest when she wanted something. And she was good at making you feel like she really cared."

Alan Peters had told me the same thing. Why I hadn't been able to see it will haunt me for the rest of my life.

Roberson had offered me my old job back teaching English and running the student lit review. But there had been too much damage done and lost trust for me to even consider going back. Oakmont didn't feel like home anymore. Paige and I agreed we needed a fresh start away from all the reminders of how we'd failed each other. A friend of mine from grad school offered me a teaching position at a small college in Vancouver where he was the dean of Arts and Sciences. I start in the summer. Things between Paige and me are improving, and I'm hopeful we can build something better.

Helen was in police custody. She'd made it to the airport in time to catch her flight from Columbus to the Maldives. But thanks to Beth or Brittany, they'd arrested her at JKF while trying to board her connecting flight. She was being held without bail at the county jail, awaiting her trial for voluntary manslaughter and three counts of attempted murder. She's trying for diminished responsibility. Pretending she doesn't remember killing Cara, acting confused and claiming to have gaps in her memory. My guess is she's mimicking the symptoms she'd seen Gerry Morton exhibit before his diagnosis. I knew I'd have to testify at her trial, but was praying she'd come to her senses and plead guilty. If she truly wanted to teach the less privileged, prison was a perfect place to do it.

Gerry Morton died in his sleep the day after Cara's funeral. They buried him next to her. Ironically, Beverly Morton's body, which had spent more than two decades hidden in a freezer chest, was still on ice in the county morgue unclaimed by any of her family members. I'd heard the woman who'd bought the storage unit made a small fortune from the contents. At least something good had happened for one person in this mess.

EPILOGUE

PAIGE NICHOLS

FIVE MONTHS LATER

The flight to Vancouver was at capacity, and Aaron and I were in separate rows with the kids. I was with Bryce and Aaron was with Bailey, two rows in front of us. It had been a day of delayed flights and long layovers, and we were all tired and cranky. Bryce had fallen asleep with his head against my shoulder, and as I gently pulled the earbuds from his ears, turned off his tablet, and tucked a pillow behind his head, I spilled my purse. Trying hard not to wake my son, I gathered up the contents. A passing flight attendant bent to pick up the few things that had fallen into the aisle.

"Thanks," I told her as she handed me a small bottle of hand sanitizer, a tube of lip balm, and a slip of paper. Not just any slip of paper, a receipt. A receipt for a pair of diamond heart earrings. The earrings Aaron had bought Cara Morton.

Cara should have never lied and told me Aaron wanted her back. She shouldn't have lied about the gifts Peters was giving her when we'd had the confrontation in my car, pretending they were from my husband. I'd gone straight home and torn up the house looking for proof. And I found it. A receipt for a pair of earrings that I'd never received locked in Aaron's desk drawer in his office. Didn't matter that the date on the receipt was before I'd found out Aaron was cheating on me. Didn't matter, they weren't something he'd given her recently. It was what the heart-shaped diamond earrings represented. He'd given her a piece of his heart. The thought of it had taken root in my mind and grown into something ugly and dangerous.

For days, I obsessed over what she'd said in the car. Until I remembered what my mother had told me. I needed to find out what was important to Cara and use it to make her stop. I thought I'd found it when I uncovered her last affair. But that turned out to be a dead end. What I discovered next wasn't important to Cara Morton, as such. It was something much more useful to me. I stumbled upon it when I finally bought Helen Watford-Raines that drink I owed her. Over a single gin and tonic at Nova, Helen unintentionally revealed that she cared very deeply for Jaida Reese. It was a day or so after Jaida had ended up in the hospital, and Helen was subdued and not her usual gracious and charming self. She was irritable and edgy. All she talked about was Jaida and how smart and beautiful she was and how she had her whole life ahead of her. She showed me a picture they took together at the Gamma mixer. And that's when I noticed the resemblance between the two women. They had slightly different features but the same height, build, and coloring.

"Are you guys related?" I'd asked without thinking. "You kind of look alike."

Helen momentarily went still and quiet. She never answered me, and I didn't put everything together until I went to Jaida's Instagram page and scrolled back to the night of the Gamma mixer, where she'd posted several pics of the event. One picture caught my eye. Jaida posed leaning against the bar smiling with a virgin strawberry daiquiri in her hand, with the caption: *You don't need alcohol to have fun. Mocktails for life!* Followed by the hashtags #alcoholintoleranceawareness #alcoholintolerant.

There were other posts linking to articles and tips on how to know if you're alcohol intolerant and how to turn down alcohol when it's offered to you. There were also posts about adoption awareness day and thanking her adoptive parents for giving her a loving home. Jaida was adopted and was alcohol intolerant just like Helen. Combined with their similarities and Helen's reaction to what happened to Jaida, two plus two equaled four.

Then I remembered something I'd overheard one day when I'd gone to Aaron's office to see if I could use his printer because mine was out of ink. This was before I'd found Cara's video on his phone and put him out. Lynette wasn't at her desk when I got there, and I started to knock on Aaron's office door when I heard him talking to someone. The door was open a crack and I stopped to listen. I heard someone he called Beth telling him about Jaida being bullied by Cara. So, I planted a seed of my own.

I called Helen under the guise of asking if she was okay and if she'd heard any more about Jaida's condition. And then I told her what I'd overheard Beth telling Aaron about Cara, only I threw in an extra twist. I told Helen that Cara had been bullying Jaida and wondered if it had anything to do with her suicide attempt. Afterward, I called Oakmont Social Services pretending to be Helen and reported Cara for elder abuse. Ironically, I had no idea at the time that Cara had actually been abusing her father, but after working for years as a nurse, I knew that it was more common than you might think, and Cara certainly fit the type. I sat back and waited for the inevitable to happen. My intension was that Helen would get Cara fired and arrested for abusing her father.

Instead, I witnessed the unintentional fruits of my labor when

I went to see Helen. While I was parked in the lot behind Tate Hall, Helen Watford-Raines rolled an AV cart covered with a dark tarp out to her car, looking around before unlocking her trunk. I was about to get out of the car to offer her help when a slight gust of wind blew the tarp up and I glimpsed something terrible. It was Cara's face, streaked with blood. I'd been so consumed with getting Cara out of our lives, I'd seriously under-estimated a mother's love for a child she probably thought she'd failed. I had to clamp my hands over my mouth before the scream could escape and slid down in my seat so Helen wouldn't spot me. I stayed down until I heard her car start and pull out of the lot.

I followed her at a discreet distance. Eventually, she pulled down a narrow unpaved road two miles outside of town near an abandoned convenience store that had been closed for a decade. I pulled into the lot, hidden behind the back of the old store, and waited. Ten minutes later, her car returned and headed back into town. Once her car was out of sight, I drove down the narrow road with my brights on following the tracks from her car in the heavy snow that was falling. The tracks stopped less than a mile near a ravine. There were clear drag marks in the dirt and snow, along with droplets of blood that the snow would soon cover. I parked and got out, slipping and sliding in my tennis shoes. I looked over the side and saw a body lying halfway down the hill.

"Cara!" I screamed.

The snow was really falling now, and I couldn't be sure, but I thought I saw her move. holding on to small trees and shrubs, and falling more than once, I descended the hill until I finally reached her. She was lying on her side, unconscious. I took off my glove and held two fingers to the side of her neck and felt a pulse. I gently turned her onto her back and ran my hands over her body for obvious injuries, like broken bones. Blood had run into her face from a nasty head wound along her hairline. I quickly fumbled for my phone to call 911. And then I saw it and froze.

Something familiar was hanging out of her pants pocket. I reached down and pulled it free. It was a bright pink and purple beaded keychain with a purple plastic letter M dangling from the end. A single key was on the ring. I recognized that keychain because I'd helped my daughter Bailey make one for her each of her favorite teachers at school. The M keychain had been made for the female volunteer who'd run a young writer's workshop at the twins' school. A woman I'd never met and whose name I couldn't remember my daughter mentioning to me. Or maybe she had, and I wasn't paying attention. Could it have been Cara all along? Did she tell Bailey not to tell me? Because why else would she have this keychain? The M had to stand for Miss Morton. I glanced at Cara's still form in disbelief.

But it was impossible, wasn't it? I had to be wrong. Then I turned the keychain over to see the tiny flower sticker my daughter had put on the back of the initial on each of the keychains she'd made, and bile rose up into the back of my throat as the keychain slipped from my hand. It had been Cara. This monster was able to get close to my baby because I'd been asleep at the wheel, too distracted and distraught by Aaron's betrayal to see what was going on right in front of me. Suddenly light-headed, I took a step back and my foot slid out from under me. I fell onto my ass with a painful thud.

And just like that, I was twelve years old again, sitting in the grass under our dining-room window holding my dead dog Sammy and sobbing into his silky coat. Ros was wrong about Jan Singleton killing Sammy. Sixteen-year-old Sammy, our Cocker Spaniel mix, had died of old age. He'd kept disappearing, and I'd find him hiding under the bushes, or the basement, and one time in the woods near our house. We'd take him to the vet, who'd give us medicine for him, and he'd be fine for a little while. Then old Mrs. Prescott from next door pulled me aside one day when I was looking for him and told me what my parents wouldn't. Sammy was hiding because he was about to die.

I was the one who'd found him not long after she'd told me. He was in the backyard, lying underneath the bushes near our dining-room window. And as I held him and cried, I heard someone else crying through the open dining-room window. I laid Sammy down and listened to my mom crying on the phone as she talked to my Aunt Pat telling her about what Daddy had done and that Jan, the woman he'd been messing with, wouldn't leave us alone. Mom recounted how she'd run into Jan at the grocery and begged her to stop. But the other woman told her she'd only stop after she'd ruined Mom and Daddy's marriage and our lives.

Mom told Aunt Pat that she was going to send Jan's husband a letter telling him about his cheating wife if she did one more thing to our family because she'd heard he was a wifebeater and would make her stop by any means necessary. I'm not sure when my mother had convinced herself she hadn't known what would happen to Jan Singleton. All I knew at the time was that I didn't want to end up like my best friend Dana whose parents had split up. She had a stepmother she hated and stepbrothers who bullied her. I made sure Mom sent that letter.

While she was out running errands, Daddy was at work, and Ros was at a friend's house. I put poor Sammy behind our garage with an empty can of dog food beside a carton of rat poison I'd stolen from Mrs. Prescott's shed. I even smeared some of it around his muzzle. At dinner, I asked if anyone had seen Sammy, and Daddy said he'd look for him. The next day, they'd lied and told us a car had hit Sammy. My mom was even more upset than we were when we buried him in the backyard, and Daddy was angry like I'd never seen him before. He could barely look at me and Ros for a long time. Two days after that, my mom had me take a bunch of mail to the corner mailbox.

One of the envelopes was addressed to a Mr. Trevor Singleton with no return address. I knew my plan had worked.

A frigid gust of wind snapped me back to reality, and I looked over at Cara. Her eyes were open now, and she reached a hand toward me as she tried to sit up.

"Help me." Her voice was barely a whisper, but I could tell she was telling me to help her, not asking. "Help me," she repeated, with more authority.

I realized something else in that moment with laser sharp clarity. She wasn't going to stop. I'd been a fool to think Cara would eventually leave us alone. And how far would she go next time? She had managed to get close to my daughter. She had gained her trust. What was she planning to do next?

"Hey," she called out over the howling wind. "Did you hear me? Help!" She was waving her hand at me like she was hailing a cab as blowing snow pelted her in the face.

Everything in me, everything I'd learned in nursing school, everything that made me want to become a nurse and help people flickered and died like a snuffed-out pilot light. There hadn't been much left, anyway. Just a tiny glowing ember. And in that moment, if I was going to help anyone, it was going to be me and my family. Aaron had started this nightmare, and I was going to finish it. The wind and snow were approaching white out levels. But all I could see was red.

Enraged, I lunged at her, catching her off guard. And fueled by months of pent-up anger, fear, and heartache, I slammed her back down to the ground. Jerking her up by her scarf and slamming her down repeatedly until I was out of breath and Cara was limp, and lifeless. Then I pushed her hard and watched as her body rolled, aided by the wind and slick snow, further down into the ravine until it stopped under a clump of bushes.

"Goodnight, gorgeous," I whispered, the frigid wind carrying my words away along with the blinding rage I'd felt only seconds ago.

By the time I climbed back up to the road, my hands and feet were numb, and I couldn't feel my face. I had to sit in my car with the heater on full blast before I could warm up enough to drive home. I made it back before the worst of the storm that brought over two feet of snow hit in time to cook dinner. And the keychain? I still have it. Only I threw the key away and switched the M for a P.

Pretending I didn't know where Cara Morton was wasn't as hard as I thought it would be. I had no choice but to live the lie or I'd lose everything. Could I have let Aaron go to prison for a crime he didn't commit? I've told myself a thousand times I couldn't have. But was it true or just what I needed to tell myself? Maybe I'm more like my mom than I want to admit. As for Helen, I might have felt guilty that she took the fall if she hadn't tried to kill my husband. And besides, as far as she knew, she *had* killed Cara. Nothing I'd told her had been a lie as far as I was concerned. I looked down at the receipt in my hand, balled it up, and shoved it inside the empty can of Coke on my tray just as the pilot announced our descent into Vancouver National Airport.

The Japanese have a centuries old art of repairing broken pottery with gold called Kintsugi. The pottery is beautiful and much stronger afterward, even though the cracks still show. Aaron, the kids, and I are getting a fresh start, a second chance. We're being mended, repaired, and made new. And even though the cracks will still show, we'll be stronger.

A LETTER FROM THE AUTHOR

Dear reader,

Thank you for reading *The Perfect Affair*. I hope you enjoyed Aaron and Paige's story. If you'd like to hear about my new and upcoming releases, you can sign up for my author newsletter.

www.stormpublishing.co/angela-henry

If you enjoyed this book and could spare a few moments to leave a review that would be greatly appreciated. Even a short review can make all the difference in encouraging a reader to discover my books for the first time. Thank you so much!

Inspired by my love of eighties and nineties thrillers, the idea for *The Perfect Affair* had been bouncing around in my head for years. *Fatal Attraction*, *Presumed Innocent*, *Jagged Edge*, and *Basic Instinct*, to name a few, all featuring both deeply flawed individuals and ordinary people pushed to their limits. As with all my books, I started by playing the *What If* game. What if someone completely upended your life and threatened your family? How far would you be willing to go to protect them? And because I've always been more interested in the backstory of a crime and the people who commit them than the act itself, I wanted to explore that in depth in this book. I hope I succeeded.

Thanks again for being part of this amazing journey with

me and I hope you'll stay in touch – I have so many more stories and ideas to entertain you with!

Angela

facebook.com/authorangelahenry

instagram.com/angelahenry_author

tiktok.com/@angelahenryauthor

ACKNOWLEDGEMENTS

I'd like to thank my readers, many of whom have been on this twenty-plus-year writing journey with me and whose support has inspired me to keep going through all the ups and downs. As well as my husband Kevin for being my biggest cheerleader, and my family and friends for their encouragement and enthusiasm for every book I've written. And I'm so thankful and grateful to my editor Kate Smith and the team at Storm for giving this book a home and being so wonderful to work with.